Family Fictions

Also by Richard Hall

The Butterscotch Prince

Couplings: A Book of Stories

Three Plays

Letter from a Great-Uncle & Other Stories

RICHARD
HALL

Family Fictions

A NOVEL

VIKING

c √

VIKING
Published by the Penguin Group
Viking Penguin, a division of Penguin Books USA Inc.,
375 Hudson Street, New York, New York 10014, U.S.A.
Penguin Books Ltd, 27 Wrights Lane, London W8 5TZ, England
Penguin Books Australia Ltd, Ringwood, Victoria, Australia
Penguin Books Canada Ltd, 2801 John Street,
Markham, Ontario, Canada L3R 1B4
Penguin Books (N.Z.) Ltd, 182–190 Wairau Road,
Auckland 10, New Zealand

Penguin Books Ltd, Registered Offices:
Harmondsworth, Middlesex, England

First published in 1991 by Viking Penguin,
a division of Penguin Books USA Inc.

1 3 5 7 9 10 8 6 4 2

Publisher's Note

This is a work of fiction. Names, characters, places, and incidents either are the product of the author's imagination or are used fictitiously, and any resemblance to actual persons, living or dead, events, or locales is entirely coincidental.

LIBRARY OF CONGRESS CATALOGING IN PUBLICATION DATA
Hall, Richard Walter.
Family fictions : a novel / by Richard Hall.
p. cm.
ISBN 0-670-83784-9
I. Title.
PS3558.A3735F36 1991
813′.54—dc20 90-50786

Printed in the United States of America
Set in Sabon

For my mother, in memory,
and for Marny
and for Jack

Contents

Family Fictions

Conflict results for the members of an American family that has hidden its Jewish roots through a legal name change.

1

MARGARET
The Marriage

She was back now. She hadn't thought she would be, ever. There had been moments, with Charlie at the Traymore in Atlantic City, when she believed she had left Judd forever. But here she was in the taxi, meter clicking, next to his hands, whitish-pinkish, with brisk unappealing black hairs on the backs, next to his tobacco smells, his witch-hazel tartness, his discolored teeth, his strangeness. She had to keep her disappointment in check. In check and tamped down like the tobacco in the pipe he affected after dinner. She had always disliked the pipe routine, the gurgling and popping, the knocking against the heel of the hand. A pretense of being grown up, but unconvincing to her. And now she too was being tamped down in the bowl, pressed by his unappetizing hand, even as she deplored the weakness that had brought her back to this marriage, this self-betrayal.

"I'm willing to forget the whole thing, Margaret, start over." He had said that a few minutes ago in Mama's apartment on West End Avenue, Mama in the kitchen but the swinging door wedged open so she could hear. But Mama couldn't hear all the meanings, couldn't register the fear and hurt under the magnanimous offer. He repeated the statement now, as they rode down Seventh Avenue to Guiffanti's, and she heard even more—the sneer congealing over the wound, the princely overtone that implied he was doing her a favor. Overlooking her transgression. But there was more to it even than that. She hadn't sorted it all out yet—they were passing Penn Station now, the Baths of Caracalla—but she would.

Of course, he had done her a favor eight years ago in marrying her over everyone's opposition. His mother had objected on principle, though she would have opposed anyone. His father had been neutral, limiting his attention to correcting her Texas accent and telling her what sights to see in New York. And his sister Hattie! Luminous, auburn-haired Hattie had told him right off that he could do better. All that had come out slowly, after the wedding, though she had sensed it before. She, Margaret Barish, just wasn't good enough for Judd Schanberg, the Prince of Wales.

And now she, who was so beneath them, whose family was provincial, ignorant, had walked out on him. The brown wren had flown away. Charlie Rysdale had learned her secrets right off. He had taken her aside last year after one specially horrible Sunday dinner, whispered, smiled, stirred her emotions with a giant ladle. And of course he was just her type—tall, with a ruddy complexion, foxy face, blue eyes and flaxen hair. Like Rudy Vallee. The kind of boy she always had a crush on back in Gideon, a private crush since none of them ever paid her the least mind. The night after that talk with Charlie she had dreamed they were heading into the dark together, along a pathway of bright doors which gradually turned into the covers of Palgrave's *Golden Treasury.*

At those Sunday dinners nobody saw what was happening. Not Judd, much too confident of his prize-winning status. Not Hattie, who should have noticed something since she was married to Charlie. Not even Selma, who missed hardly anything concerning her two precious offspring.

Only she and Charlie knew, eyes locking, smiles lurking, during those endless dinners. Yes, significant glances over the matzoh-ball soup and the brisket of beef, secret meanings over the individual salt dishes and butterballs with crisscross paddle marks and radishes cut into little red flowerets. And over the finger bowls—she'd never seen anything like those finger bowls, dirtying two dozen extra plates just to rinse off a little grease.

....

No, she still didn't have it figured out, why she was here, pulling up at Guiffanti's, sliding across the leather seat, putting her hand in that fleshy pink one. Everything in their lives was always sealed with dinner at Guiffanti's. Their first date. His proposal. Celebrating Mag's birth. Then Harris's. Maybe because it was near Judd's office on Broadway, across from the Everlasting Light, or because he never got Italian food at home. Maybe because the owner always called him by name, "Mr. Schanberg, good to see you, sir, and the missus."

And that routine started now. "Hello, Jimmy." His hearty, big-man voice, democracy at work, then a handshake. As Jimmy conducted them to a table, smiling like Uriah Heep, the joking and joshing continued, proving to her again that in hick towns like Gideon they didn't know how to talk to restaurant owners, how to order from a menu where peas were called *piselli.*

Mama had put it just right. "Too big for their britches." This was after their first visit to the Schanberg apartment, after observing the servants and the statuary and the gleaming checkerboard floors. She herself had been impressed for a while but it had worn off, like the glitter and foreignness at Guiffanti's. Now she knew. Judd enjoyed having a wife, but it didn't fit him quite, always a little self-conscious and show-offy, part of him withheld. Unlike Charlie Rysdale, who had guessed her secrets and told his own right off, so easy and confident, probing at her with his blue eyes set in that ruddy, foxy face until she had surrendered noiselessly, the flues and gates of her body opening even as they sat on her mother-in-law's Louis Quinze fauteuils with the others all around.

And Charlie stood up for her at the dinner table too, taking her side on the poll tax and the Scottsboro Boys and especially the Sacco-Vanzetti scandal. "It's a national disgrace," he said about that, again and again, his big Adam's apple bobbing, his eyes flashing, but nobody cared. She always chimed in, bringing up Dreyfus for comparison, but even that didn't wake them up. Nothing could wake them up, she realized at last, looking at Hattie with her black beauty-mark mole, at Selma with her organdy headache band, at old Henry staring fish-eyed at his food. And then her gaze had met

Charlie's, as usual, and sparkling, unsaid things had passed between them. Us against them. Outsiders against the Schanbergs. Artists against Philistines. Only she and Charlie intended to vote for Roosevelt instead of Hoover.

Jimmy Guiffanti was holding forth on the menu now. Judd joked and boomed. It was all so familiar. One more ritual in eight years of rituals. That's why she'd married, she had laughed to Charlie at dinner in Atlantic City (not eating at their hotel; Charlie couldn't afford it). "I needed someone to tell me what to do." She didn't add that Judd and his take-charge manner had made her feel comfortable, safe, at first. Charlie wouldn't have appreciated that. Her feet had hurt during that dinner, and the other ones, in Atlantic City. Charlie wouldn't rent a roller chair, so they had hoofed it up and down the Boardwalk in the heat, only her celluloid sunshade protecting her. Judd, of course, would have hailed a chair right off, peeling the bills from the wad in his pocket. Not that she minded the tiredness, which couldn't compare to the fact that, after running off with Charlie, she'd never have to go to Guiffanti's again, never have to endure Sunday dinner with the Schanbergs, never have to note Judd's modesty at bedtime. Charlie wasn't modest at all. He liked to stand around in the altogether, even next to the window, when his body, gold and hairless, caught the sun and reminded her of Mercury. And for those five days at the Traymore, when they had defied everybody, he had almost been Mercury, messenger of the gods, with word that she was beautiful.

She'd been pudgy as a girl, undefined, awkward; in the relay races they put her in the middle where she'd do the least harm. She had grown into a wide-hipped, full-breasted woman, still awkward and poorly coordinated. And there was her skin, the color of the bare patches in the side yard where the grass wouldn't take. Sometimes people asked her if she had Mexican blood. But Charlie had changed all that in Atlantic City, keeping the light on, making her look. She had watched his pale, sinewy hands trace the veinery on her breasts and thighs, proving his lust, giving her the gift of vanity, which she had thought would never be hers. "You're beautiful, Margaret," he had said over and over, and at last she believed him.

Judd ordered veal *parmigiano* and spaghetti and wanted her to do the same. But she wanted chicken *cacciatore*. His eyes flickered at her as Jimmy walked off, but what was that little revolt compared to the other one? She tried not to eat the bread sticks but there they were. Suddenly there was nothing to say, even when Judd remarked, falsely casual, "Hell, Margaret, I'm willing to let bygones be bygones."

Charlie had been a little distracted in Atlantic City, except in bed, but that was understandable. This wasn't Sunday dinner, when their conspiracy was the only freshness in the room; this was the wide world of adultery and abandonment. Charlie was playing hooky from Hattie and from his ad agency, where he handled the Auburn account. He didn't believe they could separate so easily from their mates. Her children would be pawns in any settlement. And she realized, when the subject of the future came up, that he had no clear view of it. He really had no concrete plans except to go to Paris and write a novel. Where the money would come from he didn't say. Of course, he had told her about his ambitions during their first talk, matching them with her own literary hopes, and that had been the strongest bond, the bond that had replaced all the others. She would go to Paris with Charlie. They would live in Montmartre. Charlie would write a novel, but secretly, at night while he was asleep, she would get up and write her own on her Remington Noiseless, though she wasn't sure what it would be about. But here at the Traymore, which Charlie complained was costing him twenty dollars a day, the trip to Paris, the novel-writing, seemed far away and getting farther.

Judd was looking at her now, waiting for her to speak first. She could see his pride, puffed out like a lion's mane around his head. And she knew the words he wanted, words that would heal his hurt, reassure him. They were just little puffs of sculptured wind. But she wasn't ready. She had come this far, agreed to this dinner, but she had made no promises. She had said that she would see.

She really meant that she had to find out about the children. Judd's first threat was real enough. He had told Charlie, over the phone, when they came back from Atlantic City, that if they stayed together he, Judd, would put him in jail. They had gone to the

Shelton Hotel on Lexington Avenue and, sure enough, Judd, with the aid of the family law firm, had sworn out an affidavit for Charlie's arrest. Adultery and kidnapping. A nuisance charge, spiteful, but two policemen had arrived, taking Charlie through the lobby. He had spent the night at the precinct station. And Judd had called her immediately, hoarse with venom. She was an unnatural mother. A scarlet woman. She would never see the children again. A governess had been hired and she would not be allowed to visit. All the building people had been warned against her. She had hung up the phone gasping. His accusations weren't true. She was not a bad mother. She carried the impress of her children everywhere. Even in adulterous hotel rooms she had not abandoned them. They were her own self writ small.

But Charlie, out of jail next morning, had pointed out that Judd could do whatever he wanted since she was the guilty party. "I told you it wouldn't be easy," he'd said, in a voice she didn't like, his sharp face full of self-pity and indecision. But self-pity and indecision weren't what she needed on that particular morning when she might lose her children.

If only she didn't need either man! The women she really admired were brave and independent—Ruth Hale Broun, Edna Ferber, Emmeline Pankhurst, Lucy Stone. Why couldn't she be like them? She was only brave in her thoughts. Yes, fierce in her mind and timid in the world. How many times had she spoken out in favor of free love? But when the time came . . .

Judd had finished his veal and was ready to discuss the children in general terms. "Harris is a *pisher,* what can I tell you? He pisses in his pants ten times a day." He laughed without affection. She hated those expressions, old words from a dead culture, so un-American. Harris was not the boy Judd wanted. Brown like her, with slumbrous eyelids, badly coordinated, slow to walk and talk. But he made up for that by being affectionate. He always had his arms out. She suspected he would go through life with his arms out.

"And Mag, how is she?"

Judd smiled in deep consanguinity, silvery smoke streaming from his nostrils. "Beautiful. She's the boss."

It was true. Mag ruled her father, her grandparents, everyone. She was probably ruling the new governess now. "She's gonna be a handful, whoever marries her," he added. "I feel sorry for him."

The phrase rang in her memory. Mama used to say the same thing in Gideon, before Papa died and they moved to New York, into Uncle Harris's big apartment on West End. "I feel sorry for the man marries you, always got your nose stuck in a book, look at those chickens, didn't I tell you to mind them?" And maybe Mama had been right because the man sitting across from her now had married her and he was sorry. Maybe the books had won out, as Mama had foretold, because that was the secret of Charlie's appeal. He had seduced her with book titles, suborned her with Victor Hugo and Ellen Glasgow and James Branch Cabell and his own unwritten masterpiece. The books, the books had led to disaster.

"And by the way, Mag told us about your little visit to the kids last week."

"She told you?"

"She told Aunt May. Aunt May told Hattie." His eyes twinkled malevolently behind his wire-rims, causing her to wonder at the distance, the barriers between them. Their marriage had never been more than a truce, really.

She shouldn't have called to the children but she couldn't help it. She'd been walking along Riverside when she saw them on the playground below the Soldiers' Monument. She had run down the steep path, watched them on the monkey bars, then followed their shouts to a middle-aged woman sitting on a bench. Aunt May, they called her. The new governess. She had called out softly to Harris and he had raced screaming toward her, arms out. What a heavy little sack of love he was. Mag had taken her time, climbing without haste from the top bar. By then, of course, Harris was monopolizing her and it was difficult to enclose Mag too. There had never been room enough for both, really. Still, she had to be fair. She put down the boy and hugged her daughter, registering the squirmy strength of the body, the decisiveness of the elbows, the haughty questions. She had drawn them behind some shrubs, keeping an eye out. Harris wanted to know when she was coming back, asking over and over, but she couldn't tell him. Mag asked too, but only once. Saying good-bye was terrible. She had walked weeping back to Mama's apartment. Maybe they were right—she was a bad mother. There was no way to stitch all her selves together, not her freedom with Charlie and her need for her children and her pride and self-respect and dependency.

"I don't know that it's Hattie's business if I see my children," she said.

He shrugged. "Who knows, Hattie might get custody eventually." He smiled unpleasantly.

The words went through her in a freezing tide even as she knew he was bluffing. They were here, weren't they? Eating, negotiating? Again she saw male pride like a lion's mane fluffing around his head. He only wanted an apology, really, the words of contrition. But then she would be trapped for life.

Charlie Rysdale told her he had hated Judd from the first. A mother's boy, he'd said. And she'd agreed, but if so, why had she married him? It was her own fault, living with Mama, who was bad-tempered and not adjusting well to widowhood in New York, and with Uncle Harris, a bachelor, absent on long unexplained evenings after his days on the floor at Stern Brothers. She was restless, bored. She had written some stories and sent them off to *American Magazine, McClure's, Saturday Evening Post,* but they had come back. She had gone out to Brooklyn, to the offices of the *Eagle,* applying for a job as reporter, and been told to call again in a month. Then she'd been given some test assignments by the city editor, who called her girlie. An interview with the mother of a murderer. A trip to the Metropolitan Opera to meet Jeritza. After she turned them in, working for days on each one, going over and over them, placing each word as if it were a diamond in a bracelet, the city editor had invited her to dinner. He talked about tabloid readers in the land of Moronia and dropped a few hints. There was a hotel just up the street. That's how you got a reporting job on the *Eagle.*

And then Judd had made his offer, putting an end to her indecision about the city editor and his squalid proposal. Accepting

Judd solved all sorts of dilemmas, put together the loose ends of her life. Actually he was a distant relation. Other Schanbergs, cousins, were a banking family in Austin and had written to the Schanbergs in New York about the arrivals from Gideon—Lily Barish and her two daughters, Marian and Margaret. Country people, shopkeepers, but kin. And so she and Mama had gone to dinner at the big apartment on Riverside Drive—Sister refusing, not interested, on the verge of getting engaged to Mark Giangrande.

It was her first view of the apartment she would come to know so well—huge rooms overlooking the Hudson, tapestries on the walls, Tiffany lamps, thick Persian rugs, a carved screen that had once belonged to the Shah of Iran, a full-length oil painting of Mrs. Schanberg throning over it all. And there she had been introduced to Judd—Judah originally—nine years older than she, twenty-six already, a young man with dark hair that came to a widow's peak, a fair, fleshy face, cleft chin, important nose, rimless glasses. He was wearing a gray suit with a vest and a shirt with a round stiff collar. At home people didn't dress like that, not even for company.

She was impressed—not by him; he kept looking at his mother for cues—but by the apartment, the furniture, the servants, though she distrusted the bookcases, each shelf with its own glass door that had to be lifted and slid under the shelf above before you could get at the books. People who read a lot didn't cut off their books like that.

Old Henry Schanberg, who had been raised by the Austin cousins, felt easy and down-home despite his New York business success, but it was Mrs. Schanberg, Selma, who had impressed her most. Of course, at seventeen it wasn't hard to be impressed. Mama kept saying the wrong things, as usual, and hadn't looked good either—powder specks on her shoulders, her posture bad, slurping her soup, making hideous jokes about her false teeth, but Selma, as hostess, had smiled at this unwanted distant relative and kept everyone at ease. The woman acted like a duchess, even though her eyes were sad and dark, eyes you could see tumbrils in, and Marie Antoinette going to the scaffold. Whatever Mama said, rolling down a window on their past as if it was something to brag about instead of being the most shameful thing possible, Selma Schanberg nodded and smiled. Occasionally she tinkled a little bell for the servants.

And she was beautiful. Later Margaret found out that she laved her creamy skin in seawater every morning, even in the city, and had been to Paris for a face-lift. But at that first dinner, Margaret thought she had never seen anyone more confident or admirable. Of course, Selma had been lucky in her husband, a shark in business, head of his own firm.

As she sat there that first evening, discovering individual salt dishes (you pinched out the salt) and crisscrossed butterballs and radishes like roses, it occurred to her that she was like Eugène de Rastignac after he left the provinces and appeared in the great salons of Paris. He had conquered the city and so would she. One day it would all be at her feet. The notion thrilled her so much she pressed her palm to her bosom and closed her eyes for a moment. Of course she kept the notion to herself. Mama was fool enough for both of them.

Judd had paid her special attention that evening and during the weeks afterward. Mama and Uncle Harris had encouraged it. "He's a very smart young man," Mama had said, forgetting for the moment her remark that they were all too big for their britches. She rapped her wedding band against the table and added, "If he's a little bit sissy that don't signify." But, she had protested, he wasn't sissified, he was just attached to his mother. He was crazy about baseball, had pitched for his team, had a girlfriend named Natalie. She had said these things in outrage, as if by championing him she could quell doubts of her own, and the result was predictable. She had convinced herself he was acceptable, even attractive, though she hated his whitish-pink hands and his rimless spectacles and his casual condescension.

"I reckon you've got a case on him," Mama said at last, looking pleased.

"Never you mind if I do or I don't," she'd replied quickly, afraid of getting trapped in her own pose. She didn't really know if she wanted him or not. Why did everyone have an opinion except her?

They had invited the Schanbergs back for dinner and it had not been as disastrous as she expected. At Uncle Harris's insistence they had hired a colored girl for the evening who took over after Mama fried the chicken and made milk gravy. And Uncle Harris didn't let Mama get started on any stories about Gideon. He brought out his collections of theater programs after dinner—he hadn't missed a first night hardly for forty years—and talked on and on in his wheezy, prissy voice, adjusting his pince-nez as required. He had known Hall Caine personally.

That evening Judd had caught her in the hallway and kissed her. His lips were flecked with tobacco and his breath was starchy but she had been elated. She had caught him, even though she didn't really want him. He whispered that he liked her and his mother liked her too. Later she thought that was a curious thing to say, and much later she realized it wasn't true, but at the moment she was flattered. When the Schanbergs said good night both parents kissed her on the cheek. Selma smelled delicious.

"Charlie's moving out. Hattie's getting a divorce." Judd stared at her across the table, his eyes bulging behind his wire rims (she'd made him get rid of the rimless pair right after the wedding). "That's one marriage ruined." He flickered his nostril in contempt.

She didn't rise to the bait. Charlie would have left in any event; the marriage was doomed from the start. Hattie had found him at the Art Students League, where she took life classes. Not that he was a painter; just dabbling, like Hattie. He was handsome, artistic, Lutheran, of Dutch extraction—the name was Ruisdael originally—like his famous ancestor. Just what Hattie was looking for. So he had been inducted into the secret society of the Schanbergs. And, like her, another in-law, he had been held in colloidal suspension just outside the nucleus. Welcome but not quite. Belonging but not quite. Until he grew tired of it and found a co-conspirator, another outsider, right on the premises. And now it was all over for Charles Rysdale and Harriet Schanberg. She could almost feel Hattie's hatred barreling at her across the table.

"Is Hattie going to move back with your parents?"

"She's thinking about it."

"There's no point in keeping that apartment all by herself."

"She can see Mother whenever she wants. She probably needs some privacy."

Privacy, a precious commodity in the Schanberg family. Judd called his mother every day. She had expected it would stop as the years of marriage went by, after the children, but the calling continued. There was no prying him loose—not from his mother, who lived six blocks away, or from his father, who had the big corner office at Schanberg Textile Company, where Judd also worked. "Did you talk to your mother today?" The useless question, to which she always knew the answer. He would stand in the hallway each evening under the Moorish lamp, a coffee ring from Tip Toe Inn under his arm, and complain about his mother. But the calls continued. It shouldn't have surprised her. She had seen it all, known it all, at that first dinner when he looked to Selma for cues about what to say to this young, shy cousin from Texas, and later said his mother liked her too.

And Charlie had come up against the same thing. "Can't get Hattie away from her mother," he said to her more than once, explaining why he had to refuse a chance to head up his agency's new office in Los Angeles. Well, now he could go, he could escape from the Schanbergs at last. But hadn't everyone known his imprisonment was only temporary?

She hadn't spoken to him this past week, not since she'd moved back to Mama and Uncle Harris, then told him she was going to Guiffanti's. He had understood at once, of course. Still, there was time if he knew how to make use of it. Time to make decisions, hire a lawyer, outline a custody suit. But he hadn't. He hadn't swept her into the future with him. The future was unfamiliar territory to Charlie, a hopeless abstraction, like money. And where did that leave her and her children? If only he'd been a little different.

She closed her eyes. It was so hard to be wise, so many voices to heed. Mama fit to be tied, convinced that any marriage was better than none. Uncle Harris absent, off with his fey friends at night, more worried about respectability and the latest fashions than anything else. The children tugging at her heartstrings. Hattie her enemy for life. Sister in California, married to Mark. And Judd across from her, outraged and hurt, probably with various petty revenges in mind, but still offering her . . . something. She looked at him carefully. His strangeness had worn off slightly. She pictured him in his underwear, the sleeveless cotton vest that buttoned in front, the droopy drawers, the snap-on garters encircling the calves he was so proud of. A familiar sight, not attractive, not gleaming and golden like Charlie at the window of the Traymore, yet with a hint of comfort, familiarity. Was it possible that he had changed? That he had lost a bit of his confidence? That the princeliness had eroded?

Jimmy Guiffanti hovered while the spumoni was served, directing the waiter, pouring the coffee himself. "Would the missus like some cream?" She didn't care, she never drank coffee at night, but she smiled and nodded.

The last time here had been a family party, Judd and the children, Uncle Harris, to welcome Mama back from the long train ride to Texas. Mag had misbehaved, spilled her milk, whined constantly. A difficult child even in her womb but doubly, triply so since her brother was born. Where had she gotten those genes? Not from Margaret's side of the family.

How few her choices, really. And how differently she had felt the first night she had met Charlie alone, a daring escapade that made her a heroine in her own story. He had taken her to the Algonquin for dinner—the name alone made her pulse race—and they had looked at the famous table behind its red velvet rope. The place was like champagne in her blood. And the dinner! Away from the stifling complacency of their in-laws they had talked of things that really mattered. Charlie had told her about his novel, about Paris, about going to Holland to look up his ancestors, about his boyhood in Iron Mountain. His sarcasm, the hatred trapped inside him, had disappeared and he had changed into someone sleek and funny and new. She had watched his hands, so unlike Judd's—lean and strong and hairless. The sight of them made a little cavity in the pit of her stomach. Sitting in the Algonquin with Charlie, even though they were breaking all the rules, was the fulfillment of an old promise, a promise made to herself in the side yard in Gideon, where she sat under the pecan tree while the chickens clucked and the sun beat down and she read about immortal adulteresses like Anna Karenina and Emma Bovary. When Charlie reached across the table to brush her cheek, the cavity in her stomach fell away into an abyss.

And she had told him about herself, things only Sister knew. "Christ-killer," they had called her on the way to school. "Sheeny." The boys lying in wait, the girls just behind. And sometimes she got so terrified she dropped her books and ran home, never brave, never brave enough. But Mama hadn't been sympathetic. "Just go back and tell those children sticks and stones can break my bones, g'long." And Mama would push her out the door. But sometimes she would hide in the henhouse all day, though she hated the hens more than anything else on earth, especially the smell, which clawed at her throat and was the smell of hell itself.

Of course there was Sister. Sister was beautiful; she had soaked up the beauty allowance in the Barish family, even though she had possum eyes and her feet were on wrong. Sister had tried to look after her, tried to spread her magic cloak over her younger sister, but it hadn't worked. Sister would get annoyed, or make fun of her for reading so much, or want to be with her beaux. The boys, her demon protectors, looked out for her. Even in sixth grade Sister had a beau who would fight anybody who called her names. It was a reaction she inspired in the male sex.

"But you're the one who grew up to be a beauty," Charlie had said after listening to her tales. She didn't believe him then, of course—she didn't believe it till that evening at the Traymore, with all the lights in their room shining, when he had proved it once and for all.

But why was she reviewing that dinner at the Algonquin now? It was gone, as evanescent, as unreliable, as Charlie himself. She was at Guiffanti's with Judd. "I don't see . . ." She drew in her breath. "I don't see how we could go on living in the city."

Had she given in already? Judd was studying her. She meant only that she had to get away from Selma and Hattie, from dislike that had hardened into disapproval and contempt. She didn't mean . . .

"Hell, we don't have to live in the city. It would be better for the kids anyway."

He had taken her too literally. She wasn't ready for a decision yet. She only knew that her misadventure with Charlie had ruined her forever with her in-laws. The sense that she was secretly superior to them, which had sustained her for eight years, was gone.

"We wouldn't have to send them to private schools; we'd probably save money in the long run." He was eager now, a little boyish, but still not sure.

In a rush of elation she realized how much power she had over him. It was amazing—she who had always been so powerless in this marriage. How had it come about? Could it be the power of her inferiority? She didn't like to dwell on it but she had understood, during the first years of marriage, that Judd was afraid of women, afraid of equality in women. The famous Natalie, who he always said he might have married—well, she'd met Natalie and known at once that Judd couldn't have kept up with her. A tall, assured woman with upswept hair and perfect posture and black eyes that sparkled like a fountain Coke. She was already a buyer at Russek's, purses, and had a slyly mocking attitude toward Judd. Natalie had spotted the mother bond—you could hear it in her voice when she asked about Selma—and had walked out on him. Yes, it was Natalie who had done the rejecting. And she, Margaret, had popped up from Texas at the precise moment when Judd had started to doubt the basic things about himself. She had come north and claimed a kinship (distant but still there) that eased his fears. Margaret Barish, with her inferiority complex and her schoolgirl dreams and her ridiculous twang and her brown skin—so brown you'd think she was an Arab or a Gypsy—had filled the bill exactly. All that constituted her hold over him. He had gotten a wife, a needful brown wren, without having to give up anything. He could strut and pretend, bring her to Guiffanti's, show off the children at the office, call his magnificent mother every day, forbid her to get a job, induct her into the Sunday dinners and treat her with a deadly mixture of pride and patronage. And so he had been devastated when she ran off with Charlie, the other interloper, the handsome

Dutchman from Michigan. Her flight had reawakened all his old doubts. Maybe Natalie was right. Maybe the world was full of Natalies who would always mock him, slyly but unmistakably, when they got to know him. Maybe he would end up with his mother, just the two of them, while his colleagues and customers passed winks around in a circle.

Her elation slowed down into certainty. There was no need to be afraid of him any more. There was no need to defer. She was as strong as he was, maybe stronger, because she had broken the rules and he hadn't. The words slipped out of her: "What would you think of moving to Westchester?" It was her next test, her next probe, before she could make up her mind. She had an image of the county. A place of estates, ponds, woods, schools surrounded by vast playing fields. She could imagine a new escape, not like the first one from Gideon, nor the second one with Charlie. No, a different movement altogether, to a place where she and Judd would meet as equals in a new kind of marriage. A house materialized in front of her—Tudor, half-timbered, with casement windows. Something you might see in Stratford-on-Avon.

"If you want to go to Westchester, let's go. Get your hat and coat."

She smiled faintly—an old joke. But she still wasn't sure. "What about your mother?"

A pause, followed by a shrug. Was that a declaration of independence? Or merely a shift in the alliance? "If she wants to drive up and see us, she can. She has the Packard. She's always complaining she's got nowhere to go."

Yes, the Packard, Selma's mobile kingdom, her throne on wheels. She sat in the back and gave orders to Paul, the chauffeur, through a little microphone. Judd was watching her now, even as he signaled for the check, both of them groping their way toward a new balance. If she were alone she'd take out paper and pencil and make a list—pluses and minuses—but that wasn't possible here. She had to find the answer in the most unreliable places, in her guilt and dread, her disappointment with Charlie, her children, the illuminations of a moment ago.

He took his gold toothpick from his vest pocket and applied it, a ritual she had always disliked at the dinner table. He saw her reaction and put it away. A small concession, but one he wouldn't have made a year ago.

"Enjoyed having you and the missus. And please give my best to your father." Jimmy edged the bill onto the table; it was inside a maroon leather book.

He was waiting, head down, doggedly. They had to decide. They couldn't leave without deciding. And then she saw that her escapade with Charlie, for all its irresponsibility, was nothing to be ashamed of. It had frightened Judd, it had shown her what Charlie was made of, and it had introduced her to a new self.

"I'll call some real estate agents tomorrow morning," she said. "We'll have to find someplace with good train service to the city."

He observed her for a moment, unsmiling. "You're the boss."

Outside she overcame her reluctance and looped her hand, in a kid glove, through his arm. He liked that, pressing it tight against him. The future spread out in front of her with fearful clarity. Maybe they had both known, from the moment of his arrival at Mama's apartment a few hours ago, that it would end this way. It was a sad thought—she turned her mind away from it. If only Charlie Rysdale had been different. Just a little bit different.

2

MARGARET
The Move

She found the house—Tudor, half-timbered and stuccoed—after two months of looking. It turned up in White Plains on the day Roosevelt was inaugurated. It had a huge front lawn with one dogwood and one maple tree, a stand of blue spruce where the driveway turned, ancient resin-stained pines at the street. It was a good neighborhood of large homes, quiet streets, few cars. She had known it was for her right off, as if the house had dropped into a matching cutout in her mind.

Judd took to the house and the country from the first. When he got home in the evening during the first summer, just ended, he would walk around the yard, inhaling the air, the light, the greenery. It was the expansion of the city boy into rural space, she knew, though she was surprised at the depth of his pleasure. Even tripping over croquet wickets set up by the children didn't annoy him. Wickets were part of life in the country.

It had taken them almost six months to get here. Months not only of house-hunting and investigating schools but dealing with Selma. There had been an imaginary illness or two, some dishevelment, a few scenes. Not that Margaret discussed anything with her mother-in-law. She didn't go to their apartment anymore. Judd went one night a week for dinner, the children on Saturday afternoon. That was all. Sunday was their own family occasion now, Mama and Uncle Harris joining them for a roast or fried chicken. Selma had managed to delay them, but in the end she had lost.

The subject of Charlie Rysdale never came up. Even when Hattie's divorce became final, Judd mentioned it only in passing, not naming Charlie. She was dying to know where Charlie had gone, if he had moved out West, but she held her tongue. That was part of their bargain, the unspoken one made at Guiffanti's. Judd would give up his mother and she would give up Charlie—both connections thinning out and breaking. That wasn't entirely possible with Selma, of course, but at least he was making an effort. New battle lines were being drawn; the Packard had never turned up in the driveway of their new home.

Sister, on a visit from California just before their move out of the city, had pooh-poohed the whole idea of escaping from her in-laws. "You'll only be an hour away, they've got a car as big as all creation. They'll turn up every week." This was in their New York apartment, the crates and boxes half-packed. Margaret knew that Sister was wrong, that the rift was too deep to be closed, that Hattie's hatred kept widening it, but she didn't argue. Sister had disapproved of the episode with Charlie and she didn't want to go into all that right now.

In fact, Sister prided herself on her hard grasp of reality, an antidote to her younger sister's dreaminess. And she had proved her good sense by marrying Mark Giangrande, now an executive in the Hearst empire and rising rapidly on the strength of various circulation-boosting schemes cooked up in his fertile mind. Sister was meeting famous people. Not only Mr. Hearst and his columnists—Dorothy Kilgallen and F.P.A. and Bob Considine and Sidney Skolsky—but radio stars and even movie people. In fact, she had developed a touch of the grande dame, Margaret thought, serving her tea with cookies from Schrafft's. Sister curled her pinkie over teacups now and had perfected a fake smile. It was hard to recall they had once pushed past each other, screaming, to get to the tepid bathwater during those hellish summers in Gideon. But of course that was always Sister's ambition—to put Gideon behind her for good.

The main topic today was Mama. The coming move to White Plains would leave her in New York with Uncle Harris, who was at work all day. Mama never went out, never made friends. Not in Gideon either, where she had had calling cards made like the other ladies but never used them, not once. Sister had already dropped several hints about taking Mama to the country with them.

"Judd put his foot down." Margaret wiped her upper lip with her hankie (hot for May, too hot for tea, really). "If he's finally getting away from Selma, I can't insist on Mama, can I?"

Sister looked distressed, touching her hair nervously. It was tightly marcelled, like a helmet; she had come directly from the beauty parlor. Margaret knew the cause of the distress—Sister didn't want Mama traipsing around the house in San Francisco but she felt guilty about leaving her in New York. Sister was afraid of what Mama might say when Gabriel Heatter or H. V. Kaltenborn came to dinner. Would she clack her false teeth to be funny? "Maybe we could get Teeny to come and live with her," Sister said, sipping her tea, the pinkie curled.

Margaret shook her head. Teeny Seelig was Mama's best friend in Texas, but she wouldn't come to stay. Not permanently.

Sister sighed. "Teeny would love to have Mama live with her back there."

"Mama won't leave Uncle Harris."

A dilemma without a solution. Mama would only leave her favorite brother for one of her daughters. But neither of them wanted her. In her prime, Mama had weighed 270 pounds, with upper arms like watermelons and a rocking walk the neighbor kids imitated. Sometimes she wore her blue wrapper all day. When Mama showed up on parents' day at school both of them died a thousand deaths—not only because of her appearance but because she always said the wrong thing, words that made the teachers' eyes glaze over and their mouths set in a thin line. Unlike fat people in books, Mama wasn't good-natured. She was highly critical, fast with her slaps and given to ridiculing her husband. It wasn't Papa's fault he'd been born in Romania, but Mama liked to harp on it. "I married a furner," she would exaggerate, turning down the corners of her mouth, while Papa shifted from one foot to the other. No, Mama hadn't been like the fat ladies in the circus whose sorrows were always hidden under smiles. Mama never smiled unless it was at someone else's misfortune. If you saw Mama clamp a chicken under one powerful arm and wring its neck without changing her expression, you knew what she was like.

"Well, if there's nothing you can do, Uncle Harris will have to look after her." That seemed to close the subject for Sister, but Margaret knew it wasn't the end. Mama would still be her responsibility, juggled among all the other demands. There was no help for it.

Sister was getting ready to go. She looked around for her handbag. She was meeting Mark at the Rainbow Room at five.

"Something I wanted to tell you before you go." Margaret tried to keep her voice nonchalant, but that didn't fool Sister. She knew every gradation of tone.

"What is it?" Sister's sepia eyes scurried up and down her face, the usual mixture of love and disparagement. She had never been quite good enough for Sister, but there had been only the two of them against the world.

"I've been trying to persuade Judd to change our name."

"Oh?" Sister pressed her lips together. "What did he say?"

"He doesn't see anything wrong with Schanberg."

Sister picked up her teacup, her eyes stealthy. "And?"

"I said it would make it easier for the children. They're young. We're moving. It's the right time. He wouldn't listen."

Sister lowered the cup. "Then there's nothing you can do."

"I'll try one more time."

"It's his parents."

"No, it's him. He says he can't because of downtown. Everybody at the office would disapprove."

"Well, it's called the Schanberg Textile Company, isn't it?"

"Yes."

"I wouldn't press it, Margaret. Men are funny about their names."

She permitted herself a small snort. "If they had to change them when they got married, they wouldn't care so much."

Their eyes probed at each other. Only Sister could understand. Not Mama, not Uncle Harris, certainly not Judd. He wasn't even sympathetic. "Why don't you forget all that?" he had asked harshly when she first broached the subject. "You live in New York now." And something in her had acknowledged he was right, even as she knew she couldn't forget.

"Don't make a pest out of yourself, that's my advice." Sister's tone was brisk. The subject was closed. She found her bag and took out her compact, turning her face left and right as she checked the mirror. Margaret watched her, stifling wisps of resentment. It wasn't Sister's problem. Sister had left such problems behind. She had agreed, in marrying Mark, that their children would be raised as Catholics. They had two boys now, Mark Jr. and Joseph.

The front door opened, followed by a scamper of feet. The children, coming from their after-school, supervised visit to the park.

Harris stopped when he saw Sister, his raisin-cookie eyes scanning her distrustfully, but Mag kept coming. "Hello, Sister," she said. "Are you going to see our new house?"

Sister smiled. "I won't have time, I have to go back to California. How about a kiss?" Mag obliged. "I wish I had a little girl," Sister said, holding Mag for a good look. "A little girl as pretty as you."

"Mother doesn't think I'm pretty," Mag replied.

Margaret exploded. "Who told you that?"

Mag stared defiantly. "Aunt May told me every day and you never say anything."

She looked at Sister over the child's head. "That was the governess Selma hired when I was away last autumn."

"Well, Mag, you come live with me and I'll tell you you're pretty every single day."

"All right."

Harris had gravitated to his mother. She put an arm around him. "Do you remember Sister?" He nodded, saying nothing. "Do you want to give her a kiss?" Still not speaking, he made his way over and brushed against his aunt's cheek.

"Isn't that sweet?" Sister said, daubing at the spot with her tea napkin. "Well, I must be going." She hugged Mag again.

After she left, Mag turned to her mother. "I want to go live with Sister," she said. Margaret didn't answer.

....

It was September now, and the children would be entering the big red-brick elementary school at the corner of the Post Road in another week. Mag in the fourth grade, Harris in the second. The first summer in White Plains hadn't been easy for them, though Mag, circling the neighborhood on her new bike, had made a few friends. Harris, on the other hand, had stuck close to home. But she was sure his social problems would be solved in school. He loved classrooms, paints, pencils, erasers, crayons and teachers. Surely all that would lead to friendships.

This morning, in fact, a Wednesday, all the chores associated with the move were behind her. She could hear Mildred and Ernest, the couple they had hired, talking softly in the kitchen. Mag was off on her bike and Harris was at the YMCA, at his Indian story class, which he attended only under protest, and which hadn't produced the benefits she hoped. She really had no more excuses for postponing her project. Today was the day.

She had the church picked out, having noticed it first on her rides with the real estate lady. St. Bartholomew's on Prospect Street was a brown edifice of rusticated limestone, a material that Episcopalians seemed to favor. There was a parish house next to it, also of stone, and across the street the minister's residence. His name, Allard C. Winthrop, D.D., appeared on a sign attached to the portico of the church.

She had driven past the church many times, but each time she knew she wasn't ready. Yesterday she had realized she would never be ready; it was up to her to overcome her unreadiness. It was like going to school in Gideon on certain days, no matter what. The alternative was to hide in the henhouse—but there were no henhouses around here.

She had the outfit picked out and she went upstairs now to dress. A navy suit, a white silk blouse with a little blue ribbon at the collar which she tied overhand. Her hair, which was black, bangs in front, graduated in back almost like a boy's and modeled on Katherine Mansfield, would take the white sailor-style hat nicely. And white gloves. Her makeup had to be just right, plenty of powder, the rouge blended carefully. She also did her nails, though she didn't have the patience to paint them carefully. When she finished she looked at herself in the mirror, lowering the half veil over her eyes. She really looked quite smart. She slipped into a pair of white pumps and headed downstairs.

She parked down the street from the church for reasons she didn't quite understand. Then she checked the little mirror a last time, adjusting her veil, smoothing her rouge. Her heart was beating against her ribs and her palms were damp. But that was ridiculous. There was nothing to be afraid of.

It was cool in the vestibule, by the font. She saw a man dusting the pews inside and waved, knowing instantly that was the wrong gesture. Remembering to hold up straight, she marched toward him. "I'd like to see the minister," she said.

The man, who was red-haired, with a squashed-looking face, struck her as a mental defective. He grimaced, took a cigar stub from his mouth and pointed it to a door at the left of the chancel. Taking a deep breath, she walked toward it. Inside, the room appeared to be a place where the choir hung their robes. Then she saw an inner room. A handsome young man sat behind a desk. He rose when he saw her. He was tall, with a boxy head topped by flaxen hair. She recognized it instantly as an Episcopalian head.

"I'm Dr. Winthrop." He came into the vestry, extending his hand. He seemed very sure of himself.

The sentences she had rehearsed floated lightly by, just out of reach. At last she said, "We just moved here and we were . . . I was looking for a church." It came out abruptly, almost breathlessly. She hoped it didn't sound as if she were shopping for something. But he inclined his head politely and invited her to his office. By the time she was seated, had removed her gloves and draped them over her purse, she had collected herself.

"Where did you reside before, Mrs. . . ." He nodded at the rings on her left hand.

"Schanberg," she replied, then added, as planned, "It's a German name. It used to be von Schanberg."

Dr. Winthrop inclined his head again. She had the impression he did this frequently. "I have two children," she went on. "I'd like them to go to Sunday school."

"Well, we're always delighted to get new pupils." He moved a pad in front of him. "What are their names, Mrs. von Schanberg?"

"Margaret and Harris."

"And their ages?"

As he wrote this down she wondered if she should correct him about the name. Judd would be furious. But it sounded so aristocratic.

"And where were they baptized?"

She hadn't thought about that. Her breath came short for an instant and she clutched the purse on her lap. She was just about to make something up when he intervened smoothly.

"You'd be surprised how many parents don't bother with baptism nowadays." He smiled and dipped his head. "We're always glad to arrange it here. You saw the font on the way in. A very simple ceremony, just the parents and one godparent." His smile became broader, quite dazzling. He had large square teeth like Chiclets. "Traditionally, the church has requested two godparents, but since their duties are now entirely symbolic . . ."

She'd caught her breath now. "Of course. My sister would be glad to do it. Mrs. Giangrande. She lives in California, but next time she comes east . . ."

"I'll mark that down. Sometimes Bishop Manning comes out from St. John the Divine to do our confirmations, and perhaps we can also get him to baptize . . ." He consulted his pad. ". . . Margaret and Harris." His eyes, the blue of export ware, shone on her. "That would be something they could talk about the rest of their lives."

She took out her hankie and wiped her upper lip. The room was cool but she was warm.

"Our Sunday school meets at ten o'clock. If you plan on attending our eleven o'clock communion service and the children can't get home by themselves, we have a special program while they wait for you . . ."

As he went on, his voice cultivated and vaguely English, she marveled at the simplicity of it all. There had been no reason to be afraid. The only barrier had been in her own mind. She had a sudden impulse to tell Dr. Winthrop—she liked him, he was just the sort of person she could trust—the true story from beginning to end. What a relief that would be. And wasn't the Christian church always looking for converts? What were the first Christians except converts themselves? But even as the impulse surged up, it died. She couldn't. She just couldn't.

"I hope Mr. von Schanberg will join us on Sunday too. We don't get the turnout of husbands we'd like." He laughed gently. "They say they're too tired."

Judd wouldn't come. Once maybe, out of curiosity, but never again. "My husband isn't . . . well, religious."

"There's the fellowship." He cited the men's bowling team, the men's bazaar committee, the sports program for children living in the poor sections of town. "Our men are active in those events. They're a very fine bunch. He'd make some real friends."

She wouldn't get Judd near any of that but she smiled. "I'll try to talk him into it."

"Good."

There seemed to be nothing left to say. Mag and Harris were to be dropped off this Sunday. She herself would come for the later service. And the children would walk home by themselves. She stood up. In shaking hands he pressed his other hand over hers. His palms were lean and strong, reminding her, quite absurdly, of Charlie Rysdale.

At the door she turned. "We've dropped the 'von,' " she said.

"I'll remember that." He inclined his head a last time.

Driving home, she observed the neighborhood freshly, as if a slight fog had lifted. It was full of handsome houses, well-kept lawns, old maples and elms. She had a strong, clear picture of herself as belonging here. She might even join some of the clubs she'd read about in the local paper—the League of Women Voters, the Garden Club, the Friends of the Library. They might even lead to other things, invitations to private clubs, social clubs. Everything connected in a town like this, one open door leading to other open doors. She knew about it from Gideon. The pecking order had been crystal-clear in Gideon.

Once, when she was about ten, she had asked Mama why they

didn't go to the Baptist church like everybody else. Mama had shot out her jaw, then slapped her a good one. "Our religion is older than theirs," she hissed. But that answer hadn't satisfied her. If their religion was older why did everyone disrespect it so? Why was she never elected to clubs? Why were they always leaving her out of watermelon socials and scrapbook parties? She had asked Sister these questions but Sister had refused to discuss them.

And now it was over. She had become just like everybody else. She had joined the Baptist church, or its equivalent in White Plains. She took her right hand off the steering wheel and pressed it against her chest, as if it might cup the joy within.

It wasn't until she was turning into the driveway that the image of the Haggadah presented itself. It was Papa's, the precious book he had brought in his steamer trunk all the way from Comanesti. She saw the silvery pages, the stains of spilled wine, the threadbare gilt cloth that wrapped it when the evening was over. Why was she thinking about it? It was gone now, as dead as Papa. But it was spoiling the victory of her visit to the church. Still, it accompanied her as she entered the house, checked on dinner, went up to change into her gardening clothes. It was like a limb that had been amputated. A phantom pain. It made her breath come short.

How well she remembered those evenings, especially the part about Elijah. A bit of the chant came back to her now, in the bedroom with the sun streaming in. *Eliyahu ha-navi, Eliyahu ha-tishbi.* The rhythm had lodged in her mind. That was the moment she liked best, when they poured the glass of wine and opened the front door for Elijah. It had thrilled her to know that the prophet would return disguised as a poor person. And she always knew who Elijah would be—Pancho, the crazy Mexican who slept under the courthouse. Yes, Pancho would come to their door asking for food or money or his glass of wine, and before Mama could turn him away, she would stand up and cry, "No, it's Elijah!" And they'd all look at her, knowing she was right, and let him in. And she would have been true to the spirit of Passover, to Elijah, to herself.

She stopped, holding her gardening slacks and shaking her head.

It was so foolish. The world wasn't like that. No one fed the poor, least of all somebody like Pancho, not in Gideon. Even so, as she headed downstairs, the thought of Elijah stayed with her. Maybe now, right here in White Plains, she would open the front door one night a year without telling anybody. Do it for Papa, for the things he had taught her, to appease his ghost. Pesach, he had called it, which had always made Mama snap, "This is America, Carl, it's 'Passover.' "

By the time she unlatched the little gate to the vegetable garden—time to pick the last of the snap beans before the frost—she was feeling better. She was free of memory again, and Papa had disappeared.

Judd refused to go to St. Bartholomew's but, aside from being subdued and slightly crabby next Sunday morning, raised no objection to the children going. He viewed it, she knew, as part of their new bargain, their move to the country. He had ceded more territory to her, and church was part of it.

She dressed the children carefully the first time, trying to encourage Harris into enthusiasm. But when the time came she had to drag him wailing into the parish house and pry him loose for the teacher, a pretty girl named Linda. Mag showed no reluctance—partly, she knew, because Harris was making a scene.

But when she came back an hour later for the eleven o'clock service, Harris was beaming. He was clutching a couple of lithochromes—Jesus helping his father in the carpenter shop, Jesus delivering a sermon to his elders in the temple—and showed them excitedly. He had liked the class. They told stories. The teacher had called on him and he had spoken up. Another boy asked to be his friend.

Mag, on the other hand, was furious. None of the other girls had Shirley Temple curls. There had been some teasing. One of her curls had gotten pulled from behind. She wanted to go back to New York. She didn't like White Plains. She hated church. Also, she missed Nana.

After trying to make peace, Margaret walked them to the corner and pointed out the way home. It wasn't far, a fifteen-minute walk, and almost no cars, but she had the odd feeling she was abandoning them. For a moment she wondered if she should drive them. But that would make her late for her service. At last, stifling her qualms, she watched them saunter off, Harris in the lead, waving his pictures. It would be all right. Judd had promised them a croquet game. It was good for them to find their own way home.

She entered the church, now filled with women in ornate hats and half as many men, and slipped into a pew. A few minutes later the choir entered, an angelic procession. The crucifix was held aloft at the front, then came the sopranos, altos, tenors and basses. Bringing up the rear was Dr. Winthrop, looking ethereally handsome in a magenta cassock and white surplice, the hymnal in his hand, singing lustily. She had never seen anything so gorgeous. It was like an illustration from Doré. When he saw her he inclined his head ever so slightly. It was a welcome especially for her; it gave her goose bumps.

Kneeling on the soft, oval-shaped cushion when her neighbors did, standing up when they did, sitting back when they did, she gave herself completely to the ritual. The words, the tinkling bell, the smell of incense—everything had a special intensity for her. She felt almost dizzy at times. Only when communion was offered did she feel a little uncomfortable. She hoped Dr. Winthrop didn't notice her sitting there in the deserted pew. But she couldn't go up—she hadn't even been baptized, much less confirmed. The image of St. John the Divine popped into her head—Dr. Winthrop had mentioned it. She would call them and make an appointment, for both herself and the children. When her neighbors filed back, looking mild and serene, she gave them a confident smile. It was only a matter of time before she joined them.

After the service Dr. Winthrop closed both his hands over hers at the front door. He was beatific with goodwill. "Did you bring Margaret and Harris, Mrs. Schanberg?" He had an amazing memory. She laughed, her girlish pleasure laugh, and told him. He was delighted. "Now all we need is your husband for the whole family to be here!" She agreed with that, then hurried happily to her car.

On the way home she had to fight her exultation. Judd mustn't see it; it would only complicate matters.

The croquet game was still in progress at home. Ernest, in his white serving jacket, was playing too, though he should have been helping Mildred with Sunday dinner. Still, it was good to see him there. Judd had probably invited him to join in—part of his ease with servants, his hidden boyishness. If there was a game, everybody had to play. Watching them yelling, laughing, waving mallets, she felt a surge of affection toward the world. There seemed to be a happy place for everyone.

"Harris cheated, we caught him." Mag brushed hair out of her eyes but it kept falling back.

"No, I didn't. I just put the ball back where it was."

Judd put his foot on his ball and knocked the one next to it across the lawn. It belonged to Mag, who started screaming. Harris stuck out his tongue at her. Judd grinned, baring nicotine-stained teeth.

She shook her head. She didn't understand how they could get so worked up about a game.

"Why don't you call it quits? It's almost time for dinner."

Ernest looked at her warily. It was his turn. "Go on, play," Judd said to him. From the lie of the balls she could see Ernest was going to win. In three strokes he knocked his ball against the last post.

"Okay," Judd said to the children, "congratulate Ernest. He won." Ernest looked mildly alarmed. He was really quite handsome, she thought, with wavy ginger hair and a sturdy square-cut build.

Both children took an immediate interest in something high in the pine trees. Judd issued the order again. Mag muttered something inaudible, brushing at her hair, and Harris did the same. Ernest headed around back to the kitchen door. The lesson in good sportsmanship was over, she thought; now it was time for the lesson in washing your hands.

As they made their way into the house she tried to think of what to say about her morning in church. She was dying to tell Judd about the colors, the smells, the sounds. He'd missed something marvelous. At the same time she realized that telling Judd about the beauty of the service was impossible. She looked at him, flushed pink with excitement, his thin, fine hair mussed, the sleeves of his shirt rolled up. She mustn't rush things. He would come around in time, provided she was tactful. A surge of victory went through her. She had gotten everything she wanted, almost. And she'd only had to give up one person.

But of course she hadn't given him up, not entirely. Bits and pieces of Charlie still floated around in her—the sight of him standing nude at the window of the Traymore, the first touch of his ivory hands at their secret dinner, the understanding she always read in his eyes.

She fought against these, not wanting to make comparisons, determined to stick by her bargain with Judd, but sometimes her mind raced off. She had given up Charlie to come to this house in the suburbs, but could she be sure she hadn't lost more than she'd gained? That she hadn't given away the best part of her, the pledge that was older than her pledge to Judd and the children? She watched him herd Mag and Harris into the downstairs lavatory, heard them whooping and splashing. There was no way to make a final accounting, not yet anyway.

She brought up the subject of Mama's visit over dessert, a strawberry shortcake, Mag's favorite. She just mentioned it casually, after Judd had amused the children by putting the fruit-bowl centerpiece on his head. "I asked Mama out for next week, just a few days, she needs a change."

He didn't say anything, just flickered his nostrils, and she knew it would be okay. He went to his parents' on Thursday night anyway, so that just left two evenings during which they would cross paths. Not that she was having Mama out for her own enjoyment, or for any reason other than duty. But there was no way to avoid it, any more than Judd could avoid visiting his own mother. She sighed to herself as Ernest brought in Judd's coffee. Keeping everybody happy took all her ingenuity.

The subject of church came up that evening, after the Jack Benny show, which the children were allowed to listen to. At seven-thirty, when they were sent resisting to bed, she was finally alone with Judd. He was in the wing chair by the Magic-Eye radio-phonograph, his glasses on his forehead, his eyes closed. It was a favorite posture when he relaxed. She observed his fair, fleshy face. He would never be her type, but she was no longer repelled. There were times, in fact, when he seemed almost attractive. She wasn't sure if this was due to the shift in their relations. She had retained her influence. He listened to her, grunting and grudging, but listening. She had ideas about everything—what he should do at the office, with his parents, with the future. Sometimes it seemed that these ideas, this sureness, had always been hers, just been overlaid by timidity. Well, she wasn't so timid anymore. And her new confidence had enlarged her in other ways. It wasn't only Charlie Rysdale who could trigger her responses. She was braver about her body now, listening for the beat, the surges, making demands—even insisting they leave the light on. Now, watching Judd relax in the wing chair, it occurred to her that she had made him grow up a little. Pushed him against his will, against his mother's wishes.

He opened his eyes, settled his glasses back on his nose. "How was church?" His voice was cautious; she wondered if he really wanted to hear.

"It was fine. Harris liked Sunday school a lot."

"Mag said she hated it."

She explained Mag's problems with the curls.

"I don't know whether it's right." He lifted the Sunday paper, the roto section, from the floor and started to doodle on the margins. "They'll learn all that horseshit about Jesus and the Jews."

"I wish you wouldn't curse." Her hand went to her throat. That wasn't what she meant to say.

"They'll grow up with the wrong ideas."

She thought about the service this morning. How could all that be the wrong idea? "I wish you'd come with me sometime and see for yourself."

"I always hated that religious business."

She knew. When they met, on their first evening alone, he told her he had played hooky from regular school and from Hebrew school as much as he could. He'd almost missed being bar-mitzvahed. "I don't want them to be handicapped in life," she said. "I want them to have every possible opportunity."

"I wasn't handicapped."

She thought about Selma, about mother and son. Wasn't that a handicap? And where did it come from? "Things have gotten harder. Harris will have to fight for a good job."

"We can take him into the firm."

She dismissed the idea with a wave. She didn't want Harris on Seventh Avenue. She wanted him in a career like medicine. Or diplomacy. She'd been thinking about the foreign service recently—Sumner Welles, Cordell Hull, William C. Bullitt. Ritzy people went into the diplomatic corps. Besides, South America was the continent of the future, all those natural resources waiting to be developed. "They forced you into the firm. You want to do the same thing to Harris?"

He shrugged. "Maybe he'll like it." He doodled a little harder.

"No, he won't. He has to prepare for something else. I think he should learn Spanish. You have to start young with languages."

"Spanish? What the hell for?"

She began to explain about Latin America, the continent of the future. He was listening, but she could feel his remoteness. What caused it? Lack of imagination? Disinterest in his son? Perhaps he thought these things took care of themselves, but she knew better. "I've already called the high school to see about a good Spanish teacher for private lessons. There's a Miss Niskern there."

"Why don't you let the boy alone?" The words came out in a tangled snarl. Briefly, she wondered if Judd was jealous of his son. If he resented her planning and attention. But she couldn't pursue that thought—it led nowhere, worse than nowhere. Of course, she might have to soft-pedal her plans if Judd was going to act like this, but she wouldn't change them. Harris was going to have extra arrows in his quiver and that was that.

She sat quietly for a few minutes, watching Judd doodle. "Did I ever tell you about that time with the Ku Klux Klan in Gideon?" He didn't reply. "Mama used to talk about it." She couldn't tell if he was interested. His head was bent. He was getting gray at the back. "Her father, I hardly remember him, was in the store late one night. You know, they lived upstairs, over the store."

She told it as she remembered it, as Mama had related it one evening on the side porch where they'd gone for a breath of air while Papa worked late in his own store—though he sold furniture, not dry goods, as Mama's father had done. The Klansmen had paraded on San Jacinto Day the week before, as they always did, and they were still on Mama's mind. Her story came out slowly as she rocked and fanned.

They'd all been upstairs, Mama and her mother and three sisters and four brothers, while her father closed up below. Then they heard the horses' hooves, not one horse or two, but a thunder. They had crowded to the window as the dozen or more riders called her father out. They were in white hoods, white robes. "They would have been pretty," Mama had said, rocking and fanning, "if they hadn't been so ugly."

Her father, Ben Belansky, had stood on his porch, showing no fear. The leader of the local Klavern—everybody knew he was Ted Baines in real life—said they didn't want any Jews in Gideon. Jews were the anti-Christ, the instruments of Satan. The Bible said so. They had betrayed Jesus.

But when he finished speaking there was a stirring at the back of the troop. Another Klansman spoke up. Mama continued rocking and fanning, rocking and fanning, but her voice took on new excitement. Pride, even. The man in back pointed out that Ben Belansky had ridden with the Texas Brigade, with General Hood. He had been in the counterattack at the Chattahoochee. He was a loyal son of the southland. There had been some mutters, then some approving voices. The two long sticks of wood, held in readiness, had been taken down. After some more parleying, the contingent had ridden off. Her father, who hadn't said a word, finished closing the shop, then went upstairs to his family. He had never discussed the incident with anyone.

She waited after finishing the story, just as Mama had done that hot night on the side porch. It seemed that no time had elapsed between then and now. At last Judd spoke. "When did all that happen?"

"Let's see, Mama was born the year after the Civil War, and she was thirteen or fourteen—it must have been around 1880."

He continued doodling. "You're telling me we should worry about something that happened, or didn't happen, in 1880, over fifty years ago?"

"No, I'm not saying that." She twisted sideways. He was deliberately misunderstanding.

"Yes, you are."

"I'm saying some hatreds never die out."

"Not if you keep fanning the blaze."

Why wouldn't he see? Of course, his childhood had been utterly different. A tribal upbringing in New York, surrounded by people exactly like him. Did he think the Klan was dead? All the governors and senators from the South were Klansmen, everybody knew that. A few years ago they'd marched down Pennsylvania Avenue, right past the White House, thousands of them in their robes. Maybe Judd hadn't noticed that either.

"It's all in your imagination, Margaret. What's the difference whose ass you kiss—Moses or Jesus or the King of Siam?"

"You know it makes a difference. Not to you maybe, but to everybody else."

She could see his face redden, his lower jaw bulge out. He didn't agree with her; he would never agree with her. She would have to keep quiet and do it on her own. "Maybe you're right, I do fan the blaze."

That was what he wanted to hear, all right. His face relaxed, the red fading. She went on in that vein, calming him, reassuring him. There was nothing to be gained by winning this particular argument. But the next round would be hers.

"Why don't we take a walk around the yard?" he asked after a while. He dropped the paper on the floor. He wanted to forget their discussion.

"Just let me see if everything's all right in the kitchen."

She met him under the dogwood tree, which was covered with amber leaves and red berries. When she stood next to him, he put his heavy arm around her shoulders and kissed her. His lips were warm, probing. She felt a mild quickening.

"This is the life," he said, releasing her. They started to stroll around the lawn, keeping to the edge for fear of wickets. It felt marvelously safe and private, even though she could see distant lights in the neighboring houses. This morning's sense of victory returned. Everything was going to be all right. Her planning had brought them this far; there was nothing she couldn't accomplish. They walked for half an hour in the whirring dark, talking in low tones, and then they went upstairs to bed.

3

JUDD
The Visit

He looked down at his white ducks. There was a grass stain on the knee. He'd been roughhousing with the dogs and he'd slipped. What a pain in the ass. He wanted to look spotless today for Mother and Pop—their first visit. Three years, three whole years, and only now, this Sunday, had his mother finally agreed to come out. Pop would have come any time, of course, but not his mother.

He sighed and picked up the rubber ball. Both dogs tensed, staring at his hand, long strings of slobber hanging from their jaws. What magnificent creatures, right down to the round nails on their padded paws. He'd always liked big dogs and now he had two Great Danes, one more prize of country life.

He pretended to throw the ball. Both dogs ran madly toward the street, then turned around. He laughed. He'd fooled them. What a pleasure to tease without getting tears, cries, reproaches. What was a little teasing?

He took his watch out of the little pocket in his pants and gave the stem a turn. All wound up. Noon, all of them still at that damned church. They'd better not be late; the Packard would pull in at one sharp. This time he really threw the ball. The dogs bounded after it. Frankie, the female, got there first. Johnny stood around looking confused.

This church business. He'd gone once, just to make it a family foursome, but he'd never gone back. He didn't like it. He was there under false pretenses. When they held the collection plate up high, singing "All things come of thee, O Lord," it struck him as hypocrisy of the worst kind. First they lecture you about the evils of money, then they glorify it. The minister, the famous Dr. Winthrop, struck him as a fairy. And when Margaret came back from the communion with a holy-roller look on her face, he wanted to puke.

Still, there was no stopping her if that's what she wanted. He threw the ball again, trying to hinder his thoughts. In certain ways she was uncontrollable. Well, on this one subject she was uncontrollable. Now she was saying the boy would become an acolyte in a few years. That's right, wearing a long red skirt, lighting candles, bowing, all of it. He'd have to put his foot down. Put that boy in a skirt and he'd never take it off. That would make two of them, the boy and the minister.

What a contrast to Mags, a natural athlete like him. A photo of her in blue rompers, holding a hockey stick and looking fierce, sat on his desk at the office. Now, in summer, when she was tan from her games and hikes and swims, she reminded him of a lioness. A tawny lioness. They even sparred a little sometimes, she wasn't afraid at all, though he had to be careful about hitting her breasts, her little buds of breasts. Once, when he hadn't kept his guard up, she had knocked his glasses off.

It was hard to believe he had a family, one, two, three, four of them. Families happened to other people, but here he was. And who would have believed he'd marry someone like Margaret, when he could have married almost any girl in the world? She had the worst inferiority complex of anybody he'd ever known. For her to go off with Charlie Rysdale . . . hell, he didn't want to think about that. It was all settled between them, no point to digging it up. He threw the ball again, quickly.

And she was smart. He always showed her the accountants' statements; she could read them like a book. Once in a while she visited the stores in White Plains to check on prices. She got all that from her father and grandfather, a family of shopkeepers. He pried the slobber-smeared ball from Johnny's mouth. The stupid mutt finally caught one.

And thrifty too, if that was the word. He still couldn't get her to seal her envelopes. She tucked in the flap so they went for two cents instead of three. That way anyone could read your mail. He pretended to throw the ball one more time but the dogs didn't move. They were getting wise. He turned and headed for the house. The Giants were playing a double-header with Brooklyn today. He'd listen a little.

The Packard appeared exactly on time. Harris, on the porch, saw it first. "There they are!" he cried, leaping down the steps. He was nine now, growing like a weed. Mag burst out the front door and followed. The figures in the back seat rolled down their windows and waved. Judd saw all this from the living room window, hanging on to the Giants game. The bases were loaded, dammit, he had to hear the next pitch. Margaret was still upstairs, putting on the finishing touches. She was nervous. To tell the truth, he felt a little uneasy himself. *Carl Hubbell struck him out and the Dodgers were retired!* He turned off the radio and went to the porch. No more baseball today, no more anything except headaches.

His mother emerged slowly, pulling her dress down on both sides. Then she gathered each child into a long embrace. Pop waited, then gave each a brief hug and kiss on the lips. Judd knew those pursed, rubbery lips—they didn't convey much of anything but the stale flavor of cigars.

His mother was looking up at him eagerly, as if she hadn't seen him for years instead of just last Thursday. He went down the steps slowly, aware of the familiar sizzle of resentment. He stopped to shake hands with Paul, in his chauffeur's uniform, coming around the front of the freshly Simonized car. "How you, Mr. Judah?" What a pleasure—everything was so simple with Paul, who had been born under the Austro-Hungarian Empire. "Fine, fine, thanks, Paul."

His mother was staring at him with heavily mascaraed black eyes. Reproach was buried in their depths. But what had he done? "Judah." Her voice was exquisitely modulated, a little aria in one word. She pressed him hard against her, her hand like a crowbar against his back. He could feel her balloony breasts, the hardness of the corset. And she smelled exquisite. What would his life have been like if his mother hadn't smelled like a perfume shop? If she had smelled of sweat or salami? He couldn't imagine, except that the world would have been a different place. "We can't stay for dinner," she hissed into his ear.

He reared back. She smiled in modest triumph. "Margaret's been in the kitchen all morning." Not true, but she'd given so many instructions to Mildred and worried so much she might as well have cooked it herself.

Another smile of mild triumph. "Ruth Strauss invited us to the theater. We can only stay an hour."

He shook hands with Pop, then brushed his cheek. Pop avoided his gaze—he knew what that meant. He was embarrassed by the whole thing.

They headed toward the house, a regular procession—Paul with the packages, the kids hopping up and down alongside their grandmother, he and Pop bringing up the rear. Who was going to break the news to Margaret?

Pop delayed, looking around the yard, noticing the trees, the border stones painted white, the bluestone gravel, the shrubbery. Pop liked to notice things methodically, one by one. It was one of the secrets of his success—you couldn't rush him. "Looks nice, Judd."

"You really can't stay?"

Pop shrugged, looked away. "You know your mother." He heard a little starburst of anger in his father's voice. They'd probably had a quarrel coming out in the car. And Pop had lost.

Margaret was waiting for them in the living room. She was sitting on the couch, dressed in a long evening gown of some stiff material, sky-blue, with a bunch of artificial flowers at the vee of the neck. Even he knew it was all wrong. It was only one o'clock in the afternoon, for Christ's sake.

"Hello, Mother." She stood up and came forward, her gown rustling furiously. It sounded like rain on a tin roof in the tropics.

His mother, who was wearing a black outfit with a beaded bolero jacket and a little pillbox from Lily Daché, smiled stiffly. Margaret's gown swished some more. They pressed cheeks. Pop moved forward. Margaret seemed genuinely glad to see him. The children were stamping around the gifts, which Paul had deposited on the floor, and making noises, thank God. No one could say anything until they were opened. He didn't have to tell Margaret the news yet.

When his mother was settled on the couch, still with her determined little smile and wearing the hat, he went into the dining room to get some drinks. A rock-and-rye, that's what he needed. Pop too. Let them fight it out. But returning with the drinks, he knew that was a hopeless idea. If Margaret was upset, felt snubbed or mistreated, there'd be hell to pay. They'd all be miserable. It came to him in a burst of unwelcome insight—the happiness of the house depended on her happiness.

The children were still yelling about the presents. There were about a dozen, beautifully wrapped, each tagged. His mother pointed to one. "That's for Mag."

Mag let out a squeal. "Why don't we put some of these away for Christmas?" Margaret said. Mag's squeal turned to a screech.

"These are for *now,*" her grandmother said firmly. "There will be more for Christmas."

Mag grabbed the box and wheeled furiously toward her mother. "See, you can't take 'em away from me!" she shouted. She turned back to her grandmother. "She won't let us have anything!"

That wouldn't have been allowed to pass if they were alone, but Margaret let out a hollow laugh. Her daughter's hostility always increased in the presence of company.

"I'm sure your mother gives you everything you want, Mag." Pop was fond of peacemaking, but nobody paid attention.

"No, she doesn't," Mag snapped, opening the package. A pair of long silk stockings snaked out. She whooped. Just what she wanted.

He glanced at Margaret. She was holding her breath in, one hand clenched against her midriff. She wasn't enjoying this a bit. And he hadn't even told her yet.

"That one's for Harris," his mother pointed. He noticed she was wearing both her emerald and ruby rings today. Usually she wore one or the other. The boy took the box quietly, glancing at his mother first. She nodded. It was infuriating the way the two of them communicated by little winks and nods. It was practically a secret language.

Harris had received a tatting set. It was a spool-like contraption that wove yarn into a long tubular sock. When you had enough of the sock you coiled it into placemats or doilies or some damn thing. His mother had actually given the boy something made for girls. "Mother . . ."

"Now, don't start, Judah. Harris told me that this was what he wanted. There's nothing wrong with it."

The kid was staring at him, eyes glazed. Judd recognized the look—fear, and underneath, hatred. "Jesus Christ."

"Please don't start cursing." Both women were looking at him angrily. He tapped a Lucky Strike out of the green pack and lit up. What were they trying to do? Why were they ganging up on him? He looked at Harris again. There was spit at the corners of his mouth. Nine years old and drooling like a dog.

"Well, if that's what he wants." He couldn't keep the sneer out of his voice. Harris turned back to his gift, but his enthusiasm was gone. He looked guilty. Good.

There were other presents for the children. Then Pop pointed to one for Margaret. "You shouldn't have," she said, but it was her standard disclaimer. She really loved getting presents.

Pop got up and brought it over. There was a lot of unwrapping. It was a Sunbeam waffle iron, double, on its own tray. "You can bring it to the table just like that," Pop announced. "It was made for that."

Everybody ooh'd and aah'd. "When can we try it?" Mag demanded.

"Soon," her mother replied, examining the little dials on top. They said "Off," "Bake," and "Ready." "Next time we have company."

"Let's do it tonight," Mag said sharply. Everybody laughed.

His mother was staring at him. There was one package left. He had the distinct feeling that he would have to pay for it in ways unknown. "That's for you, Judah."

Everybody looked at him. What would happen if he said he didn't want it? That the price was too high? There were too many strings attached? Harris, at Margaret's urging, scooted over and picked it up. He handed it over without looking him in the eye, then went back and crouched against his mother.

Records. They had given him seven Victor Red Seal records. He read the front and back of each one, the label visible through the hole in the green sleeve. Lucrezia Bori. Lily Pons. Martinelli. Caruso. Gigli. All his favorites. He turned toward his mother. She was staring at him with intense pleasure, tugging at him, trying to squeeze love out of him like toothpaste from a tube. Impossible, it was all impossible. "How did you know what to get?" he asked. But that was stupid. She knew everything about him.

Pop smiled. "We were talking about the time you went to see *Romeo and Juliet*."

He grinned. He hadn't thought about that in years. He'd gone to every performance of that opera in one season—twelve times in all, standing each time.

"What was that, Daddy?" Mag didn't understand. He explained briefly, but she made a face. "You stood up the whole time?"

His mother had a relaxed, contented look now—for the first time since her arrival. He understood, with something like horror, that her trip hadn't been to see the house or the children or to make up with Margaret, but to give him the records. He stood up, grabbed Pop's glass and went for refills. In the dining room, at the cabinet that served as a bar, he looked out at the shrubs in the side yard. Full of flowers—bridal wreath and mock orange, light-years away from the hideous complexities in the living room. He should have been a lighthouse keeper or a game warden, something like that. Anything to stay away from human contact. He put down the bottle of rock-and-rye and pressed his hand against his chest. He could feel his heart fibrillating, jumping around. He should stop smoking, lose weight. His blood pressure was bad. But what the hell, it would serve all of them right if he dropped dead.

When he got back, Margaret was staring straight ahead, stone-still. She raised her eyes slowly. "They're not going to stay for dinner."

"My dear"—his mother's voice was throaty with stress—"this came up quite suddenly. Ruth Str—"

"But we've been planning this for so long." Margaret clamped both hands against her chest.

"Mother." He could hear the drumbeat in his ears. "You're not walking out."

"Judah, I told your father when we left home . . ."

"I don't give a good goddam what you told him."

Pop was making moist placating sounds. "We can stay, Selma, we can stay."

He turned to Mag. "Go tell Mildred to put dinner on."

Mag jumped up. No one spoke. When she came back she said, "Mildred said sit down, everything's ready."

Margaret got up, her long dress locking around her so that she almost fell. She kept her face averted from her in-laws. Judd looked at his mother. "Now stop this."

A haughty expression settled on her face. She would stay, but she would give nothing more. He had a brief vision of more Sundays like this one, his mother and wife locked in combat, the children whipsawed between them, Pop trying to keep the peace and his own heart speeding like a bullet from a gun. It would never end. And it wasn't even Charlie Rysdale's fault. His mother would have behaved like this, sooner or later, toward any wife of his.

They filed slowly into the dining room. On the way, his mother unpinned her hat and took it off, putting it on the table by the front door. It struck him as a temporary surrender only—proof that she didn't belong here and never would.

When the soup was served by Ernest—pea soup for which Margaret had saved a hambone from last week—his mother took three sips, then put down her spoon. Everybody watched but nobody commented. The conversation, about local matters, was strained, though everybody tried. Even Pop made an unusual effort, though he didn't like to speak during meals. Through the talk about schools, teachers, lawns, dog shows, bubble-gum cards, his mother sat with a small fixed smile. He could have killed her.

When the roast was served—beautiful prime ribs—along with fresh peas from the garden and mashed potatoes, his mother took a small sample of each, then put down her knife and fork.

He continued eating calmly, buttering his bread without haste, complimenting Margaret on the cooking. Even though a pall had descended, even though the children were tense and subdued and Margaret had her tragic look, he wouldn't give in. He wouldn't let the dinner be ruined.

When dessert was served—lemon meringue pie, which Margaret had made herself—his mother asked for a very small piece. Margaret cut her a sliver, but she ate the whole thing. Then she nodded at the long drapes on the windows. They were velvet, wine-colored. "Those are very pretty, Margaret," she said. The children smiled at each other and Pop sat back, exhausted.

"Mama—my mother—made them," Margaret replied.

"Did she?" His mother's creamy cheeks bunched into little round balls. "How is Lily?"

He closed his eyes and his heart slowed down. He had beaten her. He had sat here, at the head of his own table in his own house, and beaten her.

"She has her aches and pains but she's all right."

He looked up. His mother's dark eyes were fastened on him. *You see how much I love you?* they said. *You see?*

"She's always going to doctors," Mag piped up. That was an understatement. His mother-in-law had something wrong with every organ. She'd gone to hundreds of doctors, mostly quacks.

"It's so important to find a good one," his mother murmured. She and Margaret began to trade doctor stories. But he knew where the old lady's troubles came from—from a lifetime of eating like a pig.

"Does she mind your living so far away?"

His mother knew perfectly well, from his own reports, that the old lady spent half her time with them, a cumbersome operation that required several taxis and countless long-distance calls.

"Well," Margaret replied, "she likes living with Uncle Harris. They've always been very close. They were the nearest in age."

That was true. She was very attached to the old fruit. He'd arrived in New York at the turn of the century because they rode him out of Texas on a rail. "We put her on the lawn with her crocheting and a radio," he cut in. "She loves it here."

His mother looked at him, a troubled glance. He had the impression that this was harder for her than anybody. Yes, a lighthouse keeper or a forest ranger—what a life that would have been.

Dinner was over. Everyone except his mother folded their damask napkin. She left hers in a heap. He knew the habit—a signal to the maid that she wanted a fresh one for the next meal. She never reused napkins; it was one of her trademarks.

The children wanted to show their grandparents the new Ping-Pong table in the basement. They agreed but just for a minute. Then they would have to go. After they left for the basement he was alone with Margaret. She stared at him for a long moment, then turned and went into the kitchen. He could hear her complimenting Mildred on the meal. He went to the living room, past the debris of presents and wrappings, and sat in his wing chair. Christ, what an afternoon, even worse than he'd expected. He closed his eyes. The room still smelled faintly of his mother's perfume.

After the Packard had lumbered slowly out of the driveway—the three of them standing on the gravel waving, Margaret up on the porch also waving, though with less enthusiasm—he took a few turns around the yard. It was almost four now. His parents wouldn't get back to the apartment on Riverside Drive, by way of the new Bronx River Parkway, for an hour or more. There had never been a theater engagement with Ruth Strauss. It was all a pack of lies. He recalled his mother's last embrace. It had been as devouring as the first one, as significant and troubled as her look at the table. It occurred to him that there might never be a final payment to her. He would owe forever—a debt that could not be amortized. Weariness passed through him. He was even too tired to feel the familiar resentment. There was no solution. There never had been a solution.

The living room was empty when he went back inside. His glance fell on the pile of Red Seal records stacked beside the phonograph. Maybe he could forget the afternoon with some music, some time-travel to his youth. He put on "O paradiso" and set the lever for repeat.

Caruso's voice started at once, a shining sweetness. He could see him now—a sawed-off man, almost deformed, with no neck and a mouth like a bullfrog. But on the nights he sang you could never get enough. You wanted that shining sweetness to go on forever, plating the opera house with gold. He'd taken Margaret to the Met a few times when they lived in New York, but she was tone-deaf. She fell asleep during the dark episodes—the Nile scene especially—so what was the use? Now he closed his eyes.

After the third play he was entirely relaxed, the afternoon forgotten. Nothing was as real as these sounds, as Vasco da Gama discovering love in Africa, as the miracle of Caruso. He opened his eyes contentedly. Harris was sitting on the couch opposite. He'd tiptoed in. He was studying his shoes. When he saw his father awake he half-turned away. Judd felt the ripple of tension between them, the blessing of the music fading. What could he say to the boy? He had never been able to talk to him, to get past the conspiracy between Margaret and her favorite.

"Did you like that, Harris?"

The boy bobbed his head rapidly, still turned away.

"You want to hear another one?"

Again the nodding.

He flipped the record over. "Celeste Aïda," also with Caruso. But it wasn't the same. Now his mind was active. He shouldn't have made a fuss about the tatting toy. It didn't matter; the boy would grow out of it. But there was a trigger in him, a button, that got pushed, he didn't know why, and he said harsh things. "These are songs from opera, Harris."

The boy examined him through heavy-lidded eyes. "I know what opera is."

"You do?"

"It's like a play, but they sing."

"That's right. Would you like to go to one?"

An excited nod.

"I'll take you. To the Metropolitan Opera in New York. I went when I was a boy."

Yes, he'd started young, by the time he was Harris's age he'd seen half a dozen operas. And later, at home, Hattie would play through the Ricordi scores and they'd sing the big tunes together.

"You did?" Harris was excited now, his shyness gone. Should he tell him about the Diamond Horseshoe and the stories and costumes? He'd respond for sure. It was just the sort of thing he'd like.

"This is *Aïda,* maybe we can go see that."

Harris mispronounced the strange word, but Judd heard the secret affinity, could almost see the curtains parting in the boy's mind. "It's about a man and woman who love each other and are buried alive."

Harris sat immobilized as he went on with the plot. But suddenly, in the middle, he stopped. There was something about the kid's response . . . He thought back to the trouble with Charlie Rysdale. All told, the separation had lasted three months. The boy, deprived of his mother, had become nervous, withdrawn. There had been bed-wetting episodes. He'd tried to talk to the boy, take him out, but had gotten no response. There was something wrong with the kid, something missing. He'd lost his temper a few times, spanked him, surprised at the way his fury at Margaret allied itself with his disappointment in his son.

"Can I play them sometime?" Harris came over to the machine. He touched one red label lightly, then looked at him warily. Judd could almost hear the thin strands of thought working. The kid was going to be an opera fan. But he should have known that—it was up the same alley as the tatting set and his devotion to his mother and his hatred for sports. Suddenly his own love of music took on a slightly different cast. Very few men loved opera as he did. In fact, he had never told his pals about it when he was a kid, keeping it out of sight, a passion that couldn't be shared. Even now he didn't discuss it at the office.

Harris was staring at him, waiting. That passion, that weakness, had been passed on to his son. It was plain as day. Harris might have inherited anything else—his vigor, his aggression, his athletic ability—but no, it was the softness, the neediness, that had been transferred. It was like having a traitor right in your own house.

"Where's your mother?" It came out more harshly than he intended, almost angrily, and Harris flinched as if he'd been hit. But he hadn't hit the kid, he'd only asked him a question.

"Lying down."

Big eyes on his face, testing, questioning. What was the boy waiting for, for Christ's sake? A hug? A kiss? But that was impossible. What had he gotten from his own father? Just those rubbery kisses with the cigar smoke frozen in them. And once in a while a parlor trick like peeling an apple in one long strand so you could reconstruct it afterwards. It wasn't his fault if the kid couldn't assert himself, couldn't ask for what he wanted. The battles he'd had with his own parents! He grinned privately at the thought. Hour after hour, up and down Manhattan Avenue, all the way up to 110th Street, even after the new electric street lamps snapped on and he knew that Hattie, at his mother's request, was ducking into the stoops and basements and backyards, shouting for him. Never, never would he do what his parents wanted, not till his mother came charging out, tripping over her dress, the poker in her hand. That's what he waited for—his mother in battle regalia. Then, only then, would he leave his pals and go home. It was a battle he always lost, but in losing he won, because it proved that they cared and he didn't. Why wasn't Harris doing this? Why was he standing around waiting for somebody to give him permission to exist?

"Celeste Aïda" came to an end. The phonograph clicked off. He hadn't even heard the last note, the B-flat trumpeted through Caruso's million-dollar lungs. He stood up to remove the record. He'd had enough.

When he turned around he was alone. The kid had slipped away. He could hear his light step on the stair, probably going up to see his mother. He felt remiss, almost guilty, for a minute, then dismissed it. The whole thing was a jinx.

Mag appeared in the doorway. She was wearing her new silk stockings, but they were flopping around her ankles. She didn't have any garters. She blew against the lock of hair over her eyes; it lifted for a moment, then fell. "Why don't we do something?" Her voice was a challenge, a dare. He couldn't help smiling.

"What do you want to do?"

"I'll play croquet if I can start at the middle wicket."

"That's not fair."

"That's the only way I'll play. You're older than me. I deserve a three-wicket handicap."

He grinned. "Okay, but I'll still beat you."

"How much you wanta bet? Put her there, how much you wanta bet?" She stuck out her hand and wagered ten dollars, her allowance for the next two years. He took the bet.

They tried to keep the noise down, but it was hard. They had an argument after every play, right up to the finish, when he managed to beat her by one stroke. When he knocked his ball against the pole, she ran at him and butted him in the stomach. He got a hammerlock around her neck. They woke Margaret up, but they couldn't really help it, because a fistfight started after that. Of course, she refused to concede. He had cheated, she yelled, and her allowance still had to be paid. By that time he was laughing so hard he couldn't say a word.

4

MARGARET
The Camp

She told Nora to make foie gras sandwiches, open-faced, and be sure to cut off the crusts. Nora suggested using the cutter that cut the bread into spades. They would have little spade sandwiches when Miss Rose came to visit this afternoon.

Margaret left the kitchen with a familiar sense of relief. She liked Nora—a tall, intelligent woman of thirty with milk-chocolate skin. She wore horn-rimmed spectacles. She and her husband, John, had replaced Mildred and Ernest last year. If it hadn't been for prejudice, Nora would have had a career as a nurse or secretary. Seeing her here, giving her instructions for meals, gave Margaret pangs of conscience. Nora wasn't made to be a servant. When she mentioned this, Nora gave a rueful smile and said, "They don't let colored folks in those jobs, Miz Schanberg."

Last fall, soon after Nora and John Pinckney took up residence in the tiny room off the kitchen (space enough for the double bed, a bureau, one chair and a small table), Margaret had gone out seeking better employment for them. She'd called on Joe Ronan, who ran a factory in Mount Vernon, whose wife she knew through the Ladies' Auxiliary at St. Bartholomew's. But Joe had told her the facts. "If he wants a job sweeping the floor, okay, but not on the line. The other men would resent it." It was a corrugated paper factory, with a tart smell of glue, and as Joe gave her the tour, she had glimpsed a social structure behind the working men that towered rigidly into heaven. She didn't mention the visit to

Nora, but later that night, in bed, it occurred to her that slavery was America's original wickedness, an indelible stain that could never be rinsed out.

Judd had encouraged her efforts, but she knew he was cynical about results. He didn't really believe in social progress, even though he'd voted for Roosevelt last time around in 1936. At his core, she knew, there was a profound skepticism about people, change, improvement. She was just the opposite. She was positive things were going to get better and better. It should have been the other way around. Judd, who had been raised in love and luxury, should have been the optimist. It was a quirk, a fault in his nature. She sensed the same sour strain in Selma. Maybe it was because they were city people, had never caught a whiff of the West, of movement, migration, upheaval. Because they were easterners, looking to Europe, trapped in the past.

The phone rang in the front hallway. John came out of the dining room to answer it. He had a cap made from a stocking on his head. When he took it off this evening, his hair would be straight and slicked-down.

"The Schanberg residence," he said.

It was Sister. She and Mark lived in White Plains too now—just a few miles away. Mark had been transferred from California to the Hearst offices in New York.

"What time do you want me to bring Mama over?" Sister's voice was snappish, as usual.

Margaret thought about Miss Rose, due at four o'clock. "Could you make it around six?"

"Well." A pause. "I could drop her off on my way to the train. You're busy before then?"

"One of Mag's teachers is coming out. She wants to talk to me."

"Oh?" Sister's tone softened. She was always eager to hear about Mag. She was always shopping for her too. Every time Sister turned up with some new, wasteful furbelow, Margaret thought about Sister's two closets crammed with clothes back in Gideon. Pretty soon Mag would need another closet too. "What does she want to talk about?"

"She didn't say. But she's on the staff at Camp Birchmont."

"She wants Mag to be a junior counselor!" Sister's voice jumped a notch.

"I don't see how she can be a junior counselor if this is her first year. Besides, she's only thirteen."

Sister was not to be put off. "That's what it is, I just know it."

The same thought had occurred to her but she had dismissed it. "How's Mama?" she asked.

"I made an appointment with Dr. Ellis for tomorrow. You'll have to take her. She says her stomach medicine isn't working."

Mama's acid indigestion had gotten worse since Uncle Harris's death last year, when she moved to Westchester, dividing her time between the two houses. Maybe she had an ulcer.

Sister hung up without saying good-bye. She didn't have time to say good-bye. Margaret felt the familiar irritation, as if she had been cut off in mid-sentence. Then she reminded herself of Mama's new preference and felt better. She had discovered, in the last few months, that Mama really preferred living with her. Sister ordered her around, didn't let her eat what she wanted, was always buying new yarn and insisting she start a new afghan. But she, Margaret, was still obedient, perhaps still a little afraid, though Mama was never bad-tempered now. She was old and ill and dependent—how could she be bad-tempered? If Mama preferred her to Sister, then it was an old wrong set right. It was like Cordelia and Lear. The scorned daughter, the youngest one, turned out to be the one who cared, who deserved to be the favorite.

Of course, when her in-laws came for their regular Sunday visit, special arrangements had to be made. Mama couldn't be in the house; the two grandmothers couldn't cross paths. Naturally, Mama couldn't be informed of this. Lies, conspiracies, invented errands—it was a nightmare of lying and chicanery. Even the children had to be instructed what to say. But she didn't want Selma examining Mama with her keen dark eyes, making a thousand judgments, condescending. It would have been too painful. The visits were difficult enough now, requiring her to watch what she said, serve the right food, assert herself if necessary. Mama's presence would have tipped the scale.

She'd had to explain about church to Mama, now that she was

living with them half the time. She had chosen the moment carefully, when she was setting Mama's hair after a shampoo, generally a happy time. As she started to explain, however, looking in the mirror, she had recognized the old signs of anger. The thrust-out jaw, the darting eyes, the twitching hand. Mama was getting ready to slap her a good one, just as she had done a quarter-century ago. But Margaret kept on talking, her voice level. She couldn't let Mama intimidate her. Even if Mama couldn't understand, at her age, she would have to be firm. The children's future was at stake.

And then, unexpectedly, Mama had started to cry. But what was she crying about? About the rabbi sleeping over four times a year, which she used to complain about? Ben Belansky being called out by the Ku Klux Klan? Her youth, her home, her husband? Margaret didn't know. But she couldn't let the tears influence her either. She had to wait, comb in hand, till Mama got her hankie out of her brassiere. And after that everything calmed down. When the children showed their grandmother pictures from Sunday school she nodded and said nothing. They never discussed the subject again.

At four o'clock sharp a battered Chevrolet turned into the driveway. Margaret watched it with a sense of elation, then went to the kitchen to tell Nora to put on water for tea. The foie gras sandwiches were in the Kelvinator, nicely arranged on a sterling dish with a lace-paper doily. Then she went outside to calm the dogs.

Miss Rose was a short, slim woman in her late twenties, with delicate features and dark blond hair cut almost like a boy's, though it was worn as a pompadour in front. She was wearing a white shirtwaist and tweed skirt. Over her sheer stockings she wore white ankle socks. Margaret wondered if that was part of a gym outfit. Miss Rose taught gym. She was wearing sneakers. Her feet were tiny.

She shook hands firmly and was not afraid of the two gigantic dogs who, with a little bounce, could look her right in the eye. Margaret liked women who shook hands that way. She led Miss Rose inside, through the massive front door shaped like a cathedral window, pointed at the top and with iron arrows embedded in the wood. She didn't seem impressed by the big living room with its beamed ceiling, medieval fireplace and coat-of-arms window. At least she didn't look around, just folded herself gracefully onto one end of the couch. She struck Margaret as wonderfully sporty and self-possessed. Just the kind of woman she admired. As they made small talk, it occurred to her that Miss Rose would never look shocked or disapproving, as the ladies at church did, if she spoke of her ambitions. If Miss Rose heard that she was writing stories and sending them to magazines, that she planned to get a master's degree in education, she would be pleased. She would encourage her.

Nora appeared with the tea tray. Next to the foie gras sandwiches was a little loaf cake. Nora had made it without telling her. She threw a look of appreciation upward, but the dark face didn't react. Miss Rose took lemon but no sugar. They were using the Haviland china, a wedding gift from Selma.

It turned out that Miss Rose had gone to Bryn Mawr and then to Teachers College at Columbia. As Margaret coaxed this information out—Miss Rose had to be asked, nothing was volunteered—Margaret wondered if they might become friends. She hadn't really made any women friends in White Plains, except for Florence Niskern, Harris's Spanish teacher, who was in her fifties, and marvelously independent like Miss Rose. She thought suddenly of arranging for the two of them to meet—Miss Niskern and Miss Rose. Career women, nothing like the church ladies who wouldn't discuss anything but food and clothes. The idea expanded in her mind. What about a club, made up of women with ambitions, ideas, careers? She had a clear vision of this room filling up with stimulating women, presidents of colleges, women who were really somebody.

"She's a wonderful girl, Mrs. Schanberg, a real leader. All the other girls look up to her."

Miss Rose was talking about Mag. She had let her mind drift. She smiled, remarking how much Mag liked Miss Rose. It was true. Mag always went on about her gym teachers. Recently she had begun talking about becoming one herself.

"She's good at everything, at every game, Mrs. Schanberg."

"Oh, call me Margaret."

Miss Rose looked slightly embarrassed. She seemed to have stalled for a moment. "My first name is Terry," she said at last.

Margaret shifted in her chair. She had the brief impression that Miss Rose had not come with good news. "She's looking forward to summer camp so much," she said. She picked up the silver plate and offered one of the spade sandwiches. Miss Rose declined.

"Yes, well . . ." Miss Rose turned her face to the window. Margaret felt her palms grow damp. "That's one of the things I came to talk to you about."

Margaret felt it essential to change the subject quickly, but could think of nothing to say.

"I'm afraid . . ." Miss Rose licked her lower lip and began again. "I'm afraid Camp Birchmont is a very conservative place, Mrs. Schanberg."

Margaret shook her head, feigning puzzlement. But she wasn't puzzled in the least.

"By that I mean it's . . . restricted."

"I'm not sure what you mean." Her fists clenched automatically. She knew exactly what Miss Rose meant.

Miss Rose shuttered down her eyes. She was really quite flat-chested. "I mean . . . I'm afraid it's for Christian girls."

"But we're Christian."

Miss Rose shifted uncomfortably. "I was told . . ."

"We go to St. Bartholomew's on Prospect Street." She waved her hand to the north. "Dr. Winthrop is the minister, he'll be glad to talk to you."

"I know Dr. Winthrop," Miss Rose whispered, looking around. Margaret had the impression she wanted to rush out of the room.

"It's an old German name. There's still a lot of prejudice against the Germans because of the war." Miss Rose sat rigidly now. "You can't keep Maggie out of that camp just because of a German name."

"The other girls . . ." Miss Rose forced herself to speak up. "The other girls tend to be narrow-minded."

"But she said some of her friends were going. Friends from school. And you'll be there."

"I know, Mrs. Schanberg, but in a camp situation things are a little different. There's the policy. We say grace before every meal. There's compulsory chapel on Sunday and evening prayer. All that makes the girls a little more . . . outspoken." Miss Rose touched her hand to her cheek. "I really don't like to do this."

"But I swear to you!" Her voice had risen in spite of her effort to be calm.

"We don't want Mag to have an unpleasant summer. Girls that age tend to copy each other."

"Why would her summer be unpleasant?" Her mind was buzzing, all sorts of things were crashing around in there, but she had to keep up appearances. If Miss Rose won, if she ruled out Mag, then all her hopes and plans for the last four years would be destroyed.

Miss Rose was struggling with herself. Her small feet in their white sneakers twitched left and right. She sat forward, a clean, boyish gesture. "If you insist, Mrs. Schanberg . . ."

"But I do insist!"

Miss Rose stared at her. It was not an unfriendly look, but not friendly either. For an instant it reminded her of the stares back in Gideon. Suddenly Margaret hated her. She hated her boyish haircut, her thick white socks, her neat, contained sportiness. "In that case, Mrs. Schanberg, we'll go ahead as planned."

Miss Rose stood up. Margaret did too. "We won't mention this to your daughter." They were enemies now. How terrifying, yet how predictable, that someone could change from a friend to an enemy in just a few minutes. Miss Rose put out her hand. Her fingers were cold.

"No, I won't mention it to Mag."

Miss Rose headed for the door. How small she was, more like a child than a woman. "I really didn't like coming here, Mrs. Schanberg." She stopped at the door and turned. She was sincere, but what difference did that make? "Will you forgive me?" Yes, they could have been friends, but only on some other planet.

Margaret heard herself laugh, a silly, demeaning laugh. "There's nothing to forgive, Mag is going to Camp Birchmont!"

Miss Rose slipped through the door. Margaret stayed, trying not to think. Nora looked in, then went to pick up the tea things. The loaf cake hadn't been touched, but Nora didn't comment. Margaret wondered if she had been listening. The door to the kitchen was usually ajar.

A minute later the front door burst open. It was Mag. "I just saw Miss Rose. What did she want?"

Oh, God, she hadn't had time to make up a story. "Where did you see her?"

"Coming out of the driveway. She waved but she didn't stop." Mag plunked her books and gym bag on the hall table. "Was it about camp?"

"Yes."

"Well, don't keep me in suspense."

"It was about your clothes. What to take. Labels. Tennis rackets. All that."

"Is that all?" Mag exhaled. "I thought maybe she wanted me for a junior counselor."

"They don't do that the first year."

"I thought they'd make an exception. Is there anything to eat?"

Mag had lost interest in the subject. She went into the kitchen. There was a brief outburst when she saw the loaf cake. Margaret went outside, then around to the back, the dogs following her. They pushed their broad heads into her hands, glad of the company, hoping for a pat. "Good girl, good boy," she said, but her mind was busy elsewhere.

I was told. But who had told Miss Rose?

She went into the garden, latching the little gate behind her. The dogs bounded around, complaining, but she couldn't let them in. She walked along the rows, the first shoots of scallions, radishes, lettuce, beets, carrots, bringing order to her mind. Who had told Miss Rose?

She shouldn't, she had on her good clothes, but she kneeled down to pick a few weeds. She had trouble controlling her hands—they were trembling slightly.

Judd's office manager, Irv Halperin, had moved to White Plains last year. His children were in the same school. She had asked Judd to talk to Irv, but of course he hadn't. It wasn't the sort of thing he would do. She had run into Florence Halperin several times at the station—she could tell Florence didn't like her, though she pretended to be friendly.

She rolled down her stockings. The earth felt cool against her skin. There was no telling—it might have been anyone. People would always talk.

She continued plucking at the weeds while her mind rotated through the available information. For a moment she thought of how she turned over the soil in spring before planting. That's what she was doing now—getting at the facts, exposing them to sunlight, finding a new seed to plant.

She surveyed her solution slowly, probing at each aspect, trying to predict each setback. She moved along the aisle of young green shoots, waiting for her forces to gather. It would take all her strength and ingenuity. Everyone would be opposed—Judd, the children, Mama, Sister, Selma, even Pop. Each of them would have to be dealt with separately.

She stood up, taking a deep breath. This was the last step in the series that had begun on the way to school in Gideon, as she huddled in the twilight of the henhouse, as she succumbed to Mama's persecutions. It should have come sooner.

A new calm took possession of her. She recognized it as the result of a deep resolve. She knew herself. Tranquillity came when she found her strength. It had happened when she decided to go to the university in Austin even though she was only fourteen at the time. It had happened when she persuaded Mama to move to New York. It had happened when she gave up Charlie Rysdale. And it was happening now, in her vegetable garden, on a May day in 1938.

She was still standing, extending her victory, when she heard the horn. Ga-*goo*-gah. She'd forgotten about Sister and Mama.

She met them on the front steps. Sister was wearing slacks—first time ever—and struggling with Mama's grip. Mama was carrying her latest afghan in an old taffeta slip. "There she is!" Mama cried, grinning childishly. They kissed on the lips, Mama tucking hers in so that no spit would pass. A dry, unmotherly contact.

She took the bag from Sister, who said, "I can't stay. Mark hates to wait at the station." Then Sister examined her more closely. "What's the matter?"

She shook her head, but she couldn't fool Sister. Mama went ahead, rocking slowly up the steps to the porch. She cried out for Mag, who hallooed from inside. She and Sister would have a moment alone. "What is it?" Sister asked again. She checked her wristwatch.

"The gym teacher came by."

"Oh, yes." Sister scratched the tiny mole on her upper lip—a sign you had her full attention.

"They don't want Mag in that camp at all."

"They don't." Not a question, an agreement.

"It's the name. Also they heard something. From the Halperins maybe."

"I see."

"But she changed her mind after I talked to her." She paused. "I'm not sure I should let Mag go."

They stared at each other. There was nothing they couldn't read in each other's faces. "If you don't let her go, you'll have to tell her why."

"I can make up something."

"No." Sister shook her head. "She wants to go awfully bad. Maybe it'll be all right."

They waited another moment, everything in balance, both of them trying to judge the future. Then Sister's gaze closed down. "I have to run. I'll call you in the morning."

Margaret watched while Sister got in the Buick, turned it around and drove off. She managed the wheel strongly, capably, as she did everything else. But Sister couldn't help her with this. It came to her in a rush of sorrow—something had sapped Sister's strength, prevented her from dealing directly with the hardness of life. Maybe it was all those boyfriends, or being so pretty, or Mama spoiling her. Sister would always close down, or back off, or rush away to meet Mark. She would never stay long enough to help.

Margaret headed into the house, aware of her determination renewing. Maybe she should be grateful to Miss Rose. If she hadn't come today they might have gone on fooling themselves until it was too late.

Mag was upstairs with Mama, helping her get settled. Margaret went into the kitchen for her afternoon water. She drank four glasses in the morning, four in the afternoon, out of the tap. Nora gave her a sidelong glance. "Everything all right, Mrs. Schanberg?"

Nora's voice was light, dry, but Margaret heard a vibration underneath. Yes, Nora had been listening.

"They don't want Mag in their camp."

Nora wiped her hands on a dish towel. "Last family I worked for had that trouble." Her face was flat, impassive.

"She changed her mind, though. Mag can go."

Nora hung the towel neatly. "Good. She'd be real disappointed."

Margaret was tempted to say more but checked herself. She wasn't quite ready. And she had to save her first words for Judd. There'd be plenty of time for Nora and the others. "You'd think people would get tired of hating," she remarked at last. "I wonder when it will end."

Nora let out a low laugh. "On Judgment Day, I expect."

5

HARRIS

The Name

His mother explained it to him but he didn't really understand. They were going to have a new name. But what was wrong with the old name? He'd been writing it in school at the top of every paper, right through the seventh grade. Why should he start writing another name? Who was Harris Shay? It had a cutoff sound, like a piece of him was missing.

And there was another difficulty. They were moving from White Plains to New Rochelle. That wasn't far. He'd biked there once with Buddy Murphy. But no one was supposed to know it. It was a secret. He couldn't tell anybody, not even his best friends, that they were moving fifteen miles away.

When he complained to his mother, she got her mysterious look. He knew it well—her eyes jumped around and she pushed her lips together. "You'll make new friends, Harris, you'll see." But he didn't want new friends. He liked his old ones. Besides, who would want to be friends with somebody named Harris Shay? He didn't even exist.

He wished he could ask his father about it, but he never had serious talks with his father. Once in a while they discussed music, or he played a piano piece his father liked (the Cherubini minuet or the Easy Version of the Second Hungarian Rhapsody), but that was all. Whenever he asked his father something important he said, "Ask your mother."

When his friends told him they had discussed something with

their fathers, he wondered how they got started. Were there special words you had to use? Did you have to be in the car or going to a movie? He wondered if it was his own fault that they never talked.

When his friends asked where he was moving, he gave vague answers. "Oh, away." "Out west." Then he laughed, feeling like a traitor. All this was at his mother's instructions. She had told him to make up stories. But his friends didn't like his answers. They looked at him suspiciously. His mother had never grasped the fact that your friends always knew when you were lying.

He had asked his sister about moving and for once Mag had been helpful. "We're going away because everybody here hates us," she announced. She wouldn't say anything more, even though he pleaded and promised her things. Something had happened at Camp Birchmont this past summer, though nobody would tell him exactly what. Mag had come home early. She was supposed to stay until the end of August but she turned up in July, looking thin (amazing) and staying in her room for several days. He had knocked on her door, but she wouldn't let him in. Another mystery.

He tried to discuss the situation with Nora, who usually gave him good answers, but this time she wouldn't. "Talk to your mother about that," she snapped, pushing back her horn-rims, "I don't have nothin' to do with it." He didn't know why the subject made her mad too. In fact, whenever he brought up the matter, everybody got mad. So he stopped asking.

His mother had driven them over to see their new house in New Rochelle, also to the new junior high school. He didn't like either one. The house had a steep driveway. He'd have to walk his bike up—not like here where you could come racing in from the street, pumping hard, and spatter gravel at the curve. And the school looked huge and forbidding, with Greek columns in front ("Doric," his mother had said in her educational voice), and a black-top playground instead of dirt. Who went to that school? Boys who didn't know him. Boys who would call him Harris Shay.

There was also the question of Rose Shapiro, who was in love with him. She was chubby, with wild black hair, not at all pretty but definitely stuck on him. She always sat next to him (in the S's) and waited for him to speak. Anything he said thrilled her. She would suck in her breath or roll her eyes or offer him a Baby Ruth. She was a pain in the neck but he was secretly proud. He also felt responsible—including her in certain games, walking her part way home, buying her a Melorol cone once or twice. What would happen to Rose Shapiro after he left? Would she recover? Would she forget about him?

Mag said their school records already had their new name on them—she'd peeked in the big brown envelopes Mother had brought home from school. That was another puzzle. He'd gotten those grades as Harris Schanberg; did they also apply to the new person?

Another puzzle was a phone conversation his father had had with Nana. He'd overheard it. His father had said, "How many times do I have to tell you? That's the way she wants it, and that's the way it's going to be." His father was mad too.

Moving meant he had to go through all his things and remove his name. That included the ink lettering on his tennis racket, his baseball mitt, his schoolbooks, his Big Little Books, his song music, everything. His mother gave him a knife, an eraser and a pair of scissors. She said if the name couldn't be erased or scraped or cut out, to dispose of the item. That meant throw it away. He didn't mind disposing of his Czerny exercise book, but he wanted to keep "Oh, Johnny" and "The Last Round-Up," which he'd bought with his allowance. Also, he wanted to keep his tennis racket and tennis balls and books. He worked very hard at scraping and shaving and erasing these.

There was also the matter of the books downstairs. They had a couple of thousand. Every room had a big bookcase in it. There were his father's schoolbooks, his mother's college books, all the novels and encyclopedias and dictionaries and all the stuff they were always buying. Every one of these had somebody's name inside. Mag had let out a squawk when Mother said it would be their job to eradicate these. But there was no getting out of it.

He and Mag spent whole days going through these books. If the name was written on a loose page you could rip it out, even if it was the title page. If the name was written on the inside front cover you could scribble over it with a crayon or scrape the words with a knife. If nothing worked, the book had to be thrown away.

Doing this made him feel bad. He was defacing a book. That was practically a crime. But as the days wore on and the scraping continued, something else happened. He began to feel wrong in himself. If everyone was ashamed of their name, there must be something wrong with it, and by extension with him. The two couldn't really be separated, could they?

He tried to express this to Mag—he knew better than to mention it to his mother—but Mag was scornful. "That's the stupidest thing I ever heard," she burst out. "Things are going to be a lot better when we get out of here." Yes, Mag was glad to move. She'd stopped seeing her friends since she came back from Camp Birchmont. She planned to make all new friends in New Rochelle. He checked her diary when she was out—he did this on a regular basis—and discovered she had written the new name over and over, using different kinds of penmanship. *Margaret Shay, Margaret Shay, Margaret Shay.* In capitals and backwards-slanting letters and printing. He hated the look of it.

Finally he decided to tell Buddy Murphy the truth. Maybe that would help him feel better. They were biking along Ridgeway Road, toward their favorite pond, when he pulled alongside Buddy, aware that he was disobeying his mother but determined to do it anyway. It was now or never—there were only a few more days before they moved, in time for him to start eighth grade in the new school.

"Hey," he called over, "I wanta tell you something."

Buddy, who was a year older—twelve—slowed down. "What is it, Har?"

He hesitated. Now that the time was here something was catching in his throat. He hadn't expected that. He thought it would come out easily, like everything else with Buddy. "We're . . . I'm . . ." He had to say something; he couldn't stop in the middle. "We're going to be different after we move," he said at last. It wasn't what he wanted to say.

Buddy had blue eyes, pink skin and freckles on his nose. His father was a fireman, which gave Buddy a lot of authority in the neighborhood. "Whaddya mean, Har?"

He knew what he meant, it was on the tip of his tongue, but he couldn't get it out. His mother's express command rose up between him and the words. "I'm . . . I probably won't ever see you again."

"Don't worry. I'll come see you on the train. My father said he'd pay for it."

Harris tried to evade the thoughts in his head. They were traitorous. He hadn't told Buddy they were moving to New Rochelle, where they had once biked together to buy firecrackers. Buddy had the impression they were moving across the country. "We'll be a long ways away," he managed to say, steering his bike so as not to run into Buddy's front wheel.

"Just write and tell me when you want me to come. After you get unpacked. I'll be there." Buddy gave him a true-blue look, and Harris knew he meant it.

"Okay, I'll write."

Now he felt even more traitorous. Instead of telling Buddy the truth he was adding extra lies. His mother had also forbidden writing. He was not to tell anyone in a letter either. He let Buddy pull ahead. He didn't want another true-blue look; it made him feel too bad. He watched Buddy shoot on ahead. When Buddy gave it the gas, he couldn't catch up, not even on his new Schwinn with balloon tires. But that was okay—he didn't want to talk to Buddy now anyway.

The next afternoon he had his last piano lesson with Miss Van Winkel, whom his father always called Rip. That wasn't funny but his father never gave up. Her first name was really Alma.

He didn't like Miss Van Winkel. She had a bad temper and her apartment smelled rotten. Also she had a terrible system of pasting stars in a little notebook he had to bring along—gold, silver or red stars, depending on how well he played. He didn't like her looks either, though he'd gotten used to them over the last three years. She had reddish hair, though it was white in spots, and always wore a green kimono. Every week when he rang her bell he hoped she'd wear a real dress and she'd open the windows, but every week it was the same.

Today, he thought as he rang her bell, he might tell Miss Van

Winkel about moving and all. She wasn't like Buddy Murphy; she was a grown-up. She might even be able to explain it to him. For an instant, waiting for her to open the door, he felt sad to be leaving her.

But as soon as she opened the door and he saw the green kimono and the terrible smell hit him, he knew he couldn't say anything. Miss Van Winkel was too old, too bad-tempered. She didn't know anything but music. And suppose she told his mother? His mother would be furious. The terror that came to him when his mother was angry, refused to speak, was the worst thing he knew. It produced panic, emptiness. He had a vague memory of a time when he had actually lost her, when she had disappeared. He couldn't take a chance on that happening again.

Miss Van Winkel was in a good mood today. "I'm going to miss you, Harris," she said as he took his music out of his satchel. "You're a good student, you practice, unlike some other boys I could name but I won't."

This was the first time she actually told him he practiced enough.

"You must write and tell me about your new teacher."

He wondered if she would really miss him.

"And how did you like the 'Toreador Song'? I bet you loved it. All the boys love it."

"I like the second part," he said, picking up the cushion he always used.

"You mean the chorus."

"Tor-ee-a-dora, don't spit on the floor-a, use the cuspidor-a, right behind the door-a."

He knew Miss Van Winkel wouldn't approve, and she didn't. "That's a French opera." She put a stick of camphor to her nose. "The words are in French."

"I know, I saw it."

It was true. His father had taken him to see *Carmen*. He liked the costumes and scenery, but it bothered him that Carmen got up and took a bow after she was stabbed to death.

"Oh, yes, you told me."

He hadn't told her. He never told her anything.

"Well, now, shall we begin?"

This was the bad part, when Miss Van Winkel sat on the bench with him. Sometimes she paced around the room but not today. He could smell a dozen different smells. In spite of that, he played unusually well. Miss Van Winkel beamed, maybe because it was his last lesson. She gave him a pat and didn't ask him to play the "Toreador Song" again and do it right this time.

When his lesson was over (forty-five minutes), she announced he had earned a gold star. While he rummaged around in his satchel for the little notebook he began to feel sad again. He would never see Miss Van Winkel again. She wasn't so bad. Sometimes she made him laugh. Sometimes she gave him pictures of famous composers. He'd been coming here a long time. Maybe he could trust her.

"Our name is going to be different from now on."

"What?"

"It's not going to be Schanberg, it's going to be Shay."

Miss Van Winkel stopped licking the gold star and stared at him. Her eyes were round and blue and smudged below with dark marks. "Why on earth are you doing that?"

"My mother wants to. We're moving away so we can start all over again."

He shouldn't have said that but he couldn't help it. He had to see if Miss Van Winkel could explain it.

"You can't start over again. That's perfectly insane."

"My mother says you can." He waited, hoping, then added, "I'm not supposed to tell anybody."

Miss Van Winkel closed her eyes for a moment. When she opened them, he thought he had never seen such a frightening color. "Your mother is making a terrible mistake. Tell her I said so."

Miss Van Winkel wasn't going to be any help. In fact she was making things worse.

"Will you tell her that for me, Harris?" He nodded, but of course he couldn't. His mother would be furious if she knew what he'd done. "And you must come back to visit me. All my old students come back. Where are you moving to?"

He stiffened. He couldn't tell her any more. His gaze roved around the room. It was full of shelves stacked with old music.

"We're not sure, exactly."

He tried not to look at her but he could feel the round eyes, with their frightening color, digging into the side of his face. Just then the doorbell rang. It was her next student, a girl named Janice. He took the little notebook and crammed it into his satchel with the music. He had to get out of here, before she asked any more questions.

"Harris." She was standing in the middle of the room. He could see powder marks where her skin met the green kimono. "Give me a good-bye hug."

He held his breath and moved toward her. She put her arms around him. It was like being trapped underwater. At last she let go. "You be good now, you dear boy."

He raced out the door without speaking to Janice, who was waiting with an armful of music. He ran down the hall, then down the stairs, two at a time, his corduroy knickers squeaking.

Good-bye, Miss Van Winkel. Good-bye, stars. Good-bye, smells. Good-bye forever. He felt traitorous again, but he couldn't help it.

His mother was parked in front. Still out of breath from running, he told her that Miss Van Winkel had given him a good-bye hug. She nodded but didn't speak. He knew she didn't approve of hugging. Then he said, "She wants me to come back and visit her."

"We won't be coming back to White Plains."

"I know." He glanced at his mother. She was staring straight ahead. "I told her that."

They rode for a while in silence as he thought of the things he couldn't tell his mother. There were more of those than the other kind. He wondered if it was that way for every boy his age, then decided it wasn't. His family was different, full of angers and secrets. This new one was another addition to the list.

His mother shifted the gear. Her right palm was bandaged—she had cut herself slicing twine for one of the book cartons. She had to shift with just two fingers. Her hand, with its long, tapering fingers, was very beautiful to him. He hated it when she was hurt. Last year she'd burned herself at the hot-water tap in the basement. She had to wear a bandage for several weeks. He had missed the sight of her hand, as if he had been deprived of part of himself, something essential.

Everybody commented on how much he loved his mother, but they didn't know he also hated her. Most of the time he didn't admit this, but it was there, a dark spot at the bottom of his mind. She was always turning into a stranger. Sometimes, if he came near her, she'd push him away and say, "I'm not a demonstrative person, you know that." And he would feel ashamed for wanting to touch her. Other times, when she did hold him, she would do it only for a few seconds, talking fast to cover up her embarrassment. Because he touched her so rarely, he'd learned to speed up his impressions—to take in her wonderful icy odors, the smoothness of her cheek, the softness of her breasts, all at once.

But under all this coolness was another coolness, a distance that didn't even have a name. She simply went away, even when she was in the same room. He would ask a question, show her a book, a game, but she was off somewhere else. Even when she came back she wasn't altogether present. Only in certain moods, or when something nice had happened to her, would she really pay attention to him. She would announce this in advance. "Now I'm going to give you my undivided attention, Harris." Then he had about fifteen minutes. Those were the best times, the times he lived for, but he also resented them. Why just fifteen minutes? Why not an hour? Why not all day?

Now, watching her shift the gear with two fingers, his resentment surged. His mother, whose name he wrote at the top of certain school forms (Mother's maiden name: Margaret Barish), hadn't asked whether he wanted a new name. Hadn't asked if he was willing to turn into somebody else, if he would miss Buddy Murphy and his other friends. She wasn't interested in his opinion. She didn't have time. And when he thought about that, he hated her.

When they arrived home, they found Mag on the floor scraping the last of the books. His mother told him to help, there wasn't much time left, but he wanted something to eat. "Well, be sure and come back," Mag ordered, narrowing her eyes.

He took his time in the kitchen, bothering Nora with his indecision, but finally drifted back. He found Mag reading books instead of eradicating. That's why it was taking her so long.

"This was Daddy's Latin book." Mag held up a small tan volume. The cover was loose; white netting flared out. "Look how his handwriting has changed."

His father's writing had been large and scrawly when he was a boy. He recalled photos, his father wearing glasses even when he was eleven or twelve, his face round as an egg. He took the book from Mag—Caesar's *Gallic Wars*. On the flyleaf was his father's signature, "Judah Benjamin Schanberg." It took up half the page. Under it was a sketch of a crummy-looking Roman soldier. He gave the book back to Mag and she ripped out the page, then dropped the book in the carton with the other eradicated ones.

There were more Latin books on the shelf. He tumbled them out. Cicero. Virgil. A grammar. His father loved his Latin books. Some nights he translated aloud and made boring comments. His father still admired Rome, especially Mucius the Left-Handed. Except for Babe Ruth, his father admired Mucius the Left-Handed most.

Mag got up to go to the bathroom. He opened up the first two Latin books and tore out the necessary pages. The last one had LATIN GRAMMAR I stamped on the cover in gold. It was in better shape than the others. He opened it. His father's name, loose and large, slanted across the title page, also another crummy drawing. He really didn't want to tear it out. He was sick of tearing out pages; his bad feelings were coming back.

He glanced around. Mag was taking her time in the bathroom. And then an idea came to him, an idea so dangerous that his palms went icy-cold. *He wouldn't erase the name; he would leave it the way it was.* He knew this was a terrible thing to do—a crime, really—but he'd do it anyway. He took a deep breath and snapped the grammar shut. Then he made a space inside the carton and slid it down. He stared at the carton afterward for a long time; it seemed to have changed in some important way.

When Mag came back he acted calm. She didn't suspect. But he was quietly exultant. In their new house, in their new town, he would remove the Latin grammar with his father's name in it. He would hide it. One day, when he was twenty or thirty or even older, if a stranger asked him who he was, he would pull out the book. "Look," he would say, "this is my father's book and this is our real name." And the stranger would believe him, because he had proof.

There was only one thing left to do—make a special mark on the side of the carton. He'd have to use a crayon for that when nobody was around. Mag was coming to the last book. They were done.

"I quit," he said, standing up. He hoped she would leave right away.

"Me too," she said, getting up. He waited till she went outside, calling the dogs, and the coast was clear. He found a red crayon in the desk and made the mark—a circle—quickly. He took a last look as he left the room. The carton was like treasure, buried treasure, bursting with excitement and danger.

The morning of moving day he stayed in bed late with the blanket over his head, trying to prolong the night. He could hear activity downstairs but he wasn't curious. His father had left early. He picked his nose, dropping the results in the booger graveyard under the bed. After a while he threw off the covers and looked at his furniture. The chiffonier, the armchair with the horses and dogs running across the cloth, the beat-up desk, the mirror with the blue frame—all these would be in another room tonight. Would they still be his? In the same way? How could they be, if he was another person? His mother had said he would forget White Plains and all his friends but that didn't seem possible. You couldn't order yourself to forget, or remember forward instead of backwards.

He thought of jumping up and riding over to Buddy Murphy's for an extra good-bye and a true-blue handshake, then remembered his bike had been packed. Besides, he no longer deserved Buddy's friendship; he had told too many lies.

His mother called upstairs. She was not going to call again. They didn't have time for his fooling around this morning. Hating everything, he got up. His wee-wee was standing up straight. He'd have to wait till it went down. He noticed more fuzz down there.

The moving men, the Seven Santini Brothers, were carrying out the chairs and cartons. He eyed them, mostly when they weren't looking. They didn't resemble each other at all; maybe they weren't really brothers. There was something scary about them but also fascinating. They spoke Italian to each other but English to him. "Outa da way, sonny."

By noon the house was empty. His mother was going around with a brush and dustpan. Nora was in the kitchen, wiping the counters and the empty cabinets. "Why are you cleaning up if we're leaving?" he asked.

"We're cleaning it for the next people," his mother replied. "It's not proper to leave a house dirty." Something else that wasn't proper. His mother knew hundreds of them.

At last they were ready. The movers had driven off, led by John and the dogs in the Pierce-Arrow. He would show them the way to the new house. He and Maggie and Nora were crammed into the little Plymouth with his mother. It felt strange sitting next to Nora in the back seat. She was wearing gloves and a straw hat with cherries on it. She hardly ever rode in the car with them.

"Well, here we go, thank heavens," Mag said as his mother headed out of the driveway.

"Here we go," his mother repeated, sounding thrilled.

Yes, they were both glad to be moving. He had a glimpse of Mag as a new, improved person, louder and bossier than ever. She had already put back the weight she lost at Camp Birchmont. He remembered her diary entry and her new name in all kinds of writing. He would never write his new name. Not till he was forced to at the point of a gun.

As they turned into the street he twisted around for a last look. The house rose up behind him, serious and beautiful in the noon sunshine. It had never looked so familiar, so safe. Then he hunched back down, down into himself as far as he could go. He would never come up. Never.

6

MARGARET

The Crossover

She liked their new minister, Dr. Palmsley, right off—a calm, grandfatherly man with two handsome grown sons. One son was already a minister, the other an architect. He was just as welcoming as Dr. Winthrop had been, but she was much more sure of herself now. She volunteered to teach Sunday school, which delighted Dr. Palmsley.

It hadn't been easy. None of it had been easy. She had argued with Judd for days, weeks—from the time of Miss Rose's visit in May until his consent after Mag came back from that camp in tears, the damage so deep it might never heal. It was Mag who had brought it home to him but even then he had been grudging, half-hearted. He didn't like the idea. And he had refused to lift a finger to help.

It was she who hired the lawyer in New York to make the court application. She had gone on the appointed day and stood in front of a bored judge who officially ordered the alteration for Judd and her as well as new birth certificates for the children. When she asked the judge if the old ones would be destroyed, he had stared at her angrily and replied, "Madam, we never destroy anything around here."

But she had outwitted him. At the records office, paying the new registry fee, she had flirted with the clerk, an old geezer with watery eyes, and asked him if the old certificates couldn't be lost somehow. He looked up sharply, and she slipped the envelope out of her purse and gave it to him. Without opening it he had nodded. She had walked out feeling criminal and triumphant at the same time.

Then she'd gone to the school in White Plains, insisting on an appointment with Miss Wellington, the principal. The new transfer records had to be clean. There could be no reference to the old name. The elderly woman—white hair mounded high, small hard face—didn't like any of it. "Business reasons" were not sufficient reason for changing a family name. And records went directly from school to school. Parents had been known to alter grade records. Where were they going, why did she refuse to say?

Margaret had begged and pleaded. She had gotten a little hysterical—all put on, of course, since she was quite collected underneath. They were moving out west. They didn't know which city yet. The records had to go with them or the new admissions would be delayed. The children mustn't miss any classes—school was too important.

At last the principal had written the note releasing the records in the name of Shay. When Margaret left, the principal didn't stand up, didn't wish her good luck. But she didn't care. She'd gotten what she came for. Nothing else mattered. The children would start the new school with a clean slate.

No, none of it had been easy. The children had been frightened when they started school here. That was to be expected, but even Mag was subdued and tense. And Harris. It was the move from New York to White Plains all over again, but worse. It had taken him ages to find his way there, but he'd been very young. Now, wrenching him away was extra hard. He biked home every day, went to his room to read or listen to the radio. Only with great effort, with promises of extra rewards, had she persuaded him to try a Scout meeting in the church basement last Friday night. It was too soon to tell about that.

At first she tried giving little pep talks at dinner, predicting that everything would turn out all right, but Harris groaned and Mag politely asked her to stop. Well, she would keep quiet and hope for the best. But in her moments alone, or driving around town, or teaching Sunday school, she was possessed by certitude. They were going to succeed, all of them.

Judd, surprisingly enough, had stopped resisting after they moved. She knew one reason—he was still Mr. Schanberg at the office. He had announced the change to his colleagues, probably jokingly, then hadn't referred to it again. When Stella or Nick or Ben called him at home, they always asked for him by the wrong name. She had discussed this with him, pointed out the consequences, but he had laughed. He was Schanberg in town and Shay in the country. He didn't mind.

But despite this reluctance—a form of teasing, really—there was something deeper that had led him to accept the change of name, though he would never admit it. She had sensed it from the start, since their first meeting in his mother's apartment so long ago. There was a strain of the alien in him too. The dislocation, the marginality, were there, under the joking and saluting, the bonhomie and democracy. He wasn't nearly so clear and honest about it as she was, but he had given in because of his own fears too. And that's why they were here in New Rochelle, in a house that was a dead-ringer for their old one but in an existence that was brand-new.

In fact, the newness was what excited her the most. Every time the butcher called her Mrs. Shay, or the children brought home their school papers with their names on it, or the phone rang and John answered, "The Shay residence," she got the feeling she'd been born anew. Everything was peeled away, layers of fear and hurt, so that she stepped out fresh. Gideon had shrunk to a pinpoint in memory.

And she found herself making friends, speaking up, saying things that amused or charmed the ladies at church. Caroline Elliott, who was president of the Altar Guild and chairman of the Sunday School Committee, had taken a shine to her and now, in November, just a few months after the move, was taking her here and there, introducing her around. The doors, which had never really opened in White Plains, were opening here. She had found out who she was: she was Mrs. Margaret Shay.

The first time she invited Caroline Elliott to tea at her house on Beechlane Drive, it was at Caroline's suggestion. They'd spent the afternoon pasting price stickers on items for a church sale, and

Caroline, who lived in the same part of town, had asked if she could see the inside of the house she'd driven past for years. When they arrived, in two cars, Margaret hadn't been uneasy or self-conscious for a moment. Caroline, who was large, fair, in her middle forties—her senior by ten years—was just too jolly for that. In fact, she reminded Margaret of Big Blonde, her favorite character in a Dorothy Parker story. Caroline had the same capacity for laughter, the same pleasure in a drink and a good time.

As they sat side by side on the couch having tea—it was a Thursday, the servants were off and Judd would have dinner with his parents tonight—Margaret felt almost dizzy with delight. She'd never had a close woman friend before. In fact, she'd never really had a friend outside the family. "You see, Margaret dear, I was lazy. Big and fat and lazy. And then Walter came along."

Caroline had gone to the Connecticut College for Women, planning to be a teacher. The women in the Perkins family, from Stonington, always worked, even after marriage. But Caroline was bored by children—she had none of her own—and refused. "I'm a disgrace," she remarked, "or I *was* a disgrace. I do so many things now people at home have forgiven me." She paused. "As much as New Englanders ever forgive anybody."

Margaret smiled. How simple Caroline's life had been. She crammed the complications of her own past down, out of view. She would have to meet Caroline's simplicity with her own. But that was the gift of life in New Rochelle—it was allowing her to be a new, simpler person.

Caroline turned her blue-eyed gaze on her. Margaret could feel the warmth between them. For a moment she marveled at the luck that had led to this friendship, then reminded herself that it wasn't just luck. Caroline was smart, college-educated, a cut above the other ladies. She didn't like to talk about clothes and hairdos. She had found an equal in Margaret, someone who kept up with the new plays and books, with educational theory, with the troubles in Europe. Caroline knew that Margaret had already driven over to the College of New Rochelle to see about getting an M.A. in education. All of that added up in Caroline's mind: Margaret was worth knowing.

Caroline hadn't met Judd yet, nor had she herself met Walter Elliott. Now Caroline invited them for dinner next weekend. She hesitated before accepting, even as she knew she shouldn't pause at all. It was an invitation to be accepted easily, *simply*. But her mind flashed forward to Judd's reaction. She could never be sure. He might refuse to go, or he might go and have a wonderful time. It depended on little things, his worries at the office, his mother, his mood. But Caroline was waiting. "That sounds wonderful," Margaret said, trying to pump some enthusiasm into her voice, "but I'll have to ask Judd."

"Oh, don't let him decide. I never let Walter decide anything." Caroline let out a hoot. Her large bosom jiggled.

They hadn't had a social engagement as Judd and Margaret Shay yet. This would be the first. But how could they postpone it? And where better to start than at the Elliotts'?

"Oh, he'll say yes, I just know." Margaret smiled with a confidence she didn't feel.

"Good then, that's a date." Caroline patted her. Again Margaret felt the warmth barreling between them. She could feel some of her love for Sister transferring to Caroline.

After Caroline left she took the teacups into the kitchen, debating when to break the news to Judd. Not tonight, when he got home from his mother's. On the weekend, maybe. And then, suddenly, it didn't matter when she told him. He would go. He would do whatever she asked.

There had been a silver lining to all this uprooting. It had brought them closer together. When she had stood next to Judd under the canopy at the Fifth Avenue Synagogue, she had almost hated him. Not only his physical presence but his presumptions. He was the opposite of her desire, an old defeat come true. When he had touched her that wedding night and other nights, she had felt corrupted. Yet what had first been an impossibility, later a hope, was now coming to pass. She had fallen in love with the man she married.

She wondered if it was merely habit, her gratitude to him for coming home every night at the same time, telling her about his day, listening to Harris play the piano, cracking jokes at the table, adoring Mag. She could count on him; he was reliable. Of the thousand connections they shared, wasn't that the most satisfying? She washed the teacups and started to dry them, aware that there was more to it than that.

He *knew* her. Could that be it? Sometimes, when he was examining her through his silver-rimmed glasses, his eyes a little bulgy, she had the sensation of being crystal clear. There was no need to hide; he had made her transparent, and that was an even greater gift than the gift of vanity which Charlie Rysdale had given her.

Judd knew Sister, knew Mama, knew about Gideon. He knew about Hattie's eternal hatred and his mother's deep-seated ambivalence. He knew that she still yearned, deep in her bones, to distinguish herself through literature, even though she forgot that yearning for months at a time. He knew that she was afraid of certain women—grown-up versions of the cheerleaders and club girls who had been rude to her—and that she loved being ogled by the local wolves. He knew all those things and more—when she enjoyed sex, when she was blue, when she worried about Harris, when she had to be left alone. He had seen through her and accepted everything.

And she could do the same for him. If she was transparent, so was he. She saw that the little boy, now stored in the basement or the attic, could still pop out in his mother's presence, inevitably to be followed by rage. She knew that under his joking and joshing he was rather shy, a little afraid of strangers. She knew he wasn't really good at business like his father—too careless, too spendthrift, too eager to please.

Yes, they knew each other, and that was the chief part of their life together. And their lovemaking had deepened, a joining not only of parts but of selves, pasts, totalities. They had to be careful because of the children—locking the door, turning up the radio, waiting till late—but when it happened that old relation to Charlie seemed shallow and insipid. At forty-one, Judd was all grown up. She had done the right thing in leaving him and she had done the right thing in coming back.

They were talking about having another child—not right away

but when Mag and Harris went off to college. Someone to fill the house, keep them company. Now she let her mind rove ahead, imagining the new child born to the new name. A daughter, she hoped. She would be the lucky one, surrounded by love, purified of the past. She would be beautiful, combining the best features of both families—Selma's fair skin, Judd's fine hair, her own sensuous figure, delicate features, shapely legs. Her planning—and who was to say she was not the planning genius of her family?—would deliver the last, best prize.

The back door flung open just as she put away the rest of the tea things. It was Mag with Harris close behind. They must have met in the driveway, since Mag walked and Harris rode his bicycle from school.

She gave each a hug, short but fierce. They were surprised—she never did that when they came home from school—but today she felt like it. She wanted to transmit her joy, her confidence in the future. Children were just extensions of your own ego. In a way, she was hugging herself.

"How was school?"

As she expected, the responses differed. Harris muttered something and headed for the refrigerator. If she wanted to know more she would have to dig it out. Then, in a sudden blurt, he would tell her things she didn't want to hear.

But Mag was glowing. "You know what? We had a talk from a Greek-letter sorority girl. It was voluntary, in the cafeteria. But I went. She came from the high school." Her eyes were glittering. She was in the ninth grade. Next year she would go to the high school, a red-brick building situated behind twin lakes.

"What did she say?"

"Well, she told us about sororities. Rushing. Pledging. Hell night. Everything."

Margaret heard a faint alarm go off in her head. There had been secret societies in her own high school, not Greek-letter but named after famous Southern ladies. Mary Custis Lee. Varina Howell Davis. Dolley Madison. Julia Tutwiler. The names still hurt.

"Do you think I'll get in one, Mother?"

Harris made an ugly sound. "Why would they want you?"

Margaret intervened. "What did this girl say?"

"Well, first they rush you, invite you to parties, look you over . . ."

"Yeah, when they look *you* over . . ."

"Harris."

Mag ignored him. ". . . and if they like you they ask you to join. It sounds easy."

"Why isn't there ever anything to eat?" Harris slammed the refrigerator doors.

"You can have bread and jam." He ate four meals a day.

She wondered if she should throw cold water on Mag's hopes. She was taking hold at school, through sports as usual, but they were newcomers still. She didn't know what standards those sororities used. The phone rang. Mag dashed to the front hall to get it, giving her brother a push as she passed. He spun around, cursing.

She came back, looking annoyed. "It's for Harris."

"For me?" He looked shocked. This was his first phone call after three months in New Rochelle.

"Well, go answer it, stupid."

He slouched out of the kitchen. He was almost six feet tall already. They heard him pick up the phone. The other party was doing all the talking. "Who was it?" she asked Mag.

"How do I know?"

After a while Harris returned. "That was Bob Jones." He was trying to keep the pride out of his voice. "They're starting a new patrol."

Mag let out a groan. Margaret tried to hold in her elation. "What did he say?"

"He wants me to be in it."

"Oh, Harris!"

He shrugged, but his eyes were shining. He looked covertly at his sister. No approval there.

"I think Bob Jones is so nice," Margaret said.

Mag let out a sound of disgust. "Bob Jones is seventeen, and he's still a Boy Scout."

"No, he's not," Harris replied. "He's the assistant scoutmaster."

"Big difference."

"There *is* a difference. You're too dumb to see it."

She intervened again. The bickering was endless. "When are you going to have your first meeting?"

"Friday night after the troop meets. We'll see how many new guys there are."

"Tenderfeet." Mag's tone was scathing.

"It's going to be called the Stag Patrol. Gee whiz, the Stag Patrol."

"If you need a place to meet, you can do it here. There's that room in the attic."

Harris's face crumpled in disdain. "We won't meet in guys' homes, Mother, we'll be *doing* things."

Mag picked up her books. "This conversation is making me sick."

She left as Harris began spreading strawberry jam on Wonder Bread. As Margaret watched, the last of her worries evaporated. Everything was going to be all right. They had come through. Even though war was pending, even though Hitler was going to overrun Europe, even though New York synagogues were being defaced with swastikas, they would be immune. She had done the right thing. Her memory stirred and she remembered Queen Esther. Hadn't she kept quiet about her background, on the advice of her uncle Mordecai, when she married the king of Persia? Would she have been selected as his bride if she'd told? Of course not.

Harris lifted the sandwich to his mouth. Even Harris, the problem child, was on his way.

Of course, Esther had revealed the truth later, when she was able to help her people. Well, she too might reveal it some time in the future, when it would do some good. But not just yet. Anyway, she hadn't been altogether false to her past. She had kept one promise, one ritual, the only one she'd ever really cared about. On Passover each year and without telling anybody, she made excuses to stay up late by herself. When the house was quiet, when everybody was asleep, she went to the kitchen and took out a bottle of red wine, bought especially. And there, in the dim light, at the zinc table, she poured out a glass for Elijah the Tishbite. And she waited, listening for the knock on the door, the step on the lintel. If he came she was ready, money in her apron, food in the refrigerator.

Yes, she had kept the faith, or some small portion of it. Wasn't that enough? Who could blame her, any more than they blamed Queen Esther for keeping her own counsel when she married the king of Persia?

Harris was standing by the refrigerator, with the jam sandwich. He took enormous bites. For an instant, as she watched him, she had a vision of a tall, broad-shouldered young man in a cutaway, talking confidently to the Secretary of State. Harris was going to have a great career, there was no doubt in her mind. Then she told him to watch it, watch it, he was dripping jam on the floor.

Judd liked Walter Elliott right off—a placid, handsome man with even features and grey hair. He was in the insurance business. She watched Judd relax, expand, as Walter fixed him a drink, then took him outside for a tour of the grounds. Maybe they'll be friends, she thought, listening to Caroline but catching glimpses of the men outside.

But as the evening wore on, she could see Judd wasn't enjoying himself. He was casting around for funny things to say to top Caroline. He might have been putting on a performance for a customer. It was his old fear of dominating women—the Natalie syndrome. She herself kept smoothing things over, but it didn't help. It was Caroline's house and Caroline's evening, and she was funnier than Judd, truly witty, never forced. She did imitations of the choir ladies, the vestrymen, even Dr. Palmsley. She, Margaret, was in stitches but Judd's laughter was grim.

As they were getting ready for bed that night he spoke of Walter. "He's a fine man, a really fine man."

She was relieved to hear that. Maybe the two of them would find things to do. Walter went bowling with the Men's Fellowship every week. "But your friend Caroline." Judd was sitting on a chair in his underwear. "You better be careful."

"What is that supposed to mean?"

"She's a lesbian."

"That's the most ridiculous thing I ever heard."

"I'm telling you."

"You say that about any woman who talks a lot."

"I've met them before. And she's one."

She refused to answer. He was jealous, that was it. None of them—Selma, Hattie, Judd—had ever had close friends. The tie of blood was too powerful; it precluded all others. She was at her dressing table, creaming her face, observing him in the mirror. He had his nasty-mischievous look. It meant he was in the mood for teasing. She'd just let the subject drop.

The next moment a nervous shudder went through her. Caroline had a habit of touching her, brushing against her, sitting close. She used Shalimar, a strong scent. But she herself had enjoyed the closeness, the touching. It was comforting. With another woman there were no sexual hints, no worry about losing control.

She looked alertly into the mirror. Was there something she had missed? Judd got up and went into the bathroom.

Her mind went back to their first meeting, Caroline's instant interest, her . . . well, pursuit. Why should she have taken so much interest, introduced her around so quickly, done so many favors? She recalled that someone had referred to Caroline's close friend, Diane Pope, who had moved away just before Margaret turned up.

A familiar hurt knifed through her. Maybe Caroline didn't really like *her*. Maybe she was like the rest, the cheerleaders and club girls and prom queens. Maybe she had hidden motives for her friendship.

Judd came out of the bathroom wearing only a towel. His skin was an iridescent pink, like lobster meat just out of the shell. She kept working cream into her face. She would have to wait and see. She might have to be on her guard a little.

And then another thought struck her. What if a woman loved another woman, even that way? She had loved Sister all her life, and at certain times, when she was especially unhappy, she had even imagined Sister taking her in her arms and comforting her. It was an image that brought great solace—why should she deny Caroline Elliott the same power?

"You hear about it all the time." Judd removed the towel and put on his pajama bottoms. "All these women with nothing to do in the suburbs. They get together and have a good time. Probably have a few drinks first." He put on the top. "She's a drinker—I'll tell you that."

He got in his bed. They had switched to twins when they moved here.

"Well, you're wrong."

He pulled the covers up. "It's your funeral."

She didn't tell him what she really thought. Even if Caroline were that way, she would still want her as a friend. It was like the Negroes and Mexicans and Indians back home. If you looked down on people it came around and hurt you even more. Who was she, or Judd, to cast the first stone? Hadn't they been hurt enough?

She wiped off the cream and removed her negligee. She couldn't help imagining, for the briefest moment, before censoring it, what it would be like with Caroline. To her surprise, her pulse gave a quick thunder. The next instant she was merely tense. She turned off the bedlight and lay back, marveling. Anything was possible, and she must never be the one to disapprove.

Judd was on his back snoring—the music of marriage. She had another moment when she received impressions of a life different from the one she was living, as different as the one she might have had with Charlie Rysdale. Then she dismissed these fantasies as useless and cleared her mind for sleep.

7

HARRIS

The Trial

Owen, his counselor, stood up in the camp dining room after dinner and said he wanted to report a theft. Ten dollars had been taken from his chest.

"When was the last time you saw the money, Owen?" Pa, the head of the camp, raked the room with searchlight eyes.

"Before swim class, about three o'clock. When I came back an hour later, it was gone."

Pa swept the room again. Harris, at Owen's table with the other boys in Tent Four, knew it was important to look Pa in the eye, to convince him with a steady gaze that he hadn't taken the money even though his bunk was next to Owen's chest. He did this, willing Pa to believe in his innocence, but he wasn't sure he succeeded. Pa looked at him a little too long.

"If anyone wants to come to my office between now and campfire, I'll be there." Pa looked around, then his glare came to rest on Harris again. When he spoke his voice was dangerously sweet. "If the thief confesses there will be no punishment." He waited a long, dramatic moment—he was a dramatic man, famous for bloodcurdling screams during his ghost stories—then said, "Dismissed."

Everyone jumped up. Harris looked around for his friend Daly. It was free period and they had reserved a canoe. Burke wanted to come along, of course—Burke the Spitter—so they had to get out fast. There was Daly by the door.

As they skipped and ran down to the dock, keeping an eye out for Burke, they discussed the theft. Daly had several theories. One of the day-workers in the kitchen had stolen it. The man who drove the grocery boat across Lake George from Bolton's Landing had stolen it. Old Mrs. Sarney, the camp nurse, needed it to pay for her snuff.

Harris listened to these ideas carefully. He certainly hoped one of them was true. He started to say that Pa had stared at him too long but checked himself. He didn't want Daly to know he was afraid. Even though Daly was now his best friend, he had to be careful. Daly had a way of turning nasty, acting superior.

Actually, he was lucky to have Daly's friendship at all, since Daly was a second-year camper and strategic alliances held over from the previous summer. But there was a vacancy—a camper who hadn't returned this year—and Harris had stepped into it. Something in Harris filled up, crested, in the knowledge that he had a best friend. He became funnier, happier, more skilled. Once he and Daly were true-blue pals he began to like Camp Monhegan. He liked the lake, the swimming, the overnight canoe trips, Pa's ghost stories, the woods. He was proud to be a camper. In his letters home he wrote about winning the Ping-Pong tournament for his age group, also the spelling championship. He wrote about the night they put a field mouse in Owen's bed.

He didn't want Daly to know about his fears in the dining room tonight or about certain other things. The first was that he thought Daly was handsome. Not that he used that word or any word. It was just the way Daly looked—blond, bony, blue-eyed, with budding muscles and a sprinkling of yellow hairs on his arms and legs. Harris didn't know why those things added up to a claim on his attention, but they did. He liked to look at Daly as much as possible.

There were other secrets too. A couple of times he had gone with Burke—Burke of the wet speech—into the woods, and they had pulled down their shorts and examined each other's oscars. Each time Burke had offered to milk him, but Harris had refused. He didn't want Burke to touch him, realizing at the same time that if Daly had asked, he would have said yes. Unfortunately, these trips to the woods gave Burke a special hold over him. He had to do certain things, including calling Burke Paul—a sign of humiliating intimacy—or Burke would tell.

But the deepest secret, the one he would never admit to Daly and almost not to himself, was the heart-stopping excitement brought on by the sight of two counselors—Lucas and Hatch—in bathing trunks. They were both nineteen and went to Yale. When they appeared at the lake, torsos blazing, they actually hurt Harris's eyes. He had to look away.

Knowing that Lucas and Hatch affected him like this, when the other boys were gabbling about rowing across to a girls' camp and spying on them undressing, opened up a gulf in his mind. When would he feel like the others? Why didn't he feel that way yet? Why had he been left out?

One night Hal Ellis, a boy in his tent, announced after lights out (Owen was at a counselors' meeting), "My brother told me what a fairy is." He surprised everyone by saying this, since they weren't discussing it. "A fairy is someone who sucks men's cocks all his life and never has children of his own." Ellis had sounded very superior when he gave out this information, but the tent had gone dead-silent. Nobody knew what to say. He himself had lain motionless in the dark, swearing that he would never become like that, never qualify for Ellis's brother's definition. But even then, lying in the dark, something had whizzed through him, something connected to the sight of Lucas and Hatch in their bathing trunks.

Tonight he and Daly were crossing the baseball field, pleased that they had given Burke the slip, when they heard someone calling. It was Jack Orford, trotting after them and waving. Harris's heart gave a little knock when he saw Orford. He was one of Pa's pets, a special emissary.

"Pa wants to see you, Shay," Orford said in his pleasant baritone.

His heart gave another knock. "What for?"

"Just to talk, nothing important."

Harris knew this was terrible news but that he mustn't show any fear. Daly was staring from Orford to him and back again. In another second Daly would put it all together—his blue eyes would light up in a malicious way. Harris didn't want to see that.

"Okay." He shrugged, turning back with Orford. "Wait for me

down by the canoes," he instructed Daly in a careless voice. But of course Daly just stood there.

They headed toward the camp infirmary, a little building not far from where they'd met Orford. Harris could see Jim Tomey, the camp bugler, on the porch. Tomey was tall and thin, with a huge Adam's apple. Tomey got up as they approached. "You're in hot water, Shay," he said, then laughed in a know-it-all way.

"I didn't take Owen's money."

Tomey laughed again. "You're going to have to prove that, buster. There's going to be a trial."

"Don't worry, Shay," Jack Orford said, "it'll be okay." Harris was grateful for Orford's kindness but it didn't really matter now. Nothing mattered—it was too late.

They told him to go into the infirmary and wait. He went inside and sat on one of the cots. Orford and Tomey stayed on the porch, talking. He couldn't hear them but he didn't care. Something had slipped, some connection to the other boys, and he wanted to think about it. It was like a puzzle in arithmetic.

It was his fault. The knowledge popped out of a dark corner of his mind. He was accused and was going to stand trial not for this theft, which was insignificant, but for the other crime, for being an impostor, for bearing false witness, for pretending to be someone else.

It had bothered him all year in school, at Scout meetings, even with the Stag Patrol, which he liked. When his name was called by a teacher, another boy, the scoutmaster, he expected someone to jump up and reveal the truth. He wasn't Harris Shay. Harris Shay was someone added to, or subtracted from, his real self. But no one ever jumped up. No one told the truth. He didn't even know if he was glad or sorry about that.

It was all so confusing. His mother had dreamed the whole thing up, had told him to lie, threatened awful things if he didn't. He wanted to please his mother more than anything in the world. On the other hand, how could you tell a lie, an important one like this, and not be punished? They were punishing him here at Camp Monhegan, even though his mother had sewn the new name on the labels in his clothes, carefully, with white silk thread. And the worst part was, he would never be able to tell her about this new trouble because she would be furious with him. She would believe it was his fault, even though he'd followed her instructions exactly.

He heard more voices on the porch outside. He went to the window. Two older campers, Buchanan and Keary, had arrived. Somebody told a joke, and they all burst out laughing. He went back to the cot.

Suddenly he pictured his father's Latin grammar. He had found the carton with the red circle on it and removed the book when no one was in the house. It had felt heavy and dangerous in his hands. But when he opened it he found it had changed. The signature didn't throb or sparkle anymore. It didn't promise to keep his old self alive. In fact, it was kind of dead. Besides that, it began to accuse him, even though he buried it at the top of his closet, behind his stamp albums, where his mother would never look. He didn't know why the Latin grammar had changed, but gradually he became aware that there was something terribly wrong with both names, the old and the new.

The voices outside got louder. The door flew open. Keary and Buchanan, both of them tall and powerful, entered.

"Pa sent us to talk to you," Keary said. "I'm your defense lawyer." He was good-looking except for a sharp nose which interrupted his face.

"I'm going to prosecute," Buchanan said. He was heavier and had a humorous look.

"I didn't take Owen's money. I was at lifesaving class all afternoon. You can ask Bill Bart."

Bill Bart was the swimming counselor. Why hadn't he thought of that before?

Keary took out a pad and pencil. "What time were you there, exactly?"

"Between three and four."

Buchanan shook his head. "Bill doesn't watch everybody every minute. You could have snuck up and took the money."

Harris looked at Keary, expecting him to defend him, but Keary just made a popping noise with his mouth. "Daly was in class with me," he said, suddenly remembering, "all afternoon. You can ask him."

Keary wrote down Daly's name.

"The guard will be here in a few minutes." Buchanan looked at him, smiling. "They'll escort you."

"Where?"

"To the dining room. That's where the trial's gonna be."

Harris couldn't speak for a moment. Then he said, "Why is there going to be a trial? Why don't you ask Bill Bart? Ask Daly?"

But neither answered. They both turned away, heading for the door. When they left he remembered that he wasn't going to be tried for stealing Owen's money but for the other things, and somehow that made this situation worse.

The front door opened with a smash. He sat up quickly. Four campers his own age entered. They were all wearing web belts and grinning with self-importance. One of them was Burke, Burke the Spitter, from his own tent. That was the last person he wanted to see. "Fall in!" Burke screamed. Spit flew everywhere. Harris started to say something but Burke screamed at him. "The prisoner isn't allowed to talk, fall in!"

After some pushing and pulling he was placed between the other boys, two in front, two in back. They moved out of the infirmary and up the main road toward the dining room. Burke called out a cadence as they walked.

They attracted a lot of attention. The other campers stared. Some laughed, others said nothing, a few called out encouraging words to Harris. Harris knew he couldn't let anyone see what was going on inside him. He did his best to look nonchalant. Several times he laughed and called out that there had been a dumb mistake. A few boys cheered at that, but most just kept on staring.

At the dining hall they had to wait on the porch. Harris went to the far end and turned away, not wanting the other campers to see his face. At last Jack Orford came out. "We're ready," he said to the guards. Harris came forward, still trying to look easy. "After they take you in you'll sit in a chair down front," Orford said.

Harris could see through a window. The campers were all assembled on chairs. The tables had been pushed to the wall. Suddenly he felt nervous, almost panicked. Everyone would see his humiliation. "Will you sit with me?" he asked Orford.

Orford smiled in a kindly way. "I can't. You have to sit next to Jimmy Keary. He'll take care of you." Harris knew that Keary had no interest in defending him, but he said nothing. The guard was lined up, waiting for him to step into place. He did and they entered the room, conducting him down the center aisle. Every head turned but he kept his eyes down. When he finally reached the front and sat down, he heard cheers and whistles from the boys behind him.

There was a rustle in a corner by the fireplace. He hadn't noticed before—a curtained-off section. Pa stepped out from behind a sheet. He had an Indian blanket around his shoulders; on his head was a mortarboard with a tassel hanging down. Everybody started to laugh and clap. Harris thought the outfit was silly, but he didn't understand why people were laughing. Pa, after all, was never funny, just sinister and cruel.

One of the counselors came forward to help Pa climb a table that had been set up. There was a chair on top of the table. After a while Pa managed to balance himself. "Let the trial commence," he said, looking at Harris. He rang a little bell. Everyone laughed and cheered some more.

Buchanan, the prosecuting attorney, stood up and repeated the charge about the stolen money. Then he said, "The first witness is Owen Kressler."

Harris watched his counselor walk up front. A book was produced, and Owen put his hand on it. "Do you swear to tell the truth, the whole truth and nothing but the truth?" Pa asked.

Jimmy Keary, who was sitting next to Harris but hadn't spoken to him, jumped up. "I object, your honor. That's not a Bible, it's a Boy Scout manual."

The hooting and cheering started again. "Overruled," said Pa. "Take the oath, Owen."

"I do," said Owen. Then he sat in a chair facing the crowd. He repeated what he had said earlier. He had gone back to the tent after swim class and found ten dollars missing. When Owen finished, Buchanan said "Your witness" to Keary.

Keary stood up. "What proof do you have that you ever had ten dollars at one time in your life? You owe more than that at the camp store, and it's a well-known fact you're always bumming cigarettes."

Everybody began stamping and shouting until Pa rang his little bell. "My dad sent me money last week. I was saving it to pay off my debts," Owen replied.

"Are you sure?" Keary persisted.

"This man is under oath," Pa interrupted. "Do you have any more legitimate questions?"

Keary sat down and Owen left the witness chair. Buchanan called Joe Minello. Harris, who felt numb, watched as he took the oath and sat down. Joe was big, with bunchy muscles in his arms and legs. He was the camp's best softball pitcher. "Tell us what you saw in Tent Four this afternoon," Buchanan said.

Minello spoke softly. The room became quiet. "I was walkin' past the tents." Minello examined his powerful hands. "And I saw him"—he nodded at Harris—"foolin' around."

"What do you mean, 'foolin' around'?"

"He was lookin' into Owen's things."

A muttering sounded. Harris looked down at the floor.

"You saw Harris Shay poking around in Owen's chest?"

"Yeah." Harris looked up. Joe Minello had black whiskers coming in, even on his cheeks.

"All yours, Jimmy," Buchanan said.

Keary stood up. "Last week I saw you reading a comic book with glasses on."

Minello looked surprised. "I wasn't readin' it, I was lookin' at the pictures." He said *pitchers*.

"That's beside the point. Were you wearing glasses?"

Minello scratched his neck. "I guess so."

"Okay." Keary stopped, arranging his thoughts. "Did you have glasses on when you looked into Tent Four?"

Minello blinked several times. "Whaddya wanta know for?"

Several hoots broke out. Pa said, "Answer the question."

After a while Minello shook his head. "I don't think so, nah."

"That's all," Keary remarked. "Go sit down."

As Minello passed Harris he gave a little smile but Harris didn't smile back. Keary said to Pa, "If he didn't have his glasses on, he didn't see Shay take the money."

Pa gave a sweet, dangerous smile. "You should go to law school, Keary." Stomping and hooting followed. Keary looked pleased. Then Buchanan called out, "Stan Daly."

Harris felt better as soon as he heard Daly's name. Now the truth would come out. The trial would end. He was as good as free right now. After being sworn in on the Boy Scout manual, Daly took the chair.

"Did you see Harris Shay this afternoon between . . . let's see . . ." Buchanan had forgotten the time.

"Between three and four," Pa prompted.

"I did."

"Where did you see him?"

"In lifesaving class."

Harris tried to catch Daly's eye, to let him know that he felt okay, he wasn't scared, and that he appreciated what Daly was doing. But Daly refused to look at him.

"That was class with Bill Bart?"

"Yes."

"Was Shay . . . let's see . . ." Buchanan was getting mixed up. ". . . um, did Shay leave the class for a while?"

Daly answered smoothly. "Yes, he did."

"For how long?"

"About ten minutes."

Harris froze in his seat. Daly was lying. Daly had betrayed him.

"Do you know where he went?"

"I think he went up to the tent."

"How do you know that?"

"He came back with his goggles."

Buchanan looked around at Harris, who returned his stare without flinching. "So he had plenty of time to steal money from Owen."

"Plenty of time," Daly said.

Buchanan turned to Keary. "Your witness." But Keary just shook his head. "No questions."

Daly got up, still not looking at Harris, and walked past him to his seat. The break, the separateness from the other boys, that he had first noticed in the infirmary, came back. He wasn't connected to Daly anymore. He wasn't connected to anyone. He felt dizzy and closed his eyes.

"I'd like to call Bill Bart," Buchanan said.

No answer.

"Billy," Pa said in his sweet voice.

Harris heard Bill Bart speak from the back of the room. "I'm not taking part in this."

"We're calling you as a witness," Pa said, still sweet.

"Count me out, Pa," came the reply.

Harris opened his eyes. Pa gave a little nod, then rang his bell. "Are there any witnesses for the defense?" Keary stood up and said there were, but none had responded to his subpoenas. This struck everybody as very funny.

After the laughter died down, Pa rang his bell again. He looked down at Harris. "The prisoner will approach the bench."

Harris stood up.

"Closer."

He took a few more steps. The room behind him was perfectly still. "We find you guilty of stealing ten dollars from Owen Kressler's chest." Pa smacked his lips.

Harris knew this was his last chance. He had to get every ounce of innocence into his voice. At the same time he knew he was guilty. "I didn't do it, Pa."

"We will contact your parents. We will ask them to come and pick you up tomorrow. We don't want you as a camper at Monhegan anymore."

That was nothing, just the last, inevitable punishment. "I didn't do it, Pa."

Pa paused dramatically. He broke into a happy grin. "And now, Shay, we want to thank you for a most enjoyable evening. You've been a good sport."

Screams and shouts broke out. Everybody stood up and clapped. Keary walked up to him, extending his hand. "It was a mock trial, Shay. You did real good."

The other boys were milling around him, yelling, pounding him on the back. They told him he had acted great. They'd had a wonderful time. Last year the new camper on trial had started crying, and they had to stop right in the middle. It had ruined the whole evening.

Harris listened to all this with dim pleasure. He was free. There would be no punishment. The whole thing had been made up for entertainment. He was relieved, but at the same time there was no way to reconnect to the other boys. Everything that had happened—the hour in the infirmary, the march here, the trial itself—all that had set him apart.

Jack Orford came up. "As soon as Owen made his announcement at dinner, I knew it was going to be you. It's always a new camper. I told them they should stop this, it's awful."

Harris found himself shrugging and smiling. "I knew it was a joke all along." He hadn't intended to say that—the voice didn't even sound like his own—but he couldn't let anyone know. He had to pretend. Pretending, he understood vaguely, was his only chance.

A crowd of boys followed him to his tent. He liked being admired, congratulated, as if he had just caught a pop fly and saved an inning, but he was still apart from the others. Owen was waiting at the tent. As Harris walked up the three steps to the wooden floor, Owen stuck out his hand. "No hard feelings, Shay."

Harris took Owen's hand. "No hard feelings," he repeated. The boys who had followed let out a cheer. They thought everything was okay, that he and Owen would be friends again. But they wouldn't. He knew that as he sat down on his bunk, which was next to Owen's. There was no way he could forget what had happened. In fact, he thought, as things quieted down and his tentmates arrived, he would probably ask for a transfer. How could he go on living in a tent with Owen, who had pushed him to the other side of a deep divide? He couldn't even bear looking at him.

He didn't see Daly until lifesaving class the following afternoon. Daly had been keeping out of his way, not joining in the congratulations that kept pouring in. When he saw Daly on the dock, he avoided him. They usually paired off to do the exercises, but now he didn't want to touch Daly. The thought of that tawny skin with pale hairs gave him the creeps. Daly was a snake.

At last they couldn't avoid each other. Daly was right next to him, watching Bill Bar demonstrate the cross-chest carry. Daly let out a little noise. "You sore at me, Shay?" Harris didn't reply. He had so many things to say he couldn't say anything. "I had to do it." There was a slight whine in Daly's voice. "They said I wouldn't get a letter."

Daly was worried about the "M" for Monhegan. Daly had never been worried about him.

"When we were walking down to the canoes," Harris said, aware that his voice was coming from a long distance away, "did you know what they were going to do?"

Daly swiveled his heel on the boards. "Yeah."

Daly's treachery was instantly doubled—his theories about who had taken the money were all lies. Harris turned and walked to another part of the dock. A dead feeling went through him and he wished the summer was over, that he was back home. A tremendous desire to see his parents—even his father—came over him. He didn't look at Daly for the rest of the class or walk back to the tent with him.

That evening he went out in a kayak by himself. As he dipped the double paddle in the water, first left, then right, correcting each time, he thought about the mock trial. Although it had changed his summer, he had learned something. He had learned that even though other boys, counselors, Pa, might say they were your friends, they could only be trusted up to a point. His job, now and for the rest of his life, would be to discover the exact point. Part of their untrustworthiness, their potential for treachery, came from the fact that he was a false person with a secret past. He wasn't open and honest, so how could they be? But there was another reason, which had to do with something larger, something he didn't understand exactly. It was the enmity of the world. Anyone who didn't declare himself to be your friend was your enemy. That was the way things were. He would have to think about it some more—

it was another puzzle in arithmetic—but he had to get ready for it anyhow. There was no reason to believe that just being yourself would keep you safe.

He felt better when he turned the kayak in. He wouldn't bother to ask for a transfer out of Owen's tent. There was no need. He had a clearer view of things now. What difference did it make where he slept?

When the summer ended, they all went home from Lake George on a bus. Everybody sang camp songs and he joined in. In New Rochelle his parents were waiting for him at the corner of Main Street and North Avenue. When he saw his mother, he gasped and rushed over. She was in a white summer dress with huge red and blue flowers on it. She had never looked so beautiful—by far the most beautiful mother there. He threw his arms around her, breathing in her powdery fragrance, her dark love, her happiness. Behind all that, he could feel her resistance, her desire to break away, but he didn't let go. He would hug her until she pried him loose. Finally, when she did, he stood gazing at her until she said gently, "You forgot to say hello to Daddy."

When they got in the car, he sat in the back seat. His father, driving, asked him if he knew war had just started in Europe. He said that Pa had announced it in the dining room a couple of nights ago. His mother, half-turned toward him, was still radiant with beauty. "I bet you had a good time," she said. "We got all your letters. We let Nana and Grandpa read them too."

He thought about his letters. After the trial he had found it hard to write, to sound happy, but he had managed. "Yeah, I had a good time." He tried to get some excitement into his voice.

"Well, come on, give a little," she said.

He started to talk about the lake, getting his Red Cross certificate, the overnight canoe trip, the bad sunburn, chasing the ducks, sleeping out at night. Both of them kept asking for more details. But he couldn't keep the falseness, the fakery, out of his voice. This wasn't what he wanted to tell them. He was just pretending, as he had been pretending on the evening he was arrested, and afterward. Finally, cautiously, lightly, he said, "They had a trial." Silence came out of the front seat. They were waiting. "They accused me of stealing some money."

His father half-turned. "Did you?" He sensed, rather than saw, the angry flicker of the nostrils.

"No." He kept his voice casual, offhand. He didn't know why, but he couldn't tell his parents the whole truth—how he'd felt, what he'd learned about the world. "It was a mock trial. They do it to a new camper every year."

His mother laughed in a shrill, forced way. "Then it was a joke."

"Yeah, a joke."

He settled back in the seat. Now he knew why he couldn't tell them any more. If they heard the whole story, they would blame *him*. Somehow or other the blame would double back on him.

"Sounds like fun," his mother went on. "I bet you were a hero after it was over."

He laughed, almost sincerely. "Yeah, they all said I acted really well."

"Then you were a good sport." His father's eyes were bulging at him in the rearview mirror.

"Yeah, I was a good sport."

His father nodded approvingly. "That's the most important thing in the world."

When they got home, he put his camp things at the back of his closet. He didn't want to look at them anymore, not the lifesaving certificate or the roll of silver birch bark or the beaded Indian belt or the "M" for Monhegan. All that had to be forgotten. And when his parents started talking about next year, as they soon would, he would state absolutely and positively that he would never go back.

8

MAG
The Sorority

They had invited her to the Phi Gamma party just as she expected. Cynthia Tollifer, who was a junior, had told her she was on the list. Cynthia was captain of the field hockey team—she'd made friends almost as soon as Mag turned up for practice, a week after school started.

Cynthia was pretty, with lustrous brown eyes and a mature figure. Her only flaw was freckles. They seemed to be clawing their way through her skin. "Don't worry, Mag," Cynthia said as they walked home from school in October. "You'll get in. I'm on the Pledge Committee."

Mag shifted her books to her other arm. They gave a lot of homework in high school. She didn't tell Cynthia, but she knew exactly what to wear to the party. A white angora sweater, her plaid skirt held at the overlap with a huge safety pin, and her new saddles, nicely scuffed. Mother would certainly suggest that she do her hair in an upsweep, she looked better that way, but she would refuse again. It made her look old.

"When you're a pledge, you have to do everything I tell you." Cynthia pretended to be bossy and Mag was pleasantly aware of the humiliations ahead. But they had a purpose—to make you stand out from the girls who hadn't been pledged. No makeup. No jewelry. A boy's shirt and skirt. And of course instant obedience to the sisters. It lasted six weeks, coming to a climax on hell night. Cynthia wouldn't say what happened then but it couldn't be as bad as the fraternities. The boys did horrible things to each other. Last year, when she was still in junior high, she'd seen Fred Lydon standing on Main Street dressed in his mother's wedding gown, with lipstick and rouge on his face, and a sign that said "Left Waiting at the Altar." The girls were never as cruel as that.

Cynthia said good-bye in front of Mag's house on Webster Avenue. She couldn't come in; she had a piano lesson. Mag thought of mentioning that her brother also took piano lessons, then decided to skip it. It was better not to mention Harris; he had a terrible reputation. Besides, he still had a year left in junior high. It was bad enough they were living in a tiny house, nothing like the huge place on Beechlane Drive.

Cynthia gave a lingering good-bye and walked on. Inside, Mag found the house empty except for Gran, who was upstairs listening to her programs. She went to the foot of the stairs and gave a yell. Gran hollered back.

Daddy had lost almost all the money Grandpa had made. Nora and John were gone, as well as the Great Danes. Mother was substitute-teaching at Lincoln School, and Gran lived with them permanently, paying the rent and buying some of the groceries.

Although she had moments, like just now with Cynthia, when she wished they still lived in the grand style, most of the time she didn't mind. Now they were just like everybody else, neither rich nor poor. She certainly didn't miss having a chauffeur drive her to school. She had always made John stop the Pierce-Arrow a few blocks away, but word still got around. The other kids resented it. And though she hated dragging the Electrolux around the house—now her responsibility—it was what other mothers made their daughters do too.

She went upstairs, looking into Gran's room first. Gran waved the tin of bicarb, then pressed her hand to her stomach. She was waiting for the burp. Mag went into her own room, dropping her books, then going to the mirror. It was a three-way, with side panels that hinged forward. She always checked her looks at the end of the day to determine exactly how she had just appeared to others. Sitting down, she regretted again that she didn't have a little turned-up nose. Not that her nose was bad, but it had a slight bump in the middle. She had tried tying a ribbon around the tip, knotting it behind her head, and sleeping like that, but it only made a crease. Now, examining herself in the mirror, pulling the sides forward to produce infinity, she thought for the millionth time that her features taken separately were nothing special but the overall result was quite good. She knew which expressions were most effective (a slight, mysterious smile or raising her right eyebrow very high), and what makeup was best (Regimental Red lipstick and a very little powder and rouge over pancake), but the end product was always the same. She was moderately pretty. In fact, she was moderately everything—popular, smart, funny, athletic. Her worst feature was her height. Too tall. But only moderately too tall. Not like poor Anna Kissick, who was six feet in flats and never found a dance partner the right size.

She gazed into the mirror more deeply, also aware that she had to be careful. Something shadowy lived deep in there, very far back, that she didn't want to see. Most of the time she didn't think about it, but sometimes, when she was least expecting it, it popped out. She had mentioned this to her mother, who had pooh-poohed and said it was her imagination. But Gran had been more sympathetic. Gran said the darkness in her mirror was a dybbuk—but wouldn't elaborate. She couldn't find the word in a dictionary. But sometimes, as now, she caught brief glimpses of the shadow and knew it was connected to the life she had lived before they moved to New Rochelle, the life she wanted to forget.

She could hear "Vic and Sade" ending. She'd go sit with Gran, tell her about the sorority situation. Not that Gran really understood—it was too far from her experience in Texas. There had been the Daughters of the Confederacy, the San Jacinto Day Committee, the Mardi Gras Society, and so forth, but nothing really up-to-date. That didn't keep Gran from making comparisons, and Mag liked to listen, but it was all too long ago to be helpful. What they liked best was to try out the new dance steps—the Lambeth Walk or the Big Apple—until they got hysterical, or to wash and pin up Gran's hair.

Sometimes it seemed that Gran was really her mother. She was always ready for a game of Parcheesi or robber casino or pecan-shelling or a shopping trip, totally unlike Mother. If your remarks didn't concern books or history or philosophy, Mother got impatient. Mother also disapproved of Gran's radio programs, which went on from nine in the morning until "Vic and Sade," just ended. "Why do you listen to that trash, Mama?" she would ask, making a face. Mag knew that her mother was ashamed of Gran, always keeping her upstairs when company came, always criticizing her clothes, her hats, her appearance and grammar. But she wasn't ashamed of Gran, not at all. She always brought her visitors upstairs to Gran's room and they all loved her, especially when she clacked her teeth.

And Gran, unlike Mother, took an interest in her social life. Of course, Mother pretended to be interested, but she was probably making fun of her to Harris behind her back. What neither Mother nor Harris understood, for all their intellectual pretensions, was that she was determined to escape the family curse, which was fortitude in isolation. You should be content with a good book or an opera broadcast or pasting something in an album. Well, she wasn't. She hated to be alone. She had a vocation for society. The sight of the first girl on the first playground had made her fizzy with joy. A hum had started in her throat and never stopped. She could see everybody in patterns and groups, moving around the swings and seesaws at her direction. If Mother didn't appreciate that, then it was just one more unfairness. Daddy understood her, of course, but he was away on business so much, worried about money now that Grandpa was sick, that she hardly ever saw him.

Gran was sitting in her rocker, surrounded—barricaded, really—by her heavy carved furniture, supplied by her husband on their wedding day, which she called her bedroom suit. Gran still had her hand pressed to her stomach. "How's the fallen stomach today, Gran?" she asked.

Gran grinned, then picked up the fold in the middle and waved it. Gran's stomach had fallen several years ago. Mag knew this was a gradual process, but she couldn't resist the notion that Gran's stomach had fallen with a mighty plop one day when she was getting dressed. One minute Gran was standing there, a large woman with a round firm stomach. Next minute the stomach was down, *floop,* around her knees. It would have fallen farther but Gran had snatched it. Later, after experimenting, Gran had found that a corset held her up as well as her abdomen muscles once did. But when her corset hurt or pinched, as now, she would take it off and had to hold up her stomach by hand. Gran didn't mind jokes about this—in fact she joined right in, something else that Mother disapproved of. "Go 'long," Gran remarked now, squeezing her wrinkled face.

Gran wasn't smart like Mother. She never read any books, which was practically a sin in this house, though Mag had once caught her reading a small black religious book wrapped in gold cloth. But Gran had tucked it under her when she came in. Gran's interest in God was apparently a secret, though Mag didn't understand why. She never went to church with them, not even on the Sundays Harris served on the altar.

"How was Miss Jackson today?"

Gran loved Miss Jackson stories. Miss Jackson was her geometry teacher, a fierce woman who lived with Miss Eberle, the gym teacher, in what everybody knew was an unnatural relationship. Miss Jackson favored the boys, especially the good-looking boys, which was odd considering Miss Eberle. At any rate, she hated Mag.

"She humiliated me in front of the whole class today."

"No!" Gran rubbed her wedding band along the arm of the rocker.

"She asked me to copy my theorem on the board so everybody could see my mistakes." She described the scene to Gran, who became outraged. She'd never have gotten that reaction from Mother. "Why didn't you do it right in the first place?"—that would have been Mother's response. But Gran was on her side. "I wish you'd been my mother," she blurted out suddenly.

"Now, don't say that."

"I do." Suddenly she felt sorry for herself. If Gran ran the house there'd be no private conferences with Harris, no special desserts for him, no matinees of *The Corn Is Green,* no little hints that she was stupid because she didn't go for opera and Dickens. Instead, there'd be card games and treats and new clothes all the time.

"Your mother does what's best."

Gran didn't like hearing her daughter criticized, even if it was true. Gran called it "belittlin' " and didn't approve. But the fact was, she didn't have a mother. Sometimes she was filled with hate when she thought about it. She was an orphan. No, that wasn't true, she had Daddy and Gran and Nana and Aunt Hattie. But Harris had pushed her aside, taken her place. It had happened the minute he'd been born, and she had known it as soon as she laid eyes on that reddish-brown lump at the hospital. She'd seen her whole future in that one instant.

How much easier life would be if he could be exterminated like a bug. *Quick, Henry, the Flit.* She tried never to think of him but there he was, at the foot of the table, getting in the way, trying to prove he was smarter. Of course you were smarter if you spent all your time reading. But that kind of smartness didn't count.

"Why don't I do your hair, Gran?" She'd comb it and invent a new style. Even though Gran's hair was steel-gray, it was still beautiful. It came halfway down her back if you undid the bun. Gran batted her eyes in pleasure. "Well, bless your heart."

She switched on the radio—it was time for "Make Believe Ballroom." "All or Nothing at All" was ending, followed by "Taking a Chance on Love." As she folded and combed, moving the hair this way and that, meeting Gran's eyes in the mirror, she asked about Will Porter. Will Porter, who had turned into O. Henry, who they read in school, had proposed to Gran back in Gideon, but Gran had turned him down. And Gran didn't believe Will had embezzled the bank money for which he went to jail. Her cousin worked at the bank where Will worked, so she should know.

"A nigger took it," Gran always said, and she said it again now. Mag didn't like that word, but it slipped out of Gran's mouth all the time. There were also other things they could talk about to keep them busy till dinner. They could talk about Governor Jim Hogg, who had named his daughters Ima and Ura, a cruel Texas trick which tickled Gran. They could talk about Barbara Hutton and her latest or Tommy Manville and *his* latest. They could discuss "Truth or Consequences" with Ralph Edwards, a radio show they both loved. They could talk about Eleanor Roosevelt or Frances

Perkins. Gran liked making fun of both of them for their buck teeth, their lopsidy smiles, their awful hats. Sometimes, as she listened to Gran, Mag realized she had a mean streak, but maybe that happened when you got old. Certainly Gran rarely had a kind word for anyone famous except Winston Churchill, who was going to beat Hitler.

She did Gran's hair in a new way, Southern-belle style, two long curls draping her neck like Bette Davis in *Jezebel*. It looked gorgeous, though Gran clacked her teeth and pretended she didn't like it. "Don't you dare change it," said Mag, glaring into the mirror. "It looks beautiful. I want everyone to see." She bent over and kissed one seamed cheek.

Gran squealed and kicked her feet. "Go 'long, you old hypocrite," she cried.

Mag was putting away the pins and comb and brush when Gran reached into the little purse of cracked leather pinned inside her brassiere. "I never showed you this," she said.

Mag turned around. It was a little golden horseshoe, set with brilliant diamonds. A stickpin.

"Papa had it made before he went back to Romania. He wanted to show off to his family, I reckon."

Mag turned the pin this way and that. It was exquisite.

"Is it worth much?"

"A might."

She gave the jewel back reluctantly. She would love to have it, to wear on the collar of a blouse. It would cause no end of comment. But Gran put it back inside her old, cracked pouch and she didn't dare ask. Once in a while, if she begged too much, Gran called her a gold-digger.

Cynthia said she would pick her up at eight for the Phi Gamma party. That meant her and Mr. Tollifer, since Cynthia didn't have a junior license yet. Mr. Tollifer didn't mind using his scarce A coupons for driving his daughter around, unlike the other fathers.

Mag fretted in front of her infinity mirror until the last minute. The angora sweater made her look fat. She tried some other sweaters, including one with a diamond pattern Mother had knitted for her, but none of them fit. Finally she put on the angora again, pushed up the sleeves, smoothed the fur and went downstairs.

They were all sitting around listening to Gracie Allen. "You look beautiful," Daddy said.

"No, I don't, I look fat."

"You look enormous." If only Harris would walk out the door and get hit by a car.

"I think the sweater looks nice." Mother, in her fair-minded tone. No telling what she really thought.

It was Gran who made her feel good. "Come over here, honey." Gran smoothed and tugged with her big hands, fitting the sweater farther back on her shoulders, tucking it inside her skirt. Gran refastened the huge safety pin in the skirt and got rid of the extra bulge. She went to the hall mirror. She didn't look fat anymore. Just then she heard the car honk.

Daddy got up, trailing the evening paper, and went to the door. He waved at Cynthia and her father. She didn't let him kiss her for fear of mussing something; she just yelled good-bye and ran out, dragging her polo coat. "Put that on," he yelled, but she ignored him.

"I love the sweater," Cynthia said at once.

"What's that, some kind of animal?" Mr. Tollifer was being funny. Fathers were always getting cute with girls. This came from sexual frustration—she and Cynthia had discussed it. It was pathetic in a way.

As he drove, Mr. Tollifer continued his efforts to be witty. Cynthia was wearing a new Max Factor color, Dawn, to cover up the freckles. Brenda Frazier used it. She was also wearing Evening in Paris, which filled up the car.

Mr. Tollifer let them off at Jean Palermo's house. Jean was president of Phi Gam and one of the most beautiful girls in school. Mag had examined her many times, marveling at the perfection of her nose, her widely spaced grey eyes, her light brown hair in natural ringlets that bobbed up and down like little springs. Not only that, Jean was nice, not stuck on herself.

Jean opened the door and gave them both a hug. She told Mag she was really glad she could come. She said this so sincerely, without gushing, that Mag believed her. Cynthia was right. It would be easy. Here she was in Jean Palermo's house, with two dozen other girls, some being rushed, some members, and not worried about anything at all.

Cynthia took her around and introduced her to the sisters, though she knew who they were. At school they wore the Phi Gam pin and she had made it her business to learn their names. Daddy had suggested this. "Always call people by their name, it's their favorite word in the English language." Everybody was very friendly. As she accepted a Coke from Laurie Gates, who was head of the Hospitality Committee, she had the feeling that she'd found a new family. Yes, she thought, sitting at last under some hunting prints, that's what Phi Gam was—a family. They were all sisters, weren't they? And what had she ever wanted more than a sister?

As the other guests arrived she had a serious talk with two members about problems with Tau Phi. Tau Phi boys were supposed to ask Phi Gam girls to their dances first, since they were brother-sister organizations. Some of the Tau Phi boys were dreamboats. But they weren't doing this. They were ignoring their obligations. The first sister, whose name was Melanie Blatch, thought they should write to the national association about this. The other girl, Elinor MacGowan, suggested they stop inviting Tau Phi boys to their own dances.

"They don't want to come anyway," observed a tall girl named Marion Prelinger. She had just joined their group—a rush. Mag looked at her sharply. That was a tactless thing to say. It was a black mark against her. It occurred to her that Marion, who was outlandishly tall, with bony elbows and an overbite, was someone she might have been, who she had barely escaped being. She would have to avoid her as much as possible.

"I think . . ." Mag almost said "we" but caught herself in time. ". . . I think you should talk to Chick Gergen and maybe have a closed dance just for Phi Gams and Tau Phis. Then everybody can get reacquainted." Chick Gergen was president of Tau Phi.

She had spoken hesitantly, deferentially, one hand shielding her mouth slightly in case she had bad breath, but Elinor MacGowan let out a scream. "That's a marvelous idea. Why didn't we think of it?" As the meeting began, both sisters insisted she sit with them on the couch. None of them paid any attention to Marion.

The meeting began with a welcome from Jean Palermo. Mag felt a powerful happiness spreading through her. All her life had been a preparation for this evening. When she was introduced and had to stand up, she wasn't shy at all. She had the impression, in fact, that she was quite beautiful. "Margaret Shay," Jean said, and there were smiles all around. She felt lapped in love.

The only difficult moment occurred when they were at the buffet in the dining room. Janet Dewarr, who was a cheerleader, came up to her. "You aren't from Massachusetts, are you?" she asked.

Mag smiled. "No, my parents are from the South." That's what Mother had told her to say if anyone asked.

"Oh." Janet looked disappointed. "I thought we might be related. My great-grandmother was a Shay. We're descended from John Shay, who fought in the Revolutionary War."

For an instant Mag felt disoriented, as if everything was moving out from under her—pictures, furniture, even the tank of goldfish in the corner—but she recovered quickly. Janet was just being friendly. "Well, I'm not sure. Unless there was a branch of your family that moved to Texas."

Janet's green eyes sparkled. "I'll write my aunt and ask her. She keeps all the charts. Wouldn't that be marvelous? If we were cousins as well as sorority sisters?"

Mag's nervousness disappeared entirely. There was nothing to worry about. Nothing could happen. And hadn't Janet practically told her she would be pledged?

"It would be marvelous," she replied, resisting the urge to shield her mouth with her hand. "I'll ask my mother too. Where in Massachusetts are you from?"

After the buffet was over, the members withdrew into the den. Everybody knew what they were doing. Some of the rushes, including Marion, who she'd kept away from, talked loudly to cover their nervousness. But Mag chatted quietly. She had nothing to worry about. When the members came out, smiling tight, superior smiles, Cynthia's eyes sought hers.

On the way home with Mr. Tollifer again, Cynthia confirmed

that they had voted in the study. She named several girls who had been passed over, including Marion. Cynthia was sworn to secrecy, but she could say this—Mag was to stay by her phone next Saturday morning between nine and ten. There were several sisters who weren't at the meeting tonight who had to be consulted. The vote had to be unanimous.

Mag climbed the stairs in the dark house, then paused on the upstairs landing. She was so happy she was about to burst. She just had to tell someone. But who? Mother would say something nice but wouldn't really be impressed. Daddy hated to be woken up. Harris was hopeless.

She opened the door to her grandmother's room. Gran was lying on her back with her eyes open. A dim light from the bathroom shone on her crumpled mouth. The water glass with her teeth in it sat on the table alongside. "You awake, Gran?"

Gran raised one heavy arm to her forehead. Flesh swayed from the bone. "I'm awake, honey. Did you have a nice time?"

She moved toward the bed. As she got closer she could smell Ben-Gay and camphor and Sloan's Liniment. She inhaled other things too, sweat and sweetness and decay, as if Gran's long life had been reduced to a series of smells. "They asked me to join Phi Gamma." She exhaled into the darkness, then repeated the magic words. "Phi Gamma."

"Good, honey, I knew they would."

Gran reached up and touched her hair. The smells swarmed upward too. Suddenly Mag began to cry. "There's nothing to cry about, go 'long," Gran whispered.

But she was so happy. The shadow in her mirror was going to disappear for good. Maybe she could tell Gran how she felt. But it was so weird, and Gran got snappish if she thought you were feeling sorry for yourself.

"Go on to bed, honey."

"I love you, Gran."

Gran lay back wearily, closing her eyes. Maybe she was drifting off. Maybe she had no more to say. Mag moved slowly toward her own room. She would have liked to give Gran a hug, but Gran wasn't big on hugs, just like Mother. But it didn't matter—nothing mattered except the knowledge of her triumph. She didn't look in the infinity mirror as she got ready for bed. Her eyes were red, she looked awful. But earlier this evening, when it counted, she had looked her best.

The next two days passed in a dream. She helped Mother or Gran fix dinner. She made all the beds every morning. She dragged the Electrolux around, even doing under the radiators. She also asked Harris to play a piece for her—a sign of her special favor. He played the march from *Tannhäuser*. She thought that after all these years he shouldn't be starting and stopping so much, shouldn't be saying, "Just a minute," all the time, but she complimented him anyway. That made him happy. She considered for a moment that she and Harris might become friends. Once she was a Phi Gam he wouldn't be such a liability. She might even teach him how to jitterbug.

To top it off, next day Miss Jackson complimented her on her isosceles triangles. She picked up Mag's paper and showed it around the room. "My heavens, look," Miss Jackson said in her violent voice. It was highly unusual for Miss Jackson to praise a girl.

Friday night Daddy suggested they go out for a Chinese meal. He had a favorite restaurant run by a man named Ping whom he always called Pong. Mr. Ping didn't seem to mind.

Tonight the restaurant was quite full. They were shown to a table at the back. After sitting down she noticed Cynthia Tollifer and her parents up front by the window. "There's Cynthia," she called. Everyone looked up. She wondered if she should go over or just wave. But before she could decide, Cynthia turned and looked her full in the face. Then she looked away.

That was strange. She'd seen Cynthia this morning in school, and though they hadn't talked much, Cynthia had been her usual self. She kept an eye on Cynthia's table. When the Tollifers finished and paid the bill she got ready to say hello. Mrs. Tollifer had never met her parents or Gran. She would have to introduce them.

But Cynthia and her parents walked in a straight line to the door. They didn't even turn. Mag watched numbly. Only Harris caught on. "How come Cynthia didn't say hello?"

Gran looked up, but Mag replied quickly, "She can't talk when she's with her parents." But now her hands had gone icy, and her heart had started banging.

That night she called Cynthia, but Mr. Tollifer said she was out. There was nothing to do but wait until tomorrow morning, Saturday. She found herself drifting into Gran's room. Gran was feeling low—she could tell because Gran slipped the religious book, whatever it was, under a cushion when she appeared. Mag suggested a game of Parcheesi. Before long they were laughing and accusing each other of cheating. When Harris turned up, they let him play. But even as she laughed and caught Gran skipping spaces, she thought this was the last time she would be truly happy.

She was quiet the next morning, so quiet Mother asked if she was feeling flushed, which was their code word for the curse, but that wasn't the reason. It was nine-thirty and the phone hadn't rung. She had woken up this morning knowing it wouldn't. Knowing beyond a doubt. Someone had blackballed her. Someone had found out.

She roamed around the house until eleven, then went to her room and closed the door. She had a headache. As she lay on her bed she remembered Camp Birchmont. The other girls had stopped speaking to her, put her in Coventry—an expression she learned years later. She had to leave camp in the middle of summer. When she told Mother about it, told her everything, Mother had said it didn't matter. "Who cares what a bunch of silly girls think?" But if they were just silly girls why had Mother sent her there in the first place? She had never gotten a satisfactory answer to that because there was none.

She thought of school on Monday morning. The new pledges would be without makeup or jewelry. They would be very pleased with themselves and trying not to act conceited. What would she say to them? What would they say to her?

Her headache was getting worse. She got up, dipped a washcloth in cold water. It felt good against her forehead. When Gran came in an hour later, she rolled over on her side and refused to speak. Gran got angry but she didn't care. She wouldn't speak. Not to Gran, not to anybody. What could she say? That she had known, in her heart of hearts, that the shadow in the mirror wouldn't disappear? That she hated Cynthia Tollifer? That she wished she'd never been born? She couldn't say those things to Gran or to anyone. She would just have to forget, or pretend to forget.

By evening she was feeling a little better. Everyone knew what had happened without her saying anything. Her sadness had expanded and filled the house. Even Harris was subdued, although she suspected he was secretly glad.

Still, there was nothing they could do. And she had to go to school on Monday, she had to face Cynthia Tollifer and the new pledges, she had to smile and show she didn't care. She wasn't sure, at least not yet, she could.

But that night, lying in bed, she felt her spirit surge. There were other girls. There were the teams. Most of the girls weren't in a sorority anyway. There was no reason to give up just because they didn't want her in Phi Gamma.

She narrowed her eyes into the dark. There was lots she could do. Some of the girls who she'd just smiled at, not really sought out, would love to be invited over. They might even form their own club, if they could think of a good reason. She just had to get through Monday, walking the steps into the hall, circulating between classes, proving that she didn't care.

Cynthia Tollifer was in her Latin class, third period. Mag took a deep breath at the door before walking in. She hadn't decided exactly what to do—to look at Cynthia or pretend not to see her. Miss Bowers was at the blackboard, writing. It was amazing how teachers never understood the really important things going on.

Cynthia, in the third seat of the middle row, had her head turned away. Her hair was full and dark, with a reddish tinge. Right now it looked ratty. Mag entered, taking her rear seat by the window. She came into Cynthia's view as she did so but didn't look that way. She separated her Caesar from the other books.

Miss Bowers turned, her long, sweet face illuminated with the excitement of imparting useless information. She was wearing a gauzy flowered dress and pearl earrings, too dressy really. Her gaze fell on Mag. Mag was one of her special favorites. Half the time she talked to her, even though there were twenty other students in the room. She did that now.

"I have a joke for you," Miss Bowers said, rolling her eyes, "from my beginner's class."

Mag risked a glance at Cynthia. She was facing forward. To let Cynthia know she didn't care—that was what she had to do. But how?

"I was trying to explain the ablative of respect to them." Miss Bowers's big blue eyes were fixed on her. "You remember, *with respect to.*"

Yes, she remembered, one more thing you had to memorize. *With respect to his character, Caesar was virtuous.* Daddy had to explain that to her last week, she really didn't get it from Miss Bowers.

"And when I finished, I asked one of the boys to give me an example." Miss Bowers tittered slightly. Mag smiled back. "And he said, 'The boy opened the door for the girl.' " Miss Bowers surveyed the class. Nobody laughed. Miss Bowers rolled her eyes again. "You see, *out of respect for the girl.*"

A mild reaction. It wasn't all that funny. Last week she and Cynthia would have traded glances at this point. *Oh, God, Miss Bowers.* But now Cynthia's face was set forward. How was she going to let Cynthia know?

And then, as Miss Bowers began the regular lesson, Mag grasped it. She would be perfectly friendly. There would be no sign. Not a thing.

When the class broke, she left the room just behind Cynthia. Cynthia half-turned, nervously. "Hi," Mag said, using her breeziest tone.

"Oh, hi, Mag." Cynthia turned around, smiling sweetly. "I didn't see you." She tossed her hair for a moment. It was really ratty. "I meant to call you this weekend. I just didn't get a chance."

The smoothness of the lie almost took her breath away. "I wasn't home anyway. We drove up to Lake Mahopac. We're thinking of buying a cabin there."

Not true but it seemed to work. Cynthia blinked rapidly and

studied her. Lies breed lies, Mag thought, but she couldn't help it. "It's beautiful up there," Cynthia said, in her old rushed voice. A pang went through Mag—she would probably never hear that breathy, confidential tone again. And she was right, because the next moment Cynthia was all sweetness again. "I have to hurry, Mag, they're waiting for me outside." She started off. "I'll call you real soon." She was heading for the front steps. All the new pledges would be gathered there, the first lunch hour, waiting for orders from the sisters. Mag wouldn't walk that way. Not today, not tomorrow, not for the whole six weeks of pledging. Instead she headed for the basement cafeteria. It would be full of the kids who hadn't pledged—girls and boys. She would choose one table or another, it didn't matter. She was starting over again but she wasn't afraid. She'd started over before and she always came out okay. In fact, she was getting to be an expert at it.

She sat with Marion Prelinger, who'd said all the wrong things at the rush party. Marion was thrilled to see her. Mag spoke quietly, drawing her out, making a friend.

9

JUDD

The Funeral

Hattie had phoned him at the office and he had put on his hat and coat and taken a cab right up to St. Luke's. Hattie was sitting on the radiator when he entered—she was always chilled in winter—while his mother lay still. But when Hattie cried, "Here's Judah," she started to struggle up from the bed, reaching out a pale arm. He went over and pressed her down, also planting a kiss on her forehead. She was burning up.

"You got the pip," he announced.

"Oh, yes." Irony in her voice.

"You'll be okay."

"Don't tell me that." Her voice was deep with irritation. As if, he thought, she didn't want to be robbed of her illness.

"They're trying one of those new miracle drugs," Hattie said, "the kind they use on the GIs."

His mother closed her eyes. She didn't want to hear about getting well. She didn't believe in it. She had mascara on, which made the yellow of her skin more vivid. She was badly jaundiced. "Is it one of those sulfa drugs?" he asked.

"I don't know."

His mother looked up, then patted the bed next to her. He lowered himself with care. "The medicine won't do any good." Her voice was full of satisfaction. The old, hungry look came into her eyes; she liked having him so close.

She'd had one of her angina attacks, worse than usual. The digitalis hadn't helped. In the morning, Hattie had called an ambulance.

His mother listened to Hattie's recital with her eyes fixed on him, waiting, testing his reaction. He kept his face neutral, his demeanor calm. All of them knew the real trouble wasn't angina, it was her liver. It was riddled with cancer. Under the sheet he could see how thin she was—the opulent figure, the Lillian Russell splendor, ravaged away.

When Hattie finished, his mother didn't speak, just kept her eyes on him in modest triumph. He knew what she was thinking. She'd be glad to die. She yearned for it. She had said this many times during the last four years, every Thursday when he went for dinner. She would wave her hand in a vanquished gesture and sigh for death. Pop was gone, the Packard was gone, the big apartment on Riverside was gone. She and Hattie lived together in a small apartment on West End. They didn't get along, quarreling in deep voices, accusing each other of being too unselfish. That was it. Every time one of them made a sacrifice the other screamed bloody murder. They quarreled about who took a bath first, what movie to see, where to seat guests at the table. Each wanted the other to decide, take precedence, but under that an entirely different power struggle was going on, over Hattie's new boyfriend. His mother didn't like him—Martin Stein, a refugee from Germany, not Jewish despite the name. He ranked first with Hattie—her boyfriends always did—and Mother was furious. She retaliated by being unselfish. It was hopeless. He was always being drawn in, forced to adjudicate their quarrels. They were both trapped in some kind of leftover life, and there was no way he could portion it out fairly. Only visits from the kids cheered them, but now that the children were away at college, these visits were rare. Each Thursday night he took the late train back to New Rochelle, feeling torn in half between his sister and his mother. Once he had broken down weeping while Margaret looked on unsympathetically.

"And so this Dr. Magin said he had a case just like Mother's last month and the woman recovered." Hattie looked at him, then at her mother. "You don't believe that."

His mother grunted. "Why should I believe it? That's what they're paid to say."

"If you want to get well you will." He sensed another quarrel starting. If his mother didn't get well, if she abandoned Hattie, it would be because she wanted to cause maximum inconvenience, as she did on the nights Martin came over.

"Leave her alone, Hattie."

But Hattie wanted to finish the thought. "What were all those Christian Science testimonials about?"

"They were dreck." His mother fluttered her left hand. She was wearing only her wedding rings. Her pale hands looked naked without the colored stones.

"That's not what you said at the time."

"Oh, leave me alone."

His mother had taken up Christian Science, going to the big church on Central Park West, talking eagerly about the cures and miracles. But now, when the chips were down, she wanted no part of it. He might have known.

Hattie tossed him an angry look. "You talk to her."

His mother had her hand locked around his. What could he say? His heart began to palpitate. He'd had a coronary three years ago, when the troubles at the office really got bad. He was on digitalis too. "I called Margaret," he said, to change the subject.

His mother tightened her grip on his hand. "I don't want her here." Her words came out in a growl.

"Well, she wants to come."

"Keep her away."

Hattie shifted position on the radiator. "If it will upset Mother, she shouldn't come." Her voice had a patina of reason, but underneath . . .

"Jesus Christ." He shook his head.

"Judah," Hattie went on, "you have to consider Mother first."

Hattie and Margaret were still at each other's throats after all these years. But Margaret would insist on coming, would consider it her duty. If he kept her away, she would smell rejection. There'd be hell to pay.

His mother was more animated now. She motioned to him to

arrange her pillows. Then he got up to crank the bed. "How are things downtown?" she asked.

"Downtown everything is fine." What did she want him to do, make her sicker?

"What's Wolcott doing?"

The factors were on the verge of closing him down. She knew; she got reports from Nick the bookkeeper. She probably called him this morning from the hospital, never mind the angina attack. He'd asked Nick about it, ordered him not to take any calls from his mother, but Nick swore he never talked to Mrs. Schanberg. Why would he trouble her? Business was for men. "Wolcott's given us another six months."

Her eyes searched his, testing for truthfulness. She'd been testing him for that for forty-six years, since day one of his appearance on earth. "Don't lie to me."

"Why would I lie?" He could feel his heart clattering around. God knows what was going on in there. Not only Nick but Stella kept her informed. She had suborned them years ago, even when Pop was alive. He used to overhear her phone conversations, the casual questions, the buttering up. Paul the chauffeur would deliver little gifts—perfume, cigars—on the Q.T. Poor Pop, he never knew there was a fifth column in his own house. Every day, right after she finished reading Anne O'Hare McCormick in the *Times,* she jiggled the phone hook and gave the operator the Schuyler number.

"Please don't get excited, Mother." It was Hattie. "If you get excited I'm going to ask for a sedative."

His mother laid her head back. "I'm not getting excited."

But she was. She knew all about his afternoons at the ball games too, had known for years. Stella kept her posted. Sometimes, when he got fed up with the office, the problems, the wartime scarcity of goods, the shipment difficulties, the Polo Grounds would rise up in front of him. He'd see the crowds, the vendors, the uniforms, hear the crack of Mel Ott's bat, watch the ball foul up to the little net they'd placed for him. Then he couldn't help himself—he had to get out. He'd make up some excuse. His mother never reproached him for playing hooky—she was too smart for that—but she knew. He could almost hear Stella's flat voice on the phone.

"He's gone, Mrs. Schanberg, up to the Polo Grounds, I'm sure." The two of them joined in deploring his weakness, his childishness, but he couldn't help it. If he couldn't get away, if he couldn't see the sky and the crowds and the men on the field waiting for the ball, he'd go crazy.

He should never have gone into the business. They should have let him go to medical school like he wanted. He'd be a world-famous surgeon today instead of president of a doomed enterprise. The place had been going downhill steadily since Pop first got sick.

He'd hated it from the minute he was old enough to know what the hell it was. He'd never been impressed, not even the first time he visited the office and saw his own name at the top of the stationery, ran his fingers over the raised letters, raised so high you thought you were touching stone. What was there to be proud about? Buying and selling socks and underwear. It had never been the thing he wanted to do, the thing that would make him proud. It was not his choice.

His mother groaned suddenly and pressed her bosom. Guilt raced through him. He'd been thinking about his own troubles. "What is it?" He bent over her. Her dark eyes, ringed in mascara, bored into him. For a moment he sensed that his clanging heart and his mother's cancer were one and the same. She twined her long white arms around his neck, pulling him down. He lost his balance, reaching out, but she kept pulling in a sudden access of strength. At last she had his face against hers. Was ever skin so sweet, so satiny? He fell through time, back into boyhood. His heart speeded up some more. When he broke free, forcing his way up, she studied him again, her eyes brilliant. He could read victory there. She hadn't lost him. Not at all. She might even be able to take him with her.

When he got home that night, he told Margaret he didn't want any dinner. He was *oshgespielt,* all played out, but of course she looked disapproving. She hated those expressions. He went upstairs to bed.

He felt icy, as if he had been dipped in polar seas. Yet his hands were hot, his palms a bright crimson. He knew those ruddy palms were a sign of trouble, even though everybody, including his doctor, laughed at the idea. Just before his coronary three years ago his palms had gone from their usual pink to carmine to a blazing crimson. It was the blood backing up, but nobody would believe him.

Margaret was particularly infuriating. She simply didn't believe in illness. What did she think it was—play-acting? On the night of his infarction, when the vise in his chest had threatened to squeeze him to death, she had refused to call for help until he lurched out of bed and fell on the floor. Only then had she run to the phone. He'd spent three months in bed—a hospital bed in this room—but half the time she'd suspected him of faking. She hadn't said so but he could tell. She was waiting for him to make up his mind to be well.

He could smell his mother's scent on his cheek, even now at home. It was like a brand on cattle. In a minute he'd get up and wash it off. But first he'd rest. His heart was going like a tom-tom, sending messages. Wolcott had made good on his threat. The phone call was waiting when he got back from the hospital. They were now in receivership.

The trouble was, he'd never been good at business. Pop, for all his mildness, had the instincts of a shark. He came alive when he smelled a profit. But he wasn't like that. What the hell was the difference if you made a little more or a little less? The main thing was whether people liked you.

And now he was losing the company, the one Pop had founded during the first war when he got all those contracts from the military. He didn't like the business and he had failed. Margaret and her mother paid the household bills, and both kids were on scholarships at college.

He had misjudged. It came to him on the edge of a black silence as the tom-tom in his chest missed a beat. He had misjudged when he moved the firm into big new offices, misjudged when he wrote up his bids for the army, misjudged when he borrowed to expand the mill in High Point. And now it was over. The worst had happened.

But that wasn't it. Or not all of it.

The tom-tom was going again, thank God, spreading through

him with a thick sound. He pressed his hand against his chest. His mother had done the same thing this morning.

His wife had left him. She had run off with Charlie Rysdale. He hadn't been able to keep her. He imagined his own funeral and people whispering. Why did people talk so much? He would rather die than have the kids know what had happened.

But she had come back. She had dumped Charlie. Her choice was free—almost free. And they'd been happy. Look at what they had—beautiful homes till they moved to this shithouse. Wonderful children. A family life. He had been an air-raid warden; he had driven Mag and her date to the senior prom; they had all gone to a donkey baseball game. They had sat on the front porch while the fireflies winked and the moon brightened and the Good Humor bell rang in the twilight. Didn't all that count for something?

It was hard to know for sure. She had run off, and everyone had known—the people at the office, the relatives, the friends of the family. Who had invented marriage? The mothers and aunts and grandmothers. But the young men, his teammates, knew it was dangerous, that you should never let a girl too close, that they were safe only with each other, cracking jokes, playing ball. But what could they do? They followed instructions. One of them caved in and then the rest. But he hadn't been made for matrimony. It had been a strain on his heart.

He heard Margaret's step on the stairs. She stood in the doorway for a moment, holding a tray. Seeing her face, full of worry, his bitterness began to fade. She had come back, hadn't she? There had been love between them. They had raised children together. They had done the things everybody did, the normal family things. Charlie Rysdale had been a mistake. Anybody could make a mistake. But it had been a strain on his heart.

"I made floating island," she said.

The cemetery trees were bare at the end of November. Hattie was wearing a black cloth coat with a fat fur collar. Her black veil hid her features. A small hat with pheasant feathers curling around was tilted forward on her still-auburn hair. An odd choice, he thought. In another week she'd be wearing his mother's Persian lamb or mink, but not yet. She had taken Margaret's hand before the service, then they had kissed. Now they were standing side by side at the cut in the hard ground. The coffin was waiting, the rabbi, a white scarf around his neck, was intoning. *El malei rachamin . . .*

Thank God Hattie had behaved herself. It would have been God-awful if his mother had been buried in the middle of a squabble. He looked at both women, Margaret in the mink coat he had bought her when times were good. Maybe they would make up now. Maybe the time had come.

The rabbi closed his prayer book and started a psalm from memory. Several men lifted straps under the coffin. He raised his hat and scratched his scalp. A sob sounded from Hattie as the ornate box was lowered. "Are we to be spared nothing?" she asked aloud. He didn't hear Margaret's reply—soothing, no doubt.

The headstone was a marble pillow with a fold down the center, elegant marble tassels at both sides. One pillow was incised, "Henry Schanberg, 1868–1940." The other side was blank. He looked around the family plot, discerning, under the fallen leaves, his mother's parents, Wolfe and Charlotte Lichtern, some great-aunts. He felt remarkably calm, maybe because it was so cold.

The coffin touched bottom. The men slid out the straps. Hattie broke off a rose from a standing display and dropped it in. Others followed but he did not. He had already said good-bye to his mother.

He had gone to the hospital every day last week. As he sat in her room, greeting the steady stream of visitors—strangely, it was Paul, in a grey chauffeur's uniform instead of the black one he wore when he worked for them, who had broken down—he had been calm, as now. The resentment, the turmoil, had evaporated. His mother had been gracious, enjoying the visits, almost as if she were at home.

Only when he brought Margaret for a visit had trouble started. Hattie, advised in advance, wasn't there. But when he went into the room alone to tell his mother that Margaret was outside, she had raised herself furiously, unaided, and in her deepest, most carrying voice, had growled, "I don't want her in here." Margaret had heard—that was the worst part. Standing outside waiting, a pot of hyacinths in her hand. He'd gone out to find her rigid, hurt all over her face, the pot tight against her chest. He'd broken into a sweat. What could he say? At last she thrust the flowers at him and turned toward the waiting area. When he went back inside, his mother was flat on her back, eyes open, chest heaving. He could have killed her. She was dying and it had all come out again.

Driving home that night, Margaret said, "She hated me right up to the end, didn't she?" And what could he say? What could he say to any of them?

She had died early, about four-thirty A.M. By the time he got there, a rainy windswept morning, the room had been cleared. They had been sent to the cold room in the basement, at his insistence. That was against policy, but he wouldn't leave till he'd seen her.

There were three corpses, each on a tier of shelves. His mother was in the middle, her features locked in repose. The cold and dimness bothered him but he went and kissed her cheek. It was already icy. For a moment he imagined that his kiss would waken her, and then a treacherous relief poured through him. Never again. When they left the room, he said to Hattie, "We're in the front lines now."

The cemetery service was ending. His relatives were crowding around, some he hadn't seen in years. They would be going back to Hattie's apartment in hired cars.

He had brought the Buick. He and Margaret sat in front, Hattie and Martin Stein in the back. Martin, who was blond and burly, looked like a Nazi. He had arrived from Germany five years ago, just before the invasion of Poland. Probably an ex-Bund member, he thought, just Hattie's style. Everyone was subdued as they wound along the cemetery drive, then onto Metropolitan Avenue toward the bridge. Margaret did most of the talking, trying to keep up appearances. Hattie answered, self-pity in her voice. How well he knew that tone. Things hadn't worked out for Hattie. Not quite talented enough for painting, not quite sensible enough for marriage, not quite poor enough for a job. Mother and Pop had spoiled her, and now she was an overweight, sorrowing, middle-aged woman. She would be his responsibility.

Or would she? Maybe Martin would take charge of her. But no, Hattie's bad luck would prevent that. Martin had a wife and child in Germany, though that fact was rarely mentioned. He was also an enemy alien.

Hattie started talking about a vision. She'd seen Pop sitting in his old chair last week, smoking a cigar. It had been a sign that he was waiting for Mother, knew she was about to join him in the next world. "Can you understand that?" she said in a loud aggressive voice, as if any skepticism about her hallucination would be a sign of stupidity.

Margaret murmured something, but Hattie went on in a juicy tone, "Now they're together, they were so in love." She started sniffling. He wasn't sure they were in love—he'd seen damn few signs of it for the last twenty years—but he kept his mouth shut.

The talk shifted to the kids, Harris at Harvard, Mag at Michigan. The atmosphere in the car changed. Hattie put her hankie away, voices rose. The kids were hope, newness, the future. But Martin was bothered that they weren't here. "They did not love their grand-mutter?"

Judd felt Margaret stiffen beside him. "They'll go to enough funerals. Why start so young?" she said in an insincere voice.

"But their own grand-mutter?"

"We don't feel that way in America. Once you go away to college you cut yourself off from the family."

Another rumble from the back seat, something about respect for the dead. Martin couldn't be told, not right now anyway, that the children were to be kept away from ancient rituals. That pact had been sealed long ago. Hattie and Mother and Pop were not to interfere.

Martin said he had visited his grandmother's grave in Charlottenburg every year on the anniversary of her death. Judd started to speak, to set Martin straight, but Hattie changed the subject. Too bad. He would have told Martin that Mag and Harris adored their grandmother. He would have told him about running down the drive to meet the Packard, the big car laden with presents, embraces, devotion. If Martin had seen that! They had called both children last night, too late for them to attend the funeral. The timing had been Margaret's idea. Harris in Cambridge, Mag in Ann Arbor. Both had been upset, Mag working up to hysteria. She was coming anyway. She was leaving for the airport. She'd get a military transport if necessary. But he knew Mag. It was just a release of emotion. There was no way she could arrive today and she knew it.

He wished she'd been here, though. She should have been here to listen to him read "Crossing the Bar," at his mother's special request. *Sunset and evening star and one clear call for me.* As he read it he heard his mother's melodious voice in his ear, as if she were reading the lines through him. Mag would have heard it that way too. *And may there be no sadness of farewell when I embark.*

He had to keep his mind on the road. A lot of crazy drivers in this part of Queens. He spared a quick glance for Margaret beside him. Her face was set, her lips tense. He knew that look. Her resolution was raging. He'd never known a woman—or a man either—with will power like that.

The children would never see these graves, never decipher the Hebrew lettering, never even know the cemetery was connected to the Fifth Avenue Synagogue. If they asked where Nana was buried, Margaret would give them some vague answer, as she had four years ago with Pop. After a while they'd stop asking. Margaret's will power would win out. There was no force in the universe to compare to that. But Mag should have been here today. She should have seen her grandmother buried. She should have heard him recite the poem. He would have liked to lift his eyes from the page and see her face.

Ah, he'd have to forget all that. It was a jinx. Maybe Margaret was right, the kids were better off. Why load them down with all that family history? In the back, Hattie was sniffling again. It was going to be a long difficult afternoon, and he wasn't sure how he felt about any of it.

In the following days he noticed that his palms were turning even a deeper red, going from crimson almost to vermilion. At mealtimes—there were just the three of them now, the old lady sitting at the foot where Harris used to sit—he would hold up his hands. "Look." But neither of them would pay attention. They'd trade glances. Sometimes he'd get sore and say, "I'm a sick man," but that made the old lady laugh. She would squeeze her face and knock her wedding band on the edge of the table. She was seventy-two, and she'd been going to doctors for twenty-five years. What did he know about sickness? Margaret, of course, didn't believe in any of it. She thought he wanted sympathy, which she never gave.

His chief pleasure, now that the kids were gone, was listening to the radio. He liked to listen to the music programs until Raymond Gram Swing came on at ten with the news. The war was going well, after years of worry. The Germans were retreating on all fronts, the Japs too. It was only a matter of time now. Thanks to Roosevelt, of course, the greatest President this country had ever seen, despite Westbrook Pegler's slanders. Greater than Washington, Lincoln, Jefferson. Just hearing that elegant voice with the built-in wheeze gave him confidence. He'd always liked Roosevelt, right from the beginning. A real aristocrat.

But the music programs were his favorites. He liked Jessica Dragonette and Vivien della Chiesa and John Charles Thomas and James Melton. There was the "Firestone Hour" and the "Bell Telephone Hour" and "Radio City Music Hall" and the "Metropolitan Opera Auditions of the Air." He'd sit in his chair after dinner, push his glasses to his forehead and listen, while Margaret knitted and the old lady crawled upstairs to hear "Amos 'n' Andy" or "The Goldbergs." Music had never refreshed him so much, penetrated so deeply. Sometimes, listening to "The Song of the Flea" or "Un bel dí" or the "Good Friday Spell," he would play with the notion that music wasn't simply a sound but a country, a kingdom, with its own meadows and lakes and valleys. You could enter this kingdom, walk around, observe, explore, be free of things like sickness and gravity and death. When the music came to an end, when it was time to leave that world, he felt lightened and refreshed.

Sometimes, if the trip was especially satisfying, he would speak up. "Did you hear that?" he would say to Margaret. "I ask you, did you hear that?" She would nod, but she was afraid of dropping a stitch. The only programs she liked were "Information Please" and "The Quiz Kids."

After the music programs were over, he would sit quietly until it was quite late, doodling on the edge of the newspaper, trying to recapture his music travels. But in the days just after his mother's funeral he became aware that he was waiting for something else, something new.

At first he thought he was waiting for the result of an important ball game, though the Series had finished a month ago (Cards won). Then he thought it was the future sight of Mag in her cap and gown, striding to the podium for her college degree, her tawny mane flying. Then he told himself he was waiting for a phone call from his mother, asking if things were better at the office.

But the weekend after the funeral, Thanksgiving weekend, when Mag had managed to get home from Ann Arbor on a train, he found what he was waiting for. He was waiting to pitch a no-hitter. It was very clear.

Five years ago, at the Con Edison Exhibit at the World's Fair in Flushing, they had all passed through a door and found themselves on a cobblestone street lit by tall gas lamps. Con Edison had re-created the World of Yesterday, to contrast with the World of Today. Actually, they had rebuilt the street of his childhood. He had been tremendously excited when he saw it; it had brought everything back. Now, in his armchair after dinner, he was waiting to pass through the same door, onto the same gaslit street, but this time not as a stage set. It would be the real thing. Everything would be as before—the coal dealer, the milk wagon, the Lithuanian social club, the crippled pencil vendor, the boys waiting in the vacant lot. And now they would recognize him. They would yell, "Judah! Judie! Hey, Schanberg, how's the arm?" He was expected to pitch today.

He'd eaten too much spaghetti tonight—Margaret made delicious spaghetti—and he had indigestion. Maybe he'd go upstairs to bed. Lying down would ease the pressure. Margaret had already gone up. He hoisted himself out of the armchair, still aware of the game he had to pitch, and headed upstairs.

She was in the bathroom. He'd rest a minute, then take an Alka-Seltzer when she came out. He stretched out on the bed, happy in spite of the pressure in his gut.

They were waiting for him to walk to the mound, all the guys. He was wearing his lucky railway cap. His knuckleball, the most famous pitch in the neighborhood, had led the Manhattan Avenue Bandits to victory year after year. Once they heard a big-league coach was coming to scout him, but nobody showed up.

Margaret flushed the toilet, then opened the door. He didn't open his eyes. He was in top form now, tossing pitch after pitch, his whole repertory of curves, sliders, knuckleballs, even the dead ball. He was playing the only real game in the world, and he was as good as anybody, good as the best, even Christy Mathewson or Rube Marquard or Ferdie Schupp. It was beginning to look like a no-hitter, ninth inning, nobody on, the bottom of their batting order coming up.

Margaret called his name, but he didn't answer. He had to concentrate. One last pitch and he'd done it. A no-hitter.

Margaret's voice was sharper now, insistent, but his mother's was louder; she drowned out everybody else. It was getting dark. He was late. "Judah, you wretch!" She sounded like a guy when she got mad. But it was too soon. He had to stay out, celebrating. The street was the place after a game like that, everybody shaking his hand, saying it was one for the record books.

He'd go home later when he felt like it. And she'd forgive him. She always forgave him if he didn't stay away too long, didn't hop a trolley to another part of town. As long as he was nearby, it didn't matter how much he tormented her. She even enjoyed it. She actually got a kick out of it. At last he headed home. He climbed the eleven steps of the stoop and flung open the door. She was there all right, steaming. But he laughed. Right in her face. "Whaddya getting excited about? Here I am. Look." He held his arms out wide to include her in the joy of his presence, his great victory. "Here I am." And then she opened her arms too, forgiving him for everything, welcoming him home.

10

HARRIS
The Seduction

Harris was in his room in Lowell House waiting for Willie Mortimer. He tried not to look out the window at the enclosed quadrangle, tried to concentrate on his Lope de Vega, but he was too excited. Words, books, even the *siglo de oro,* couldn't still the thrumming in his mind and his chest. Willie had said he'd bring over his new "Emperor Waltz" after dinner, but the way he said it—a light in his green eyes, his lips peeled back to reveal vast amounts of gum—had made Harris's knees tremble. Maybe tonight. Maybe it would happen tonight.

He'd met Willie last fall—his own second year at Harvard, Willie's first. Harris had scooped him out of the cafeteria line, chatting with him, inviting him to a table in the bow window. Willie was flattered by a sophomore's attention, listened respectfully to Harris's advice, instructions. He came from Revere and, as the term went on, it was clear that he had to struggle to keep up. He was getting poor grades.

Harris got up for the fourth time and went to the window, hoping for an advance view of Willie's square head, the blondish hair cantilevered over his forehead, the thick shoulders, general meatiness. Willie had made the House intramural football team right off, but his mother wouldn't let him play, not till he'd made good grades.

He sat down again, pleasantly aware of the changes, the new self, that had emerged after almost two years at Harvard. A few days after checking in and meeting his new roommate, a slow-speaking but clever boy from Lancaster, Pennsylvania, named Tom Chauncey, he had written a letter to the Massachusetts General Hospital. He directed it to the Chief of Surgery.

> Dear Sir,
>
> I am a student at Harvard. I believe I am a homosexual. I would like to have an operation to change this. Could you let me know when you could do this and how much it would cost. Thank you.
>
> Harris Shay
> Lowell House K-22
> Cambridge 38, Mass.

The hardest part had been writing the word "homosexual." He had never put that down on paper before. The letters seemed to resist being joined together. Actually, he had only learned the word the year before when he read an article in the New York *Journal-American* headed "Hitler a Homosexual." The article stated that Hitler was a degenerate, since he surrounded himself with tall, handsome, blond bodyguards. Harris had studied the article, trying to tease out its meanings, aware that it had some sinister application to him. But he wasn't exactly sure how. He would have to ask his mother—always a risky procedure. After she read the article, she got her tight, closed look, and he knew he had strayed into forbidden territory. "Homosexual means a man who likes men better than women." She spoke rapidly and left the room immediately, leaving him flushed and guilty. He shouldn't have asked. He didn't bring up the subject again but the headline danced around in his mind for days, the type now thicker and coarser: HITLER A HOMOSEXUAL.

To be safe, he mailed his letter to the hospital at a box up on Massachusetts Avenue, not in front of Lowell House. Walking back to his rooms afterward, he understood that he had taken a terrible chance. His secret, attached to his name, was now moving through the world. Anything might happen. The hospital might notify the college and he would lose his scholarship or be expelled. They might write to his parents. They might even write to the Boston *Herald* or *Globe*. But he had no choice. He couldn't be like this for the rest of his life.

He had never told his secret to anyone. Well, almost. He had sort of talked it over with Chuck Watlinger in high school. Chuck had a bad reputation, especially after he dyed his hair henna during his senior year, but Harris drifted toward him irresistibly. He knew he was compromising his own reputation, the result of constant posing, pleasing and becoming sports editor of the high school newspaper, but he couldn't keep away. Chuck fascinated him.

Every weekend Chuck took the train from New Rochelle to New York and picked up strangers at the Men's Bar of the Astor Hotel on Times Square. He would hint at what happened next, licking his lips, swaying his hips, opening up vistas of such depravity that Harris could hardly look at him. "He took me to see the floor show at Billy Rose's Diamond Horseshoe—those girls are giants—and held my hand under the table." Or, "He had these sample cases full of tropical uniforms, so I went back to the Statler and tried them on." Chuck delivered these stories with an air of weary nonchalance, as if they were the most normal thing in the world, but Harris wasn't fooled. He knew Chuck's behavior would lead him into a life of vice and loneliness, maybe even crime. At the same time he knew it all applied to him in some deadly way, like the headline about Hitler.

Sometimes he resented the fact that Chuck kept after him, waiting for him after school, phoning him at home, and would refuse to speak to him. But at some point he always gave in, agreeing to meet, to hear more stories. Even as he dated girls, went to dances, ran for school offices and edited the newspaper, he kept some part of himself apart, traveling in his thoughts to New York with Chuck Watlinger, joining him in his pickups.

Chuck had a large collection of books about prison with titles like *Man Alone, Thirty Years on the Rock, I Was the Warden's Son*. After he saw Harris leafing through one, he offered to lend it. "You'll find it pretty interesting, Harris, about all the sex that goes on in prison." Harris swallowed hard but took the book. He carried it home in a brown paper bag and locked his bedroom door before opening it. As he read, his throat got dry and he had to take deep breaths. But he read each one straight through.

He knew that he had found the place where he wanted to be. He wanted to be in a cell at Sing-Sing or Alcatraz, which was fixed up to look like a honeymoon cottage, with pictures and draw curtains and a radio next to the bed. There, a handsome man with delicate features and bulging muscles, a cross between Helmut Dantine and Charles Atlas, would devote himself to making him happy. He would save tidbits of food for him, call him the kid, and hold him in his arms all night. All his shameful and forbidden feelings would disappear, not only because these things were okay in prison but because it was a case of true love. When they were both released, they would find a room somewhere and continue as before. Even when he was old and grey, the man would still call him the kid.

It was hard keeping the prison books hidden, even for the short time they were in his possession. Somebody was always cleaning up, and Mag was a terrible snoop. Not only did she check his room when he wasn't there, but she tried to read his mind. She would stare at him, sending X-rays into his brain. Sometimes she was horribly accurate. She was always announcing that he was running around with the wrong people, especially Chuck Watlinger. He finally stashed the prison books behind his other books—*David Copperfield* and *Porto Bello Gold*—but even there she might easily discover them.

One afternoon, walking home from school, Chuck gave one of his weary, affected smiles, and asked, "Do you think you'd like to go to prison, Harris?"

Since he hadn't really told Chuck how much he liked the idea, he hesitated. If he spoke up, Chuck would know, and that would give him power. On the other hand, he wanted to confess, to tell Chuck about the dryness in his mouth and the images that paraded across his bed at night. At last, very quietly, reserving most of the meaning for himself, he replied, "I think I would, just for a short time."

Chuck brayed victoriously. "I thought so, you little sneak."

Furious with himself, Harris hurried ahead, but Chuck caught up. His voice was slimy, patronizing. "You think you can fool me, but you can't. I knew about you right from the beginning."

Harris thrust at him, pushing him off, but Chuck went on talking. "You're going to end up in the same place as me, and you won't be so hoity-toity about it. Hah! In prison, having sex with everything in pants."

Harris started to run, but Chuck caught up and threw his arms around him. "I'm gonna seduce you right now," Chuck hissed in his ear. "I hate virgins."

Harris flung him off so hard he fell in a pile of leaves. As he raced off he could hear Chuck having hysterics on the ground. He was laughing so hard he was crying.

After that he stopped seeing Chuck. He even dropped a few remarks about Chuck's perverted tastes, to let people know he wasn't that way. But nothing stopped Chuck. Every so often he'd come up to him in the halls and ask loudly, "When are we going to prison, Harris?" Harris pretended not to hear. But as graduation time rolled around, and he began to pack for college, which would begin July 1 on a speeded-up wartime schedule, he decided to have an operation. He'd write to a hospital in Boston and get it over with right away. Nobody would ever know except him.

After mailing the letter, Harris checked the box at the foot of K entry every day, racing to get there before his roommate did, even if he had to cut class. He knew he couldn't explain it to Tom—a return address from Massachusetts General Hospital—even though he was good at lying. He couldn't imagine a lie good enough for that.

The reply, when it came, was brief.

Dear Mr. Shay,

There is no surgical cure for the condition that you have. We have turned your letter over to Dr. Gerald Westfall of our Psychiatric Division. Please call him to discuss treatment.

The letter was signed by a woman, a secretary. Harris read it over and over, trying to picture the people involved. Who was the secretary? Was she proper and Bostonian, with her hair drawn back in a bun? Was she kind and overweight, moaning with sympathy as she drew the page from her typewriter? And what about Dr. Gerald Westfall? Suppose he looked like his father? Besides, he'd always been afraid of doctors. What should he say to him when he called? "Hi, I'm Harris Shay, the homosexual who wrote that letter"? He'd never even said the word aloud. How could he say it to a stranger, a doctor, over the phone?

Why couldn't they just give him an operation? He'd pictured it dozens of times—it would be like having his tonsils out, only farther down. Now they were making it complicated. They wanted him to sit down and discuss it. He'd never been able to discuss it with Chuck Watlinger, who had practically begged for details.

He tore the letter into tiny pieces and flushed them down the toilet. He'd have to forget about the hospital. His plan hadn't worked.

Suddenly he caught sight of Willie Mortimer rounding the corner from the dining hall. He had his green bookbag over his shoulders, no doubt containing the "Emperor Waltz." Harris felt his pulse quicken. That hospital business had been so stupid and naïve. Everybody knew there was no surgical cure for this. It came from your family relations, especially with your mother. Freud had explained it all. But it wasn't as tragic as he'd once thought.

He'd made a great discovery at Harvard. It was okay to be a sissy. The sissy boys were in the ascendant. Well, that was a slight exaggeration. They didn't actually run things, but they weren't at the bottom of the heap either. This place wasn't like the rest of the country. When he encountered his first true local specimen—a young man with a dainty manner and a passion for Regency silver—he had heard the old warning voice in his ear. Stay away. But then he noticed that Andrew Strong, who came from Duxbury, had no trace of the furtive, oppressed manner of the sissy boys at New Rochelle High. He was quite confident and very popular. People sought him out in the Yard, in the House. His table was always full and included all sorts—lacrosse and rugby players, a tutor or two, some older 4-F types, other sissy boys. One Saturday evening, when Andrew waved him over, Harris found himself very much at ease. Nobody looked funny when Andrew remarked that Charles Kullman had sung the Duke of Mantua very poorly that afternoon, or when Paul Innis criticized his English instructor for not including *The Picture of Dorian Gray* on the supplementary reading list. He watched the faces around the table, the faces of men who brought Radcliffe and Wheaton girls to Sunday dinner and took them to their rooms afterward, and saw indifference or acceptance of Andrew. Something strange was going on. The codes he had mastered with such effort didn't apply here. Talk that would have gotten you stomped to death in the woods behind New Rochelle High didn't raise an eyebrow. There was none of the baying and bragging, the warlike posturing, he knew so well.

Slowly he began to make friends with the sissies. Many of them, like Andrew Strong, had gone to prep schools. He knew nothing about such schools but began to picture them as places where the sorrowful silence of sissyhood could be averted. Maybe it was because there were no fathers—natural enemies—on the premises. Maybe it was because the sissies outnumbered the athletes. Maybe it had something to do with being rich or having ancestors who came over on the *Mayflower*. If you were part of what his mother called the upper crust, you didn't care what people thought.

He also began to hear people described as charming. This was a new category. Until now, charm had seemed old-fashioned or alien, reserved for certain movie stars like Franchot Tone and Joel McCrea and Katharine Hepburn. But at Harvard it was a fact of everyday life. Charm could be sitting right across from you at lunch.

Harris began to study charming people. They were always smooth and low-key. They told light tales about hardship, frustration, deprivation. Also about parents, grades, sex, teachers. Anecdote was the coin of their realm. Most of the time Harris listened spellbound, trying to get a fix on this baffling new quality. Finally he decided people with charm let you in on a big secret: they were lovable. No setback or criticism could alter this fact—it lay too deep in their bones. And they let you share in their lovableness even as they hid what was really going on. Yes, the essence of charm, Harris decided, was concealed self-appreciation. He would probably never have it.

As he made friends with this new crowd of sissies and charmers, he also began to relax sexually. His ugly scenes with Chuck Watlinger faded. He joined in the innuendo, the bawdy jokes. When Lester Backs, his best friend, remarked, "For a prize he's going to win a night with a V-12 sailor," Harris laughed as hard as everybody else. He learned to show no surprise when tutors and instructors came to their parties, leering and joking about Arcadia. He took down the Vargas drawings from *Esquire* which he had pasted to his bedroom wall with little Veritas stickers and replaced them with prints of the Cellini *Perseus* and the *Discoboulos*.

Sometimes, however, as he listened to his new friends talk about the Theban Band and Damon and Pythias and the Australian Embrace and *le vice anglais,* he would cave in with remorse. It would arrive unexpectedly, frightening and disorienting him. He would want to run out of the room. It was always accompanied by the sight of his father, puffing on a Lucky Strike, flickering his nostrils in anger. Even though his father had died at the beginning of his sophomore year—a heart attack in the middle of the night—Harris would see him, disapproval and contempt erupting from him in a fiery hail. At that instant he would become speechless, would hate his friends for their tastes—it was only at Harvard, after all, where they could talk like that—and wish he were not like them. But if he held on, didn't give in, his father would fade away and his new freedoms would return. Besides, in spite of the hinting and joking, he was sure nobody actually did anything. It was all talk, parlor athletics.

He began to be amazingly happy. Because he would be drafted when he turned eighteen, each moment was to be treasured, enjoyed. And he was aware of his luck, the savor of his life. Walking up Mt. Auburn Street, past the Lampoon building, or over to Mike's for a strawberry frappe, he would say to himself, "I am happy, this is happiness." He loved the classes, the professors, the Yard and its elms—tall maidens with their arms in a vee above their heads. He loved the bookstores on Massachusetts Avenue, the sculls and wherries on the Charles, the towers and spires of the buildings. He loved Widener Library, the vast reading room, the long afternoons there. Most of all he loved being away from home.

One afternoon, walking along the river with Lester Backs, he interrupted their usual discussion of communism—they were both violently in favor of it—by exclaiming, suddenly, "I like Harvard even better than prison." He shrieked with laughter. The words had come out of nowhere.

After he explained, Lester told him that his own adolescent daydreams had revolved around Irish bartenders. He had always wanted to stand next to a slim Irishman with prematurely gray hair, shake cocktails together, then go off to a furnished room and get cosy. Talking about their fantasies like that was intensely liberating. As they walked back toward Lowell House Harris felt that one of the doors that had sealed him off from everybody had flung open.

Willie's heavy foot sounded on the landing. Harris was at the door, waiting. He admired Willie's massive bulk one more time. It was a body he had observed often in the swimming pool in the Indoor Athletic Building. It might have been created by Michelangelo's chisel.

"How are *you*?" Willie's smile revealed the usual amount of gum. He was a vast smiler. He strode in, a mighty presence, straining his tweed jacket, his button-down shirt, his tight chinos.

"What did they give you for dinner?"

"Creamed finnan haddie."

Harris let out a groan. On Friday nights he went to the Hayes-Bickford and had Salisbury steak with mashed potatoes for ninety-five cents. He hated fish.

"It was good, you shoulda tried it." Willie liked everything, that was part of his appeal. He liked the food, the housemaster and his wife, the townies, the Old Howard, Johann Strauss, Jr., everything. For Harris, who had just discovered critical judgment, Willie's refusal to discriminate was childish but endearing. It was also an opportunity to instruct him.

"I brought the 'Emperor Waltz,' also the Grieg piano concerto." Willie fished them out of his green bag, grinning happily. Harris found himself laughing along. It was a pleasure just being next to Willie, not only because of his football-tackle shoulders and hands like pulley blocks, but because he was so enthusiastic.

Harris put the waltz on his phonograph, a gift from his uncle Mark. He had sharpened the cactus needle with the rotary grinder a few minutes earlier—a lot of trouble but steel needles damaged the record.

"This is called the two-four waltz. It starts with a march." Willie, still grinning, sat on a captain's chair with the Harvard seal stamped in gold on it. "It's very advanced for its time period." He began tapping his feet to the music. When the tempo changed to three-quarter, Willie raised a finger. "Hear that? Now we're in a waltz."

Harris sat on the couch opposite. The gulf between them, the width of the room, seemed impassable. Now that Willie was here his fantasies seemed absurd. They existed only as a series of impossibilities, like finding true love in Alcatraz. What could get Willie out of his clothes? How could they touch each other, do things he hadn't even imagined specifically? He had no experience in these matters—only what he'd read and heard.

The record came to an end. "Wanta hear it again?" Willie loomed up, magnificent, unreachable.

"Sure."

He watched while Willie reset the arm. His hands, for all their size, were delicate in their movements. And then, fighting the sensation that he was falling from a great height, he patted the cushion next to him. "Sit over here, Willie."

Willie hesitated, his green eyes jumping around, then he lumbered over. His lips were peeled back, but Harris knew it was a grimace of nervousness, not joy. He sat down, hunching forward on the cushion, hands clasped. Harris could think of nothing to say. Willie, next to him, was even farther away. Now they couldn't talk, couldn't trade the trivialities that made it possible to pretend something was going to happen. Nothing was going to happen.

And then a new thought struck him. Why was Willie here, sharing his favorite records? He might have been in Boston with other friends, maybe going to a burlesque show at the Old Howard. He might have gone to the dance at Adams House. But no, he had passed that up. For all he knew, Willie wanted to do something right now, maybe liked the idea as much as he liked creamed finnan haddie and the "Emperor Waltz."

Holding his breath, not sure what could happen next, Harris dropped one hand on Willie's thigh, which was hard as a rock. Willie didn't move. He was just about to inch his hand higher—though he certainly didn't want to raise it *too* high—when the waltz ended. Willie jumped up. He kept his back to Harris as he took off the Strauss and replaced it with the first Grieg record. Then he crossed and sat in the captain's chair again. They didn't look at each other.

Harris didn't really know what to do. Willie settled back in the chair and began to drum his fingers on the arm, as if he were helping Moura Lympany along. Was it up to him to make another move? Did Willie secretly want it? Or was he really horrified by the idea? The gap between what he wanted, what he had imagined and what was happening, was vast. So many things stood in the way—Willie's clothes, his averted gaze, his own dread, even the crashing chords of the Grieg piano concerto. He had the impression that his desires could never mesh with the world.

The next minute he realized, in a rush of panic, that he had no choice. He couldn't go back, he couldn't continue as someone who *did not know*. He would have to cross over whether he liked it or not. He rose and went to stand in front of Willie.

Willie looked up at him. "What'sa matter?"

Harris wanted very much to rest his hands on Willie's shoulders, to run them down the sleeves of his tweed jacket, but he hesitated. "Nothing's the matter." Standing here was embarrassing. In another second he'd have to move. "Why don't you stand up?"

To his surprise, Willie rose slowly. They stood facing each other. Harris could hardly breathe.

"I thought you asked me over to hear the music," Willie said, smiling a little.

"I did." And then, amazed at his daring, he slid his arms around Willie's chest. It felt as if he were embracing marble. Willie was still for a moment, allowing the movement, then put his arms around Harris. He patted his back lightly. "I don't do this stuff anymore," he said.

Harris felt the stone arms and thighs. He began to flush, waves and tremors rolling through him, but he didn't say anything. This had nothing to do with words anyway. Quickly, before he could think about it, he moved his face against Willie's, registering the bristly dots of beard, the otherness of a skin that was not his own. His existence rushed upon him. If he was going to live, it would be as someone who did this, who touched men, who took terrible chances.

Willie gave him a last pat on the back and dropped his arms. He stepped to one side. "I gotta go."

Harris stood watching as Willie removed the Grieg, which was still in the middle of the first movement, and slid it in the first sleeve of the set. He didn't mind that Willie was leaving. He had a lot to think about. He had to consider not only the electric otherness of Willie's skin, the impress of his arms and legs, but also his own future here at Lowell House. He was no longer someone who just talked about it—he had made a move. He had crossed over. Nothing would be the same again, not in the dining hall, not in the library, not on the squash courts. He had to think about all that.

Willie gave his customary grin as he left, lips pulled back, vast amounts of gum. He didn't seem embarrassed in the least. They were still friends. Next time they met nothing would be said. He still didn't know what Willie had in mind when he accepted his invitation tonight—maybe he would never know, maybe Willie didn't know himself—but it didn't matter. He himself had changed. It had required only the smallest, briefest, of movements.

He sat in the captain's chair vacated by Willie and thought about Chuck Watlinger. For the first time since high school he wished he could talk to him. He wanted to know how Chuck had gotten free so soon. How he had handled the snubs and gossip, how he had shrugged off his parents' curiosity, how he had managed to live in the world knowing what he did about himself.

Then, quite unexpectedly, he remembered Hal Ellis at Camp

Monhegan and his definition of a fairy. At the time, lying in the tent, a premonition had whizzed through him. Now it had come true. He was a fairy. He didn't like the thought, the word, but he couldn't twist away from it. It comprised the existence that had overwhelmed him when he stood close to Willie. Would he be able to cope with it? With the lying and pretending that a fairy's life required? He had a big pocket for secrets, the space that had been dug in his mind when he became Harris Shay, but did he have room for this too? It would require constant alertness, cleverness. Just thinking about it made his head swim.

Then he began to feel a little better. Maybe there was a hidden fit, some congruence he had overlooked, between being a fairy and living in the world. Maybe there were places you would be welcome, corners and crannies where you could be yourself. He'd heard stories about New York, of course, but they had always struck him as so guilty and criminal—from Chuck's adventures at the Astor Bar to something about Grand Central Terminal he had heard recently—that he had ruled out any application to himself. Now he would have to reconsider. He had to find the places where his desires could flourish, and if that brought him into contact with criminals, well, there was no help for it. He would be a criminal himself.

Finally, quite tired and confused, he went to bed. Toward dawn he had a dream about Willie Mortimer. Willie and he were living in a prison cell together, and every night, in their single bunk, Willie held him in a love grip so powerful it was impossible to break. When he woke up from the dream next morning, he found his pajamas crusty with semen.

"Well, now, I've made dinner for you boys, but first we'll have a drink." Lester's aunt Vicky lived in Watertown, not far from Harvard Square, and encouraged Lester to bring his college friends over. She was in her mid-forties, childless, and needed relief. Her husband, Joe Grune, managed a movie house in Boston, which kept him away every evening. They didn't spend much time together anyway, and when they did they quarreled, Harris was told by Lester.

"Here you go, Harris." Vicky—she hated being called Mrs. Grune—handed out highballs. Harris knew it would be too strong but he took it. There was no way to avoid a party with Lester and Vicky.

"Hair of the dog," said Lester. He tossed off half his glass, then grunted appreciatively. It was a Sunday afternoon.

When he first started coming to Vicky's house, he had resisted drinking, which had annoyed her no end. "Oh, for heaven's sake, Harris," she would snap if he asked for sherry or, even worse, a Coke. "Have a real drink; it's not going to hurt you."

And so he had learned about liquor from Lester and Vicky. If they weren't having a drink, they tended to be short-tempered and critical. Not that he kept up with them, of course, but he always drank enough to get tight, sometimes drunk. Over time he began to respond automatically to the leaded crystal glass in his hand. It meant honest talk was coming. Talk about angers, needs, promises, raptures. It meant arguments as intricately structured as a labyrinth. It meant that, eventually, there would be some sloppiness and a taxi back to Lowell House.

These tipsy afternoons in Watertown, when the sun went down on Vicky's backyard, became part of his education. Not only did he learn about the chemical flowering in his mind, but he discovered that other families, seen from the inside, were wonderfully different from his own. The Backs-Bannon-Grune family (Welsh and Danish mostly) discussed sex frankly, had no social ambitions, saw no difference between whites and blacks or Christians and Jews, spent money on trifles and luxuries and were always throwing parties. They were almost the exact opposite of his own family—sort of an anti-family. Sometimes he wondered why they liked him, had adopted him, in fact. Maybe his conventionality was a challenge, or maybe he brought some balance and stability to these Sunday afternoons. When he was there Vicky didn't rage about her husband and Lester didn't pass out. A third person kind of steadied them. Still, it could have been any third person—why him? Nevertheless, he loved being here, loved hearing them talk about scandalous things, loved thinking that his mother would be shocked.

Occasionally, as the drinking went on and the conversation got looser and louder, he would consider telling them about his past. He would rehearse the sentences in his mind, practicing nonchalance. "By the way, we used to be called Schanberg; I bet you didn't know that." But that was stupid—of course they didn't know it. Or, "We changed our name from Schanberg to Shay when I was almost twelve. My mother didn't want people to think we were Jewish." But that was stupid too—not only bigoted but raising questions he had no answers to. Were they Jewish inside all that Episcopalianism? How Jewish? He didn't know. Aside from the matter of the name there were other unanswered questions. What about Nana's matzoh-ball soup, Gran's kreplach, and all the phrases he had heard, which had been passed off as low German but which he now knew were Yiddish? He didn't have it figured out yet. "Some people change their names; we did too," he might say, followed by a rapid change of subject. But that wouldn't work either. Lester and Vicky never let him get away with evading things. They went after him like terriers digging up a bone.

And so all his rehearsing had produced no result. He couldn't open his mouth. Even though Vicky and Lester would, he knew, have laughed or dismissed the subject—even while understanding its importance and probably returning to it some other time in a kindly way—he couldn't speak up. It was the old trouble. His mother's injunctions, the fear of displeasing her, stood in his way—even here in Cambridge with his new friends, his new life, his anti-family.

After one of his failed attempts he would become silent. Vicky would observe him for a while then let out a sigh. "Harris is sulling." Lester would peer at him tipsily. "Are you sulling?"

They would force him out of his retreat, refuse to let him hide, and the conversation would resume. But even as his good humor returned, he would be aware of some permanent loss. He hadn't spoken. He hadn't uttered the truth. He hadn't let the submerged part of him rise to the surface. And so, in an important way, he was still a stranger to them.

This afternoon Vicky had started her usual complaints about her husband. "I only see him in the morning, and that's when I don't want to see anybody. I need privacy in the morning." She paused to sip her drink. "I don't look decent till the middle of the afternoon, for crying out loud."

"Why don't you get a night job too?" Harris asked.

"Why would I want a night job?" She turned on him, outraged. "I've got the Friends of the Drama at night. We're doing two productions this spring, *Junior Miss* and *My Heart's in the Highlands*."

"Well, Auntie"—Lester's voice was superior and needling—"he's been managing that movie house for fifteen years. You should be used to it by now."

Lester didn't resemble his aunt at all. She was slim and doe-eyed, with glassy skin, while he was heavy, broad-faced, with strong, handsome features.

"I don't want to get used to it! For all I know he's got a mistress!"

Harris knew that her objections were a sham. She really liked having her evenings free. She didn't care if Joe had a mistress. She had told him about one of her lovers—a bad actor in her amateur company. "He was only good for one thing," she had remarked, "but he was *very* good at that." Then she had burst into peals of laughter.

"Well, if he's got a mistress"—Lester sounded snotty now—"why don't you get yourself a good lawyer? Maybe you can blackmail him."

Vicky looked genuinely puzzled. "Why would I blackmail him? He's my husband."

That was another thing he'd learned in Watertown. Serious things weren't taken seriously. You could make light remarks about anything. Even death wasn't a terror in this family. Lester's brother had gone down on a merchant ship in the Atlantic last year. But a few weeks after his death, when Mrs. Backs came to Cambridge for a visit, Harris had found her amazingly resigned. "Well," she said in her mild, rich voice, "every family has a loss these days. Wherever I go I see gold stars in windows." She was heavy-set, with a broad, handsome face like Lester's. He had sensed no agony, no irreparable loss. She had shed this terrible event just as her sister Vicky had shed Joe's infidelities.

The comparison with his own family was alarming. When his

father died last fall, his mother had gone to bed for two months. Gran had to take over the house, and Mag had transferred from the University of Michigan to the Columbia School of General Studies, so she could live at home and help out. Death in his family wasn't a passing tragedy, it was a crumbling, a collapse. People who had seemed strong just fell apart. There was a flaw, an unseen fault, in the inner structure.

Lester was tired of his aunt's willfulness. "You're going to do exactly what you want anyway. Why do you ask for our opinion?"

She let out a shriek. "I don't recall asking for your opinion."

Lester shook his head and switched to Karl Marx, always his favorite topic. He was very much afraid that the rule of the proletariat would be indefinitely postponed. The commissars wouldn't give up their power. "The ruling class never abdicates voluntarily, they have to be forced out," he said now, looking at Harris. "Just think about the dynasties in this country. Morgan. Gould. Roosevelt. Taft. The new rulers take over by forcing the old ones out. Now, what methods do they use?"

His voice took on a singsong, familiar to Harris. It was Lester's tone of intellectual ecstasy. In a few minutes he would get onto the nature of reality. This involved the chairness of chairs and the tableness of tables. He would point out, yet again, that everything in his Aunt Vicky's living room was a debased reflection of a pure form that existed someplace else. Harris could never pin him down on where these pure forms were—in fact, Lester claimed that asking such a dumb question was proof that Harris had missed the most thrilling part, the nature of the theoretical.

Lester might rave on for ten minutes, ending up with the tree that falls in the forest with nobody around. Did it make a sound? Harris hated that conundrum. Whichever side he argued, Lester took the other side and won. Harris particularly disliked a certain smile that played on Lester's lips when he forced his opponent into an untenable position. He wanted to get up and smash Lester's face. But Lester would keep going until Vicky got sore. "I want you to stop this nonsense right now, and I mean it," she would yell and only then would Lester shut up.

Although Harris's field was Government, and he had read Plato,

Machiavelli, John Stuart Mill and all the rest, political theory, like Lester's abstracting, was basically meaningless to him. He simply didn't grasp the reason or relevance of different forms of government, or if he did, it was only for a few minutes, to be followed by the old miasmal murk. What did it matter how political systems were set up, how leadership was justified, defended, swapped, abused? Who were those vast agglomerations—the bourgeoisie, the proletariat, the colonialists, the rentier class? Sometimes he thought they were things dreamed up by idle and overrefined minds in order to fill textbooks. For that matter, he didn't really understand what power was. It seemed a vague and pointless abstraction, light-years away, not nearly as vital as making friends or coming to terms with his own life. He was studying Government because that was required for the diplomatic service, which his mother had been pushing all his life, but he was sure it wasn't for him. It would require an added layer of lies and deception—wasn't that what diplomacy was all about, telling lies?—that he knew he couldn't manage. He had his hands full now.

Lester had started on the elite. Everyone at Harvard was a member of the elite whether they admitted it or not. But he, Harris, didn't feel upper class, not at all. He felt just as fringy and hard-pressed as ever. And what about after he graduated? There were no jobs waiting for him in the State Department or on Wall Street or anyplace else. His father had died broke, and his uncle Mark wouldn't lift a finger to help him. It would be strictly up to him. He pointed this out.

"You refuse to understand, Harris." Lester was highly exasperated. "Just walking into a personnel office with a Harvard degree gives you a tremendous and unfair advantage."

Harris shook his head. "Maybe for ten minutes. After that you're on your own."

"Ten minutes! What do you think I'm talking about, for Christ's sake? If you'd gone to City College you wouldn't even get in the door!"

"Well, all this is beside the point because in about six months I'm going to be marching up and down in a platoon."

"You just won't understand, will you?"

Harris sighed and refused to answer. It was hopeless anyway. Lester was passionate about ideas. They seemed to occupy the place in his mind that love and friendship did in his own. Apparently it had always been that way. Lester told him once that when he was small, seven or eight, he used to sit in a cleft rock in his family's garden, under a black walnut tree, and worry fiercely about the universe. He worried about the stars going out, about the earth slipping off its axis, about the Ice Age coming back. He believed that if he worried about these things hard enough they wouldn't happen. Ever since then, with time out for meals, Lester had been worrying about abstractions and fending off disasters. Harris didn't really object to Lester's preoccupations—it was all quite stimulating—but he couldn't let himself be drawn in too deeply. Lester got the upper hand right away.

"Who wants to help me with dinner?"

Vicky stood up; she'd had enough of the discussion. Lester's eyelids suddenly drooped. He was going to doze off for a few minutes. Harris followed Vicky into the kitchen and sat at the counter. She handed him a large pair of shears for cutting up the head of lettuce.

Harris enjoyed being alone with Vicky if she wasn't too drunk. He could tell her things about his mother. Vicky had, with his assistance, taken a strong dislike to her. "You mean she didn't speak to you for two days because you got a D on your report card? What's a little D, for crying out loud?" He would nod, pleased that Vicky, who was close to his mother's age, disapproved. "You never discussed sex at home, ever? Good God, what did you talk about?" More nods, more vindication. "They actually drank cider and told people it was whiskey? I don't believe it." More nods, more happy outrage from Vicky, and maybe a refill for both of them.

In Vicky's kitchen his family life was revealed as a hotbed of puritanism. With each exposé he felt more privately dissolute. His true nature was surfacing. One day he would be as alcoholic and carefree and guiltless as Vicky or Lester. It was just a matter of spending more time with them, drinking more, copying their attitudes, criticizing his relatives. The intensity that had disfigured his past would end. He would become blasé.

Tonight, as he cut up the lettuce, he debated telling Vicky about the evening with Willie Mortimer two nights ago. He would have to keep it light, casual, but it would be a big step. But he wasn't sure how it would be received. Vicky was only partly approving of such things. Sometimes she announced, rather snidely, that so-and-so in the Friends of the Drama was "one of them." She would usually add, with a giggle, "I don't care what they do so long as they don't do it in the street and frighten the horses," but disapproval had been expressed. Still, he'd like to tell her about Willie.

He watched her open the oven and stab the chicken with a large fork. She wiggled her bottom as she did so. Harris had the impression that she was flirting with him. He hoped she wasn't getting any ideas. "I have this friend," he began, "Willie Mortimer . . ."

"Oh?"

"I really like him a lot."

"Well, college is a place to make friends. Not that I'd know." She wiggled again. She had gone to a finishing school in Des Moines. When she came to Watertown, after her marriage, she had gone to the Curley School of Expression on Tremont Street in Boston for acting lessons.

"Actually," he continued, feeling nervous, "you can make friends anywhere."

"I suppose."

She was looking around, bored. They weren't getting anywhere. "I think . . . I think . . . my urges . . . my real urges . . ."

He stopped. She was staring at him in a frightened way. "Oh," she groaned, "let's not go into all that."

He laughed loudly, falsely. He'd gone too far. There were some things you couldn't discuss, no matter what. "I mean . . . I really like this guy, Willie Mortimer." He stopped. It was a lame ending.

"It's natural for men to like each other. Joe has Charlie Ingersoll; they go to the harness races every Thursday afternoon." She was speaking quickly, helping him over the rough spot. She slugged the rest of her drink. As he watched her a familiar loss went through him. He would never be able to tell everything. He recalled his kayak ride after the mock trial at Camp Monhegan. What he had glimpsed then was still true—you could trust people only up to a certain point. Even here, in this house, it was true.

"Call Lester," Vicky said, "we have time for one more drink."

It took him two more months, until June and the end of term, to get up his courage. He thought about it every day, reading in the library, walking to finals, sitting by his little white Philco, following the D-Day invasion. It was always there, the knowledge of the next step that couldn't be avoided. But it wasn't until Paxton Allward dropped a remark as they left Portuguese class together that it gathered into a clear direction. "God, Shay, you should see the queers on the benches in the back of the Public Gardens. No wonder they call it Fairyland."

Paxton had been on his way to the Park Street station after walking his date to Louisburg Square. He had noticed men sitting, standing, around the benches just inside the park. He hadn't gone in—"You won't catch me lurking in there"—but had observed the action from the street. Harris hadn't heard about the gardens from his friends, and it was ironic that Paxton, who was only a class acquaintance and a lacrosse fiend, was the one to tell him. But as soon as he heard, he knew. He would have to go. It was the logical next step.

He made several reconnoitering trips during the day, checking out the benches, tracing the paths, eyeing the strollers. The area seemed to carry no imprint of crime or degeneracy. Mostly it was full of children, their guardians, meandering servicemen killing leave time.

But one Saturday morning in mid-June, after his last exam and just before a twelve-day break when he would go home, he understood that the time had come. All day he felt edgy, drifting around the Yard, going for a swim, dropping in on Lester, ascending to the Tower Room to bang on the piano for an hour. But even as he felt apprehensive he was aware of a furious excitement, making his activities more vivid, tingeing his conversation with suspense. He didn't tell anyone where he was going—not even Lester, though he had related what happened with Willie Mortimer. Lester, he knew, would make an abstraction out of his desires, put them in some context that had nothing to do with the way he felt. They would end up discussing illicit sex from a political or social point of view. He might end up not going at all.

When evening came, he put on freshly pressed khakis, a checked button-down shirt and a gray sweater with a crew neck which he had bought at J. Press. He hoped he didn't look like a Harvard man. Most of the time he liked it, but not tonight. If he'd had some rougher clothes, he would have worn them, but he had little money for extra clothes. Variations of the undergraduate uniform were all he had, except for a blue serge suit.

He took a preliminary stroll around the back of the Public Gardens at seven, though he didn't sit down. It was still too light. The daytime people were walking around. His excitement increased as he realized there would be a complete change of cast after dark.

To kill the last hours of daylight he decided to go to a movie. He had a choice—*Gaslight, Destination Tokyo, Meet Me in St. Louis,* all playing nearby. He decided quickly on the first. He liked Ingrid Bergman, who was saintly and sexless. Her knockers didn't hit you in the face. Unfortunately, it was playing at the theater Joe Grune managed. He certainly didn't want to run into Joe tonight. Still, if he wanted to see *Gaslight* . . .

On his way to the movie house he passed a bookstore. As usual, he couldn't resist stopping. The books, printed on wartime recycled paper, were awash in romance and beauty. *The Robe. Forever Amber. Green Dolphin Street. A Tree Grows in Brooklyn.* He could imagine stepping inside their lurid covers, hearing the bindings snap behind him, locking him into another life. He had to tear himself away, back to the gray pavements, the closed faces of the crowds, the anxiety and confusion of the last few weeks.

Luckily, Joe wasn't in the lobby of the theater. He bought his ticket and went quickly inside to a seat. It never bothered him to enter in the middle of the movie. He liked to follow hints, allusions, backtrack in his mind, then put the whole thing together when he saw the beginning. *Gaslight* was especially complicated, which gave him a lot to think about, taking his mind off the rest of the evening.

At ten o'clock, after having sat through the movie one and a half times, he made himself leave. He didn't even want to, but he had an obligation to go through with his plan.

This time he was out of luck. Joe Grune was at the exit, talking to the ticket-taker. "Harris!" he yelled, putting out his hand. Vicky always said her husband had missed being a leading man by six inches. He was small and dapper and wore patent leather shoes. "What are you doing here all by yourself?"

Harris stammered something about end-of-term, going home. Joe introduced him to Monty, the ticket-taker, a pink, bald man.

"I'm meeting some friends at Locke-Ober's," Harris said, getting control of himself.

"Locke-Ober's? They stop serving at ten."

"Not inside. In front. We're going to take a walk." The words just slid out, instantaneous lies.

A knowing smile curled Joe's lips. "You goin' to Scollay Square?" He turned to Monty. "Harris is goin' to Scollay Square and find himself a girl." He scanned Harris with new respect. "Listen, I can give you an address. You want an address? But you gotta promise not to tell Vicky."

"That's okay, I got some." He patted his pocket, then smiled, a thin smile of man-to-man complicity.

"Watch out for them hookers," Monty said.

"You sure?" Joe winked. "You don't have to be ashamed, Harris, it's the most natural thing in the world."

"No . . . no, that's okay." His stammer was coming back. He was running out of inventions. Joe was still examining him, testing his resolution. He had to get out. "Listen, I'll call you when I come back next term." He put out his hand. Joe's grip was enthusiastic.

"It's always a pleasure, Harris. You have some fun. And don't worry, it's no business of Vicky's."

"Don't catch anything," Monty said.

Outside, walking down Tremont Street, Harris felt his head whirling. He hardly noticed where he was going. He had been detoured, sent off course, by Joe Grune and his assumptions. How could he think of going to the park now? It had moved out of reach morally. The place he had reserved for it in his mind had been declared out of bounds.

He continued walking until he got to the Park Street station, at the corner of the Common. Maybe he should go back to Cambridge, postpone everything until next term. Maybe going home, seeing his mother and Mag and Gran, would end his confusion, bring back some old certainties. He would see his room, his collections—license plates from every state, matchbook covers from over a hundred nightclubs, to say nothing of four stamp albums. The worries that had plagued him since his evening with Willie Mortimer would disappear. All his fears would disappear, in fact—his dread of going in the army, of picking a career, of facing a life of crime and degeneracy. He would backtrack. He would talk to his mother—she was always glad to talk as long as he said the right things. He would be undefined again, no longer a fairy.

But he didn't go down into the Park Street station. His feet wouldn't take him there. They just kept going, past the State House and toward the Public Gardens. There was no way to stop. Some other force had taken over.

When he got to the corner of Beacon and Charles, he stood for a long time looking into the park. His head was light but he stood still, peering through the shrubbery and toward the benches and walks. Dim figures, barely catching the light of the tall lamps, were moving around. Most of them were alone. There were servicemen too—soldiers, a sailor. They all seemed remote. What would he say to them even if he did cross the gap between here and there? What would they suggest? What could possibly take place?

And then, as in his room with Willie Mortimer and the Grieg concerto, he realized he couldn't go back, not to Cambridge, not to New Rochelle. It didn't matter what Joe Grune had assumed. He couldn't continue as someone who didn't know what went on in this place. Finding out would tell him what the rest of his life would be. At the same time he understood that if he didn't live this new, unknown life, he wouldn't live any life at all.

A few minutes later he stepped into the park. It closed around him, separating him from everything outside. He recalled the books in the window of the Bodleian Bookstore. He had wanted them to snap shut behind him too.

People stared at him so curiously as he walked around that he chose a bench, dim and shielded by shrubbery, and sat down. He would be less conspicuous. If someone came up, there would be no one else watching. He could have a private conversation.

Several people passed by, staring down at him and murmuring "Good evening." Each time he replied politely. He wasn't sure if he needed to do that—the usual rules of behavior were suspended here, inside the cover of a novel, but the words rose naturally to his lips. But of course they didn't mean the same thing—nothing was equivalent to its old meaning in here. "Good evening," he thought a little wildly, might mean "Can I love you for the rest of my life?" or "You're going to be arrested."

About ten minutes after he sat down a lanky man, pretending not to see him, sat at the other end of the same bench. The man continued looking away, half-turned. Harris debated moving on, but when the man lit a match he saw that he was about thirty, with blondish hair slightly receding in front and tightly curled on his head. He was wearing square-cut spectacles, and his features were pleasant. Feeling his palms go sweaty, Harris decided to stay. Before putting away his pack of Camels, the man turned and offered him one. Harris wondered if this was the usual procedure—first an elaborate pretense, then a friendly move. He took the cigarette, though he didn't smoke. The man slid over to light it. "I've never seen you here before," he said.

Harris laughed. His hand was trembling as he puffed on the cigarette. "I've never been here before."

The stranger nodded. "You a student?"

"Yeah." He didn't want to discuss Harvard. "I'll be drafted in a few more months."

He felt the man's eyes on him. Maybe he wouldn't pass muster on close inspection. He had never thought he was good-looking. Half the girls he asked to dances in high school had turned him down. But apparently the man approved, because he spoke again in a husky voice. "What's your name? Mine's Wilson."

Harris gave his first name, but the stranger didn't offer to shake hands, to his relief. That ritual had been suspended here too.

"I guess if you're a student, you can't take anyone back to the dorm." He paused. "Not people you meet in the Boston Public Gardens, anyway." He laughed slightly. Harris smiled, somehow relieved that their shared transgression was out in the open. It felt good, an antidote to all this skulking in the bushes.

"No, I can't."

The man waited for a while, drawing on his cigarette, then said in an unnaturally casual voice, "I live a few blocks from here. Maybe you'd like to come up."

Harris knew he did, but he wasn't quite ready to go. His fear and shyness came back. What would they talk about on the way? What would the man want to do? The space in his mind which he had kept carefully blank through all these years would now be filled in.

He glanced at the man. His appearance, like the words in the park, was deceptive. Under the double-breasted sharkskin suit was another person, a whole new form of existence which he'd been forbidden to touch.

"Come on, Harris." Wilson stamped out his cigarette. "You don't have to worry. We won't do anything you don't want to do."

Wilson had read his mind. They stood up and began to walk toward the exit on Beacon Street. Several people stopped and stared. Wilson ignored them, chatting about the neighborhood, the war, the fact that he was 4F. Harris knew he was trying to put him at ease but it didn't help much. He was stammering, saying meaningless things. At the same time he was terribly excited.

Wilson lived on Charles Street, in a wooden house with a wide front porch. As they stepped up to the porch, he put his finger to his lips. Harris tiptoed upstairs behind him, his heart pounding.

After Wilson locked the door to his apartment behind them he removed his glasses. Harris got a good look at him. He had a triangular face, broad at the top, tapering to a sharp chin, and cloudy blue eyes. They were the same height, both over six feet, though for some reason Wilson seemed taller. He was attractive—more than that, romantically handsome. A welter of images came to Harris—Wilson visiting him in Lowell House, Wilson shaking hands with his friends, Wilson sitting across from him at Locke-Ober's. His life would be drastically different from now on, a direct result of this night's decision.

"You want a Coke?"

He did. On the way to the kitchen Wilson flicked on the radio. "Long Ago and Far Away" poured out. Harris sat on the couch, aware of the strain in his Jockey shorts. He rearranged things in there.

When Wilson came back, he sat down on the couch. It was like the park—they were side by side—but now there was nobody else around. He waited, wondering what Wilson would do next. But Wilson began to talk. "I have a brother your age—what are you, eighteen?"

"Yeah."

"I raised Johnny. I put him through Oberlin. Our parents died when he was young."

Harris stifled his disappointment. Wilson seemed to be slipping away, rejoining the throng of people who never took their clothes off. He continued talking about his brother Johnny, who was in the senior class at Oberlin, also the ROTC. Wilson said he was going to get a commission. His voice expanded as he talked about this, and Harris could tell he was proud.

Wilson was eyeing him. "I see you're hot to trot."

Harris smiled, embarrassed. He didn't know what he was. Wilson leaned over and cupped Harris's chin in his hand. Then he kissed him. His lips were probing, muscular. Harris felt as if he'd been slightly electrocuted. When Wilson pulled back, he examined him again. "Bring your Coke in the other room."

The bed was covered with a paisley spread. Harris stood with his Coke, waiting for the next order. Wilson motioned to a bureau. When Harris put down the glass, Wilson said, "Okay, let's go." He started to take his clothes off—first the sharkskin jacket and pants, which he hung in the closet, then his shirt and tie. His socks were held up by garters, the same sort Harris's father used to wear. Harris started to undress too, pulling off the gray crew-neck sweater, the button-down shirt, then the shoes and chinos. He left them in a heap on the floor. They no longer concerned him.

Wilson's chest was covered with tight ringlets of tawny hair. His shoulders were wide and bony, his arms veined. Harris noticed an appendix scar to the right of his belly button. The sight of Wilson burned at him, and he wondered why he should have been kept away for so long, why so many obstacles had been put in his path. At the same time he knew that what they were doing was absolutely forbidden.

They met in the middle of the bed. Wilson moved over him at once, cradling him, holding and squeezing him, biting and tonguing him all over. Harris gave himself to this; it struck him as another form of early happiness. No one had touched him like this, held him like this, since Nana had arrived in the Packard and emerged onto the driveway with her arms out, smothering him in her fur coat, her rare smells. But this was even better. He was doing it with the handsomest man in the world, and they were buck naked.

Wilson stopped, looked down at him, then kissed him on each eye. Harris wrapped his arms tightly around Wilson. He had finally come home. Home was a radiant man who would kiss him on both eyes. There was nothing to be ashamed of. The wrongness he had felt before had receded—disappeared, in fact.

"Can I brown you, baby?" Wilson's voice was warm in his ear.

"What?" He opened his eyes wide. He had just felt Wilson's hand on his behind.

"In there. If it hurts, I'll stop."

He didn't answer. What did that have to do with love, with coming home?

"Turn over." Wilson got up. Harris heard a drawer open.

"I don't . . . think I want to."

"You'll like it." Wilson came back, a jar in his hand. "I did it with Johnny all the time."

"No." Unpleasantness had invaded the room. He could almost hear something tearing apart. Then he wondered if he should agree.

Maybe that was the price he had to pay for what he really wanted.

But Wilson had put down the jar and was moving over him again. "Okay," he whispered, "we'll save it for another time."

He slid down, kissing and tonguing as he went. Harris felt a sizzling as his cock slid into a warm place—Wilson's mouth. The sensation was exquisite. He felt as if he were being swallowed by a ripe peach. An instant later he shot. Wilson tugged and gurgled and swallowed, then came up, licking his lips. "Tapioca pudding," he said. Harris lay still, worried. Had he acted correctly? Or made a mess of things? But he couldn't have stopped if he'd wanted to.

Wilson told him to lie still, then climbed up and thrust between Harris's thighs. He rubbed up and down, clenching and straining, until a final thrust. Harris squelched his distaste—warm stuff was squirting over his legs—and remained still. At last Wilson fell off. A towel was produced. First Wilson wiped his own chest and stomach, then handed the towel to Harris. "Clean yourself off," he said.

Harris felt quite soiled. He'd like to take a shower, but wasn't confident enough to ask. Besides, he wanted to lie next to Wilson again, feel his arms around him. That was more important than washing up. He wiped himself off as best he could, then waited. "Throw it on the floor," Wilson said.

They got under the covers. Wilson rested an arm across Harris's chest. Harris wondered if they would lie like this all night. He ran his fingers along Wilson's forearm, picking at the long, silky hairs. It was hard to believe he was really here, touching Wilson's skin. He recalled the gulf that had yawned between him and Willie Mortimer. Now he'd crossed over. All the way. Not with just a hug, a hope, but with his whole body. What came next? Would they make plans for the future? Would his earlier impressions—a trip to Lowell House, dinner at Locke-Ober's—come true?

"I wish you could spend the night, but my cleaning woman comes first thing in the morning."

Harris stared into the darkness.

"Where do you go to school, by the way?"

"Harvard."

"Then it's just a short ride. I was afraid you went to Amherst or something." Wilson laughed briefly, then switched on the lamp.

Harris got up slowly. He didn't understand why he couldn't stay. He'd leave early, at dawn if necessary, before the cleaning lady arrived. But he didn't say so. Wilson didn't want him to stay and that ruined it anyway.

As Harris got dressed Wilson talked about Harvard. He knew some other undergraduates, had met them in the gardens too. Harris might know them, he said, though he didn't offer any names. Harris realized he was being discreet. For the first time he was glad he hadn't told Wilson his own last name.

In the living room Wilson gave him a kiss on the forehead. "You're sweet, Harris. How can I get in touch with you?"

Harris gave his room number in Lowell House, without offering his last name, which Wilson didn't seem to mind. He wrote it on a pad by the phone which, Harris could see, had its number taped over.

"I'll drop you a note," Wilson said, smiling as he rose. "We'll get together again."

Harris didn't know what to say as he found himself guided toward the door. A handshake and good-bye seemed all wrong. He had thought it would end differently. But when he hit the street the shock and disappointment began to wear off. His hopes rose again. He would hear from Wilson. They would take up where they left off. The other things would happen too—the visits and meals and excursions. He had taken the step; he had crossed over. He had met someone who could love him. Everything else was fading in comparison—Harvard, his courses and books, his friends. He laughed into the night and flung out his arms. There was no way to reverse the amazing events of this night. The rest of his life might not be so bad after all.

11

MAG

The Wedding

She was in front of her infinity mirror when the sadness reappeared. She would never sit here again, watching herself recede into ever-smaller versions. All that was gone, including school, college, and the long hours when she worried and primped and revised her face late into the night.

She could hear Mother and Gran arguing in the kitchen. They'd been up since dawn, she didn't know why, since there was nothing to do. Sister had arranged for the wedding breakfast at the Westchester Country Club. "You bet it will be ritzy," Mother had said, breaking the news, but they had both felt the old resentment. If they wanted to succeed socially they had to ask Sister for help—the Shay family could never quite manage it alone. True, Mother had her bridge ladies and her lunches with Caroline Elliott and *her* friends, but she had never . . . well, taken off. And she was busy all the time teaching sixth grade anyway. Even if she had been in demand she would have no time.

And Gran. Gran belonged to something called the Order of the Eastern Star. Once a month she got dressed up and went to a tea meeting and that was it. The ladies had met here a few times, but Mag didn't particularly like the look of them—bad grammar and cheap jewelry. She had caught Mother and Sister trading pregnant looks when the subject of the OES came up.

No, if they wanted to impress Howie's relatives, who had come all the way from Omaha and were now staying at the Roger Smith Hotel in White Plains, they had to turn to Sister for help. And she had suggested the Westchester Country Club. In all the years she and Uncle Mark had been members—playing golf, going to dances, taking Mark Jr. and Joe to the teen events—they had never once suggested that she, Mag, come along. Not once. Not until today as a wedding present.

She could hear Mother shouting downstairs. "Mama, I asked you not to do that." They argued a lot now, like they were reviving some old dispute from Texas. Sometimes she had to intervene. Gran wanted Mother to go out, circulate, meet men, but Mother wanted Gran to mind her own business. Three women in one house. It had never been the same since Daddy died.

That terrible night, more than two years ago, was still an unhealed memory in her mind. After Mother came rushing into her room (it was a miracle she was home for Thanksgiving), everything had gone into slow motion. Daddy in his clothes stretched out on the bed, eyes wide open behind his glasses, Mother standing helpless, saying over and over, "He's dead, oh, my God, he's dead." Daddy not responding to her calls, her pressure on his chest. She had raced to the phone, calling Dr. Stokes, demanding that he come at once. And what had Dr. Stokes said? "Well, if he's dead, there's nothing I can do." She had started screaming at him to come, even at midnight. At last he agreed. He had, to give him his due, been apologetic afterward.

Mother had said it several times, but she knew it wasn't true. "He couldn't live without his mother." Daddy wasn't dependent on Nana, not like Harris was dependent on Mother. It was the other way around—*Nana wouldn't let him go.*

She mustn't let her mind wander today. But it was too bad Daddy had never met Howie, that she'd never had the benefit of his opinion. Not that she'd made a wrong choice. Howard Snepp was the one for her. When he touched her, minor thrills raced up and down her spine. But there was more to Howie than sexy fingers and a confident manner and blue eyes and a decent height. Howie had a bright future at the Amarillo Oil Company. He was already a district supervisor in Maryland. Everybody liked Howie. She smiled into the mirror, watching it repeat a dozen times. She was marrying a real American.

She had mentioned that to Harris a little while ago when he was on a weekend pass from his desk job at Fort Dix, and he'd gotten furious. "What are you trying to say, that we aren't?" He'd actually spit the words at her, almost drooling, like years ago. She didn't care to explain, though she knew exactly what she meant, and he did too. He had started shouting, but she had shouted him down. She could still boss her little brother around.

Howie more or less ignored Harris. They had gone to the movies a few times, the three of them, but Howie was twenty-eight, a former captain in the air force, with dozens of missions over Germany, and Harris was twenty, due to leave Fort Dix and return to Harvard now that the war was over. They were worlds apart. She had observed Harris trying to impress Howie with some of his book-learning, but Howie had laughed it off, naturally.

In a few minutes she'd put on her hat and corsage. She was wearing a wine velvet jacket with big moon-pearl buttons, and a matching skirt, no jewelry. There was just the corsage that Howie had sent this morning—white orchids with purple centers.

Nobody understood why she didn't want a big wedding. Gran had offered to pay for it, but she'd been firm. She was starting a new life. Besides, who was there to invite? She didn't see any of her high school friends. As for Michigan—well, she had attended Columbia for her last years, to be near Mother and Gran. She had lived at home and commuted, made few friends. But it was at Columbia that she'd met Howie. He had picked her up outside Low Library, which was amazing, since she later found out he had never once stepped inside. He was just passing by. He got his buddies to write his papers for him, he said.

He began talking the minute he met her. He was like Daddy that way—he could make a friend out of anybody. "They all know Howie!" she had laughed to Mother after her second date.

They had discussed Howie's marriage proposal, which came in May, just before graduation for both (she getting a B.S. in Business,

Howie an M.B.A.). Another student, also getting an M.B.A., had proposed at the same time. But Craig Frost was shy, uninspired. He hadn't kissed her once, whereas Howie had kissed her after lunch in the West End Café on the very day he met her. Besides, Craig was too short.

Mother had tried to be logical about it. "Let's decide which one Daddy would have liked."

"Oh," she'd cried, "Daddy and Howie would have hit it off right away. Can't you just see it?"

But Mother frowned. "Craig is going to make a lot of money, I can tell."

"Howie's going to make millions. Everybody is just crazy about him."

Finally Mother gave in. Daddy would have preferred Howie, for any number of reasons. Mother did too, though she wouldn't come right out and admit it. She liked it that Howie's mother was head of the Omaha chapter of the WCTU and that his father had the Olds dealership, now reactivated after the war, the first models arriving from Detroit. Still, there was some chemistry between Mother and Howie that wasn't quite right. Maybe because he was the opposite of Harris.

Besides giving her minor thrills when he touched her, Howie made her laugh. She liked men who could do that—Daddy always had, with his corny jokes and puns. But there was more to it than that. She'd discussed it with Althea Krafft, one of her few friends at Columbia.

They'd been on a double date, Howie and her, Althea and a friend of Howie's. They had compared the two men afterwards, and Howie had won hands down. He'd kept them in stitches all evening.

"Funny men, men who can joke about things, make better mates." She'd been thinking about this recently. Althea looked uncertain but she went on. "It's a sign of vitality. It shows they're confident, they have a good outlook on life."

She paused, hoping Althea would agree, but she still looked puzzled. "Men who can laugh have more power. It'll show up everywhere. Even in their offspring."

This time Althea broke into a smile. "You mean it's a way of keeping tabs on their genes?"

"Yes. It's the opposite of crying or complaining." She recalled a play by Eugene O'Neill in which one of the characters had done almost nothing but laugh—affirming life through his laughter. "It's a new form of natural selection. The funniest man wins."

They went off into giggles, but there was no doubt in her mind. Howie was the one for her. Even Charles Darwin was on her side.

She clipped on the corsage. It was huge, running from shoulder to waist. She debated removing some blossoms, then decided against it. Howie had chosen it especially. She fitted the hat, a felt band that ran across the top of her head. She observed the results, then pressed the side wings of the mirror back. It was the last test and she had passed it. She would never need these views of herself again. She was becoming a new person, Mrs. Howard Snepp. There was really no reason to feel sad.

She had discussed their family history with Howie after talking it over with Mother. Mother had said she must tell everything; no marriage could be based on untruths. She had gotten her dark, pained look when she said this, and Mag knew the remark had not come easily. She also knew that Mother never let momentary weakness interfere with the correct decision. And she was right. Your husband was the one person who had to know everything.

Still, she was reluctant. She had erased all that from her mind years ago, why bring it up now? Then, watching the grimness on Mother's face, she had another idea. Not a lie, just a slight alteration. "Suppose I tell Howie"—she toyed with her engagement ring, which Howie had bought at discount through a diamond merchant he'd met on the train—"suppose I tell him about the old name . . . but tell him Shay was actually Nana's maiden name." Her face lit up. "That we adopted a previous family name because everybody hated Germans so much."

"You mean say it was in the family all along?"

"That's better than saying we picked it out of a hat."

"He'll find out eventually."

"How can he find out about Nana's maiden name?"

Mother shook her head. "It always comes out. Lichtern. It'll be on some old paper you thought you'd thrown away."

"I'm not taking any old papers with me. And Howie never looks back, never even talks about when he was a boy."

Mother considered some more. Mag could see silver points of anxiety in her eyes. They both hated this subject. "I really think it's better," she urged. She could see assent forming slowly, in the relaxing of Mother's jaw, the unclenching of her fists.

"I suppose."

"Nana wouldn't mind. If she knew."

"Oh, Nana." Mother made a face and turned away. Of course, Mother and Nana had never been on really good terms; it had been an armed truce for as long as she could remember.

"Aunt Hattie too." That was a mistake. She shouldn't have mentioned Aunt Hattie. Mother got her martyred look, then stood up. "I'm sorry, Mother, don't go. We haven't finished the discussion."

But she wouldn't sit down again, even though there was a lot more to say. Biting her lip, looking hurt, she left the room. Wasn't that typical? Just when they were getting along, when they were really communicating, something went wrong. A wave of bitterness washed through her. Mother couldn't sit still long enough to discuss the most important thing in her life—her relationship with Howie. If it had been Harris . . . she put that out of her head. She had more important things to consider. Still, she was sick of these family feuds. Aunt Hattie and Mother were deadly enemies. Daddy had hated Gran, called her horrible names. Uncle Mark would never make friends with Daddy. Nana and Gran couldn't sit in the same room together. Nana had refused to let Mother into her hospital room when she was dying. And of course she and Harris had never gotten along for an instant.

If only she'd been born into a normal family. Where aunts and sisters and in-laws and grandmothers loved each other. Where they had big reunions. Her own family, the one she would have with Howie, would never be like this one.

She got up from the dressing table, smoothed her skirt and

checked her new nylons. Thank heavens she didn't have to use Liquid Stockings for her wedding.

She thought about Aunt Hattie again. She shouldn't wish she would be here today, but she couldn't help it. What a difference it would make to see her in the church—her beautiful auburn hair, her crystal skin, her big pearl earrings, her large frame oozing with love. Her last living relative on Daddy's side. But it was totally impossible.

Aunt Hattie was convinced Mother had poisoned Daddy. Killed him because she hated him, had always secretly hated him. Aunt Hattie had told her this a few months after Nana and Daddy died, when Mag was visiting in the apartment where she now lived alone.

"I would have taken my evidence to court," Aunt Hattie had said in a reasonable tone, "but it would have harmed you and Harris. It would have ruined your lives to have your mother convicted as a murderess."

She had stared at Aunt Hattie, too shocked to speak. Her aunt's eyes, so much like her own, were boring into her. She didn't know what to think, but a dim loyalty forced her to speak up. "Daddy died from a coronary, from the strain of losing Nana, because he started smoking again. The doctor told him not to."

Aunt Hattie shook her head. Mag had the impression her aunt was off somewhere, alone. "I have evidence that some pills were given to your father just before he died. Pills that were poison."

"Daddy was always taking pills for his heart."

"These were different, Mag. I talked to the druggist. Your mother ordered them without telling anybody."

She could feel Aunt Hattie's hatred everywhere—clinging to the curtains and rugs, the big Persian screen, the marble statue of Diana and the Tiffany lamp. This accusation would confuse her forever if she didn't resist. "I don't believe that."

An unkind smile played on her aunt's lips. "You don't have the facts. I do."

"Mother filled prescriptions all the time. Dr. Stokes was always trying something new."

"This one was from another doctor, not Stokes."

Mag tried to remember. In the years between his first attack and his second, fatal one, he had consulted several specialists. She pointed this out.

Another lethal smile. "This was from a doctor who had been her lover. Your mother had many lovers. You're old enough to know that now."

Aunt Hattie began to move around the room, touching each beautiful thing as if it were a magic talisman. Again, Mag had the impression that her aunt was alone, speaking to herself, and her heart sank. There was craziness in the family on top of everything else. What should she do? She would be forced to choose between Mother and Aunt Hattie. The rifts, the divisions that she detested, would create another split. She felt tears forming in the corners of her eyes. Wherever she turned, she found pent-up hatred, ancient enmities. It was her heritage. Where had it started? In the dry places of Texas, on the gray felt upholstery of the Packard, at the family dinners in New York and New Rochelle? She didn't know. But it had been a constant all her life.

"I could go to the D.A. tomorrow and have her indicted." Aunt Hattie seemed to be swelling with rage. "She could go to prison for life."

"But why would Mother want to poison Daddy? She loved him."

Aunt Hattie turned swiftly, her eyes blazing. "You'll have to ask her that; she's the only one who can tell you. But I'll say this—she never loved him."

At last she had managed to change the subject. But even as they spoke of other things, calmed down, Mag knew this would be her last visit to this apartment, her last time alone with her aunt. She was going to lose her beloved Aunt Hattie, just as she had lost all the others. There was no help for it. It was a family curse. And she didn't even know how it had started.

But when she got home that night, back to New Rochelle, where Mother was just beginning to recover from her depression, to talk about teaching again, she had learned some more. Mother had told her an amazing story about Charlie Rysdale, whom she remembered vaguely—a tall man with hair the color of butter. They had run off together. She never dreamed Mother capable of a romance like that—with Aunt Hattie's husband, of all people—but it was true. They had almost married. Only at the last minute had Mother agreed to return to all of them.

Mother didn't want to tell this story. She said she had promised Daddy she would never reveal it. "He was so humiliated by the whole thing," she said, twisting her hands together.

But that explained it—Aunt May, whom she still remembered clearly, Aunt Hattie's hatred, Nana's grudging behavior. It was all rooted in Mother's passionate affair with Charlie. More craziness, but also beautiful. She believed in love like that. It made sense of the world. It was the way she felt about Howie Snepp. But it had alienated her from Aunt Hattie forever.

When she came downstairs in her wedding outfit, Mother and Gran inspected her carefully. It reminded her of other inspections—makeup, dresses, halitosis ("Let me smell your breath," Mother would say, and she would puff deeply into Mother's face). This was the last time. She would never descend to find Mother critical, Gran approving. Another moment of loss swept through her. Who would tell her that her slip was showing ("It's snowing down south") or that dandruff had rained on her shoulders ("Let me brush you off")? Or that she'd look fine if she'd just hold up straight? She repressed tears. Daddy should have met Howie, he should have been here to give her away. She started to dab at her eyes.

Incredibly, Mother was dabbing at her eyes too. Mother almost never cried. "My little girl," she mumbled now, "I'm losing my little girl." Mother came over and hugged her. It felt wonderful, Mother holding her like that, but she had a taste of the old bitterness. She had never been Mother's little girl, much as she had hoped to be, and it was too late now.

She stopped sniffling and detached herself. That was enough. She'd have to check her makeup in the car. Which reminded her, she wanted to talk to Harris. She wanted him to act serious and dignified in church. This once he would have to take Daddy's place, even though Uncle Mark was giving her away.

"Where's Harris?" She heard the usual command in her voice.

"He's out back wiping off the car," Mother said. She had put her hankie away.

"Well, I hope he hasn't forgotten what I told him."

"Don't worry about Harris, Mag."

Mother, sharp and self-possessed, defending Harris again.

Today's ceremonies had to go off without a hitch. Not only Howie's parents but his aunt and uncle and brother were here. Mag looked at Gran. She was wearing her new dress, hydrangea blue, with her graduated amber beads and a blue straw hat with paper forget-me-nots at the front. She looked fine. But Gran's appearance was no guarantee of anything nowadays. At a restaurant two weeks ago, Gran had come back from the ladies' room with her dress tucked inside her bloomers in the back. Nothing like that must happen today, not at the Westchester Country Club with the whole Snepp family looking on.

She was beginning to get tense, which would make furrows over her nose. She made herself relax. "Tell Harris to bring the car around." Mother went off while Mag helped Gran with her coat. Gran's arms were enormous; they almost didn't fit in. But when Gran was ready, buttoned up, she reached into her coat pocket and took out a tiny package. She looked a little embarrassed. "Surprise, surprise!" she said.

Mag took the package. "What is it?" She didn't expect anything else—Gran had already given her the sterling from Georg Jensen.

"Open it and see."

It was the diamond horseshoe stickpin, now set as a ring. She let out a gasp. It gleamed and sparkled. She slipped it onto her pinkie—a perfect fit. "Oh, Gran, I'll never take it off, never, never." She flung her arms around her grandmother.

"Go 'long now, you old hypocrite," Gran said, blinking back tears.

A few minutes later they were all in the car. Harris, at the wheel, was in a spotless uniform with sergeant's stripes. She began to give him instructions. She could see he was getting ready for a smart retort but, to her surprise, he held his tongue. Maybe he was nervous too. Maybe, for the first time in his life, he wished his father was alive.

She sat in the back next to Gran. That was her choice. She held Gran's hand, rubbing the crispy skin, the flat gold band. It felt so good, so familiar, and for a moment she was full of grief again. Then she held her other hand up to the window. The diamond horseshoe glittered in the morning sun.

"I wonder how Howie feels," Harris observed as they turned into the church parking lot. "The condemned man walks the last mile." He let out a snicker but nobody laughed. His remark was completely inappropriate.

Several people had suggested they spend the first night in Saratoga or Ithaca, but Howie had hooted down the idea. "Heck, I drive all day in Maryland, ten hours is nothing." So they were going to reach the Mohawk Inn at Niagara Falls around midnight. Personally, she would have preferred to stop halfway, but she had deferred to Howie. She wanted to get used to that. But they'd be exhausted when they arrived.

She glanced at Howie's hand on the wheel—strong, lightly furred, reminding her of her father's. He would probably be too tired to do anything tonight. She had mixed feelings about that.

There had been only one bad moment in church. Harris had been solemn, Uncle Mark had been relaxed, Howie's brother Earl had produced the ring without fumbling. But when she was standing there, listening to Father Palmsley (he used to be plain Dr. Palmsley) read the last vows, she had gotten faint. It had come on suddenly and she had to grab Howie.

She should have been in a bridal gown with a pearl coronet and a tulle veil and a silken train. She should have been surrounded by ushers and bridesmaids, by pots of arum lilies and a photographer snapping pictures. The church should have been filled with friends and relatives. She should have had a bouquet to toss. She had been cheated.

Gran and Mother wanted a big wedding but she had refused, and now, for one awful moment, the pain came back. She hated New Rochelle. She hated the schools and the houses and the people. They had never let her in, never made room for her, and she wouldn't pretend, with a fancy wedding, that they had. She had recovered quickly, letting go of Howie, but the moment had left her shaken. She was standing there in her wine-colored suit with the moon-pearl buttons and a little felt band in her hair because she had turned her back on this town, but it wasn't fair. It wasn't fair and she would never forget.

"Why'n't you settle back and catch some sleep?" Howie glanced at her.

"I want to keep you company."

"Shoot, I'm used to driving alone."

"Howie, this is our honeymoon."

"Well, sure it is, but we're gonna sleep on our honeymoon too."

He was so good-natured. She'd been so proud of him at the wedding breakfast. Maybe she would just close her eyes for a while. But when she did, images danced around.

The breakfast at the club had gone like a dream—to be expected, with Sister in charge. Rolling up the long yellow-gravel drive to the huge building that looked like a French château had been suspenseful. Then, inside, they had passed through a long series of rooms filled with flowered chintz furniture—rooms for every function imaginable, cards, dances, movies, meetings, banquets. They had stepped onto verandahs full of wicker furniture and graced with men in linen jackets and white flannels, women in sailor suits and one-piece tennis outfits. A swimming pool and golf course gleamed in the distance. You'd never know the country had been at war just two years ago.

She had caught Mother's eye as they went into the private dining room, each of them suppressing a tiny smile. The Snepps, all of them as talkative as Howie, had been reduced to murmurs. Sister had presided over the table, signaling the waiters, asking just the right questions, never taking the spotlight off Howie and her. No wonder Sister was such a success. And for once she was grateful for Sister's elegant diction. Mother made fun of it sometimes, calling it the Adelaide Hawley effect, pointing out that no one would suspect that Sister had once said "pen" for "pin" and "pin" for "pen." But now Sister sounded like the Duchess of Windsor. Only once or twice, when Sister cut off Gran, who was starting on one of her stories about Gideon, did Mag get annoyed. They were ashamed of Gran, but Gran never complained. Watching Sister glide under Gran's remark, changing the subject, she swore that she would never be ashamed of her grandmother. Whenever Gran wanted to visit them in Baltimore, she would take her around, introduce her to everyone, announcing clearly and proudly, "This is my grandmother. Her father was a hero in the Civil War, and she is a Daughter of the Confederacy." There'd be no hiding Gran in her house.

They had to toast the bridal couple with tomato juice. Too bad, but Mrs. Snepp had strong convictions. So did Howie's Uncle Earl and Aunt Regina. Howie had laughed—he was used to the teetotaling—but she had felt a little disappointed. Even knowing they would order champagne at the hotel tonight didn't make up for it.

Yes, it had been a dream, something out of the movies, and when she and Howie had said good-bye at the front entrance, stepping into the Olds the parking-lot boy drove up, she had had the brief impression that she *was* in a movie, something with Andrea Leeds or Cobina Wright Junior. She had never been so happy.

The car swerved and she opened her eyes. Howie was passing dangerously. She started to warn him, then bit her tongue. She would have to break herself of certain habits. Howie reached over, tucking his hand around hers. "Have a little shut-eye?"

She shook her head. "Thinking about the breakfast."

"It was real nice. Your Uncle Mark and Aunt Sister did okay by us."

"Do you think your parents liked the country club?"

"Like it?" He let out a whoop. "They loved it. They never saw anything like it in their whole darned lives." He floored the gas pedal and scooted around another car.

This time she couldn't help herself. "Be careful, Howie."

"Shoot, that gal was only doing thirty."

She sighed. "It would have been fun to spend the afternoon at the club. I wonder if we'll ever go back there."

"Sure we will. Uncle Mark will ask us back next time we visit."

She doubted that, but she kept quiet. Howie was very impressed with Uncle Mark. No doubt he was impressive—all those famous friends, a huge house, and now a weekend farm upstate. But she had always thought him uninteresting. Small, repulsive, Italian-looking. Forever in a polka-dot bow tie, clutching a pipe. He never said anything brilliant, despite his reputation.

She settled back. Now she was really sleepy. They weren't even halfway there. As she began to drift off she thought contentedly of her talk with Howie, the one she and Mother had worried about. It had gone as they hoped. Howie didn't care about the Schanbergs, about any of that. When she mentioned that her grandmother on her father's side had originally been named Shay, he didn't even blink. It didn't matter. When she finished, he gave her one quick, penetrating look—as if a blue light had gone on deep in his eyes—and that was the end of it. Her conscience was clear. Mother was satisfied. The subject would never come up again. She was Mrs. Howard Snepp, now and forever.

She half-opened her eyes for a moment and surveyed Howie. His face was benign. For an instant she was swept by the alarming notion that she had no idea what he really thought, then she rejected that. She had chosen Howie, had given her life to him, because he was a man without secrets. She had had enough of those for a lifetime.

Their bathroom at the Mohawk Inn had a heart-shaped tub. Howie caught on right away. "It's for two people, don'tcha see?" He let out a little whoop. "Let's try it."

But she was too tired to take a bath. She couldn't believe Howie had any vitality left at midnight. But he did. He had ordered the champagne right at the front desk. The manager had smiled (smirked, actually) and now the bottle was icing in a tripod bucket next to the bed.

She wasn't dead over the idea of the chiffon nightgown either. To tell the truth, she really wanted to get into her flannel pajamas, put up her hair and sleep. She sat on the edge of the bed, fighting these ideas, listening to Howie in the bathroom, gargling. The sound had plain implications and she wasn't in the mood for those either.

A faint shudder went through her. Suppose something went

wrong? Many marriages failed on the first night. She could hear him spitting the gargle out. He was going to come out and take charge. She hated people taking charge of her.

The door opened. He appeared smiling, but she caught a certain tension. She had the sensation that they were caught in a script, with roles they weren't ready to play. Why didn't they just . . .

"Go on, honey, get ready."

She forced herself to hold up the chiffon nightgown. "I bought this for tonight." She tried to get a little enthusiasm in her voice.

"You don't wanta wear that."

"Why not?"

"Save it for tomorrow night."

He was bare-chested, in boxer shorts. Howie had a good physique, very natural and manly, with brown curly chest hair. They had lain on the beach many times. His hairiness had always thrilled and alarmed her at the same time.

"Go on, hurry up." He stepped out of the bathroom door.

"Please don't rush me." She didn't mean to sound irritated. She took her cosmetic case and headed toward the bathroom.

"Who's rushing you?"

As she closed the door he was pouring champagne into two glasses. Inside she undressed slowly, thinking about pain. She had a very low threshold of pain. Something Virginia Matters, the housemother in the dorm at Michigan, once said popped into her mind: "Virgins come high." All the girls had made fun of her afterwards, said she was living in the last century, living up to her first name, but Mag had been secretly impressed. It had something to do with her self-respect, which she thought of as impregnable, a high tower in a lonely wood, and closely related to virginity.

When she came out wearing the nightgown, Howie was sitting on one side of the bed. He'd turned off all the lights but one—a lamp in the corner that gave off low red and purple gleams. "They sure think of everything," he observed. "Come on, get in."

She approached the bed, resisting his bossiness. She got in slowly, to keep from mussing her hair. He handed her a glass of champagne. She held it up. "Here's to us," she said.

"All the way," he replied. "Now why don't you relax?"

She thought he was really trying to relax himself, but she didn't say so. She was quite tense. She took a sip, then another. For some reason she thought about a championship game of field hockey in high school with their archrivals, Mount Vernon. She had won that game with a brilliant shot at the last minute. It had taken all her nerve and concentration.

Howie put down his glass and nuzzled her neck. "Go on, relax, honey."

But she was relaxed. Anyway, it wasn't something you could order yourself to be.

He moved up to kiss her. They had done this many times, and the sensation, the taste of his breath, was pleasantly familiar. Maybe this wouldn't be so bad. She could feel her limbs loosening slightly, a faint liquefying of her nerves. Howie's hand began roving. She didn't grab it, as she always did, though it brought some of her tension back. She decided to think of the hockey game again; it would help her concentrate.

Howie shifted part of his weight onto her. The champagne glass was in the way and she couldn't reach the table. "Just a minute," she said. He reared back, his eyes obscure. She twisted sideways to get rid of the glass.

She didn't enjoy any of it—the thrusting, the sweat, the weight—but it might have been worse. The pain had not been great, just a sudden tingle like a bee sting. And it was all over very quickly. Maybe he hadn't enjoyed it. Maybe she had been uncooperative. The manuals said the foreplay should last at least twenty minutes. They'd had limited foreplay unless you counted the champagne. But that wasn't her fault.

Now she was quite soiled and wet, and she didn't know if it was blood or not. She had to get up and wash; she couldn't lie here another minute. She nudged Howie and he rolled away.

When she came back she was in her pajamas. Seeing Howie lying on his back, staring at the ceiling, she felt a sudden uprush of love. That was over. She had the impression they had reached home port after a long, difficult voyage.

She got into bed but remained propped up. Howie, making dim noises, nestled against her. He rested his head on her breast. As she played with his hair, listening to his low, regular breathing—he was practically asleep already—contentment seeped through her. She felt almost purified. She had married the right man. There had been no nerves, no incapacity, on Howie's part, beyond that first hint of tension at the bathroom door. She recalled her talk with Althea Krafft about natural selection. Her wedding night was one more proof. Howie had overcome her reluctance simply by ignoring it. That was the best way, the mark of a winner. She knew where her reluctance came from—from the dark strain in her family line. But Howie would free her from that, would carry her over the rocks and reefs, the hatreds and deaths, into a new life.

She bent down and kissed the top of his head. He was like a boy. The soreness in her groin kept her awake for a while but when sleep came it was dreamless and refreshing. She woke up bursting with things to say.

They met a nice couple in the Sweetheart Coffee Shop next morning. Sue and Lyle Gilgan were from Toledo, also on their honeymoon. Howie started chatting over the booth partition, and before long the Gilgans were sitting next to them having second coffee.

She liked to observe the sequence of events when people came into Howie's orbit. First the reserve, a cover for shyness, followed by surprise, then easiness, then total surrender. The men as well as the women. But it wasn't only Howie's cheer and confidence that won them over, it was his appearance—his chestnut hair, blue eyes, florid cheeks bunched into balls. He was like a Norman Rockwell cover.

Of course, certain snooty types didn't respond. She'd noticed this when they were dating, going to clubs and dances and parties. They would give Howie the once-over, note his extroversion, trade glances and move off. She had learned to spot these people, steering Howie away, distracting him. But even when it occurred, he wasn't bothered. He would hoot and talk to somebody else. Only later, when they were alone, would he refer to the snub, a question spinning out of his cloudy blue eyes. It had registered. How deeply she couldn't tell yet.

The fact was, plain people liked Howie best—Sue and Lyle Gilgan, for example, who were now turning toward him like lilies to the sun. Lyle ran an auto supply store, was hoping to open some branches. And Sue told them they'd had a trial honeymoon last month ("Takes the pressure off, you know what I mean"). They had poured out these confidences—intimacies, really—five minutes after sitting down.

Mag listened as Howie described their own wedding yesterday, the country club ("Mag's uncle, he's a big shot in the newspaper business"), the long drive here, the heart-shaped bathtub ("We haven't gotten around to that, have you folks?"). He just opened up his mouth and talked. It was amazing.

She chimed in, holding her own, happiness sparkling in her. She could see, in the eyes of their new friends, that they had no reservations about her. There were no hidden meanings in what she said. She was Howie Snepp's wife, she was one of them. And all without even trying.

The Gilgans were taking the eleven-o'clock *Maid of the Mist*. Why didn't they come along? "Sure we will," Howie answered for both of them. She agreed, though it would have been nice to be consulted. As they headed for the Olds (Howie insisted on doing the driving), Sue took her arm. "I'm so glad we met you," she said. "We're both awful about talking to strangers."

They spent the day with their new friends, viewing the falls, stopping for lunch, arranging to meet for dinner in the Bridal Room. They had millions of laughs, but as the day wore on, she began to wonder if Howie was talking too much. The Gilgans didn't object, but gradually, she noticed, they stopped talking. Howie's remarks flowed over, around and under the boats and platforms and snack bars, through the mist and spray, even in the Cave of the Winds, where nobody could hear a word. At one point, when Howie had interrupted Lyle one more time, she debated interfering. "You were saying, Lyle . . ." The words were on the tip of her tongue. But she didn't—it was between the men and she was training herself to be a wife.

After dinner they went to the Golden Anniversary Lounge for drinks. The Gilgans were leaving early in the morning, so this would be good-bye. Lyle ordered Seagram's and Seven, Howie Canadian

Club with ginger. She and Sue stuck to Cokes. She was really quite tired. She would love an hour by herself. Howie had begun talking about signs, how important they were. His company spent a lot of money designing signs for the gas stations; Lyle would have to do the same thing for his stores.

Lyle didn't look very interested, and Sue was fidgety. It didn't seem very appropriate for their last get-together, and she tried to change the subject, without success. Of course, Howie was a salesman, and that's what salesmen did—they talked you into believing something. Still, she could feel the evening veering off course, slipping away. She hated to think that all their goodwill—affection, really—was going to be dissipated. She glanced at Lyle as Howie got onto problems of sign illumination. Lyle looked almost sullen. He was staring at his hands, which, she'd noticed this morning, had deep grease marks in the creases and cuticles. Howie seemed oblivious to Lyle's discomfort. She thought briefly of a large ocean liner and a small motorboat—Howie was bearing down on Lyle like the *Queen Mary*. Suddenly, for the first time, she wondered if Howie's free and easy ways denoted not strength but a flaw—a flaw she had overlooked till now. But no, that was impossible, and disloyal besides.

At last Lyle spoke up. "You wanta know somethin', Howie, you think you know a lot more'n you do." His voice wasn't hostile, but it wasn't friendly either. Mag thought of a knife with a dull blade.

"Okay, hold the phone." Howie's eyes danced around and his jaw sagged. "I've been in this business a heckuva lot longer than you."

She looked at Sue, a significant glance. "Maybe we should say good night, Lyle," Sue said. Mag felt her forehead ice up. The day, the occasion, was going to be ruined, just as she feared. Her head jangled with a flood of remarks, anything to keep the peace.

"Just listen here, Lyle, we spend as much as two thousand dollars on a single sign, that's how important it is." Howie's voice was deep but throttled back. She could see a line of sweat where his forehead met his hairline.

"I think we should change the subject," she broke in. Her voice was louder, firmer, than she'd intended.

"I do too." Sue seconded her.

But the men were glaring at each other. "I can't afford that kind of sign and it don't matter." Lyle pulled his hand into a fist.

"Of course it matters. If you say it doesn't, that just means you're in the wrong business." Howie emitted a little boom of laughter—exactly the wrong sound.

Lyle half stood, his arms dangling over each thigh, fists clenched. "You're full of it, Howie."

Sue stood up quickly and grabbed her husband. "We're going upstairs right this minute," she said. Lyle didn't take his eyes off Howie, who was still seated.

"Will everybody please calm down?" Mag's head was suddenly throbbing. She couldn't imagine a worse ending to the day.

"Heck, I'm calmed down. It's Lyle that's hot and bothered."

"Mag." Sue looked at her imploringly. "It's been wonderful meeting you and we wish you all the best." She tugged at Lyle, who let himself be pulled around. He dropped his fists. They walked a few paces then stopped. Lyle turned and came back.

"G'bye, Howie." He put out his hand. Howie took it, looking mild.

"You look after your pretty wife, Lyle."

Mag felt herself go limp as the Gilgans walked off. She didn't even know how it had started. One minute they were friends, the next minute at each other's throats. Maybe the men had had too much to drink. Maybe Lyle couldn't let himself be steamrollered any more in front of Sue. But suddenly the precariousness of social relations—the very thing she thought she'd escaped forever—came back. There would be no end to it, not even with Howie. In fact, managing her friendships might even be harder—she would have to control not only herself but her husband. She glanced at Howie. He was signaling to the waiter for another drink. He winked at her.

"Are you all right?" she asked.

"Sure I'm all right. Why the heck wouldn't I be?"

"You're not upset or anything?"

He let out a familiar hoot. "He was just blowing off hot air. I knew what was coming the whole time."

"But, Howie, maybe you pressured him too much. In front of Sue." She thought again about the endless flow of talk during the day. Should she mention that?

"I didn't pressure him; he just couldn't take it."

As the waiter replaced both their drinks—her own Coke too, though she hadn't asked for it—she observed Howie closely. He was utterly calm. The whole thing had washed off him. He wasn't even sweating anymore. He was sipping his drink and gazing innocently around the room.

She closed her eyes in mixed relief and irritation. If a scene like this had happened in her own family, involving strangers or guests, there would have been recriminations and sulks for a week, followed by a round of apologies. But maybe that was wrong. Maybe Howie, whose emotions didn't descend to the depths of grievance and revenge, was right. And maybe she didn't need to worry after all.

"I'm really exhausted," she said.

Howie looked at her solicitously. "You wanta hit the hay?"

"Yes, I do."

When they stood up, the waiter scurried over. "Well, how do you like that?" Howie remarked with a chuckle. "They stuck us with the whole darned bill."

12

MARGARET
The Farm

Harris's voice on the phone sounded more hostile than usual. She could sense the old accusations gathering force, collecting in a black pool at the other end of the line. He was coming for the weekend. He'd be on the 7:10 in Hudson tonight. After hanging up she felt the usual blend of pleasure and alarm.

She went to the couch in the bay window and watched the herd in the pasture across the road. It was June, and the new calves were stumbling around. It had been one of her first discoveries after moving up here—calves played around like puppies. They dodged and chased and fell down. She had mentioned the discovery to Sister, whose pasture this was—part of the Giangrande place, Maple Hill Farm up the road—but Sister hadn't been amused. "If you knew how much trouble those cows are or how sick they get, you wouldn't enjoy them." Sister and Mark always had manager problems besides their herd problems, so that their weekends, which were supposed to be for rest and recovery, were filled with crisis. They had to go over the milk production records, the feed bills, the machinery repairs, the labor headaches. What Maple Hill Farm gave them was trouble, aside from the tax break. But that wasn't the point. The point, Margaret knew, was to have the largest dairy place in the county and a farmhouse built in 1775 filled with Early American furniture. Spending the weekend with account books and an alcoholic manager was the price they had to pay. It went with the territory—more than a thousand acres of it.

She made herself leave the calves and go to the kitchen. She'd fix something special—a devil's food or a lemon meringue pie. It was a reflex she couldn't control, like reading the stock tables every day or going to auctions for bargains. Harris had to have a treat. She'd been fixing treats for him all his life, and even now, when there was so much tension between them, the treat couldn't be stopped. She decided on the devil's food.

Before beginning she glanced at the sheet of paper in the Underwood on her desk by the window, the window which overlooked the little well with its cute wooden housing. She was writing again. It had started quite suddenly, her second year here, after all the renovations were done and winter had set in. The typewriter had called her over one day, just like that, and she had begun writing about Gideon, the unpaved streets and simple houses, the schoolgirls and eccentrics, the prejudices and talk and food. She could hear it all so clearly, even now, the twang and slang, the ignorance and provinciality, the meanness and sorrow. It rang in her head, ready to be tapped onto a page. The story in the machine now was about an encyclopedia salesman who had called on them one evening, telling Papa about the *Book of Knowledge* and how it would help his girls at school. But what Papa didn't know was that the salesman was making eyes at Sister, who was sitting very demurely, an enormous white bow in her hair like a butterfly. And what Sister didn't know was that she, Margaret, had seen her and the salesman at Gem's having an ice together, earlier.

But she had come to a dead end with the story, as happened quite often. One moment she was racing ahead, and the next her fingers were frozen on the keys. An infinite number of branches had opened in front of her. Which one to take? If she got lost on a wrong turning, she'd have to destroy days of work. In the last month she had learned the virtue of pausing. Fiction was like piecrust dough. After working it you had to let it cool. This story about the encyclopedia salesman was now cooling. Too bad she couldn't put a dish towel on it and pop it in the refrigerator.

She hadn't told Sister about the writing. She didn't want to see the reaction. Kindness and condescension, because Margaret was a widow, because Margaret was alone now that Mama had died—if that was the word for the way Mama had simply dissolved on her mahogany bedstead. And of course, Margaret had these awful problems with Harris, who was totally unlike Mark Jr. and Joe, who were both married, with babies, and important careers coming along. "That's nice," Sister would say in her grandest, most condescending manner. "Keeps you busy." Sister, of course, had countless activities to keep her busy, looking after Mark, entertaining his business associates, running two enormous houses, keeping tabs on her two sons and daughters-in-law and grandchildren. No, Sister's life was much too full for her to be impressed by these scribbles. Of course, once she got published, that might make a difference. She could imagine dropping the news quite casually to Mark and Sister on one of their weekend get-togethers. "Oh, by the way, *The New Yorker* took one of my stories about Gideon." Mark would be genuinely pleased, would get up and kiss her cheek, and Sister would be impressed in spite of herself. Yes, the Duchess of Maple Hill Farm would actually register approval. Unfortunately, none of her stories had been accepted yet. She could paper the walls of this kitchen with rejection slips.

As she got out the cake pans and measuring cups she wondered if she should invite Francis for dinner tonight. If Francis were here, Harris wouldn't have a chance to get started. The conversation would be general. On the other hand, she was still a little uneasy about Francis in front of Harris, who always eyed him in a funny way. It was difficult for grown sons if their mothers had . . . well, male friends, but it was especially difficult for Harris, who was all twisted up about sex. God knows what thoughts ran through his mind. But she didn't want to pursue that subject right now.

Without letting herself hesitate further she went to the wall phone and dialed Francis at his shop. When he answered in his mild, flat voice, she heard the electric saw whining in the background. He did custom carpentry. They'd met when he came to take measurements for her kitchen cabinets. Now she invited him for dinner at seven-thirty, apologizing for the lateness of the hour because she had to meet the train. But she would leave the front door open.

"Okay," he said, waiting for further instructions. There would be a pitcher of drinks in the icebox; he was to help himself. "Okay," he said again.

Francis Grecky was new in her experience—a man who waited for her to speak, to make decisions. At first she had been put off by it, but gradually she had come to like it. Francis was comfortable with women who asserted themselves. That might be a failing of some sort—she really wasn't sure—but it certainly made him easy to be with.

That was another item she hadn't passed on to Sister—she wasn't really alone anymore, despite being a widow, despite Mama's dissolution and death. Francis visited two or three times a week. It had all been very easy and natural. A week after he installed the cabinets he had left a quart of strawberries on the back porch. A week later there had been a flat of peony shoots. There had been no name on either gift, but that only made it clearer. When she called, he said in his mild voice that yes, he had left them, he thought she could use them. There had been no request for return favors. A few weeks later he had offered to replace the muffler on her car.

After the muffler she invited him for dinner, making pork chops with apple fritters, eggplant casserole and rhubarb pie. She had found herself a little self-conscious about entertaining him—she was forty-seven years old, after all, and her figure was almost gone. And she had to wear high heels to show off her legs, her major good point, which made a clatter as she moved around. But after they settled down to eat she found herself relaxed. Even more than that, sinking into familiarity and comfort. Francis was the opposite of Judd in almost every way. Not only in his flat voice and habit of waiting for her to speak, but in his table manners and physical presence. He was a small square man with a thick mane of gray hair, blue-gray eyes and delicate features. Of Hungarian extraction, Catholic. When he picked up his knife and fork, holding them in small, square, hairless hands, he cut everything on his plate into equal portions, even the apple fritters. Only then did he put down the knife.

It occurred to her that this habit came from a lifetime of taking measurements. Later, as she got to know him, she realized that he had extended the measurement-taking to everything. His blue-gray eyes marked off faces, words, events, into manageable segments. He converted the variable and the insubstantial into inches and feet. It was his way of understanding. This meant he didn't always follow when she talked about plans for the future—about writing novels, getting a Ph.D., teaching at one of the new community colleges. But if she was patient, if she explained, he could break her passions and hopes into small particles. Then he could absorb them. He even made useful suggestions.

Yes, she thought, as she sifted the flour with the same sifter she'd been using for twenty-five years, Francis was the opposite of Judd. She and Francis might not even have gone upstairs if she hadn't taken the initiative. He would have come by for dinner once a week—that became a routine rather quickly—and cut his food into tiny squares and waited for her to speak. Waited and waited. Sometimes she thought of Barkis in *David Copperfield.* Francis was willin', but he had to be given a push. She had invited him upstairs when it finally became clear that he would never invite himself. And up there it had been the same way—subdued, stepwise, measured. The pleasure had come in small increments, but it had been sufficient for both. But even after that first time, he still waited for the invitation. And now she rather liked that about him.

When the cake was in the oven, she went out to the garden with a basket. Only a few things were in—asparagus, which she had to allow to seed again this second spring, some scallions and the first pea pods. Should they eat the pea pods, with their unripe kernels inside? If they did, that meant no full-grown peas in July. On the other hand, eating them now meant they could consume the shells, which would only be thrown away later, a dead waste. She did a few calculations in her head, including weight, vitamins and flavor. The ideal solution, of course, would be to wait until July, eat the ripe peas and feed the shells to the chickens. However, she had no chickens. She hadn't overcome her old dislike of them, even though she appreciated their economic value.

Finally she decided to pick a few baby pods, enough for Francis and Harris but not for herself.

As she worked, honks sounded from several passing cars. She

turned each time to see someone waving at her. People were getting to know her, Mrs. Shay, who was a widow and had two grown children and was the sister of Marian Giangrande, who came up weekends to the big place nearby. It was amazing how quickly she had become known. At church in Chatham, or at a bake sale at the firehouse, or at the auction house in Copake, strangers would come over. "You're Mrs. Shay, aren't you, bought the Tuddenham farm?" She heard welcome, placement, in their voices. She was a known quantity—a widow, a mother, related to the largest landholder in the county. In some ways it reminded her of Gideon, but with a difference. These were the same country people, country ways, but there were no reservations about her or her family. She wasn't an outsider; she was one of them. One with old Mrs. Hutchison, her neighbor, who sat on her porch all day waiting to see if cows strayed onto the road. One with the Hagan family next door, who managed a big greenhouse and sold cut flowers as far away as Albany. One with Mr. Serocki, a widower, who performed yard chores at the County Home.

As she picked the last of the pea pods her thoughts went back to Judd. He'd been gone more than ten years now. Their years together had faded in her memory, like the colored panels on the quilts she bought at auction. How he would have hated this place—too many rubes, he would have said. The volunteer fire department, which was the men's social center, wouldn't have held him for a minute.

No, if Judd were still alive, this transplanting, this return to her roots, wouldn't have happened. She'd still be a suburban housewife, still trying to please him, cotton to his needs. She didn't like to think about it—it was disloyal—but she was happier now. Independent for the first time in her life, though it had taken her years to achieve it—years when she thought she never would.

A car stopped. It was Marilyn Hagan asking if she wanted some cut peonies; they had more than they could sell. "I thought you might have some company for the weekend, Margaret"—they were already on a first-name basis—but she declined. She had dozens of peonies in bloom from the flats Francis had given her last year. Marilyn went on about the coolness of the weather. "I bet you're used to much hotter Junes." Margaret laughed and agreed, then Marilyn drove off with another wave.

That was another placement—she was a Texan. A special sort of Southerner, an expatriate in these hills and valleys west of the Berkshires. Coming from Texas gave her special qualities—slightly humorous, outlandish, but nevertheless respectable. And, hardly noticing, her old accent, the one she had worked so hard to erase, had crept back. She began peppering her speech with *you-all* and *I reckon* and *don'tcha know*. Her vowels sneaked upward and her laugh got shriller. But she couldn't help it, even as she reminded herself how she had always hated professional Southerners. It seemed to be what people expected of her.

On the way back to the house she thought again about Francis's first gifts of strawberries and peony shoots. Maybe she would write a story about that. "A Wordless Wooing." Not that she would make fun of him. She might also write about her dilemma. He was serious and she was not. She didn't want a husband. But it took all her skill to keep things as they were with Francis, moving neither forward nor back. His first wife had treated him badly, messed around with men picked up in roadhouses, yet managed to win custody of their son, Carl, an exquisite boy of thirteen with his father's pale skin and blue-gray eyes, whom Francis adored. Now he wanted to erase all that with a new wife. The question was in his eyes all the time. If she kept avoiding the subject, laughing or skipping around it, she would lose him.

She washed the pea pods and put them on the kitchen table in the sun. Maybe the baby peas inside would get a little bigger that way.

Harris emerged from the train wearing a gray flannel suit. The sight of him drained her instantly, the peace of the day, of every day, evaporating. He had taken her hostage the moment he was born. Yet she hardly knew him now—a tall, darkly handsome young man with a secret life.

He got in on the passenger side, leaning over to kiss her cheek. She turned and put both arms around him, an impulsive move. He had complained—one of his many complaints—that she had never been physical with him. Never held him, never really touched him. She had defended herself, pointing out that she'd wanted to, but all the books, all the psychologists, told you not to hold a child too long, not even to pick up a screaming baby. It only encouraged clinging, dependency. It was especially bad for boys. She had always put her faith in the experts—how was she to know that Dr. Spock would decree just the opposite a generation later? Now, as she clasped him, she could feel the tension in his shoulders. Bars of metal. Fear combined with her tension. Had he come up to accuse her of something new?

She started the car. "Francis is coming for dinner." She tried to sound offhand. "He's probably there now."

"He has a key?" His voice was light, but she heard the curiosity behind it.

"I left the door open."

"God, you can't do that in the city, not even for ten minutes."

"How are things at work?"

"Not bad. I wrote some new jingles. They'll use them on TV, besides on the car cards."

His voice took on new pride. He wrote copy for Tweedy-Lord, a big agency on Madison Avenue. He'd had his choice of three such jobs when he graduated from Harvard—an English major with good grades. She'd been disappointed over his change of career, had warned him about the insecurities and treacheries of advertising agencies—Charlie Rysdale had wanted to leave that business twenty years ago—but Harris had ignored her. He wasn't interested in diplomacy and the State Department. All that was a bum steer, pressure that shouldn't have been put on him. He should have been allowed to make up his own mind, not been forced to overcome her influence. He wanted to live in New York, wanted to be with his college friends who were moving there, wanted something literary. Advertising was a logical choice. Except, she thought, turning onto the dirt road that was a shortcut to the house, except that most of the time he hated it. Everybody at Tweedy-Lord wanted to quit and write a novel.

She changed the subject to Mag and Howie and Roland, who had visited last month. Harris had complicated feelings about his sister, but he always liked to hear the news. Roland was huge for his age—at five he had the weight and height of a boy of eight. Tall on both sides. Mag was a wonderful mother. And Howie—she had come to trust him, she said, to follow his advice about investments. Howie was always traveling, talking to people, getting ideas. He had a feel for what was happening, what companies were growing, what research departments showed promise. And he was so even-tempered, so cheerful, able to get along with Mag, who had never been easy to get along with.

Harris let out a slightly superior grunt. She knew the cause—he considered his brother-in-law crass. But she let it pass. Her mind focused on Mag. Amazing how it had all turned out. Her daughter, who had been an endless botheration as a child, was now full of love and admiration. "You're a positive role model for me, Mother," Mag had said last month, sitting in the kitchen, Roland squashing her thighs. "The way you manage your life, your independence, everything—I want to be just like you."

Her heart had melted when she heard that. To think that Mag approved of her! And it was just the opposite with Harris, who had been the cause of endless worry and attention as a child. Now he didn't have a good word to say about her. She had done everything wrong. She was all the bad mothers of the world rolled into one. Yes, it was amazing.

"Tony Calero moved out." He interrupted her thoughts, speaking dryly. "We were fighting all the time."

"Maybe he'll change his mind again."

"Not this time. I won't let him back in."

Tony Calero was his special friend. Harris sometimes referred to him as the Cuban Spitfire. She had met him several times—he'd even come up here one weekend, when she had put them in separate bedrooms, though she had heard the patter of bare feet in the middle of the night. He was a fair-skinned, dark-eyed, aquiline young man with limited English, four years older than Harris, and wonderful at repairing things. She had kept him busy with a hammer and pliers all weekend. "Well, you know best."

"Yes, I do, and I'm through."

She didn't know what to say. Whatever she said would be wrong.

But she knew what she thought. There was no satisfaction to be found in that life. Hadn't she watched her own uncle Harris for the first thirty years of her life? What had he ever found except sorrow, shame and loneliness?

She hoped it wasn't her fault that Harris had turned out this way. She'd shouldered so much blame, accepted so many accusations, she couldn't take on this too. When he started spouting the latest psychoanalytic theory, she said he was wrong. "Mark my words, Harris, they'll find it's genetic. Hereditary. Not the way you were raised. I never wanted you to be like this."

And though he looked grim and disagreed, she knew she was right. Anything else, any additional responsibility, was beyond her strength. Besides, even if his problems were hereditary, he could still change. Anybody could change, if they wanted to badly enough.

Francis had parked his Ford on the shoulder of the road, leaving the driveway free. Now she was glad she had invited him. The first night was the worst, full of Harris's accumulated grievances, but tomorrow morning, after a good sleep in his own bed, surrounded by his old things, Harris would perk up. He would be his old sweet self.

Francis rose from the gentleman's chair in the parlor, which had been covered in green rayon, shaking hands with Harris, then brushing her cheeks with his lips. She tried to make the greeting sexless, laughing and wriggling free, but she could see Harris watching. As she headed for the kitchen she cautioned herself. There was no reason to feel guilty.

"Francis, why don't you pour Harris a Purple Jesus?"

Francis followed her into the kitchen while Harris went upstairs to change. The pitcher—gin and grape juice—was in the icebox. Francis poured the drinks, and a second for himself, while she lit the stove. Then he sat down to watch. He liked kitchens. All the craft people around here, when they came to discuss repairs or renovations, gravitated to the kitchen, even though she invited them to sit in the parlor. She wondered again how it would feel to have Francis on the premises every night, watching, measuring, listening. And again she knew she didn't need him here, not all the time.

Harris turned up in dungarees and a polo shirt. He had brought her a little bottle of Shalimar—the five-dollar size. Caroline Elliott had started her on that scent, and now it was the only one she used. She gave Harris another hug, thanking him, and this time he seemed to enjoy it. He even hugged her back. Maybe the country magic was already beginning to work.

Everyone was cheerful. They talked about President Eisenhower—Harris said he played golf all day and bridge all night, when did he have time to run the country? "That's why everybody's doin' so well," Francis remarked, "they're lettin' us alone." It was an unusual remark for Francis, and they both gave it some extra appreciation. She was swept with contentment. Everything would be all right. She had never lost her faith in progress.

"Aren't we having fun?" she asked suddenly, aware that she was giddy after only two swallows of her drink.

"Oh, yeah," said Harris, half-agreeing, half-condemning. She knew what he thought. He said he had been oppressed by her optimism all his life. But that wouldn't stop her.

The dinner was a huge success. She lit candles and everything was delicious. No one noticed that she didn't serve herself any pea pods. After cutting his pot roast into small cubes, Francis made a serious effort at conversation. He had just finishing installing a free-standing spiral staircase in one of the great homes along the Hudson. The house belonged to a famous stage actress.

Harris got interested, asking about the house, the actress, the grounds. "When I finished the job"—Francis's voice always seemed to come from far away—"Miss Granville said she'd give me two orchestra seats to her next play." He pronounced it or-*ches*-tra.

Harris beamed. "That's great, Francis. You can take Mother; she loves to go to the theater."

Francis gave a quick, embarrassed smile, and his eyes skittered down the wallpaper. A surge of joy went through her. Was Harris finally giving his seal of approval to Francis?

"We used to go all the time," Harris continued, "when I was in high school. Even before."

He started listing the plays they had seen, always matinees, just the two of them taking the train to the city, he cutting school, she playing hooky from her chores at home. *The Little Foxes. The Corn Is Green. The Second Mrs. Carroll. Angel Street. Twelfth Night. Harvey. Victoria Regina.* Even when it was hard, when money was short and two dollars for a ticket was a lot, she had done it. She just had to get away from Mama and Judd, from all their woes, and burrow her way into those brilliant lives onstage. If she hadn't, she would have suffocated.

After Harris wound down, she added, "Well, that was a long time ago. I don't miss them anymore."

"I bet you do."

Harris's eyes probed at her. He wanted her to be the same, to take him on adventures, just the two of them. But she didn't contradict him. She simply changed the subject.

The devil's food cake was a success too. Francis examined it carefully and Harris clapped his hands. It was the sour-milk recipe she had cut out of *Good Housekeeping* in 1933. They each had two slices.

As they sat back, stuffed, she glanced at Harris. All the tension was gone from his face, now softened and ruddied by candlelight. Her optimism surged again. He had taken a wrong turning, but he would straighten out. He would overcome his childhood just as Mag had overcome hers. It was like her faith in the stock market. Even when it went down she knew in her bones it would rise again. And it always did.

They decided to have coffee on the back porch for the last of the light. She and Francis sat on the glider facing the yard; Harris sat in a wicker chair at right angles. She felt Francis close his hand over hers in the cleft between the pillows. She debated pulling away—it made her nervous with Harris so close—but she didn't. It was almost dark anyway. The glider squeaked as they pushed it. An insomniac robin hopped around.

"Oh, to be a virgin now that spring is here."

She grabbed her hand away from Francis. "Oh." She turned away, the pain releasing in a long ribbon inside her.

"Oh, gee, Mother, I'm sorry . . ."

She could hardly catch her breath.

"I didn't mean . . . it was just a joke."

She waved at him, but she couldn't turn and look. She took out her hankie and pressed it to her nose. Her body was filling up with shame.

"Oh, God, what did I do now?" He stood up, gesturing angrily, an elongated form in the darkness. Then he stamped into the house.

"He didn't mean anything, Margaret." Francis touched her back. She wished he wouldn't.

She couldn't explain it—not yet. But there was accusation buried somewhere in his remark. That she was sure of.

"Come on now." Francis was out of his element, floundering around. She should say something, try to save the evening.

She took a deep breath. "He was just being mischievous. He didn't know what he was saying." But her voice was unconvincing, even to her.

They went back to the kitchen. Francis agreed to another cup of coffee. She could hear Harris overhead, tromping around. A phrase that had occurred to her after his last visit popped into her mind. *Never have children.* She didn't even believe it, but here it was, rolling around again. *Never have children.*

She tried to make conversation, but it was impossible. Her thoughts were elsewhere. Francis seemed to have shrunk—she had no more connection to him. Her destiny was upstairs.

At last Francis rose. She walked him out to his car. The night was black and star-strewn. It reminded her, unpleasantly, of the dress she had worn at her wedding reception at the St. Regis—black velvet sewn with occasional dull sequins. She hadn't looked good in that dress, and she didn't look good now. Francis kissed her, just a press on the lips before she broke away. Harris might be watching from his bedroom.

When she got back to the kitchen, he was washing the dishes. She let him do it as she cleared the rest of the table. It might help them in some way. But what had happened, really? She had overreacted absurdly. But she couldn't help it.

At last she was ready to speak. "I know you didn't mean anything, Harris, so let's just forget the whole thing, okay?" Her voice was calm, judicious, though her heart was pounding. Maybe they could put it behind them now, pretend it never happened.

A strangled sound came from his throat. "I really can't say anything, can I?" He turned from the sink, his hands soapy. He was on the offensive now. "There are so many hang-ups in this family. About our past. About sex. About everything. It's pathetic." His eyes bulged, reminding her of Judd's. "No wonder I can't bring any of my friends here. No wonder we never have an honest conversation."

She could feel the ground sloping under her. "It's over and done with, all right? We'll both feel better in the morning." She gave a bright, false smile. "I don't know about you, but I'm going to bed. Just turn off the lights."

She went over and brushed her face against his, third time this evening, a conciliatory gesture with no spark of meaning. Nor did he respond. But what could she do? She had to keep trying. Her motions had been laid out in the most intricate labyrinth at the moment of his birth, no matter what he did. Now he simply stood and glared at her. She turned and left the kitchen quickly, before he could think of something else to say.

Upstairs she undressed and lay in the dark. After a while he began to play the ancient upright in the parlor. It usually put her to sleep—he played very well nowadays—but not tonight. For some reason her mind reverted to Mama and her talent for punishment. Were Mama's itching fingers, the slaps that came out of nowhere, behind her reaction tonight? She didn't know.

The upright had a tinny sound, but Harris coaxed out some mellowness. He was playing the "Raindrop Prelude," one of the few pieces she could identify. He had always wanted to play the piano, insisted on taking lessons when Mag refused. He had also wanted to play with Mag's friends, with dolls. Remember the tatting set? Time and again she had thrust him out the front door with a baseball glove, a bat, a helmet, ice skates. What more could she have done? And yet he blamed her for all his problems.

Never have children. All her scheming and plotting, her hopes and encouragement, had come to nothing. It was like Penelope and the tapestry. What she had woven by day, Harris had undone by night. Tears started in her eyes, but she wiped them away with the sheet. All tears were tears of self-pity, Mama used to say.

The prelude came to an end. She began to think about Uncle Harris again. Maybe it was in the blood. Harris had inherited his tastes from his great-uncle, who had been forced out of Gideon in a scandal so terrible nobody had ever been willing to make her privy to the details. He'd spent forty or fifty years, his whole adult life, in New York with his friends, his first nights, his playbill collecting, his secret nocturnal errands. That was it—a genetic linkage. There was nothing she could have done to prevent it.

She recalled Uncle Harris's friend Zinny Dawes, who used to drop by the apartment on West End. Uncle Harris always served him Cocomalts. The minute she laid eyes on Zinny she'd known—his eyebrows were plucked! She had actually come across a grown man who tweezed his eyebrows. It had made the world topsy-turvy for a moment. Little did she know that one day, in her own family . . . Her mind moved on. Caroline Elliott loved to gossip about Paul Poyntz, the choirmaster. Sister was always dropping savvy hints about famous actors—Maurice Evans, Joseph Schildkraut, Alfred Lunt. Together they had giggled and slandered and felt superior. And now it was coming back to haunt her. She should have known. She had never been in a position to belittle anyone.

She heard a new piece begin downstairs. He hadn't meant anything on the back porch; it had just been some old fear of her own. An image of Charlie Rysdale flitted into her mind—a ghost. She dismissed it.

The music was beautiful. She was almost asleep. *Never have children.*

"Well, now, Harris, I said to your Aunt Sister, 'When Harris visits tonight, we'll have some real good talk.' "

She watched Harris grin. He always responded to his uncle. Only a man can give him that, she thought, sitting on the couch next to Sister. The library, at the back of the Giangrande farmhouse, was a new addition. It had a good view of the huge pond the government had just paid for.

Mark chewed his pipe and signaled to the books all around. He read few of the volumes he bought—he didn't have time. "Now take Bernard Shaw there, he was a fella I'd like to sit down and talk to." He gave Harris a conspiratorial smile. "You and me and Bernard Shaw, Harris."

Harris looked delighted. "You know," he said in a careful voice, "those Shaw plays still don't have their pages cut."

Mark nodded. "Don't have the time."

"I'd be glad to cut them."

Sister let out a cynical laugh. "Keep talking, Harris, maybe you'll get 'em someday."

It was the Ayot St. Lawrence edition, already a rarity. Harris had had his eye on it for years. He really thought his uncle Mark would give it to him, but Margaret knew better. Everything was for his own two sons.

"Hell, I didn't even know what it was," Mark continued in his humorous voice. "This book dealer called me up and said, 'I got twenty-five volumes of Shaw, you want 'em?' I said, 'Put 'em in the mail.' "

As they continued teasing, Margaret turned to Sister, who was sewing rag circles for a bedspread. But her motions were slowing down. They always slowed down as the cocktail hour progressed, until they ceased entirely. Sister had been talking about the Columbia Hunt Club. "You don't have to hunt," Sister said, putting down her needle and picking up her gin and bitters, "just drink." She couldn't hide the satisfaction in her voice. She gave her little society smile, which Margaret thought was rather wasted here in the library. She and Mark had just been asked to join. They had already met most of the people on the Membership Committee. Tomorrow, Sunday, there would be a luncheon to meet the rest. Margaret asked about the dues, just to be polite. She didn't really care and they could afford it anyway. "If you don't keep a mount in the club stables, the dues are quite reasonable," Sister replied.

Now it was a mount. Once it had been a horse or a pony, and before that it had been a critter, but now it was a mount. Margaret watched as Sister took another deep sip of gin. It was her third, though she tried not to count. Sister's hair was streaky—she was turning blond by degrees. She recalled Sister in slacks years ago. That had been the latest thing too.

"Does anyone get blackballed at that club?"

"I'm sure they do," Sister said, in a remote tone. Margaret's thoughts sped back to high school and Mag's tragedy over the sorority. There had been a leak through the school office—some papers from the school in White Plains that had gotten through in spite of all her efforts. The principal's secretary, a dried-up woman named Miss Scanlan, had passed the information on to someone in Phi Gamma. An act of pure malice that she had found out about years later, only by chance. That kind of evil chance never happened to Sister.

"You know Mrs. Barston down the road? She named her new baby Zeena." Sister smiled brilliantly. "She waved me down on the road this afternoon. She said, 'You know, Zeena, like the flower.' "

Margaret smiled, but she felt sorry for the farm women. She'd like to see them all go back to school. Now television was making it worse.

"I doubt she went beyond the fourth grade," Sister added. "None of them have."

Sister's face in repose was angular, almost stony. When had the bones started to jut out, Margaret wondered, when had the softness disappeared? Or had the new stoniness come from within?

"She's another one whose husband walked out the door and never came back. Maybe he couldn't bear the idea of a kid named Zeena." Sister whooped with laughter, then waved her glass at Mark. He refilled it at the Early American hutch that served as a bar. Margaret watched—maybe she was wrong in her count.

Mark began one of his routines. "This morning, Margaret, we had a real bad case of the why-don't-yous." He grinned, his molars biting into the pipe stem. He had never been handsome, a short man with dark eyes and a nose broken from his days as a lightweight boxer, but his appearance always inspired confidence. Maybe because of the jagged nose in the baby face. Or because of the flat, California tone. Or because of something less definable—a refusal to exaggerate, a respect for everyone, an unswerving honesty. " 'Mark, why don't you put in a pool? Mark, why don't you stock the pond with trout? Mark, why don't you sell steaks through the mail? Why don't you build a guest house?' " He waved his pipe. "I counted thirty in all. Isn't that a record, Babe?"

"Oh, sure." Sister waved impatiently. That was new too, along with the jutting hardness of her face and the unkindness of her comments about the farm families. She didn't play the loyal wife anymore. At least not after a few drinks.

But Harris laughed. He loved jokes. "Why don't you print a proclamation, tell them 'why-don't-you' is forbidden at Maple Hill Farm? Do it on parchment, in a script, with *f*'s for *s*'s?"

As he and Mark went on trading jokes, she thought about this morning. As soon as Harris came downstairs, hair on end, face swollen with sleep, she knew that last night had been swept away. Even the awful scene on the back porch had disappeared. He wanted to forget it and so did she. And they had. She fixed him eggs and bacon, with thick slices of molasses bread she'd made a few days ago. Their talk was simple, unencumbered—about the picket fence she'd ordered, the Dutch corner cabinet she was refinishing downstairs, Francis's offer to build her a chicken house. Harris actually took pleasure in hearing about these improvements. They helped him slip away from the complications of his own life. But that was always the way on his second day here.

Deep in her mind, so deep she hardly acknowledged it, was the hope that Harris would come and live with her. He'd have to have a job, of course—Albany was only forty-five minutes away—but he would return every night. Things between them would be sweet and uncluttered again. They wouldn't quarrel. There would be no reproaches. He might even meet a nice girl in Albany. If he really put his mind to it, he could.

Harris had begun to ask his uncle about the *Brett & Wagner Encyclopedia*. A Bohack where he shopped was featuring them. He'd been proud to tell his friends that his uncle Mark had dreamed the whole thing up.

Mark didn't go into details—it might seem like bragging and he never did that—but he provided a few glimpses. The hardest nut to crack had been A&P. Once he convinced them, everybody else fell into line.

She watched Harris absorb this. He was eager for glory, and his uncle's exploits could be his, at least partially. Mark no longer worked for the Hearst organization. Now he was a sales manager for a nearly defunct encyclopedia. But a few weeks after joining them he had come up with an idea so simple, so brilliant, that it had revolutionized the selling of reference books. But no one who knew him had been surprised. He had simply convinced a few key managers at the supermarkets to sell one volume a week. The first volume went for twenty-five cents, the second for fifty cents, and the remaining eighteen for $1.99 each. The customers came back every week until the set was complete—and bought a lot of groceries besides. Twenty weeks of assured traffic. Now he had dozens of imitators around the country.

Harris's face glowed as he listened. He made suggestions for other series of books—medical, fix-it, home decorating—that could be handled the same way. Mark listened approvingly, his pipe between his teeth, and once again Margaret noticed how Harris expanded in his uncle's presence. She was sure Mark had already considered these ideas, but he didn't let on. A sudden loss filled her. Judd had never taken an interest in Harris. How would he have turned out if he had had a father like Mark? Mark had given his two sons endless love and respect. He had treated them as equals. And they had turned out extraordinarily well. She quashed these thoughts and turned back to Sister. "What are we having for dinner?"

The reply was brusque. "We butchered a calf last week; I don't know what Lincoln decided."

Lincoln was their cook-chauffeur, an illiterate black man, who had been Sister's confidant for thirty years. Believe it or not, Margaret had sometimes been jealous of Lincoln. Her thoughts lapsed into a familiar groove. It was Sister who had spotted the Tuddenham farm, insisted that she buy it, move here, start over. But did she really want her next door? Or was she a burden? Sometimes she caught an expression on Sister's face, as now, that frightened her. Were they both—she and Harris together—just family obligations? Poor relations?

"How about another drink, Margaret?"

"No, thanks."

"Come on, I'll fix you one."

"For God's sake, Mark, she said she didn't want one." Sister's voice cut through the smoky air. Mark went rigid. Margaret flinched. But Sister caught hold of herself. Margaret could see the effort—the pursing of the lips, the lowered eyelids—and the anger was pressed out of sight.

"Don't you think we're ready to eat, Babe?" Mark's voice was gentle, placating.

Margaret watched Sister struggle again. She never drank with dinner or after. Once they left the library she was through. But sometimes it was hard to get her to leave. "I'm starving," Margaret said. Sister lowered her eyelids again. The struggle had resumed. Margaret knew how it would end tonight—they would go into the dining room in a few minutes—but one night it wouldn't end that way. Sister would stay in the library until somebody came to get her. After that, there would be no more self-control.

They made small talk throughout the meal. Sister steadied herself with the pot of tea that Lincoln always placed beside her the instant she sat down. Even the society smile reappeared briefly, as if she were reminding herself of her place in the world. But Margaret said little unless someone spoke to her directly. Sister's anger had been biding its time for almost fifty years and now it had arrived, like the last car at a border crossing. But Sister's anger shook her own world—like seeing Zinny Dawes with plucked eyebrows. What did Sister have to be angry about? She didn't know. She couldn't imagine. And then another thought struck her. Maybe too much good luck was really bad luck. Maybe Sister's easy victories had made the gods angry.

When Harris came downstairs in his city clothes at four o'clock on Sunday afternoon, he was in tearing good spirits. He cracked jokes, sat at the piano for five minutes and rippled out cadenzas, went outside for a last smell of the lilac tree by the front door. She said he was like Antaeus—he had been revived by touching the earth—and he laughed. When he piled his suitcase into the car he said he'd be back soon, it had done him a world of good.

As they took the shortcut through the Giangrande land, alfalfa and corn sprouting on both sides, she couldn't help mentioning his coming up here to live. She didn't mean to, it just slipped out. But he wouldn't commit himself. He only promised to think about it. But even that, she thought as she swung onto the main road, Route 66, was more than he'd ever offered before. Her heart gave a swell of anticipation.

They were leaving the stoplight at the intersection with Route 9 when the words shot into her ears. She wasn't ready and they exploded like little bombs, even though his voice was steady and cheerful. "I'm thinking of changing my name back to Schanberg, Mother."

Her left hand went to her throat. "Why? Why would you want to do that?"

"It would be telling the truth." A nervous laugh. "I feel like I've been living a masquerade most of my life."

If her foot hadn't been on the gas pedal, she would have rocked her body back and forth. "If you do that, I'll have to leave here. Give up the house. I don't know where I'd go."

"Oh, God." He put his hand to his forehead and turned to stare out the side window. They were at it again, jammed up against impossibilities. It had only been a temporary truce. She swerved to avoid a jackrabbit on the road. She was doing seventy, and her mind was splitting to pieces.

"You should never have taken our name away, Mother, it was a terrible thing to do."

"I did it for you, for you and Mag."

"I've thought about that a lot. You didn't do it for us, you did it for yourself."

She could feel disaster building between them. "I cut off my arm for you and now you say, 'Look, you're a cripple, you only have one arm.' "

"Would you stop that, please? I can't stand it."

She gripped the steering wheel so that her knuckles showed white. There was a way to erase this, words that would undo the words that had been said. She only had to find them.

"I went to see Aunt Hattie."

"You went to see Hattie?"

"Yes, on that trip to California last month. She lives in Santa Barbara." He paused and she felt the venom gathering on his lips. "You were married in a synagogue and you didn't tell us. Nana and Grandpa are buried in a Jewish cemetery and I didn't even know where it was. Don't you think I had a right to know?"

She had passed the stage of speaking. She stared straight ahead, steering down Warren Street, through the Negro section of town, turning left toward the train station. If she could will him not to speak, never to speak to her again, she would, although her heart would break.

"It was nothing to be ashamed of, Mother, don't you see?"

"You don't know anything about it." She had found her voice again, the power of speech.

"Hitler killed millions of people and all you did was complain about the refugees moving to New Rochelle. Don't you see the immorality of that? The horrible immorality?"

They were at the station. She didn't turn the ignition off, just set the gear in neutral. "Don't come up here anymore, Harris." She was surprised at the quiet authority of her voice, but then again, why was she surprised? She had always known what her choices were. "Stay away from me."

His face crumpled, and he lifted his valise from the back seat. "Don't worry, you'll never see me again." He got out, slamming the door, but she had heard the break in his voice, the hint of panic.

She backed out, turning the car around quickly. The tall young man with the suitcase stood looking after her. But who was he? She hardly knew. He had disappeared into a landscape full of enemies and strangers.

She drove home slowly, trying to concentrate through the white whirl. Mama had said she wasn't pretty. She had said it over and over. "Margaret isn't pretty, Margaret's plain." What did that mean, and why was she thinking of it now?

She drove the car into the garage and went in the house. It was her fault, everything was her fault. She had been wrong from the beginning—wrong face, wrong figure, wrong skin. She had married conscience? So what if he wasn't sensitive? What difference did that make?

Mag came back on and made her promise to visit again. She didn't want to let her go, didn't want to hang up, but finally she did. Mag was like medicine. Mag's voice, her family, her place in the world—all that was proof of her own worth. Finally they said good-bye.

She went upstairs to lie down. Her bed was like another room when she was upset. The scene in the car at the station returned, but now she was able to think more clearly. Mag had blown away the white fog. Mag and Howie and Roland.

It wasn't true. His accusations were false. Maybe there was a grain of truth, an iota of truth, but he didn't have the facts. He hadn't been there. He didn't know. And he had gone to see Hattie—Hattie, who believed she had murdered Judd.

Oh, God. She rolled over, some of the pain returning, and put her head under the pillow. Harris had such terrible power over her. It had happened the moment she saw him at Women's Hospital, an ugly dark infant who had been hers, ineluctably hers, because no one else wanted him. He had laid siege to her heart and it had never lifted.

And now she had banished him. But of course she hadn't. He was still hers, forever hers. His face at the station reappeared, crumpling again with pain and anger. But she couldn't help him. She hadn't been able to help him, really, since he left for college, and now he was beyond all reach.

She didn't want to believe it, it was unfair to Mag, to her grandson, but it hammered at her until she thought her head would split. *Never have children.*

above her and that had been wrong too. She went to the bac porch and sat on the glider, staring into the distance. She had onl gone off like this once before, after Judd died. Did that mean Harri was dead too?

She almost didn't hear the phone. It might have been ringing for a long time. But she ran inside, slightly disoriented, thinking she was back in New Rochelle and someone else would pick up. It was Mag, her voice crisp and cheerful. She couldn't have asked for a better gift. The room condensed, came down, took shape again. "Honey," she cried into the receiver, "I'm so glad to hear from you, I can't tell you."

"I figured Harris would be on his way to the city and you might need a friendly call."

Mag had been thinking of her, her welfare, her peace of mind. It was a miracle. "Oh, darling," she said.

"We think of you all the time, Mother. Roland always asks, 'When is Grandma coming back for a visit?' "

"Does he?" Someday, when she was old and feeble, Mag would look after her.

"Did Harris behave himself?"

It was a party line—she had to be careful. "He thinks I'm a terrible mother, I did everything wrong."

"Well, just refer him to me, I'll set him straight."

"He's full of old grudges. He goes over and over the same things."

"If he had children of his own, he'd forget all that." The assurance, the self-righteousness in Mag's voice were infinitely soothing.

"You're right, I know you're right." Of course, that was it. Harris had created no new world to replace the old one. That's why he was still trapped in the past.

"I used to be furious that you preferred Harris, but now I know you loved me too. You just expressed it differently."

A pang went through her. But she'd make it up to Mag. She vowed and declared she would.

"Howie wants to say hello, Mother."

She didn't pay close attention as he jawed away, but she appreciated the noise. Howie had a simple, grateful view of things, and her reservations about him were trivial. So what if he had an easy

13

HARRIS
The City

The blond man sat across from him in Vaseline Alley, near the Central Park Zoo, as twilight came on. Eyelock at fifty paces. Harris didn't know whether to cruise back, he was kind of tired, but habit was strong. Besides, it was better than being alone, as he had been all day, drifting around the city. He'd called in sick again and he needed to talk to someone. The sentences had been piling up in his head like thunderclouds.

The man was sending out heavy signals from piercing blue eyes under eyebrows also blond. Handsome, about thirty-five, vaguely European. Harris liked foreigners. They asked different questions than Americans. They seemed less critical too, as if by just being born here he had an assured place in their esteem.

The man got up. His suit, double-breasted, was tightly buttoned. He was smiling and looking away at the same time.

"Mmmmmm . . ." A hum of bees in a meadow emerged. "How air yew? May I sit?"

Harris gestured. The bench creaked as the man lowered himself.

"Beauti-ful evenink." He looked at the sky as if asking it to confirm his judgment.

"Yes, it is," Harris replied, his first remark. He felt himself relaxing. This was going to be okay.

"You are from here?"

Harris pointed behind them, across Central Park. "I was born over there."

"Mmmmmm . . . I don't meet many people born in city. They come from . . . outside."

"Oh, there's a lot of them, they just don't like to admit it."

The man smiled. Harris was sure he had missed the point.

"Where are you from?"

"I am from Poland. Polish." He pronounced it carefully. "I am in food business. Import." The man swiveled his head and stared at him. "Nize boy."

Harris shifted uncomfortably. It was too soon for that stuff. He wanted to talk, to hear the man's story, to float some version of himself. That was the thing about strangers, especially foreigners—you had your choice of countless autobiographies. He knew how to make them convincing. Today, as he walked around the city, he had thought of writing a book made entirely of fake self-introductions, depending on the circumstances. A different autobiography for sex, for business, for parties, for travel. At the end of the book the reader would be asked to decide who the introducer really was, to define his character, if any.

"My name is Stefan." The man's hand was thrust at him. His grasp was long and hearty. Harris wondered if that handshake was Polish in some way—most Americans got off the line very quickly. He gave his own first name.

"You live near here, Har-eese?"

It was still too soon for that. Harris made a vague sound. Then he said, "I'm in the advertising business."

"That is gut business, I think." Stefan reached in his pocket and took out a crumpled pack of Caporals. Harris declined. "You make publicity?"

"Sort of. I write what they call copy. That's the words in the ad." He had a sudden vision of himself as occupying a glamorous world, very American, very different from the food-import business.

Stefan made a clucking sound. "You must be very smart, I think. Making publicity not easy."

"Oh . . ." Harris gestured with his hand. He was getting a fix on things now. He was the young creative genius, his mind paved with stars, any of which might burn with a million-dollar idea. "I just dream things up. It comes easy."

His words had the desired effect. Stefan took a deep drag on his cigarette and couldn't think what to say. Harris remembered Tony Calero, whom he'd met on Central Park West, just across the park from here. Tony had taken him home to a small furnished room on Seventy-fourth Street, the walls covered with signed photos of Libertad LaMarque and Sarita Montiel and Bobby Collazo. The room had struck him as marvelously exotic, a few square feet of Latin America dropped into Manhattan. He himself had become instantly musical—a concert pianist who had been discouraged by his parents from pursuing the career he wanted. Tony had been excited by all that. Sex had been wildly gymnastic, and they had continued with each other for almost two years, when everything fell apart. Tony had never had the least idea who he was.

"You live alone, Har-eese?" Again, Harris shrugged off the question.

"I'm thinking of leaving my job. I don't like my boss."

Stefan's lips peeled back in a soundless laugh. "Naughty boy. You have gut job and you want to leave."

"My boss is a bastard."

"Boss is very important." Stefan wiggled a finger at him. It struck Harris that their conversation was really primitive, something out of a first-grade reader. Maybe he should move on. He shifted uneasily on the bench.

"Come, we go." Stefan closed both eyes for a moment. It was a sign meant to be encouraging. And then, quite surprised at his reaction—his surrender, really—Harris stood up.

"Okay." He would take Stefan home. He was beginning to feel a little sexy. Maybe they could talk later, in more relaxed surroundings. "I live at Ninetieth Street and Second Avenue."

"We take taxi, I pay."

Stefan followed him out of the park. In a shadowy spot, away from the lampposts, Harris felt Stefan's hand brush his ass. Stefan probably wanted to fuck him. Europeans always wanted to fuck you. That was one reason he was in such a hurry. Harris stopped abruptly. "I don't do that."

"Come, come, naughty boy," said Stefan. "You like."

Harris repeated the statement and Stefan closed both eyes again.

This time Harris didn't know what it meant. But as they got in the taxi, he said, "Remember."

In the apartment, Stefan paced around, smoking, looking at the pictures, orienting himself like a cat. It was a railroad flat, a string of four rooms, the kitchen in the middle with a bathtub next to the sink. The toilet was in the hall, shared with the neighbors across the hall. The rent was eighteen dollars a month.

The front room, the only one with windows, overlooked Second Avenue. In the summer, now, with the windows open, the roar of traffic entered in crashing waves—first silence, then a coming surge, then the boom. Harris unfolded the louvered shutters from niches in the walls and closed them. That muffled some of the noise. Then he turned toward Stefan, who promptly stubbed out his cigarette. This was the moment Harris liked best.

They embraced standing up in the center of the living room. Harris skimmed his fingers across Stefan's shoulders, arms, back, chest. He was working in Braille, tracing ridges and valleys, plains and hills, that were invisible. Yet it was territory he would soon know intimately. But it was best to stand here, not yet knowing. By running his fingers along the seams of Stefan's clothing he was touching every handsome, undiscovered man in New York.

He had become a connoisseur. The city was full of vibrant, alarming men, and he had mastered all the movements of approach and disrobing. It was a precise minuet, with the early notes, in some illogical way, more satisfying than the last. Now, here with Stefan, whose last name was unknown—a gap, a lacuna, that enabled him to be anyone, really—Harris felt the old, electric surge. There were no reasons, no theories, to account for it, no matter what Freud or his mother or anyone else said. He simply liked men—their haircuts and wrists, their necks and courtesies. If God hadn't wanted him to love men, he wouldn't have made them so beautiful. And the ones he didn't know were the ones he liked best.

Of course, he still had his attacks of wrongness once in a while. Even with all his experience, he sometimes felt as he had when he first embraced Willie Mortimer back at Harvard—embarrassment, shock, a sense of the unbridgeable otherness of a strange man. There were so many reasons to feel wrong—movies, magazine articles, conversations at work, only referred to men and women together. The idea of two men kissing, doing other things, was laughable or horrible. Almost inconceivable, although he'd discovered a few precious novels, like *The Heart in Exile* and *Finistère*, that referred to the subject in doomed ways, ending in death. Even so, his feeling of wrongness always disappeared, to be replaced by a sense of inevitability. This was his nature; there was no use fighting it.

"We go back now," Stefan said, drawing away. His blue eyes were slits. The odor of tobacco was strong. He motioned toward the back room, where he had spotted the bed. Harris followed him in, grateful he hadn't had to serve the preliminary drink.

Stefan kicked off his shoes and stripped quickly. He left on his white anklets. His body was milky in the half-light, well-defined but with soft muscles. There was something European about the body too, Harris thought, something peasanty and unhygienic, though that might have been the smell. Stefan smelled acrid. Harris held his breath at first, then gave in to it, almost enjoying it, as if it were the odor of sex itself.

Stefan attacked him quickly. Harris wondered if he was married, if something was being released that had been choked off for a long time. Stefan moved desperately, thrusting, sucking, biting. Harris had the impression that for Stefan, as for himself, today's partner was only a stand-in for all the others he couldn't have. Finally he forgot all that in the mounting excitement. He didn't let Stefan fuck him. They ended up doing a sixty-nine, which was awkward and a little smelly. Stefan's cum had the same odd, bitter taste as his skin, but with a tinge of tobacco.

Afterwards they lay for a long time, Stefan smoking again. His last name, it turned out, was Barilovsky. He had been in America for two years, before that in London, and before that in various places with the Free Polish Army—Russia, Iran, Yugoslavia. He had been an officer in the parachute corps.

As Harris listened, playing idly with the blond hairs on Stefan's stomach, helping him with the English words, he didn't know if he liked hearing these details or not. They were losing their magical anonymity. Soon it would be his turn to talk. On the other hand,

Stefan was a foreigner. He could offer Stefan certain services—tour guide, American friends, slang—that would anchor him more firmly in his new country. He, Harris, could become indispensable. That was what he had thought would happen with Tony Calero, but Tony was too flighty and arrogant to make it work. Stefan seemed much more needy. Lost, really.

But did he really want some kind of steady relationship? He had rarely heard of any that lasted very long or produced much happiness. Everything was against them. And since that scene with his mother last month, since she had banished him, he had needed to meet more strangers. Some days, after work, he went straight to a bar or to the park. The velocity of sex had increased. His thoughts came faster too, also his dissatisfactions. Everything had speeded up, like a runaway film in a projector.

Stefan was quiet, his story finished for now. Harris wondered how much to volunteer about himself. That was always a dilemma. Too much and he felt overexposed. Too little and he remained a stranger.

As he debated, the image of Aunt Hattie's house in Santa Barbara came to him. It was very beautiful—a white cube with wavy red tiles on top and tufted palms in the yard. She had stood framed in the doorway as he got out of the taxi, her arms held out theatrically as he made his way up the brick walk. He could see that she'd gotten fat, but it wasn't until he was pressed against her, her hug enveloping him, that he registered how vast she was. He thought, quite traitorously, of an old remark about Isadora Duncan in her later years. Aunt Hattie, who had once been the nymph in the temple, had become the temple itself. At the same time it was wonderful to absorb her warmth, her sense of the past. He had let himself be invaded, soaking up her affection like some nutrient soup. Nana and Aunt Hattie had never been stingy with the hugs; that was why he had adored them.

Her house was furnished in the western style—Arab pots, Navajo rugs, goatskin chairs, cactus plants in wicker planters. But here and there he spotted a few of the old things from the apartment on Riverside Drive—the huge carved screen that Nana claimed had belonged to the Shah of Iran, the little framed tapestry of a forest fire, the Tiffany lamp with its roses and lilies. He kept looking at these as Aunt Hattie told him about her husband, Max Rothman, who would be home later. He knew she was married—that information had seeped back east to Mag, who had informed him and Mother—but he was a little nervous about meeting Max. It was difficult to imagine Aunt Hattie living with a man. It was in the same category as his mother and Francis Grecky.

"Now tell me about yourself, Harris."

It was a loving command to reveal all. He began to tense up. He hadn't seen Aunt Hattie for almost ten years, not since Daddy died, and a lot had happened to him. He certainly couldn't tell her about most of it. Her eyes, a little beady and close together, focused on him. He started to talk about his job at Tweedy-Lord. No problem there, he'd had a lot of recognition, success. She listened for a while, then brushed away the subject. "Tell me about yourself, Harris. How are you? Are you happy?"

He began to squirm. He'd forgotten how direct she was—Nana too. But how could he tell her anything like the truth? It wasn't publishable. He squirmed some more as he stammered about his friends, his apartment, his occasional weekend visits to his mother.

"Do you have a girlfriend, Harris?" There it was, the question that could never be avoided. He had traveled three thousand miles to quiz Aunt Hattie, and she was quizzing him instead. Suddenly he noticed her moles. She had a lot of them, next to her eyes, in the center of one cheek, on her chin. They used to fascinate him as a kid, and now it seemed they had gotten larger too. Yes, they had expanded with Aunt Hattie, growing from the pressure of all the fat. He had the sudden impression that she was measuring him not only with her eyes but with her moles.

"You don't want to talk about yourself, I can see that."

"No . . . no . . . it's not that."

"That's all right, Harris, I have no right to pry." She looked away, hurt mixed with annoyance in her voice. "Tell me, how is Mag?"

It was a relief to talk about his sister. He told everything he knew—Howie's job with the oil company, Roland growing up, Mag's social success in Baltimore, the fact that she had been invited to join the McHenry Club, the most exclusive bunch of ladies in town. Aunt Hattie kept her eyes on him throughout; the moles seemed to have receded.

"You know I never hear from Mag. Not a word."

They were on dangerous territory again. "Yeah. I know."

"I didn't want to force the issue. I'm not her mother. Though I loved you two children as if you were my own."

He took a deep breath. Why hadn't he foreseen any of this? Why had he thought he could zip out here, find out what he wanted, then leave? Things didn't work that way, not in this branch of the family.

"I hear your mother has a new lover."

Harris stared at her. How had she found that out? "Well, she has a friend, his name is Francis Grecky. I'm not really sure what their relationship is."

"I know your mother and believe me, he's her lover."

More dangerous territory. He didn't want to go into his mother's sex life. He didn't know the details and it was none of Aunt Hattie's business anyway. And he didn't want to get her started on her murder theory. He had no idea what his response would be, but he'd have to defend his mother.

Perhaps she sensed this because she let out a sigh, then stood up. She was wearing a muumuu—teal blue with white frangipani blossoms all over it. The Q and A was over. Her face had cleared, smoothed away into its remarkable youthfulness. She was his old aunt Hattie again, loving and trustworthy.

She showed him to his room—it was late afternoon and he would have to leave in the morning—then said, "I know what you came here to ask, Harris, and we'll have our talk later." After that she left him. She had just heard Max's car in the driveway.

In the morning, over breakfast, she told him what he had come to hear. They were all Jews. German Jews and Polish Jews and Romanian Jews, rich and poor, educated and ignorant, shrewd and stupid. They had come from villas and shtetls, from ghettos and farms. One of his great-grandfathers had been a personal physician to the kaiser, another had founded a bank, another had starved to death.

Aunt Hattie kept her eyes on his face as she told him this, worried, he knew, that he would react badly. But he didn't. None of it surprised him. He hadn't known the details, but he had known everything else, almost from the beginning, hadn't he?

Stefan was getting steamed up again. If they lay here anymore it would be hard to stop him. But Harris wasn't in the mood for another go-round. He jumped out of bed, to Stefan's disappointment. "You stay," he said, patting the vacated sheet. Stefan squeezed both his eyes shut but Harris got dressed. Stefan did too, finally. The back room smelled awful.

But Stefan was in no hurry to leave. He accepted Harris's offer of coffee. As he put on the water for Nescafé and checked the bottle of milk for sourness, his thoughts reverted to Aunt Hattie and her revelations again. Had he been wrong in throwing all that up to his mother without warning? But he hadn't done it out of malice; he had done it as a trial balloon. Though he had sounded confident in the car, he wasn't. He was seeking her permission for reasons he couldn't fathom—reasons buried in the murk of his childhood, the difficult love between them, his endless need to please her. The prospect of reclaiming his name had seemed the next stage in his growth, a logical development. He was twenty-seven years old and the time had come to reconnect. But her prohibition had thrown him for a loop. She hadn't changed. She was still dark and forbidding on that subject. And he couldn't get free without her—she still had him in some ancient vise. He had kept the secret all these years, as ordered. Not even Lester Backs, who knew everything else about him, had been told. He had hoped, in the car driving to the station, they could both be rid of the burden. Secrets isolated you—didn't she know that? Didn't she want to be free? But she didn't, and she wouldn't turn him loose either.

The coffee was ready. Stefan put in three spoons of sugar and filled the mug to the top with milk that was on the verge of turning. He drank with the spoon still in the mug. They went into the living room to sit down. Stefan seemed very much at home. He picked up a copy of *Life,* an old one, the mid-century issue, which Harris had been saving. He thought it would be worth a lot of money in 1975 or so.

Last week, for the first time in years, he had taken out the old Latin grammar with his father's name on it. He had studied the signature for a long time, trying to figure out all its meanings. For his mother it was a shameful taboo, literally unspeakable. For Mag the same. For Aunt Hattie it was a source of pride. That's what she had said—"You mustn't be ashamed of your background. You have some very distinguished ancestors, Harris." But under that claim, he knew, was the desire to hurt his mother through him. And what about his father? What had he thought when he scribbled his name in the book? And what had he thought later when he became Judd Shay and his children were growing up with new identities? Why had he never spoken? Why had he never given them a clue? He had closed the grammar with a snap at that moment. If only his father were alive, to cut through all the meanings to the decisive one. And then, sitting there, he wondered if he had to invent the meaning for himself. Maybe nobody else could do it. The only trouble was, he didn't know how.

"We meet again, Har-eese? I like that." Stefan had finished his coffee. He was peering at him. It was time to trade phone numbers. And then Harris had an idea. It took him by surprise and his heart began to pound.

"I didn't tell you my last name, Stefan."

Stefan blinked. "Your family name."

"Right. It's Schanberg. Har-ris Schan-berg." He spoke slowly, feeling slightly disoriented. He hadn't spoken that name aloud in fifteen years.

Stefan blinked again. His eyes dimmed. "That is German name."

"German-Jewish."

A thoughtful pause. "You are Jewish?"

Harris hesitated, heart thrumming, then nodded.

Stefan waited a moment. A slight smile appeared on his lips, still swollen from their play in the back room. He seemed to expand. Harris felt his forehead dampen. Had there been a change in the balance between them? Had he been assigned a new role? Or was he imagining all that? Stefan's smile widened. "You have money. Why you live in place like this?"

"I don't have a lot of money. I'm what they call a junior copywriter."

Stefan turned his head sideways, teasingly. "You are not telling truth. Come, I know."

Harris stared at him. A thousand years of European history floated between them in a poisonous cloud. He repeated his remark about being a junior copywriter. This time Stefan laughed shortly. Harris began to get angry. Maybe he should ask Stefan to leave.

"Well, doesn't matter, we have good time anyway." Stefan batted his eyes again, then made writing motions with his hand. "You give me telephone number, I call."

Harris, still irritated, got some paper. They both wrote, though he had to repress the urge to put down a fake number. He didn't want to see Stefan again. He had all those annoying habits, plus the terrible smell. To say nothing of the language barrier.

Stefan shook hands at the door and gave a slight, stiff bow. An old Polish custom, Harris thought. The Polish guards at Maidenek and Treblinka had probably given that same little bow. Stefan repeated his promise to call. Harris closed the door before he had quite finished speaking.

After Stefan left he sat down, feeling drained. Maybe he hadn't been fair. Maybe he'd misread the signs. Stefan had liked him, wanted to get together again. Why was he inventing obstacles? They'd had a good time in bed despite the aromas, and a second time might even be better.

He was like a snail without a shell. Before he tried those little tricks of revelation again he'd have to make sure his defenses were in place. He gave a hollow laugh. He would have to learn how to be a Jew.

He glanced at the clock. Just a little after nine. He could play for a while if he kept the soft pedal down. The desire to make music raced through him. Nothing could quiet his mind like music.

There was some Schumann on the rack of the little Sohmer upright in the middle room. He closed the window on the airshaft—

Mrs. Rothenburg downstairs was probably already in bed. Well, he couldn't help that. It was legal to play till 11:00 P.M.

He began the "Carnaval," skipping the crashy parts. Schumann had hurled himself into the Rhine and then gone crazy. He pictured the crag, something from a neo-Gothic painting, and the body falling. Of course, he'd been picked out at once. Had Clara alerted some friends? "Robert is going to throw himself into the river today. Can you be there? At half-past one? Afterwards we will have some wine."

He was playing badly, carelessly. In a few minutes Mrs. Rothenburg would start banging on the riser. But he went on with the Florestan section. Schumann had two selves, Eusebius and Florestan, sad and happy. Which was on top when he threw himself in the Rhine? An interesting point. Did Schumann wish he weren't manic-depressive? There was something wrong with everyone on earth—too short or too tall, too dark or too fat, too shy or too bold, too manic or too depressive. But—and this was the kicker—everybody was convinced that if they could just remedy *that one thing,* they'd be okay. "Get rid of my acne, doctor, and I'll be happy." You just needed one little fixer-upper.

But that was just another trick of the mind. Happiness didn't come, no matter how many jobs, diets, friends, hairpieces or lies you added to your life. Happiness didn't come at all; there were thousands of things in the way. You ended up in the Rhine one way or another.

A clang ran up the riser, making some of the piano strings vibrate. A surge of fury went through him. She was at it with the wrench. She disturbed people more than his piano did. He swung into the finale. The chords crashed, his breath came short, he started to sweat. In the distance he heard the wrench clanging, an anvil chorus, but he didn't let up, going fortissimo to the last cadenza. Then, for good measure, he did a glissando from bass to treble and back down. That would show her. He slammed down the lid and threw open the window to the shaft. "It's legal to play till eleven o'clock, you hear me?"

The clanging stopped. He heard a guttural exclamation. In Weimar, when everybody was imitating Liszt, they had to pass a city ordinance forbidding people to play with their windows open. "*It's legal!*" he roared, then closed the windows and left the room. He was trembling.

In the living room he checked the clock again, his mind racing. Hell, it wasn't too late to go out. He'd hit some of the bars. Or take a cruise up sexy Lexy. If he brought somebody home, he wouldn't get to work tomorrow either, but he didn't care. He certainly couldn't stay home, not now, not after that session with the Polish guy, he'd forgotten his name already.

He'd have to give himself a quick sponge bath at the kitchen sink. As he washed, using a cloth with a crocheted border—Gran had crocheted those borders onto every washrag in the house, make-work to keep her calm—he thought about the *Reader's Digest*. The night he came down from the farm, after the trouble with his mother, he'd picked up a copy at Grand Central. The *Digest* was his father's favorite shit-bowl reading, every morning on the crapper with Harry Emerson Fosdick and Norman Vincent Peale and J. P. McEvoy. He had picked up the copy to end his confusion. The *Digest* would speak to him in his father's voice, explain why he was having so much trouble, why his mother had cast him out. On the subway home he flipped through the little pages. The jokes and fillers gave him a homey feeling. It was all here, waiting. The wisdom that had made it the Little Giant, the repository of advice for millions. It was just a question of finding the right article. His father was always circling things for them to read.

But the magazine was full of sanctimonious crap. A cross between the Boy Scout Manual and the Book of Common Prayer. His father had been an idiot. He ripped the magazine in half and mashed it in the garbage with the potato peelings. How had he ever believed he could find something in there?

He was clean now—relatively clean—and began to dress. He'd take the Third Avenue el to the Blue Parrot. He liked the el, riding in the air. Last week he'd seen a stunning man in his car, an Italian who might have marched with Caesar in Gaul or fought with Pompey. A Roman warrior, flat and hard. He had stared and stared until the man got annoyed. Even then he sneaked glances at him.

A thrillionaire, that's what he was. He had been addicted to books, to knowledge—it was a family failing—but now he was addicted to thrills. That was the great thing about New York; you could find as many of those as you wanted. It was just a matter of going out and talking to people, not being shy, taking chances.

He found himself whistling the "Carnaval" finale on his way to the el—David against the Philistines. It didn't matter if he never went back to work. He hated his job anyway. He hated everything except what he was going to do now, tonight, and tomorrow and tomorrow. The *Reader's Digest* could stuff it. They could all stuff it. He'd gotten free of their rules and regulations. He was living a new kind of life, on a new kind of planet. He was a thrillionaire.

14

MAG

The Chickens

Mother's farmhouse was the safest, most beautiful spot on earth. And the heart of the farmhouse was the kitchen. Mag looked around while giving Lily—named after Gran—her one-o'clock formula. The room was painted yellow, the color of sunshine, and there were chintz half-curtains at each window. The stove was huge—four gas burners plus a wood-burning extension, cast-iron, with disks you could lift with a tooth-like prong. Mother used the wood-burner all winter, filling it with pea coal, claiming it cooked the food and warmed the whole house for half the price of running the furnace.

Lily had stopped feeding, was playing around with the nipple. Mag extracted it, watching for signs that Lily was going to whoopse. Roland was upstairs napping, she hoped, though it was possible he was tearing off bits of his grandmother's flowered wall-paper. He liked the taste of glue.

Her eye went to the desk at the window which Francis Grecky had made for Mother when he was still coming around. It was full of books and papers, some of them sticking out of half-closed drawers, all to do with Mother's dissertation. She was fifty and getting a Ph.D. in psychology. It was amazing. She had chosen that over Francis Grecky, said he didn't suit her, she had other fish to fry. Of course, he'd found someone else right away. The wonder was that he had hung around so long, hoping Mother would change her mind. Obviously he didn't know her very well.

Lily was showing signs of sleepiness so she took her into the dining room and settled her on the couch in the bay window, covering her with one of Gran's afghans. Some gifted writer could tell the story of the family in those afghans. Unfortunately, that wouldn't be Mother. She'd given up writing along with Francis. Said it didn't pay and was just asking for rejection. Shortly after that, she'd taken up residence at the University of California, Riverside, a long way to go for her course work, but all the universities around here had turned her down because of her age.

Mother should be back from Poughkeepsie any minute. Some of the chickens, at the broiler stage, eight to ten weeks, had keeled over last night. They'd been discovered this morning, on the early egg-collecting trip. Mother had brought one of the corpses inside to show Roland. "See the swelling, the discharge from the nostrils?" She had pushed the dead animal in Roland's face. "I have to go to the chicken doctor to find out what killed it."

Roland had made a face—fascinated and horrified. "The chicken doctor?"

"Yes. All he does is look at chickens all day, then he makes a diagnosis."

Mag remembered that little trick, dropping in big words so the child would learn. But it didn't work with Roland. He didn't ask what "diagnosis" meant, unlike Harris, who used to eat up big words with a runcible spoon—that was another one. Then Mother had turned to her. "If I don't find out what's wrong, I could lose the whole brood. There's a lot of distressed breathing out there."

Well, there was a lot of distressed breathing in here too, though Mother chose to overlook it. In her own opinion, it would be good riddance if the chickens died. They were endless trouble. Mother had always said she hated chickens and here she was practically sleeping with them. Last time she had visited the farm, chicks were peeping in a cardboard box under a brooder lamp in Mother's room. Yes, upstairs next to her bed. Mother had said she wanted to keep an eye on them. And now, Saturday, her own first full day here, when Mother should have been spending time with her and Roland and Lily, she was off to Poughkeepsie.

But that wasn't all. Before leaving this morning, Mother had popped the dead chickens, the diseased ones, into the freezer, discharge, swelling and all. It would be just like her to serve them for dinner one night without saying anything. She'd have to keep her eyes open. She wasn't going to let Roland eat diseased chickens, no matter what.

She really didn't want to be alone this morning; she'd had a bad night. But obviously the chickens came first. Suddenly her irritation swelled into anger. Mother still didn't believe that her problems were on a par with anyone else's. Not even the chickens'. Some things never changed.

No, that was unfair. When she'd called two days ago, telling everything, breaking down and weeping, Mother had declared, "Come right away. Bring the children. I'll pay the airfare." That's what she'd wanted to hear, and now she was at the farm, in this beautiful land of barns and creeks and hills, everything turning gold in October, and Mother was doing all she could to help. And she would help—that Mag knew. Mother might be peculiar, but when you needed her she was there.

She observed Lily asleep. A large baby, as Roland had been. The pediatrician had said they were the biggest children he'd ever seen. Suppose Lily grew up to be impossibly tall? She recalled her own embarrassments, the humiliation of towering over a boy whose head reached her shoulders, a boy who pumped her around the dance floor like she was the Trylon and he was the Perisphere. Once, at a high school dance, one of them had asked, "Hey, how's the atmosphere up there? Thin?" She still couldn't think about it without a shudder. Hurt—that's what the teenage years were, though the pain didn't end there necessarily. But at least if you were *pretty* and the *right height*—she italicized the phrases in her mind—you might have a good time. She had expressed her fears about Lily's future size to Howie, but he laughed. "What're you worrying about? It's years away." But that was her nature. She worried. When she was pregnant the second time, she had prayed it wouldn't be a girl for this very reason. Yet how thrilled she had been when they told her. A girl! She had immediately envisioned the chain of women lengthening, holding hands across the centuries. This Lily's great-grandmother had been a daughter of the

Confederacy. A great-great-grandmother on the other side had been a member of the lesser German nobility. A proud heritage no matter what Harris thought about it all. Years ago she had written him that peace of mind depended on what you chose to remember. She chose to remember good things. He'd replied, in that superior way of his, that forgetting was a form of immorality in their case. He'd missed the point, of course. She didn't forget; she just didn't dwell on certain things.

She went back to the kitchen, keeping an ear out for Roland. No little feet moving up there. She went to the fridge and removed the platter of chicken salad she had made for lunch when Mother returned. She examined it, then smelled it. All she could smell was the curry and mayonnaise. You don't suppose there were diseased chickens in the freezer prior to this morning? She would have it out with Mother; this couldn't continue.

She set the table in the dining room for lunch, glancing at the papers on the desk from time to time. She knew about Mother's dissertation; she was collecting the data right here in an elementary school. "The Masculinity of Boys as Related to Family Variables." Mother had cooked up a questionnaire with a scale of masculinity, one to ten, depending on whether the boy liked sports, indoor games, girls' games, and so forth. Then she had designed another questionnaire, which she applied to the parents. All this had been approved by her adviser at the University of California. She was very excited by the results, claiming she had discovered some new factors in the relationship between boys and their fathers, factors affecting identity, self-image, sexual tastes.

Well, there was no question where her interest in that abnormal subject had come from. Even though Mother hadn't seen Harris for several years, communicated with him only by cards at Christmas and on his birthday, he was still with her. He would always be with her. He was even dictating the subject of her Ph.D.

Not that she resented it, despite an occasional twinge of jealousy. All that was behind her. She knew how Mother felt about them both. Mother had chosen her, and her children, over Harris. There was a residue of love—no mother could avoid that—but Harris had forfeited his place. He was in the wrong and had made no effort to apologize. But of course he was incredibly selfish; all those people were.

She was finished setting the table, using the good china, the Haviland, which Mother would probably object to. Well, it was a special day, wasn't it? To have her and Roland and Lily here with her? What better way to mark it than to use the finest china, a family heirloom, and eat in style?

Harris had been arrested for indecent behavior in Central Park two years ago. But she wasn't surprised—that was all part of it. He had called Uncle Mark from the police station, turning to the family he despised when he got in trouble. Uncle Mark had gotten him out with an expensive lawyer and (probably) some bribes. He had been sworn to secrecy, of course, but he had told Sister, and it hadn't taken long to work its way back to Mother. She had been terribly upset, actually calling Baltimore during the day, when rates were high. It had taken all her own cleverness and authority to convince Mother this new escapade was not her fault. She had done all she could, she had been a good mother, this was Harris's responsibility, etc., etc. But she had only partly succeeded. She could hear the old sorrow in Mother's voice, the endless self-blame. It had taken all her own will power not to make odious comparisons about Mother's emotional investment in her—but she had resisted the impulse. She was beyond that pettiness, thank heavens. Besides, she understood motherhood now.

She heard a car in the driveway. Now they could continue their discussions. She had some new ideas, the product of her sleepless night. But it wasn't Mother; it was Loretta Meade in her beat-up Ford station wagon. She was carrying something. Mag went to the front door.

"Oh, Mag." Loretta's voice was bony, like her. "We had so many grapes we didn't know what to do with them. Your mother said you'd be here, so . . ."

Mag ushered her into the parlor, taking the bundle—it must have weighed ten pounds.

"Your mother makes grape juice. I just hope she hasn't started with her own grapes."

"I don't think she has. She went to Poughkeepsie, to the agricultural station."

"Oh, more chicken troubles. We've been having trouble with the lambs this year."

Loretta sat down. "I'll just stay a minute." She pulled out her holder and cigarettes. They talked about Roland and Lily for a bit. Mag hoped their voices wouldn't wake them up. She liked Loretta, who lived with a woman doctor named Carlene. Loretta was wonderfully straightforward. She looked after the house and garden and sheep while Carlene did her doctoring in Hudson. When she first met them, she had mentioned to Mother quite casually that the two women must be in an unnatural relationship. Not that she disapproved, really, since they had such a beautiful house and hundreds of friends around here who accepted them. But Mother had contradicted her. Said it was impossible. Insisted so emphatically that Mag had let the subject drop. Sometimes she didn't understand Mother at all.

"You know," Loretta said in her hard, enthusiastic voice, "we just love your mother. Everybody around here does."

Mag nodded. The social success that had eluded Mother for so long had finally arrived. Something had changed in her—some ease or confidence had been released. When Howie and Roland were here—the whole Snepp family—Mother ferried them around like trophies. But Mag had sensed another, more subtle message under that. Mother was showing off her own friends to them, proving that her awful childhood in Texas had been erased. Mag didn't know which thrilled her more—being approved after all these years or seeing Mother's pride in herself.

"The other day," Loretta went on, "we had a party and your mother couldn't come, she had to work on her dissertation. I can't tell you how many people asked for her."

Mother was no longer desperate, Mag thought. Desperation was something people could smell, then they turned away. Social success was like a loan from a bank—you only got it when you didn't need it.

"She's such an unusual person." Loretta stabbed the air with her cigarette holder. "Can you imagine getting a Ph.D. at her age?"

"Oh, I know, we're all so proud of her."

And it was true. She'd resented Mother's bookishness for years, but now she bragged about it to her friends in Baltimore. "My mother is simply brilliant; wait till you meet her."

After Loretta left, making her promise to visit with the children tomorrow, Mag recalled Caroline Elliott in New Rochelle. She used to come home from school and find Mother and Mrs. Elliott side by side on the couch, the curtains drawn, the room reeking of Shalimar. They were having tea—tea that went on for hours. Mother had always made close friends with a certain kind of woman. Not that Loretta and Mrs. Elliott were similar. It was just that . . .

The front door flew open. "Mycoplasmosis!" Mother yelled. She tapped her pocketbook. "I've got the cure right here!"

Mag gave a little cry of delight. Some women got vaguer with age, but Mother had become more definite. Her outline had hardened. Maybe it was giving up Francis or working on her Ph.D. or learning to live alone, but now she bore only a slight resemblance to her old self.

"Everything all right?" Mother was seized with enthusiasm. "Oh, honey"—she pulled Mag into a hug—"I thought about you all the way there and all the way back. I've got some wonderful ideas."

"Really?"

"Yes." Mother headed into the kitchen, shedding her disreputable old car coat as she went. "I thought it might be aspergillosis but I was wrong." Mag drifted after her. "It was the discharge that gave it away. It's also called CRI—chronic respiratory disease. I have to go right out and put the aureomycin in the feed."

"You're going to do that now? I have lunch ready."

"I have to kill the sick ones too. But that can wait."

That reminded her. "Are you going to eat those sick chickens?"

Mother's eyes danced around. "I'll boil them a good long time."

The irritation that had disappeared during Loretta's visit returned. "Well, I'm not going to eat them. I certainly don't want Roland to eat them."

Mother was at the door, waving her hand. The chickens were not going to waste, and that was that. She darted out to the yard, her bag still in her hand. Mag watched her disappear behind the henhouse, then shook her head and started to put lunch on the table. If Mother had married Francis Grecky, she wouldn't be like this.

Not that Francis Grecky was entirely suitable—he certainly couldn't compare with Daddy—and Mother would never have gone back to graduate school if she'd married him. Still, there would have been advantages. It was so hard to balance the pros and cons. She did admire Mother, as she'd told Loretta, but there was the other strain, the oddness. She'd always wanted a mother who would be like the other mothers.

Well, that was only partly true too. In a way, she'd been impressed with Mother's abilities, the way she could solve quadratic equations with a flick of a pencil. How many mothers could explain sine and cosine, to say nothing of *Moby Dick?*

Her thoughts moved on. Francis Grecky had been devoted to Mother, starstruck in a way. Mag had often wondered how it had been in bed—better than with Daddy?—but Mother had been outraged when she asked. "What a question, Mag. Don't you have any inhibitions at all?" Well, she didn't, not where sex was concerned. She had a perfectly healthy curiosity. Another of Mother's peculiarities—she refused to discuss sex. And now Francis was gone for good, married to a younger woman, always a lurking danger with a man his age. And Mother had no regrets, or so she said.

Mag recalled her thoughts of last night. She had lain awake for hours, still strung out from the plane trip, from managing the children by herself. She'd had a slight revelation in the dark. She had faced life as if it were a test in geometry. If you studied, you got a good grade. Of course, there were different courses and subjects in Life—parenting, sex, husband, social life. But your grade depended on the usual things—how hard you studied, how you prepared for the final. But last night in the dark, the outside air brimming with the calls of peepers, she had understood that this notion was warped and childish. Nobody got an A in Life, it was a contradiction in terms. Why had it taken her so long to see that?

Now, seeing Mother round the corner of the henhouse, Mag

realized that her foolish idealism, her delusion of perfectibility, had come from Mother. Mother's optimism, which was a form of control, had hidden the truth. It had preserved them both in error. And the saddest part was that if she tried to explain it all to Mother now, her words would be dismissed with a wave of the hand.

The salad was delicious, and though Mag inspected it for disease again, she didn't find anything. She also tried to give Mother her full attention while keeping an ear tuned for Roland and Lily.

The essential point, Mother said, was to see that Howie's checks were covered. If they weren't, if the brokerage house made good on its threats, Howie could go to jail. That would be an indelible stain on his future and the future of the children.

Mag nodded. Howie couldn't go to jail. Neither of them would ever live it down.

"Now you must remember, honey, he hasn't committed a crime, only been guilty of bad judgment. If the funds are restored to Harmon Trask, there will be no record and you can forget it." Mother paused. "If you want to."

That was a new, ominous note. She knew what was on Mother's mind—divorce. Sometimes she thought Mother had been trying to break them up since the day they got engaged. But Howie hadn't committed a crime, as Mother had just pointed out. He had simply covered a margin call with a bad check. When they sold him out, the uranium stocks being almost worthless, he still owed Harmon Trask some money. That had resulted in another bad check. There had also been some borrowing from friends. The catch, the unthinkable part, was that Mrs. Dexter Trask, Jr., was the daughter-in-law of a senior partner in Harmon Trask as well as a moving spirit in the McHenry Club, and her own sponsor. There could easily be a leak. Ten thousand dollars was a lot of money. And Mag knew about leaks, how much damage they could do.

"Everybody's been speculating in uranium stocks, Mother," she temporized. "The people at Howie's office just talked him into it." She shouldn't be making excuses, but she couldn't help herself.

"You know, he asked me about it, Mag. I told him by no means. He should stay with the blue chips."

She remembered the conversation. Mother read the *Wall Street Journal* every day, cover to cover. She was a genius at investing. But Howie had ridiculed her. "You're too conservative, Margaret." He'd laughed, hooting down her further objections. "I got no time for Du Pont to hit a hundred."

"Mark my words, Du Pont will hit a hundred before those uranium stocks hit ten." But Howie hadn't paid attention. And now he owed a small fortune, his credit was gone and disgrace was just around the corner. Her head started to pound. She put down her fork and pressed her fingers to her temple. Some old pain had started up there. She'd kill herself before she let them kick her out of the McHenry Club.

Mother continued, ignoring the gesture. But wasn't that Mother's way? Will power was all. "I was thinking about it in the car, Mag. You have to have your own career, independent of Howie. No matter what happens, you have to be able to look after yourself and the children."

Her glance went to Lily on the sofa. How could she have a career with two small children? But Mother read her mind. "There are ways," she said.

She began to talk about nurseries, day-care centers, financial assistance, including some from her. She talked about stick-to-itiveness. How many times had Mag heard that hateful word? It had been applied to everything in her life—field hockey, algebra, Regents exams, finishing *Lorna Doone*. However, it did not apply to her marriage. Stick-to-itiveness was not required there. Just the opposite, apparently. She began to feel trapped. What kind of career could she have? Her real career was her family.

"You can't control what Howie does. You can only control yourself and the children."

There it was again. On her honeymoon, when she learned how much fun a couple could have, she had thought she was free of Mother's instructions forever. But she'd been wrong.

"I came across something in yesterday's *Wall Street Journal*." Mother got up and went to the desk, in the kitchen. Mag watched her rummage around in a drawer crammed with junk. Mother was a terrible slob except in her mind.

The clip was headed "Post-War Children Lack Reading Skills," with the subhead "Programs Required to Offset Influence of TV. Will Tomorrow's Office Workers Be Illiterate?"

Mag read the article at the table. It sounded hopeless. Was she supposed to become some kind of reading expert? She had planned to be a phys. ed. major until she switched to business.

She put down the clip. "That's awful. I don't want to teach reading."

"It will make you independent."

There it was again. The strategy to make her divorce Howie. Mother had never liked him, that was the trouble. She recalled their early meetings in New Rochelle, after Daddy died. Howie had joshed and joked, gotten Mother out of her depression when no one else could, but he had never earned her whole-hearted approval. And Mag knew why. Howie wasn't peculiar enough for her. Wasn't odd or eccentric or queer. He was a normal man. Mother had never felt comfortable with normal people.

"You could check the University of Maryland. Or Johns Hopkins. Or even Georgetown. Some of them must give M.A.'s in reading education. If you make up your mind, you can do it."

How could she drive to a university that was miles away? And look after the house and the children? When Mother went for her Ph.D. courses, she had picked up and moved right to a dorm on the campus in Riverside.

Lily stirred in her sleep. Mag got up and felt her. She stood looking out the bay window, at the herd in the pasture across the way, as Mother began to clear the table. "I can't do it," she said.

"Of course you can. You'd be a wonderful teacher. You love children."

"It would be the end of my marriage. I might as well get a divorce right now."

"Why?" Mag knew that look—the knitting of the brows, the fixing of the dark eyes. Now it struck her as slightly faked. Mother wasn't really worried; she was just being sly.

"Why? Because Howie wouldn't stand for my supporting the family. It would undermine his self-respect. That's the way men are."

"But you wouldn't be supporting the family. You'd be doing it as insurance. In case he loses his job."

"If we pay the ten thousand dollars he owes, he won't lose his job. He won't lose anything."

Mother hadn't said anything about contributing the money. She was willing to pay for more education, but was she willing to keep their marriage going?

"I'm only saying, Mag, you should be prepared for the worst."

"I'm always prepared for the worst! I've been prepared for it all my life!" She didn't mean to flare up, but she couldn't help it. It sounded like Mother wanted her marriage to fail.

The argument had woken up Roland. She went to the foot of the stairs and called, telling him to wash his face and come down. A low whine floated past her. She'd have to go up. She wondered if the price of Howie's bail-out was her cooperation in this new plan. A career as a reading teacher. It wouldn't surprise her; she'd never gotten something for nothing from Mother. Harris, of course, always got whatever he needed. When it was learned, after much delay, that the judge who dismissed his sex crime had stipulated that he get psychiatric treatment, Mother had actually funneled the money to him through Uncle Mark. That, besides repaying Uncle Mark for the legal fees and everything else. All without a thank you from Harris, of course, who should have known where the money was coming from. And with no strings attached. But here she was, condemned to years of slavery because Howie wrote a few bad checks.

Upstairs, Roland was standing at the wash basin playing with the faucets. She scrubbed his face, especially the gunk in the corners of his eyes, holding him tight. He started to howl. "Stop it this instant." She gave him a shake. "Do you have to wee-wee?"

"Yes."

She watched the thing while it spouted. How small it was, yet it would earn—had already earned—extra amounts of attention for its owner. Mother was always saying, "Youth must be served," but she really meant, "Boys must be served."

He had finished. He was aiming it around the bathroom now. She reached down and tucked it in his pants.

"Ouch!" He let out a scream. "You hurt my wee-wee."

"No, I didn't. Hurry up."

"I can't."

Insisting on his privileges even now. Maybe he'd tell Gramaw she had hurt him, show his little thing to prove it. Gramaw might offer to kiss it and make it well. She wouldn't put it past her.

She'd really like to lie down, but she couldn't. She had to watch Roland. She didn't want him in the yard while Mother was hatcheting diseased chickens. The yard would be full of blood and feathers, and he'd have nightmares tonight. She opened the medicine cabinet and took out the Empirin bottle. Her life had been relatively simple, and now it was full of complications.

She made Roland sit in the kitchen with a coloring book while she washed the lunch dishes. She caught glimpses of Mother outside catching and trussing the offending chickens. As she put on the rubber gloves she recalled something Mother had said about Howie: "He has no guilt." A form of disapproval, a special deficiency. As if he had no brains or no neck. *No guilt.* What was so wonderful about guilt? Look what guilt had done to this family. She'd never have married Howie if he'd been the remorseful type, moping around, giving in to moods, blaming himself for every little thing. That's why he was fun to be with, because he never worried about right and wrong. Maybe he'd overdone it sometimes. Once he had siphoned gas out of a car parked near them, just enough to get them to a service station. "They'll never miss it," was his comment, and though she had her doubts, she had gone along. And he had sold their power mower to a neighbor, knowing it was on the verge of stopping forever. She'd had her doubts about that too, bigger ones, but Howie had joked about "buyer beware." She'd made the mistake of discussing these episodes with Mother, also a few others, and Mother had instantly made up her mind. "He's a sociopath; he has no guilt." But her verdict was wrong. Most American men would do anything they could get away with.

She recalled how Daddy had hated that tight, judgmental side of Mother. He wouldn't have disapproved of Howie, not for a minute. He knew about business. His own father had been a buccaneer, a robber baron. God knows how many bad checks he'd written. That's how Grandpa had made his fortune—cheating everybody.

She was beginning to feel better. Mother was going to give them the money; she was just stalling. Maybe she'd promise to go back to school, then renege after a semester. Eventually it would be forgotten. Mother, despite her old favoritism, now preferred *her*—she had to remember that, not let old rivalries cloud her judgment. Harris was gone, swallowed up in his perversions. She didn't have to act as if they were battling for the last scrap of meat or slice of pie. She was here with her children, the focus and center of Mother's attention. Howie, her husband, was at home waiting. What choice did Mother have except to help?

The phone rang. Her heart skipped. It was probably Howie. She would have to make a decision. She stripped off one rubber glove and went into the dining room.

"Is that you, honeybunch?"

The familiar voice was a little forced. She knew every gradation. "It's me."

"How's it goin'?"

"We're all fine." She saw no reason to reassure him yet. "We love it here."

"I know you do. Heck, I do too. How's Margaret?"

"She's fine. She's outside killing chickens."

He let out a whoop. "Isn't she something? Boy!"

She let a pause develop. Then, her voice softening, she said, "How are things down there?"

He made a smacking noise. She wasn't sure what that meant. "I miss you and the kids."

"You do?"

"Sure. When you comin' home?"

"I need some more time to think."

"If you want me to come up there . . ." He trailed off. He hadn't said a word about their troubles. But he wouldn't. He would pretend, or wait. She wasn't sure how much of that was pride or stubbornness or strategy.

"You're not doing anything foolish, are you?" She had a vision of him writing more checks.

He hooted. "You mean am I going out with any blondes?"

"That's not what I mean."

"Well, I'm just doin' my business."

She let another pause develop. "Mother says she'll . . . um, help us."

"She did?" She heard the relief under the jauntiness. "All of it?"

She took a deep breath. She had committed herself to both of them. Again, she felt the trap closing. "Yes, all of it."

"Shoot, I knew she would. She doesn't blame a guy for trying."

After hanging up she went outside to tell Mother about the call. Roland was already there. He had slipped out while she was on the phone. Mother was in her work shirt and filthy slacks, demonstrating how she intended to kill the chickens. A bloody plank with screw eyes at either end was on the ground. Old pin feathers were stuck in the dried blood. Next to the plank were six trussed chickens, blinking rapidly. The cords around their necks and legs would be passed through the screw eyes on the plank. That would keep them from jerking around and spattering blood when their heads were lopped off. Roland was scootched down, investigating this. In another minute she would yank him away. "That was Howie on the phone."

Mother glanced up, a faint nod.

"He wants me to come home, but I said I wasn't ready."

The faintest of nods again.

"I didn't mention the other business. About going to school." Mother was waiting for her surrender. "I'll try it."

"Just try it, honey, that's all I ask."

"And you'll help us out?"

A rush of triumphant affection swept over Mother's face. "Of course I'll help you."

Mag really wanted to say more, to express her doubts, her resentments, the fact that Mother had ignored her truest feelings, her relationship to Howie. But she let it pass. What was the use? Mother would never acknowledge her own secret motives. And she had gotten what she wanted—the ten thousand dollars—hadn't she?

"Would you boil some water, honey? Use the big Revere pot. I can dip the whole chicken."

"I don't want Roland to stay here."

Roland let out a squall and rushed to his grandmother. "I'll watch him," she said.

"He shouldn't see this."

Mother waved, a grand and careless gesture. "Relax, Max."

Against her better judgment Mag went inside. She stayed in the kitchen as the water heated in the Revere pot. Plucking the chickens was almost as grisly as killing them. She glanced out the window. Roland was squatted down again, following Gramaw's pointing finger as she explained what was going to happen. Mag remembered that finger—it used to run under the line of print in her Dick-and-Jane reader, pulling, insisting, intimidating. If the finger went backwards, started over, that meant she had made a mistake. Now it was pointing out how the chickens were going to be executed. Somehow, she wasn't exactly sure why, there was a close resemblance between the two operations.

She wondered if Roland would come to share Howie's casual view of right and wrong. Did you inherit such things or were they trained into you? The former, she suspected. Howie's mother had been a model of rectitude—head of the WCTU chapter in Omaha until her death. His father, despite a taste for liquor, had earned a reputation as an honest dealer in cars. They had raised their sons strictly. But in Howie's case all that training hadn't taken root. Something deeper had intervened. Would Roland turn out to have an easy conscience too?

The water had come to a boil. She managed to carry the heavy pot outside and set it near the plank. One chicken was corded in, blinking and twisting its scrawny neck. Mother had the hatchet in her hand. "Let's go down and look for fishies in the stream," she said to Roland.

"I wanta watch Gramaw kill another chiskin."

She looked around. There was already one headless corpse on the grass. She hadn't noticed.

Mother lifted the hatchet, gasped, aimed and brought it down with a resounding thlunk. The head was severed; the little body thrashed around. "How was that?" Mother turned and smiled at both of them. Mag stepped back. Roland had a strange expression on his face. It struck her that Mother, with her tomahawk and coarse silver-gray hair and beige skin, looked like a Comanche Indian on the warpath. All she needed was a band around her head.

"That's it!" She grabbed Roland and dragged him away in spite of his caterwauling. She didn't stop until they were screened from the butchery by a stand of sassafras. Still, they could hear Mother's cries of triumph, the hatchet thlunking, the water splashing. She covered her ears. Years ago, when she was growing up, she thought she had strayed into the wrong family. She had married Howard Snepp hoping to be reborn into the right one. But that hope had been tarnished too. The feeling of being trapped returned again, the third time today. Neither Mother's way nor Howie's was exactly right for her. There would have to be another way, if only she could find it.

She cast her mind back over the years. There had been the nightmare of summer camp, the sorrows of the sorority, Daddy's early death, Aunt Hattie's bitterness, her brother's disgrace. Through it, behind it all, had been her mother's peculiarity. Mother had survived by denying all the loss, burying the sadness. But that was a shallow view of things. Mag didn't want to forget; she wanted to include everything. She wanted to combine all the people in her past, the lives and deaths, the love and imperfection and pathology. She didn't want to deny any of it. She would become strong only by admitting and accepting all of it.

Roland was pulling at her. She yanked him around sharply. Her eyes were filling with tears. No one could give her what she needed. Not Howie, not Mother, no one. She would have to find it herself. Could she do it? She didn't know. It would mean reversing and undoing half the things she had trained herself to be.

She heard the hatchet hit the plank again. Another little death. She had to go inside to check on Lily. She dragged Roland past the killing ground. Five tiny corpses lay on the grass. The air was dim with feathers. Several scrawny-looking cats had turned up out of nowhere. The hatchet swung again. *"Place de la Guillotine!"* Mother sang out.

Roland squealed with delight as they went past. He loved to see Gramaw acting weird. He might never forget this scene. She clutched him more firmly.

As soon as Mother gave her the money she'd go home. She had a lot to do. Things would have to change with Howie. Maybe she wouldn't sacrifice herself so much. Maybe she'd stop modeling herself on the other wives—on Muffie Trask, for example. Maybe she'd even resign from the McHenry Club. That was Phi Gamma all over again.

She had been repressing her powers ever since she turned adolescent, always hoping to be popular. But why did she have to be popular? Why did she have to be just like everybody else? She had hungered and thirsted to be ordinary, the American disease, but she wasn't ordinary. She was uniquely herself. She could feel something new surging through her. She took a deep breath.

She looked out the kitchen window, still holding tight to Roland. Mother was stooped over the pot, a headless chicken in one hand. She was pulling out the pin feathers. Mag stood rooted. A remarkable woman but so peculiar. It was hard to believe she was really her daughter. And yet she had inherited something from Mother. Something hard and enduring and implacable.

15

HARRIS
The Dinner

Patrick was in a tizzy; the cornbread hadn't risen. Harris got up from the butterfly chair, where he was working on a manuscript, and went to the kitchen. Patrick, his face brick-red, threw the dish towel on the floor. "That oven's no good, how many times do I have to tell you?"

"That cornbread looks perfectly fine to me."

Patrick's face, square and granitic like that of the Old Man of the Mountain, which they had seen a few summers ago, was twisted in pain. "I can't make turkey stuffing with that."

Harris pressed his thumb on the cornbread. It sprang back. "What's the difference if it's heavy?"

Patrick slammed a cupboard door. Obviously it made a big difference. Harris glared back, then turned on his heel. The scene was a fake. Patrick was in a tizzy because Mag and his mother were coming. He wanted the turkey dinner to be perfect. His anxiety shouldn't be interfered with.

Back in the living room he heard pans being banged around in the kitchen. Another batch of cornbread no doubt. What was he supposed to do? How could he calm down Patrick when he himself was in orbit? He hadn't seen his mother for seven years.

Patrick's grim face appeared in the doorway. "If we're going to have fresh cranberry sauce, you can fucking well pick out the stems."

Harris sighed and put down the manuscript a second time. Editing was the most soothing thing he knew. He'd brought the piece home yesterday with the intention of working on it in the hours before his mother and Mag arrived. Editing was like basket weaving or stringing beads. Utterly soothing. And he did it well. When a sentence was just right it gave off a low chime in his ear, probably like the sound Alice B. Toklas heard when she first met Gertrude Stein, Pablo Picasso and Alfred North Whitehead.

The kitchen was too hot and Patrick was hopping around, so Harris brought the cranberries back to the living room. Mag had suggested the dinner over the phone from Philadelphia last month. "Mother would appreciate it a whole lot, Harris." There was something in her voice that had made him agree. It was time to make up. In seven years all the cells in both bodies had died and been replaced.

He pawed through the berries looking for stems. Mag and Patrick had met a few times and the vibes had ranged from neutral to positive. Harris permitted himself a small chuckle. Patrick couldn't be controlled. At first Mag had been offended, then she had come around. There was something in her that responded to honesty nowadays.

"Well, Howie comes to see us every other weekend," Mag had remarked in the restaurant on Waverly Place where they had gone for Mexican food, everybody's favorite, the first time. "We haven't given up on our marriage; we're just postponing a final decision while I get my degree."

"Does that mean you don't have sex anymore?" Patrick had looked at her calmly, unswervingly, his brown eyes full of sincere curiosity.

Mag had become outraged. "That's an extremely personal question! I hardly know you!" Her fair skin had mottled, and she had turned to her brother, expecting help.

But Patrick wasn't fazed. "It seemed logical to me. Don't we want to know each other?"

Harris, instead of giving his sister support, had laughed. He couldn't help it. It was the kind of question Patrick always asked. Their first time together Patrick had asked dozens of things like that. He had started to walk out several times, but each time Patrick had said, "I bet you've been walking out on questions like that all your life." So he had stayed. That had been more than three years ago, not long after his trouble with the police, when he was still seeing Dr. Fike. Before Mag had gotten her degree in remedial reading and started teaching in the Philadelphia school system.

"If the cranberry sauce is going to chill, we'd better cook it right now." Patrick was in the doorway again. He really looked distraught.

Harris gave the cranberries a last paw-through and handed them over. "We should have done this last night," he remarked.

"Next time your mother comes we'll take her out," Patrick said.

Harris looked around the room. It was quite different from his old place on Second Avenue. That had been neat as a pin; this was in a state of disorder. Patrick's books and papers—he worked at a high school in Ridgefield, New Jersey—were scattered all around. Slippers, sandals, huaraches, full ashtrays, neckties, stacks of coins. Last week they had seen a mouse threading its way from the kitchen to the radiator by the front window. Now there was a saucer with cheese along the route. In the town near Galveston where Patrick had been raised, field mice always came inside for winter. "They're cute," he said. "Their eyes sit on top of their heads like raisins." Harris wasn't sure city mice were all that cute, but the saucer stayed. You could see little tooth marks in the cheese.

He'd better start cleaning up. They'd be here in less than two hours. Strange how he'd gotten used to living in a midden. Tidying up had been a bad habit for so many years, but he had tried to tidy up the wrong things. Patrick had pointed that out early on. "Oh, leave it," he'd say, again and again. And gradually Harris had learned to leave it. The dirty clothes heaped on the floor of the closet. The sneakers and odd socks under the bed. The toilet paper that gave out before a replacement had been brought in so that Kleenex had to be used and once, God help them, wet newspaper. The shelves, besides being full of books, were weighted with hideous curios—scraps of wood, shells, rocks, rotting pine cones—each with significance only for them. The apartment, he thought now, was like a display case. Anyone might walk in and make a hundred shrewd guesses about their life together, starting with the three-quarter bed ("princess-size," Patrick said) in the next room. His mother would have no trouble picking up the signals. She would see his life with Patrick with X-ray eyes, though of course she'd gotten a full briefing from Mag these last few years. A little zing of nervousness went through him. He didn't want his mother here, passing judgment. At the same time the thought of seeing her gave him an almost throttling joy. Seven years was a long time. They had talked on the phone once or twice each year, and of course there were the cards with brief notes, but he had been deprived of the sight of her, the messages in her movements, the touch of her hands. Sometimes the deprivation had been unbearable—he thought he would rush up to the farm and beg her to forgive him—but he had never given in. He was in the right. She would have to come around. And today was the day.

He'd been cleaning for a while when Patrick looked in. He seemed calmer. "It's going to be all right," he said. "I mixed some biscuit dough with the cornbread."

Harris nodded. He couldn't blame Patrick for being tense. Tension was filling the apartment, throbbing all around. It had been with them from the moment they got out of bed this morning. It wouldn't be their usual happy Saturday.

They had met one morning on the checkout line at the Gristede's on Bleecker Street, which was like a sitcom except they had gotten into an argument. He had placed his cart incorrectly, at an angle, and a man his own age had yelled, "No jumping the line!" then smashed his cart into Harris's. Several times, in a fury. Harris, quietly angry, went to the back of the line, but when he left the store, the man was waiting for him on the sidewalk. He was apologetic without actually apologizing. He furrowed his brow, nodded, shifted his packages and spoke about fairness. Fairness was very important to him. He walked along with Harris and invited him to his apartment, which was not far away, at the corner of Christopher. "Don't worry about your stuff," the stranger said. "We'll just put it in the icebox with mine and have a cup of coffee."

Harris, still angry, refused, but he had to walk in that direction and the stranger kept talking. He had been in New York only a few months. He was from Texas originally but had spent the last ten years in San Francisco. Now he was teaching high school English in New Jersey. As Harris listened, his anger waned. Patrick McClellan—that was his name—had an odd appeal. There was some kind of protective device missing. Harris found himself smiling, then opening up a little.

"Here we are," Patrick McClellan had said at the doorway to his walk-up. "I have Martinson's, that's the best."

Harris had doubts about the coffee and the offer, but followed him upstairs. The place was barely furnished. They sat on a canvas cot that served as sofa and bed. He had the impression that Patrick McClellan's life, despite the graceful talk, was in no better shape than his own. He had lost his job at Tweedy-Lord. He was doing office temp work, typing statistics. His mother, he knew, was paying for his visits to Dr. Fike, but he hadn't been able to acknowledge her help. It would have given her the upper hand all over again—another problem he had to work out with his shrink. As Patrick moved around his apartment Harris saw that he was handsome in a lean, hollow-cheeked, backwoods way. Daniel Boone at the Cumberland Gap. Harris felt a familiar yearning in his gut.

Before the coffee was ready they were kissing, and after a few sips they had their clothes off. Patrick's body matched his face—ridged and bony. A vee of black hair ringed his clavicle, but below that his pectorals were staring-white. It was the body, Harris reflected later, that now suited his tastes. He had refined them over the years, moving from the bulgy classicism of Willie Mortimer to the stringy muscularity of the American frontiersman. They had achieved orgasm lightly, easily, and afterward Patrick had spread the luminous goo over both chests and tummies. Harris wanted to get up and wash almost immediately, but Patrick had held him down. "Oh, leave it," he'd said—the first of hundreds of times he was to issue that instruction. Harris left it.

Then the questions had started. Each time, as Harris started to duck or lie or remove himself physically, Patrick had made his crack about walking out. He seemed to know all about Harris right off. Harris wondered if it was because Patrick came from Texas, like his mother.

At last there was nothing left to hide. He had told all, lying on the floor of Patrick's barren flat in the middle of the day, a comforter the only way to ease their bones, not even a drink to lubricate the passage of so many secrets. He'd told Patrick about the Schanbergs, about the trial at camp and his trouble with Mag. About the sissy boys of Harvard, his bitter quarrel with his mother, right up through his arrest and overnight imprisonment in the Central Park precinct. He had never told anyone the whole story, without fabrications, and now, telling it for the first time in sequence, it all made sense. It made sense, he realized later, because of the way Patrick listened.

"I was locked up too," Patrick said when Harris finished. "Twice. Yesirree bobtail." They turned on their sides to look at each other. "Once in the navy when I was court-martialed for sucking somebody's cock in the head after lights-out and once five years ago when Mama died and I didn't know what to do with myself." He didn't sound ashamed, Harris thought, more as if he were talking about TB or athlete's foot. The second time had been worse, Patrick said, although the navy hadn't been any fun. He'd made a fuss at the Dallas airport—they wouldn't let him on the flight back to San Francisco—and the airport police had intervened. They'd taken him to their locker room and banged him against the steel cabinets, also hit him with their nightsticks where it wouldn't show. Then they'd locked him in the psycho ward at a nearby hospital. "But I wasn't crazy"—Patrick knitted his brows, as if he were trying to define craziness in a new way—"I was just going to pieces because Mama died." A friend from the coast had flown to Dallas to get him released in his custody.

After a while they showered together, then Patrick announced he'd walk home with Harris. There was something in his tone that made Harris wonder if he was a chronic migrant, a bird of passage looking for a place to land, but he put the notion out of his mind. Patrick's curiosity was natural. They were neighbors and he wanted to prolong the afternoon.

Patrick inspected the apartment on Charles Street in the Village with great care. Harris had moved there a few years before, just after receiving a raise at Tweedy-Lord, before his real trouble started. "This is great," Patrick said, examining the upholstered chairs, the teak bookcases, the desk from Sloan's, the Karastan rug. Again Harris wondered if perpetual motion was Patrick's natural state. It was a back apartment on the third floor. Patrick raised a window. "Lookie there," he said, leaning out, "nasturtiums and dahlias right in the middle of New York City." After that he turned around and put his arms on Harris's shoulders. "When my sublet finishes next month, I'll move in with you."

Harris smiled and broke away. That was impossible. He wasn't ready to share this limited space. He could think of dozens of good reasons why not. He was used to solitude. He didn't know this guy at all. Maybe Patrick would turn out to be a bore—a nonstop talker or a drunk or an on-and-off psychotic. A phrase in a Madame de Sévigné letter occurred to him—"He deprived me of solitude without affording me company." Suppose that happened with Patrick? How would he get rid of him?

But Patrick had read his mind. "Don't decide now. I'll come by at six o'clock and pick you up for dinner. I found a place where they make great ribs."

Harris felt impinged upon, pressured. He had no plans for this evening but he liked to be free—to walk around, drop in Mary's bar on Eighth Street, where his friends collected on Saturday night, or do nothing. Patrick would interfere with all that.

But there was something else. Letting Patrick into his life would mean telling the truth, always telling the truth. He'd become aware of that as they lay on Patrick's comforter, their bones breaking on the floor boards. He'd have to stop his evasiveness, his equivocating. But those were the habits of a lifetime—how could he break them? It would deform his character.

Patrick rang his bell at six exactly and he went downstairs.

The ribs place was called Miss Lucinda's, and it was on West Street by the river. Patrick knew the owner, a handsome, middle-aged woman who wore a mob cap with pink ribbons flowing down her back. "Hiya, honey!" she called when they entered.

"Hi, Lucinda," Patrick replied in a mild tone. He fished a paper out of his jacket pocket. "I brought you that poem, 'To Lucinda on Going to the Wars.' You'll love it."

The woman sputtered with delight. "Well, aren't you something? Who's your friend?"

"This is Harris Shay," Patrick said. Harris put out his hand. Lucinda's dark hand was warm, almost feverish. Brown, Harris thought, brown is the color of life. "He used to be Harris Schanberg," Patrick went on, "but his parents changed it."

"Well, isn't that something?" Lucinda said again. "Now you and your friend sit over there, I got some ribs gonna break your heart."

Harris followed her in a nervous sweat. Several people had turned around during their little exchange. What did Patrick think he was doing?

After they sat down and ordered beer, Patrick turned his soft brown eyes on him. "Did that upset you?"

"Of course it did."

"Good. It was supposed to."

Harris's whisper was venomous. "I wish you'd mind your own fucking business."

But the next minute he began to feel better. Patrick's rudeness, tactlessness, had helped him, had let some air in. So what if he'd been unprepared?

Patrick made a plane out of his right hand and dipped it through the air. "You gotta let the stink blow off."

Harris found himself grinning in a twisted way. At this point he didn't even know how he felt.

Six weeks later Patrick moved into the Charles Street flat. It had been hard at first. Not for Patrick, who'd grown up in a large family, four brothers and two sisters, and had never liked being alone, but for him. He'd felt cramped, pushed into a corner. But when he complained, Patrick said, "Well, push me back, Harris, push me back, don't just sit there acting squirrelly." So, with Patrick's help, he had learned to push back.

Still, it hadn't been easy. Patrick had his dark side too—moods, fears, intensified by liquor. His insistence on fairness came from an abiding paranoia. His older brothers had bullied him while his daddy looked on approvingly. It was up to little Pat to defend himself. He hadn't been able to, and his mental balance could still teeter in any battle where he sensed too much power on the other side. Harris had been able to help him with that.

And so they had managed. Managed for more than three years, despite their damages, their ups and downs. Now they were notched together. It wasn't one of those infatuations, an uneasy half-love, that Harris had known with others, with men who had conspired in his evasions, helped him avoid things and eventually departed. With Patrick there was a tidal pull, as if they had met before. Even though they jerked free at times, got irritated by each other's rough edges, they always joined up again. They were incomplete without each other—a fact that enraged them both from time to time.

As the years went by, as their routines became more settled, Harris found he didn't miss his old life. He was tired of parks and bars, of phone calls that didn't come, of groping his way for a piss and coming back to a stranger in his bed. With Patrick he rediscovered lost pleasures—a walk, a game of cards, playing the piano, cooking dinner. Simplicities that had been missing for years.

And their fit at home gradually spilled over into work. Patrick was promoted from teaching; he was an assistant principal now—managing faculty and students with the same fairness he always insisted on for himself. And Harris was able to leave the office-temp limbo and start a small publishing operation, booklets that corporations distributed to their employees on health, safety, recreation. He had hooked up with a printing company. He was his own boss, making good money at last.

And Patrick had helped him with the name business too. He began confessing to his friends, starting with Lester Backs. Some of them were shocked, others sympathetic, others disapproving for his having kept quiet so long. Whatever their reaction he discussed it with Patrick, who had never needed other people's validation as much. Harris began to see that he had a dual identity, like the Anglo-Indians and the French-Canadians. He wasn't Harris Schanberg, he wasn't Harris Shay, he was both. They enclosed and encompassed and defined him. Only by accepting his doubleness could he put his past together—serving on the altar at St. Paul's, Gran hiding her Haggadah, his mother teaching Sunday school, Nana's matzoh-ball soup, and all the cemeteries.

He had gone out to the Elysian Gates in Queens, following Aunt Hattie's instructions, and walked among his family graves on a crisp day in October. He had observed the Hebrew lettering, the eroded names and dates, the marble carvings, and wept. This was where he came from, this was who he was. But even as he dried his tears he recalled the other cemetery in Westchester where Gran and his father lay buried under angels and crosses. That was where he came from too. As he walked back to the elevated train stop, stopping first at the florist shop across the street to order flowers for Nana and Grandpa, he decided that he was Christian on Monday, Wednesday and Friday, Jewish on Tuesday, Thursday and Saturday, and Buddhist on Sunday. That seemed to take care of everything, at least to the extent possible.

He also went to a Sabbath service in a magnificent Sephardic synagogue on Central Park West. It was cold and gloomy and poorly attended. The service struck him as rooted in sorrow, due not only to the sound of the canticles intoned by the rabbi but to the great age of the men who watched and prayed. Only when the doors to the sanctum were opened and the Torah scroll paraded around did something stir in him. This was the source of his mother's reverence for words, the root of her bookishness. "*Baruch atah Adonai,*" he murmured at appropriate moments, having been coached by the friend who brought him, but real excitement, a sense of homecoming, eluded him. It was too late, he thought, watching the rapturous faces of the two boys—sons of the rabbi—who dashed around doing sacred chores. He recalled his mornings in a white surplice and red cassock helping Dr. Palmsley with the bell and candles, the wafers and wine. Too late, even with a yarmulke on his head and a tallith around his shoulders. There was no escaping his duality.

One night, telling Patrick about these visits, he had wound up with his old theory about one-thing-wrong-with-everyone. "And so," Harris summed up, "I always thought the one thing wrong with me was that I had this other identity. If I just didn't have that, I'd be fine. Now I know that's bullshit. I'm fine just the way I am."

"I'll drink to that," Patrick said, hoisting his beer. They were waiting for their ribs at Miss Lucinda's.

"And maybe that's the end of the subject for good."

"I doubt that," Patrick said, frowning. "You never come to the end of some things."

Harris looked around the living room. He was through cleaning up for today's visitors, though most of the junk had merely been transferred to the bedroom. Still, the room looked reasonably neat without erasing their passage through it.

Patrick had emerged from the kitchen looking flushed and was now in the shower. He would be there for some time—he suffered from cysts and one had just drained in his groin, another sign of tension. As he began to change his clothes, Harris deliberated. It was an idea he had taken up and discarded a dozen times in the last month, ever since Mag's call. He had discussed it with Patrick, who, for once, had made no suggestion. "It's up to you," he'd said, "either way." Harris recalled Patrick's remark about never coming to the end of some things. He might be right, though he himself had disagreed at the time.

He finished dressing, then went to the bookcase, still debating. There was no reason to hurt her. No reason to be dramatic. This was supposed to be a happy time, a rapprochement. But his fingers had a will of their own and they removed the little volume. It was light in his hands. He didn't open it, didn't need to look. He put it on an end table next to the couch. He'd be able to get to it if necessary, that was all.

The doorbell rang at one-fifteen. He and Patrick were dressed up and slicked down, looking at each other. The sound triggered a wild beating of his heart. He ran to buzz them in, then took a deep breath. Patrick slipped into the kitchen as he opened the front door.

He could hear Mag's encouragements as they climbed the two flights. His mother was going slowly. He could see her head bobbing below him. It was gray, but still familiar. There was no other shape in the world quite like it. He could see her hand on the banister. That set off another alarm.

"We're coming!" Mag called out in her brightest voice.

"Slow but sure," he heard his mother say, one of her pet phrases.

At last she was in sight, half a flight below. Her eyes swept upward in a dark arc and caught him. Was there ever a look like hers? He stepped back automatically. He didn't want to be caught in that darkness. The next instant he was on the landing, arms out. Her glance had gone bright and shallow. The danger was past. "Here we are!" she cried. They embraced. She was wearing a new scent and her face was icy. He remembered the touch of that skin. She patted his arm twice before breaking away.

"We had a hard time finding a parking space," Mag said. "We're blocks away."

He kissed his sister. She felt young and firm after his mother. Everybody was talking at once.

Patrick stood in the living room, dish towel in hand, looking composed. "Hello, Patrick," his mother said, not waiting for an introduction.

"Hello, Margaret." Patrick went to shake hands, but his mother grabbed him excitedly and brushed her cheek against his. It was, Harris knew, a sign. Patrick was to be included in the new order.

As he took their coats he was able to see his mother clearly. She looked much older and her face was thin. He noticed a greenish tint under the makeup. She went to the couch and lowered herself slowly. "This is so nice, Harris." Her voice was high, girlish. "A lot more light than your place on Second Avenue."

He snorted. "That dive."

"Eighteen dollars a month; what did you expect?"

"Oh, God." Mag came over, rolling her eyes. "I'll never forget that toilet in the hall."

"The worst part," Harris said, "was sharing it with my neighbor. He never locked the door." Everybody laughed. The small talk eased the awkwardness.

Mag was in full bloom, her skin lustrous, her chestnut hair falling to her shoulders. She was thirty-six now, two years older than he. The little changes he had seen accumulating for the past year, since she and Howie had gotten together again, since they had moved to Philadelphia and she started teaching, had coalesced into an aura of ease and power. It was clear that she'd won battles invisible to him. It showed in her calmness, her general sparkle. He had always thought she had it easier, but now he knew her struggles had matched his own. He recalled her troubles at camp, in high school, with Howie. He had simply failed to acknowledge them. His own exertions had blinded him to hers. Now, watching her settle into a chair, he was suddenly proud of her, proud to be connected. The sensation was new and it surprised him.

Patrick and his mother were chatting about Texas. Tentative probes, circling around the usual mix of pride and provincialism and hate shared by escaped Texans. If they had a chance to explore, without interruption, they would become friends. Harris could already tell, in Patrick's knitted brow and heartfelt speech, he was aiming at that. Pleasure swept through him. It was wonderful to watch Patrick and his mother get acquainted.

He took drink orders. Mag wanted a Coke. Scotch and soda for Patrick and him. "I'll make you a Manhattan," he said to his mother. "I got cherries especially."

She looked gleeful, but Mag said, "Make Mother's very weak; she's not supposed to have anything."

His mother didn't really know how to drink. She would gulp a Manhattan to get at the cherries. One and she was giddy, two and she was drunk. He went into the kitchen.

In there he heard Patrick's low, uninflected voice blending with the others. The afternoon was going to be okay. They were going to get along, maybe even enjoy themselves. His worry had been unnecessary.

When he came back, Patrick was addressing his mother. "You went to the university in Austin, didn't you?"

His mother waved her hand. "They had to take everybody in the state back then. No entrance exams, you just needed a high school diploma."

Mag objected. "She was only thirteen when she went there. She was practically a genius."

"Fourteen." His mother smiled, accepting the Manhattan.

"And she graduated at seventeen," Mag went on, "the youngest graduate in history. Tell him, Mother."

Patrick looked impressed. "Seventeen is all?"

"Oh, I never had any dates, I just studied all the time. And I went in the summer too. I didn't like staying home. My parents made me visit relatives and sweep the yard and shell pecans."

"Her professors loved her," Mag intervened again. "I tell all my friends about my brilliant mother." She stared at Harris. He was supposed to say something. His mother had always been smart, not like the other mothers. But he had never really been impressed by that. Brains weren't what he wanted from her.

"I haven't seen you since you got your Ph.D.," he said, trying not to sound apologetic or guilty. It was his right, wasn't it? A choice he had made?

"You haven't seen her since she got her job either," Mag asserted. "She has a wonderful job at St. Mary's Hospital in Poughkeepsie."

Harris glanced at his mother. She was leaning forward, not really relaxed. The Manhattan had been consumed. She was waiting for him to say something too. He felt a little thrill of importance. His approval was required. Then the old ambivalence shot through him—he wanted to approve and deny her at the same time. "It's terrific you got the job," he said, pumping some enthusiasm into his voice. "Do you really like it?"

His mother's eyes widened. "I tell them I should pay *them,* I like it so much."

"They call her Dr. Shay," Mag offered. "When I phone they say, 'Dr. Shay's office.' " She looked around at the three of them in triumph.

"Big deal." His mother settled back at last. But he could see she was delighted. She'd always wanted a major career and now she'd achieved it. She was in charge of the testing program in the psychiatric wing. She gave Rorschach and Szondi and Stanford-Binet tests all day, plus individual evaluations.

Mag said her case histories were passed around the hospital. "They've never seen any so well-written."

His mother waved again, then gave a deprecating laugh. "It comes from reading George Eliot so much."

Patrick was glowing with pleasure. Harris knew what he was thinking—if only his own mother had been like this. Patrick was hungry for a change of mothers, retroactively. "Did you like George Eliot?" he asked now.

The two of them started to compare notes. Harris was sure his mother still had the complete set of novels at the farm, the set she'd sent away for when she was in her teens. Patrick had taught *Silas Marner* many times, he said, and the kids always hated it. His mother advised *The Mill on the Floss* or *Daniel Deronda*. Her voice took on the rapturous tone Harris knew so well. He suppressed a spurt of irritation. It was her optimism spilling over. George Eliot always triggered it, not only because she was a woman writer but because she had set up housekeeping with a man she wasn't married to. "Mary Ann Evans," his mother rhapsodized now. "She defied convention in the Victorian age. The first emancipated woman." Her head tilted back and her mouth gaped open.

Harris felt his irritation mounting. His mother was getting started with a new audience. Those cornball sentiments, that disfiguring intensity, hadn't disappeared with the Ph.D. in psychology. They were still underneath, waiting for a little sympathy or interest to pop up again. And Patrick was interested—he was frowning and nodding. Harris knew those signs too. On Monday Patrick would write a long memo to the head of the English department.

"*The Mill on the Floss,*" his mother cried out, pressing her hand to her breastbone, another familiar gesture. "Maggie and Tom Tulliver, they're based on George Eliot and her brother." Harris found his irritation thickening into anger. More bullshit was on the way. Their own lives had been turned into fictions thanks to her. She had rewritten them all as literature. Then another thought struck him. Did his mother know that Henry Lewes, George Eliot's live-in boyfriend, had been Jewish? What would happen if he threw out that bit of information right now?

Mag cleared her throat imperiously. A vertical furrow appeared between her brows. Another familiar sign—she was being left out. A literary discussion was under way, which she particularly hated. "I forgot," she announced loudly. "Roland sent you both a present. Where's my pocketbook?"

His mother's little puff of pride evaporated. Harris watched as she condensed, sank back. That was something new—taking a back seat to Mag, dropping out of a discussion of books. She almost looked guilty for a moment.

The drawing Mag produced included birthday greetings. "Roland wasn't sure when Patrick's birthday was, but I told him to congratulate you anyway," Mag said. The two men in the crayon drawing were riding camels. "I told him about your trip to Egypt last year," Mag explained. "It made a big impression, but he forgot the pyramids."

They talked about Mag's kids after that. George Eliot didn't come up again. Harris relaxed, though his palms were sweaty and he knew his irritation was just offstage waiting for the next cue. Once or twice his eye fell on the little book he'd put on the end table.

Dinner was delicious, including the cornbread-biscuit stuffing. Mag talked about her job, Patrick about school. Harris chimed in with news of his own little publishing company. He had just gotten a huge order for a booklet on plant safety. It would be distributed to half the blue-chip companies in America. His mother's face lit up at the news, and he found himself suddenly thrilled. He still wanted to please her, even after all these years.

His mother didn't eat much. Harris watched her push the turkey and sweet potatoes and cranberry sauce around while she kept saying everything was delicious. Mag watched, lips compressed.

Over dessert the talk switched to the Kennedys. Mag thought Jackie Kennedy was gorgeous. It was good to have her in the White House after a long line of frumps. Harris was reminded—Mrs. Roosevelt had just endorsed one of his booklets. He could use the line from her newspaper column, "My Day," in a promotional mailing. "Even Uncle Mark never got Eleanor Roosevelt." He laughed.

It was the wrong thing to say. His mother stared at her plate and Mag looked at him significantly. Uncle Mark had died of a massive coronary last year and Sister had killed herself two nights later—liquor and pills. She was fifty-nine. He hadn't seen his mother then either. So much had happened, so much they hadn't discussed. He might have gone up to see her after Sister's suicide, but he hadn't. He had rationalized it at the time, but now he regretted it. He should have paid a visit. He should have been more generous.

"Well," Mag said brightly, her company tone, "do you want help with the dishes?"

His mother looked up, a forced brightness, back to the present.

"Harris is going to do the dishes," Patrick said calmly. "I cooked."

"Whoops!" Mag cried. "I'd like to see that."

As he worked in the kitchen he heard the Texas talk start again. Patrick began a story about the day his father took all the children to the town jail and asked the sheriff to lock them up for a while. This while had expanded into hours, days, in Patrick's memory. It was one of the deep impressions of his childhood. "Daddy wanted us to know what jail felt like so we'd never get in trouble."

Harris heard the laughter of the women. Another quaint Texas anecdote. But his mother wouldn't understand this one. A jail cell, deterrent punishment, were not in her lexicon. No one in this family had ever gotten into trouble. Almost no one.

They hadn't discussed his arrest either. Nor his humiliation at having to call Uncle Mark. Uncle Mark had gotten the charges dismissed. He could hear the lawyer still, a thin, handsome man in a blue pinstripe: "There is no proof that a prima facie breach of the peace has occurred." And the judge's lecture, stipulating psychiatric treatment pending a rehearing of the case in six months. And then it had been quashed.

No, none of that had been aired. It was a chapter of his life now closed. Besides, neither his mother nor Mag could possibly understand his state of mind at the time. It was beyond their experience. His mother might give Rorschach tests to rapists, murderers and psychopaths, but the distance between her and them would never be abridged. She would be fascinated, stimulated—that went with the territory—but the gulf wouldn't close. It wasn't just her bourgeois origins either; there was some deeper naïveté—or hypocrisy. He heard a cell door clang in his mind, open or shut he couldn't tell. He had been forced onto the margins, the fringes—his old discovery, at Harvard, that he would have to become a criminal in order to survive, had come true in a way. And he had faced it, accepted it. Some part of him had dropped out of America for good. But he'd had to do it alone—his mother had stayed on the other side of her glass wall, secure in her optimism, her misplaced faith in upward mobility, her denial. All her promises to him, her predictions, had been false. Worse than that, they'd been foolish.

The conversation in the other room interrupted his thoughts. My God, they were back to George Eliot. The years, the Ph.D., the job at the hospital, were all dropping away. He could hear the gush in her voice. The fictions were flying. It was as if she were pressing against him in the old way, with the old lies. If he didn't push back, he'd go crazy again. But that's what he'd learned from Patrick, wasn't it? To push back? Wasn't that the chief lesson of the past few years? To tell the truth, no matter what?

He dried his hands and went back to the living room, walking carefully, holding himself in. Patrick glanced at him, then frowned. Patrick could tell from the way he walked. His mother too. Her voice rose a notch. He had the feeling this was like a collision in a dream. There was no way to avoid it, even though he wanted to. He picked up the little volume. Everyone turned toward him. *Now now now,* he thought.

"Remember this?" Mag coughed and shifted in her chair. He had the sensation he was vile, which was an anagram of evil. "Daddy's Latin grammar."

His mother's eyes danced around. "Oh, yes."

"It still has his old signature." He flipped to the title page and held it up.

Mag peered at the writing. "Where on earth did you find it?"

"I saved it. I kept it out of the ones we were eradicating, remember?"

"Of course I remember."

"He used to ask about it. Everybody said it was lost. But I had it. I kept it hidden all these years."

He could see the play of tension in his mother's jaw, lips, neck. Her fingers closed into a fist. He only had one more statement; then he would be done. Maybe they could even pick up where they left off, though he doubted it. "I should tell you, Mother, I don't lie about our name any more." His head buzzed furiously for a moment. "I've told everyone I know."

He waited, everyone waited. She swiveled her gaze to the window, the houses across the yard, then back again. "Well, good, Harris, I'm glad you don't." The hand on her lap unclenched, the fingers curling outward like petals.

"You don't mind?"

"Naw." She gave a little chuckle, though it was forced. "I stopped caring about that years ago. I've told people too."

He looked at Mag. "A lot has happened to us, Harris. You don't know because you haven't been around."

Were they telling the truth? It didn't matter—the magic words had been uttered. A space opened in his chest, a piece of sky. Vile was also an anagram of live.

"I think you should do what you want," his mother continued. "You have to live your own life."

He took a deep breath. "I'm glad to hear you say that."

She nodded. He could see she was casting around for a change of subject. She didn't want to make a big deal out of it. Maybe that was another form of evasion, but he'd let it pass. He'd made his point.

"Do you remember Miss Bowers?" Mag asked. She turned to Patrick. "She was our Latin teacher in high school. I was crazy about her." She laughed. As they talked about Latin—Patrick regretted his high school hadn't offered it—Harris watched his mother. She had gone off in a brown study. She had left them.

He recalled the old sensation of sitting with her when her thoughts were far away. Her frequent remoteness had made him feel ignored, but now he could understand. Part of her had been unfulfilled as a mother and housewife. She'd had other dreams, equally pressing.

Then another thought struck him. He had always prided himself on his rebellion, his escape, his rejection of her. But now, looking at her, he wondered if he had given himself too much credit. Maybe it was she who had let him go—all these years of not calling him, hardly writing, demanding nothing. Daddy and Nana came to mind—Nana had never let go of her son for a minute. He shook his head, appalled. His mother's greatest gift might have been the one he had never acknowledged. She had made up her mind to release him.

His mother finally came out of her reverie. "Oh, those Latin declensions," she chimed in. "Your father used to recite them in bed when we were first married. I thought they were the most boring things I ever heard. I guess he didn't want to forget them."

Everyone laughed. "Marriage," Patrick said. "Isn't that the hardest thing?" He glanced at Harris.

"Everything's hard," his mother said, "every single thing."

He and Patrick didn't talk much after the women left. It was five and Patrick wanted to take a nap. Harris was glad to be alone. He sat in the living room, replaying the afternoon.

He was free. He could feel some vestigial muscles, sinews clenched all these years, loosen in his chest. It was another crossing. He'd had several crossings to make, more than most people, but now he was safely over. New choices, freedoms, opened up ahead. Maybe a year abroad with Patrick. Maybe teaching piano. Maybe writing fiction—God knows he had a head start on that. It didn't really matter what he did, as long as he felt free to try.

But he was thinking only of himself, ignoring the other thing, the irrefutable math of his mother's appearance. He had known the instant he saw her, also known why Mag had insisted on this meeting. But only now, sitting alone, could he explore the meanings.

Mag had taken his mother to the bathroom. She held onto Mag's arm on the way. When Mag came back alone, he asked, "Is she sick?"

"Yes."

"How sick?"

Mag looked at him dramatically. "Very sick. There's a spot on her lung. But she doesn't know it. We told her it's just a fungus infection."

"A fungus?"

"Something curable she picked up in the garden. They've just started her on chemotherapy."

"If she's on chemotherapy, she must know what she's got."

Mag shook her head. "Not Mother. If she doesn't want to believe it, she doesn't."

He had no reply for that. When his mother came out again, he got up and helped her to the couch. It was the first time he'd touched her since that brief embrace at the door. He could feel her thinness, her dryness. She was like a strawflower. He handed her down as delicately as he could.

Later, when Patrick woke up from his nap, they discussed the afternoon. First came the food. Patrick liked to review his kitchen triumphs, always prefacing his remarks with an old joke, "Weren't those hush puppies *good*?" He did that now.

After the culinary postmortem Patrick knitted his brows and spoke slowly. "I really liked your mother."

"Obviously."

"She's like a lot of women I knew growing up. A fine strong Texas woman."

"If that's all she'd been, my life would have been much simpler."

Patrick shrugged. "You have to take the bad with the good."

"Let's not have any philosophy, please."

"I'm just telling you . . ."

"Patrick."

They sat quietly for a while. Then Harris said, "I'll have to go see her. Regularly. Either at Mag's or at the farm."

Patrick nodded. "It'll be good for both of you. You can finish your business."

"I guess so. It'll be easier than before, anyway."

Later, in bed, after giving Patrick a good-night kiss and marveling again at the naturalness of their fit, Harris thought of the Latin grammar. Mag had said she'd like to borrow it and show it to her kids, tell them about their grandfather. Another change in the inner workings of the family.

The unveiling of the grammar had been a letdown. The big moment had fizzled. He snickered into the dark—his father's signature wasn't Rosebud after all. Too much time had gone by. Or maybe there was no Rosebud because there was no single key to anything. They all lived in many rooms with many doors and locks and each one had to be found individually. He started to express this dubious insight to Patrick, then heard a light snore. Patrick was off. It could wait until tomorrow. And he was tired—exhausted, in fact. It had been a long day.

Patrick was mumbling in his dreams. Harris reared up, listening, but he couldn't sort out the words. Some long-repressed trauma of Patrick's, no doubt. They were both haunted by everything that had ever happened to them. But then so was everyone else. Finally, dismissing this thought, he turned on his side and went to sleep.

16

MARGARET
The Dream

She turned over and over, round and round. She couldn't get comfortable anymore. There were no beds, no pillows, that could make her comfortable, let her draw a good deep breath.

The medicine was making her sick. She'd taken it gladly, starting in the hospital in Poughkeepsie. She always followed instructions where health was concerned, but now she wasn't sure. When Mag walked in with the awful capsules, she wanted to refuse, point out that the capsules, not the fungus in her lungs, were harming her. But she always took them, Mag waiting to retrieve the glass of water.

A fly circled, landing on the sheet. *Seven at one blow*. She'd read that story to Harris when he was a boy, and it had become his favorite. He used to run around the house with a fly swatter yelling, "Seven at one blow." Maybe she'd read it to Roland tonight, though Roland didn't take to stories the way Harris had. He didn't sit there, out of breath, out of time, trapped in the place where things were truer than true. Roland tended to squirm and interrupt and liked to have a gun in his hand. When he got bored with the story, he made shooting sounds. Mag said she shouldn't read to him, he was perfectly capable of reading himself, but she couldn't stop. It was one of the few things that still gave her pleasure, though sometimes she had to stop because her breath ran out.

She rolled on her side, though it was harder to breathe in that position. It compressed her chest. But she was bound and determined to get well. She got up every morning and afternoon here in Mag's house in Darby, just as she had in Vassar Hospital. She walked the length of the hall in both places. Here, of course, she didn't have to worry about the IV stand, that clumsy hatrack rolling with her, nor about the patients and nurses getting in the way. She just had herself to worry about.

She'd never smoked a cigarette. Lived in clean air most of her life. Followed health diets, from Gaylord Hauser on. Yogurt and blackstrap molasses—whoever heard of such a thing, Sister had said. But she'd persevered. She knew what was good for her.

But it was a temporary condition, wasn't it? Even though she'd lost her hair, tufts and patches of gray up there, and she had to wear a wig when people visited. Did that mean it was worse than they let on? She couldn't be sick that way, not really sick. *Pshaw, there's nothin' wrong with you, you just want attention,* that's what Mama would say. She was malingering. It was almost time for her morning walk now. She turned on her back again. In a few minutes.

She always knew Mag would take care of her. When Mag arrived at the hospital in Poughkeepsie, sweeping into the room like a tornado, taking charge of nurses, doctors, food, medicine, she had felt a deep comfort. It was almost like being back in Gideon with Sister, Sister combing her hair and straightening her dress and making sure she was fit to be presented. She had started to sniffle a little, she'd been all alone, Sister gone and Harris not coming around—and Mag had gotten indignant in that grand way of hers. "You should be glad to see me!" she'd burst out.

"Oh, honey, I am, I am," and she had put up her arms and it was like Sister, except Sister had never hugged her so uncritically, so unconditionally. It was remarkable. Maybe that love had been curled up in Mag all these years, a thumbnail bud waiting to bloom. Or maybe it was something between mothers and daughters. She tested that idea as she would test a clothesline before hanging out the wet wash. Mag would bear the weight of her illness. Mag would make her well.

Time to get up. Slowly, patiently, first one foot on the floor, then the other. She clutched the bedstead while she put on her kimono, first one arm, then the other. Straighten up, do it slowly, little by little. She would walk herself well, it was just a matter of making up her mind.

Yes, walking would cure her. Maybe she'd have a good day today. When Mag came home this afternoon with both children, all of them full of news about their various schools, she'd be able to pay attention. Not doze off. Maybe even go downstairs for dinner when Howie came home.

If only she could have some chocolate. The urge rushed over her—a good sign, she hadn't thought about chocolate in weeks. Pie, candy, pudding, ice cream, it didn't matter just so long as it was chocolate. Mama, who believed in a treat if you'd earned it, used to give her a nickel to go to Gem's. There it was always a chocolate soda in a tall glass inside a metal holder, the spoon sticking through the foam. She could taste it now, through the enduring bitterness of the medication. Some afternoons at the farm, if Mark was away on a business trip and Sister was bored, she'd call on the phone. She could tell instantly, from Sister's first words, what Sister had in mind. *Let's make a chocolate pie.* And they would, in her own big kitchen, the two of them like conspirators or children. And when the pie was done, even before it had cooled properly, they would dig in. At the end of the afternoon there might be one small slice left. They would part in guilt and gluttony, hardly saying good-bye, but the restlessness, the boredom, had been overcome. They had had a treat. They had gone to Gem's.

She fought away the next thoughts, but they scrabbled back. She had not been enough for Sister, not enough of an inducement for her to stay on the earth. It had been the final rejection, the final judgment. Of course, Sister was drunk when she did it, too drunk to know what was happening, but still the truth screamed at her. *Sister had never needed her as much as she had needed Sister.* She had not been enough, even though she lived down the road, available any time for drives, shopping, movies, chocolate pie. It was the curse of the demon protectors, Sister's old weakness. The softness, the carelessness of spirit, the need to be prized—all these had made Sister vulnerable. She had never been cauterized by pain. No scar tissue had formed. Mark, with his endless love and attention, had misfitted her for life without him. Though it wasn't his fault either—he had simply loved her to death. Of course, the roots of something like that went down and down, back and back, to their embarrassment over Mama's hugeness, over Papa's accent and all the rest. What was the use of going over it? Better to concentrate on getting well. But Sister had always said she would refuse to turn sixty and she had stuck to her word. She had always laughed when Sister said that, always knowing that when the time came . . . but Sister had proved her wrong.

My Thoughts: That's what her scrapbook-diary said on the cover. She wrote in that book every day, in the yard under the pecan tree or upstairs with Sister in the other bed. Mostly she wrote about books, whether she liked them, *Madame Bovary* better than *Cousin Bette, The Reds of the Midi* better than *The Hunchback of Notre Dame.* A provincial girl derailed by too much reading, but when she got to Austin, to the university, they didn't believe she had read all those books. Professor Dunbar, who had eczema on his hands and scratched himself raw, doubted her in front of everybody. But she had the characters and plots to prove it. Finally he had bowed mockingly and said, "Miss Barish, we defer to your superior wisdom." How she had hated him then.

Would she never be free from the prosecutions of memory? There were exercises to clear your mind, but she had never bothered. She enjoyed her thoughts too much, the brown studies, the wool-gathering. They were her essence, her core. Daydreaming.

There, she'd walked enough for now. Slowly, patiently, back to bed. She could feel her blood charging through, making her heart pound. A good sign. It proved she was vital and alive. She might even go through the pile of *Wall Street Journal*s next to the bed, her subscription transferred here to Pennsylvania.

They didn't know it, she'd kept it secret, but Mag and Harris would be well off. All those dimes and dollars Papa had collected from the Negroes and Mexicans who bought furniture on the installment plan, that he had passed on to Mama, and from Mama to her and Sister—she had built up her share. Everyone made fun of her for scrimping, for saving the used paper napkins to wipe off the stove, for living off the income of her income, but she couldn't stop. Not that she thought money came first, or even mattered much. It just gave you the freedom to do what you liked. And she'd been right. She'd paid for Mag's master's degree, helped Harris out of his scrapes. Both her children were witnesses to the liberating power of money.

But nothing compared to what Roland and Lily would be. The children were rolled up in America, inside the fold of the nation. Nothing would keep them from flowering, from prospering, as God intended. She had a sudden picture of them entering this very room, faces aflame with the brightness of belonging. Nowadays all the books and newspaper articles condemned what she had done. The new ethnicity, they called it, the age of minorities. But what was so wonderful about being a minority? What was America about, except the freedom to start over? Harris had called it a masquerade in one of his tirades—she couldn't exactly remember which one—but he was wrong. She had gone along with him that afternoon in his apartment with his friend, told him what he wanted to hear about the book he had saved, and all the rest, but she had reserved some private meaning for herself. You could invent yourself anew if the need was great enough. Wasn't that why her ancestors had come over, because they refused to live the life they'd been born to? Wasn't that true of all the immigrants? Harris called it camouflage, but everyone covered up some part of the truth in their lives. If everyone told the truth all the time, how would people get along? And Roland and Lily were the proof of her wisdom. They had sailed around the bend into a new, broader sea, the epic space of America.

She was tired now, even from that little walk. It was discouraging, but she wouldn't give in. The next walk would be easier, and the one after that. She would never stop trying.

Her head drifted back to the pillow. She would rest her eyes a little.

She'd been thinking about Roland's future. She had some ideas. Tourism was the coming thing—jet planes crossing the Atlantic, hotels springing up everywhere, prosperity sweeping the globe. It was the new frontier. Cornell had the best hotel school in the nation. Roland could get in on the ground floor. He had no special talents that would lead him to something creative or intellectual. But he could be a manager, an executive. She had a picture of him, tall and fair and blue-eyed like his father, standing in the atrium of some great hotel, flagship of a chain like the one owned by G. David Schine. He would be shaking hands with the president of General Motors, who always stayed there when he came to town.

The garage doors banging woke her up. She checked the clock. She had slept the early afternoon away. The taste in her mouth was terrible—acrid and medicinal. She forced herself to sit up, just as they all rushed in. Roland got to her first and pushed a brown paper bag at her. "I gotcha Dixie cup, Gramaw."

She took it, not trying for a kiss. He was eleven and didn't like kissing.

"He asked what he could buy you, and I said she loves chocolate ice cream." Mag was glowing. "He spent his own money."

"I didn't mind," Roland said.

"Thank you, honey." He wriggled away.

Lily had made a valentine for her, even though the date was several weeks away. She took it, praised it, and asked for a kiss. Lily proffered her cheek, giving out little peeps. Kissing her was like touching a nectarine.

"How do you feel?" It was more a command than a question, but she didn't mind. She never minded any of Mag's bossiness now—just the contrary.

"I think I'm better. I walked for about twenty minutes."

"You did?" Mag's face lit up.

A slight exaggeration but justifiable. If she told Mag about the hole in her chest, the hole she could feel herself falling into, it would make it worse.

"Why don't you go downstairs and get Gramaw a spoon? She doesn't like this little wooden thing."

She started to object but Roland whipped off. Mag took the bag and extracted the Dixie cup, then removed the lid. "Remember when they had movie stars on these, Mother? Once I had two

Deanna Durbins and I traded one for Tyrone Power. I'll never forget. He was my heartthrob."

"I remember."

"No, you don't remember, you're just saying that."

Mag had trapdoors through which you might suddenly fall. You never knew when it would happen. "I remember; you were crazy about Tyrone Power."

"You couldn't remember because you never paid any attention to me."

Just as suddenly the rain cloud swept off and Mag was beaming again. Roland appeared with the spoon. It didn't mean anything with Mag; she just flew off the handle, always had. It was her way.

She started digging out the Dixie cup. The chocolate was cool and luscious on her tongue. It neutralized the bitter taste.

Roland climbed on the foot of the bed. "Gramaw, did you really know Davy Crockett?"

"If you're going to tell him stories, Lily and I are going to put the groceries away." Mag swept out, first giving her a reproachful look. She didn't like these little tales. But what was the harm, really? They were just like Grimm or Hans Christian Andersen.

"Yes, honey, I sure did."

"Did you, um, meet him? Wha'd he say?" The boy's blue eyes sought hers.

She invented quickly, without effort, as if she were writing a story about Gideon. Davy was in town looking for volunteers for his fight against Santa Anna. All the young men ran into the street, buttoning their jackets, waving their Colts and Winchesters. She had run out with them. "I want to fight," she said to Davy Crockett. Now her voice was strong and sure, her breathlessness of this morning, her dyspnea, miraculously vanished. "I can fight, Davy, I'm as good as any man."

Roland's eyes were fixed on her, unwavering.

"Look at my muscle." And now, here in bed, she held up her arm to show how she had demonstrated her muscle to Davy Crockett. "I can ride and kill Mexicans just like the rest."

Roland sucked in his breath. She had him now. He was hers for as long as she went on talking.

"But the other young men, they said, 'She's just a girl.' " Her lip curled, the sneer of those who didn't believe in girls. " 'She's no good, she can't do anything.' "

"Lemme prove it," she answered back, standing very straight and tall. "Lemme prove it right here."

And she'd taken her rifle, aimed at the sky and brought down a big old crow that was flapping by. The crow fell at the foot of Davy Crockett's horse. "How's that for a girl?" she asked.

And then Davy Crockett told her to wait a while, he wanted to have a conference with his lieutenants. So she'd waited, the boys still sneering, while they talked. She hadn't looked left or right, just straight ahead, ignoring the boys. And at last Davy had ridden back, his horse chewing the bit and pawing the ground, and said, "We won't take you today, Margaret, but we'll let you join up with us next time. Don't worry, there's gonna be lots more fights, this is just the first."

She hadn't felt bad when they rode off because she'd been promised. She knew that Davy Crockett never went back on his word. The Alamo proved that. He'd come get her, no matter what.

"Did he come back, Gramaw?"

It didn't matter what she answered to that. The impression had been made. He had glimpsed wondrous possibilities.

"Did he? Huh?" Roland was wriggling, bad-tempered in his disappointment. Of course she had to finish the story. That was part of the bargain.

"Yes, he did come back to get me."

"Gramaw is making all that up, Roland." Mag's voice in the doorway was sharp. "She likes to tell stories."

"No, she's not." Roland stood up. "Are you, Gramaw?"

"That's just the way it happened, Roland."

"My goodness." Mag was quite irritated now. "Fairy tales are one thing, but telling whoppers about . . ."

She looked at her grandson. She felt slightly dizzy from the efforts of the last few minutes. "Remember what I said, honey."

"Come on, it's time for your homework."

"I wanta stay with Gramaw."

"She wants to sleep. Don't you, Gramaw?"

She nodded her head. She barely noticed when Mag removed the unfinished ice cream or drew the curtains. She would sleep for a while, and then she would get up and walk again. Walking would make her well.

She didn't wake up until midnight. Mag had let her sleep clear through. She shouldn't have done that, and now it was too late to complain. Everyone was asleep. The house was still.

She'd had a frightful dream, exploding in her mind like snow out of a black sky. It was terrible the way dreams took advantage of you. She turned her mind away, trying not to remember, but it came back.

She and Papa had been in some foreign city, standing on the sidewalk outside a theater. They had been surrounded by every type of Jew—businessmen and peddlers, professors and shtetl teachers, Jews from Bucharest and Galicia, from Bessarabia and Bialystok, in frock coats and fringed tallithim, in broad-brimmed hats and furs, their wives standing apart in shawls and long dresses and wigs. All of them blowing on their fingers and beating their sides in the cold, waiting to go inside. And she'd been happy, excited. This was a special treat. She'd never been to this kind of play before, she was looking forward to it. But when they got inside, she found everyone speaking a hoarse guttural language she didn't understand. The smell of cabbage was intense. A man came through selling prune cakes and tea in glasses. She began to feel sick. She tugged at her father's sleeve but he paid no attention. He had run into a friend, someone from Comanesti, and they were talking about their school days. And then the room darkened, the curtain went up and a rabbi walked onstage. A rabbi who was a character in the play—Rabbi Judah Loew of Prague, who had created a golem to protect his congregation. But when Rabbi Judah turned toward her, she saw that he had the face of Judah Schanberg—*Judd*—as he had looked when she first met him, with a widow's peak and a fleshy face and cleft chin and rimless glasses. She had tried to cry out, pressing through the softness of the dream, but something had stopped her. An enormous terror had flooded through her. And the next instant she understood what Rabbi Judah

Loew was saying. He was speaking to her. He was telling her she would die. The golem had gotten out of control. It was on a rampage and would destroy all the people it had been created to save.

She awoke from the terror, grateful it was only a dream. She couldn't make sense of it. She didn't want to anyway. It was just something sent from the Middle Ages, from the collective tribulations of the race, to plague her. Maybe she should call Mag. Mag could keep the dream, all dreams like that, at bay. "Mag," she whispered into the dark. But she shouldn't wake her up, not on a weeknight. She lay inert, exhausted. The dream had robbed her of her strength, the strength to keep on walking, trying, planning. "It's finished," she whispered, and again, louder, "It's finished." She would never go back to her job, to the job she loved, where they gave her so much respect. Dr. Shay, with her own office and her own secretary. She tried not to cry. There was so much to cry about, but she mustn't. Mama would punish her.

After a while her thoughts moved on to Harris. He had visited last week with his friend. She couldn't remember the friend's name now, but she'd liked him right off. Maybe that connection would last despite the forces ranged against it, though she doubted it. But even if it didn't last, Harris had made it over some inner barrier. An aberrant strain in the family, traveling from Uncle Harris to his great-nephew. Perhaps that had been necessary too, part of a plan she had been powerless to interrupt or understand.

And Mag was happy with Howie again. Marriage was Mag's natural medium, and now she'd shaped it to suit her needs. Howie was a good man—you just had to watch him. Mag had been right to leave and right to come back.

A thin smile came to her lips. She'd said the same thing about her own marriage, long ago. History repeating itself. Maybe wives always had to walk out once, to wake up the husbands, startle them into manhood, assert their own equal powers.

And now there was no more unfinished business with her children. The estate—she heard it as *es*-tate—was in order, the will and letter of instructions in the safe box. It would be share-and-share-alike, except for funds set aside for college for Roland and Lily. But when hadn't it been share-and-share-alike, when hadn't she been fair, despite her wayward preferences in the old days? Her fairness was bred in the bone.

She had dreamed about Judd just now, for the first time in years. Maybe it was compensation, a righting of the balance. She'd been thinking about Charlie Rysdale recently. That was the barrier she had crossed just as Harris had crossed his. But she hadn't been dead-sure, hadn't proved it, until a few years back. She let her mind drift again.

Charlie Rysdale and his second wife had moved to Edgarville, not twenty miles from the farm. She didn't know till she saw the sign go up—Thelma Rysdale, Interiors. She had asked around. Yes, Mrs. Rysdale had a husband, a retired advertising man named Charles. Even then she didn't quite believe it till she saw a picture of them in the local paper. They were summer people, with another house in Boca Raton. The decorating business was mostly a hobby for Thelma.

She thought she saw him once on the street in Edgarville, coming out of the paint store, but she wasn't sure. She didn't stop the car. There was so much she was afraid of knowing. She had her doctorate, her job at St. Mary's, Sister and Mark still alive. Her life had no empty places, least of all for Charlie Rysdale. She hoped she didn't run into him at a party. Her mind caved in at the thought of finding things to say to him.

But her luck didn't hold. Anne Plaisted, a ritzy woman who had bought an old Federal house, invited her to a Christmas party. She was on all the invitation lists nowadays—not just because she was Marian Giangrande's sister but because she was somebody in her own right. Newcomers always wanted to get acquainted.

She could see the invitation now, printed but with a handwritten note at the bottom. "Do hope you can come. Anne." She knew right off he'd be there. Thelma Rysdale had worked with Anne Plaisted on the house interiors. She mentioned it to Sister the following weekend but Sister hadn't been especially startled. "What do you suppose he's like?" she'd asked, then answered her own question. "He could always talk a blue streak; it's probably worse." Margaret hadn't discussed her own anxieties.

She had dressed for the party with special care, choosing her tightest girdle, a red wool dress, high-collared, with a little flare to the skirt, black nylons and black pumps. She changed the veil on her hat, this one peppered with little dots to make her a bit more obscure, mysterious. Her makeup had taken almost half an hour, but at last she had eradicated the pouches and stains, alleviated the brownness. With the veil down, her eyes sparkling behind the dots, she might even remind Charlie of her youthful self. Not that she wanted to, of course, but she might as well look her best. She took her sneakers out to the car for the drive; she'd put on her heels when she got to the Plaisted house. She could hardly breathe for the girdle.

She made a point of not looking for him right away. She chatted with Anne and her husband, a stockbroker, then moved to the punch bowl, greeting Loretta Meade and some others. Then she saw a tall, stooped man with a big nose and sand-dune hair standing by the window. He wore aviator glasses. She recognized him at once—a thicker, coarser version of the man who had sailed out of a blue summer afternoon and landed at her mother-in-law's dinner table.

"Margaret." His voice was moist, plummy, the kind he must have used for presenting ad campaigns to clients. He came over and clasped her free hand in both of his. He wore a diamond pinkie ring. His calluses were rough, probably from playing golf. "Anne said you'd be here. I'm so darned happy to see you. You look wonderful."

She extricated her hand. Now that the moment was here she wasn't shy at all. She could think of dozens of things to say. He was a stranger, wasn't he? She could chat with him as with any stranger. They went over the news. He knew that Sister and Mark lived up here. "Mark's done really well. I hear about him all the time." Then he asked about Mag and Harris. She gave a censored version of events. He said he had met his wife soon after he divorced Hattie, moved to California. They had a stepdaughter, Megan, Thelma's child, now in graduate school.

After the news had been covered, they stopped. She felt tense for a moment, draining the last of her punch. What came next? What would he ask? What did she have to find out? There was both too much and too little to say. She stifled the urge to walk off.

Charlie was uneasy too. His blue eyes—the only familiar part of him, really—darted about. Maybe he was looking for his wife. Maybe he wanted to be rescued too.

And then she knew what she wanted to ask. It gathered in her mind, a whisper at first, then louder. Maybe it was rude, maybe it opened the gate too wide, but she needed to know. It was the only piece still lacking. But she'd have to be careful. She couldn't let on. She gave a nervous laugh and put her hand to her cheek. Then she spoke lightly, nonchalantly.

"I was wondering—" he was studying her now, she could read alarm in his eyes—"I was wondering if you ever wrote that novel. The one you used to talk about, remember?"

Yes, the novel. They had talked about it after the Sunday dinners at Selma's and when they sat near the famous table at the Algonquin and in Atlantic City after they made love. The novel had been the lure, the promise. They would share his success and fame and then her own. It would make everything she'd dreamed in Gideon come true.

He let out a guffaw. "I never got around to that, Margaret. They made me head of the L.A. office and I met Thelma and she wasn't interested in that sort of thing. We were busy, you know." He eyed her a little sheepishly and laughed again. "I wrote a couple of books about scoring with direct mail. They're pretty well known. Somebody told me he saw them in the catalogue at the New York Public Library."

She smiled and murmured something. She could feel a shift deep inside her. She hadn't missed a thing.

Just then his wife came up, a woman in her late forties with a round Irish face. The woman stared, examining her carefully. Of course she had heard the whole story. After a while Margaret excused herself. When she looked back, they were talking with some new arrivals. She left the party without saying good-bye to Charlie. She didn't want to make false promises about meeting again. The connection had been broken. All that had been laid to rest.

Laid to rest. She pressed her hand to her chest and coughed. Even that was taken care of, the plot in Westchester next to Judd and Mama. Neither of them had been buried in the other cemetery, the one in Queens, even though it meant separating Mama from Papa. Nor would she. That was the last of her planning—a Christian burial. Christ was her Redeemer too.

But why was she going on like this? She didn't have cancer. She had a fungus infection, one of the spores from a mushroom or dandelion setting up house in her lung. They'd seen a spot in the X-rays, about the size of a quarter. That didn't mean a thing. She'd probably had it all her life.

On his visit here Harris had remarked that if will power were the only requirement, she would be queen of the world. They'd both laughed at that, and Mag had agreed, so it didn't matter about her dream or waking up scared or visualizing the cemetery. You can be anything you want to be, and she wanted to be alive. She had a thousand things to do.

She wiped her eyes. Tears of self-pity, that's all. She was finished with those too.

"Gramaw?" The hoarse whisper sped through the dark.

"What are you doing up, honey?"

"I wanted to ask you something."

"Well, you can ask me in the morning. Go back to bed."

A low whine. He almost never took orders, unlike Harris at that age. But that was a good sign, wasn't it? "I want to ask you now."

She debated a moment, then turned on the light. "Just one question, then you have to go back to bed."

He grumbled in, neither child nor man, and leaned against the bed at her side. "Mom said you didn't really know Davy Crockett." He probed her face. He was all new; he hadn't been written on yet.

"Is that what she said?"

He nodded.

She summoned her fiercest voice. "Well, I did. I vow and declare I did."

He stared at her, conspiracy in his eyes. He believed her now. She had established the truth of imagination. No matter what happened to him, wherever life took him, some fragment of this conversation would remain. She was inside him like a time capsule. "Will I grow up to be like Davy Crockett?"

Suppose she had only tonight, this last night, after all? "You can be anything you want to be, honey."

His face, with its golden skin and light eyes, took on some of her fierceness. He stamped his foot. "Oh, boy!" he said. "Oh, boy!"

She lay back and closed her eyes. She could rest now. She had passed it on. There was no stopping any of them.